a lite too bright

a
lite
too
bright

samuel miller

KATHERINE TEGEN BOOKS
An Imprint of HarperCollins Publishers

Katherine Tegen Books is an imprint of HarperCollins Publishers.

Library of Congress Control Number: 2018933385
ISBN 978-0-06-266200-2

Typography by David Curtis
18 19 20 21 22   PC/LSCH   10 9 8 7 6 5 4 3 2 1
❖
First Edition

for great purpose.

also, for my roommates.
anthony,
& sheppard,
& dylan,
& addison.

i always felt there was some Greater love waiting for me,
just around the bend of the orange horizon.
i'm learning now that the world is a circle, & what i thought
was ahead of me is actually behind.
but my eyes are open,
& i can see that i'm coming up on it again.

—*arthur louis pullman*, **a world away**, *1975*

PART ONE.

truckee.

MY HANDS ARE gripping the steering wheel as water rushes all around me, through the cracks in the window, collapsing the sides of my Camaro with pressure.

If you think about it, sinking is a lot like being shot into space. You're floating, untethered by gravity, and everything around you is in weightless slow motion, moving with you from one world to the next.

You expect too much from me.

Every one of my limbs is bound by a different seat belt, five of them locking me in place as I drift farther and farther from the surface. It's darker down here. The water is colder. You never get down this far when you're swimming.

You need me too much.

If you can keep your eyes open long enough, you get to watch a ballet of debris. All the little things you carry with you when you drive—the CDs, the books you never read, the empty bottle of three-dollar wine, the cast, the ring—they all float around you as if in orbit, tiny planets in your solar system.

The seat belt around my torso is gripping tighter, forcing out the last of my air.

"Alright!" A voice is calling to me from a million miles away. I don't even turn to look. The voice is above the surface.

BANG.

The window shakes. Someone's trying to break it open. Someone's trying to get me out.

"Alright!"

BANG.

I should move. I should help them. I should reach back, let them know that I'm alive. I should tear off the seat belts and try to find the door handle.

But I don't move. I keep my hands on the wheel, my eyes fixed forward out the front window. The last of my air leaves me in tiny little bubbles.

I watch them, one by one. They'll fight their way to the surface, but I won't. I'm comfortable here.

"Alright alright—"

2.

"ALRIGHTY THEN, FOLKS! We're about to make our stop at the incredibly scenic and naturally beautiful Truckee Amtrak station, home of the mourning dove, the nightingale, and the Exxon oil refinery, on your right.

"Those of you going to Tahoe, you'll be exiting out the door on

your left; those of you not going to Tahoe . . . well, why the hell aren't ya? I'm working, what's your excuse?

"We're ahead of schedule today—yes, folks, miracles do happen— so we've got, oh, just a hair less than forty-five minutes till we'll push off for Reno. Next train's not until tomorrow, so make good 'n' sure you're back on time; that's 8:35 a.m., for any sports fans out there keeping track.

"If you'll take a humble recommendation from a man who's seen this route a time or two in his day, this 76 gas station here has the best taquito you'll find outside Mexico City, and that's the hand-to-God truth.

"We'll see you in forty-five or we'll see you next time; that's all, from your brilliant and loyal conductor."

3.

THE TRAIN LURCHED backward and I sat up.

"Everything okay, Arthur?"

My dad had been looking at me, and I knew what he was thinking. It had been three weeks since I'd been in court, and every time I opened my eyes fast enough, I caught his private, woeful, single-parent stare: two parts pity, one part confusion, two parts *what the hell am I supposed to do with this thing now?*

He'd practiced this look for years after my mom left. Our

house was big enough that most of the time he could ignore me, but when we did run into each other—over breakfast or when the A's played or if we both got to the garage at the same time in the morning—he'd crease his forehead at me like I was an ancient Egyptian baby left on his doorstep. And he'd had about that much say in the matter: my mom had always done all the parenting, but my dad kept the house, so she decided I would stay with him.

Now that I was a criminal, he was finding it even harder to disguise his misfortune.

He pointed over my shoulder, out the window of the train. "Prepare yourself. Hurricane Karen."

My auntie hugged me as soon as I was far enough onto the platform that she could get a clean shot. "Arthur, we're just so happy you decided to come stay with us!"

"Auntie, it's, uh, it's so good to see you," I said.

The Truckee Amtrak train platform is more of a glorified slab of pavement, placed in the middle of a town unaware that it's not 1950 anymore. The only activity in the town is crammed right there around the concrete slab—one gas station, two breakfast spots, one visitor center, and six bars. A guy waiting in line for the train bathroom told me, "In Truckee, everybody does one of two things: they drink, or they don't." I think he might have been an example of the former.

"Oh my goodness, Tim is beside himself—he simply *can-not wait* to show you the deck! *Did you know*—"

I noticed that she'd emphasize a three-word phrase like she

was a game show host, not really talking to me but instead to an audience seated slightly above my head; an audience who *could not believe* that someone would give away *all this money.*

"*Did you know* that we have been working on this deck for almost—well, guess. How many years? Almost? Do you think?"

"Uh, maybe sev—"

"Eleven! Eleven years!"

Game show audience gasps.

"Wow, that's—"

"*Did you ever* hear of such a thing? Deck's almost as old as the marriage!"

Game show audience laughs.

"Oh, no, that's, that's awesome." I gritted my teeth in a smile.

It didn't seem worth it to clarify, but I hadn't *decided* to come stay with them. I was given the option of an extended "vacation" at their Truckee cabin or on a farm in western Nebraska with my family's resident red-state lunatic great-uncle, Henry.

I figured I'd be *slightly less likely* to *commit a homicide* in Truckee than I would in Nebraska.

"He's had a rough week. Month, really," my father said, clasping my back as Karen waddled toward her Ford Escape. "Might not be very talkative."

"Oh." She spun on me. "We know all about that. And I just have to say . . . Arthur, we are very, very proud of you. Skipping college, and—and your hand, and this girl . . . all of this is so hard, and—well, we know you'll be back on your feet in no time." Tiny tears formed in the corners of her eyes as she grabbed the back of my head and pulled me in for a hug.

"Thanks, Auntie Karen," I said into her boobs.

Game show audience sighs.

4.

I THINK TRUCKEE must be one of the places you go when you've thrown in the towel on doing anything extraordinary in your life, and you figure, "Fuck it, I may as well do some skiing before I end it."

My uncle Tim and auntie Karen were the least extraordinary people I knew. Uncle Tim installed water systems in people's homes, like a Culligan Man without the brand recognition, and Auntie Karen bought shit at garage sales and sold it on eBay. They'd lived in the same cabin for twelve years, and spent their entire marriage bragging about some meaningless renovation.

Living less-than-impressive lives was a disease that ran uncontrollably in my family. My mother had figured that out, and left us when I was nine. My dad, also an Arthur Louis Pullman, sold life insurance. He didn't make an impressive living, but we existed comfortably in grossly expensive Palo Alto, California, off the royalties owed to the only exceptional member of the family: my grandfather, the late, great author Arthur Louis Pullman the First. We moved into his house after my grandmother died, when I was five, and we'd been there since, even after he died five years ago. It was weird. People knew that it was weird. My dad and I didn't belong in a house like that. We didn't belong in Palo Alto. I was the poor kid at Palo Alto High.

But it was a nice house, and the cabin was a nice cabin, so everyone in my family got to play pretend-rich because my grandfather had done extraordinary things in his life. Even though we didn't talk about him anymore. Even though his torch was being carried by a life insurance salesman and a B-team Culligan Man.

"Arthur Louis Pullman the Third, as I live and breathe!" Uncle Tim shouted, just as he had every time I had walked into a room for eighteen years, grabbing my biceps and shaking me. He was much shorter than me, wearing a polo and khaki shorts, exactly what you'd expect from a water installation specialist. His mustache made him look like a white, middle-class Mario.

"Look at this guy. You feel stronger. There's muscle mass there. You been working out or what?"

"No, um, not really."

"Oh. Well, eating healthy?"

"Not really."

"Huh. Well, you're newly single. You masturbating a lot?"

The phrase *newly single* burned in my chest but I pretended I didn't feel it. "I guess, yeah."

"There it is!" my dad shouted, Karen slipping a drink into his hand.

"You know," Tim added, "people really underestimate how

much that helps build arm and wrist strength." He raised my left hand and squeezed the cast lightly. "Look at this. That hurt?"

"No."

"Good. That means it's healing. Just don't try anything here," he said, slapping the wall with one hand and grabbing his drink with the other. "These things are reinforced plaster." He laughed at himself. "C'mon, Arthurs. Let me show you the deck."

The view of Donner Lake from their house was one of the only redeemable parts of Truckee. The lake sat in the middle of a valley, surrounded by mountains that were covered by pine trees, all the way up to the timberline, where snow and clouds took over. The pine trees were formed into rows, nature's perfect geometry, creating layered patterns of evergreen around the crystal-blue lake. It was the kind of place where you could take photos for postcards or preloaded computer screen savers.

"Took us eleven years to build this thing," Uncle Tim said, proudly smacking the wooden railing of the deck.

"I heard."

"Said you can't build a deck on a solid rock foundation like this. You know what we learned from that?"

"That they, uh, they were wrong?"

"No. That they were right. Shouldn't have done it. It was an eleven-year pain in the ass."

"Oh."

"Lesson here, Arthur, is that usually when people tell you

something's impossible, it is."

"It looks—"

"Would you speak up? You talk like a goddamn rabbit."

I cleared my throat. "It looks nice now."

"Eleven fucking years, Arty." He looked back into the house at his wife. "No deck is worth eleven years."

"Oh."

I felt a small fire in my chest. I hate when people tell me to speak up, and more than that, I hate the idea that it represents. My friend Mason called it the *tyranny of volume*—the belief that whoever speaks the loudest should be heard the clearest. It was one of the fundamental things we hated about the United States, and people like my uncle Tim. But I couldn't talk to Mason about that kind of thing anymore.

He took a sip from his glass. It was a mixed drink, but from the smell of it, I could tell it wasn't a proportional mix. "How's that car of yours working out?"

My father rolled his eyes. "He spends all his time out with it."

"Hey now," Tim said. "If you'd had a car like that when you were his age, you'd've set up a tube for food and shit so you'd never have to leave the thing. What's it get to sixty in, Arty?"

"Uh, under four."

"I've got a buddy with an Audi who says he can do three point three. What do you make of that?"

"It's not faster than my Camaro."

"I don't know, he says—"

"It's not."

He took a step back. The benefit of rabbit voice was that when you spoke up, people noticed. "Right. Anyways . . . how's the therapy going?"

"Okay, I guess."

He finished his drink in one gulp and turned to face me, shaking the ice. He wasn't smiling. "Look, Arthur, I'm your uncle, and I hope I'm not out of place, but I feel like I have to say this. I don't know if your auntie told you already, but . . . we're proud of you. We really are, for all the, uh, all the stuff that you're doing. You took a couple serious whacks, right in the pisser, and you, you made it through without—well, almost without a scratch."

He nodded toward the cast on my left hand.

My father took over. "You're at the hardest time for it, too, you know. It's the kinda shit, gets better as you get older. Bad things happen, people leave you." He paused. "But you learn to take shit like that on the chin. You get tough. Doesn't freak you out as much."

"You find your own ways of coping. Channel it into"—Tim forgot his drink was gone and tried to take another sip, ice spilling onto his face—"productive habits. And you know what? That hand is gonna heal, good as new. You'll be playing tennis again before you know it, we'll find you another scholarship, and it'll all be just like it was. Your future'll be right back on track."

I didn't say anything, instead counting the trees that lined the far end of Donner Lake.

"What? Arty?" My father waved to get my attention. "Why are you—did we miss something here? What'd I say?"

I cleared my throat. "What about Kaitlin?"

"Yeah." He ran his hand over the railing of the eleven-year deck. "Might have to let that one go. Restraining order is serious business. Same thing with Mason, after you—you know, after court . . . happened. Probably want to give that some space."

I nodded again.

All of this was the same thing Dr. Sandoval had told me, the same thing anyone tells anyone whose life is fucked up to the point that it's no longer recognizable. "Everything will get better"—but I'd lived in the world long enough to know it wasn't true. "The scholarship will come back"—no, it won't. "UCLA will still accept you"—no, they won't. "Life will get back on track"—no, it won't. Not without Kaitlin, it won't.

But that's not how they wanted me to act. "Thanks, Dad, Uncle Tim. That, uh, that means a lot to me," I said, and they smiled at me like you might smile at a dog that was trying to clean up its own shit.

For dinner, my auntie made ham loaf, beans, and mandarin orange Jell-O salad. I knew she'd made it for me, even though I was a vegetarian. It had been my favorite meal when I was seven, and no one had bothered to ask if my food preferences had changed.

"Dear God," my father prayed to the four of us around the table. "Thank you for all of the gifts you've given us. Tonight especially, oh God, we thank you for the gift of life."

I think he hated praying, and I know he hated going to church, but he did it, probably because my grandfather had always done it, so to stop would require him to question the way things were, and that was something my father didn't do. He was hopelessly obligated to the status quo.

I didn't feel obligated to anyone, least of all God.

"No matter how hard it gets, we're so glad to be alive. And to share that gift with each other." He shot an eyes-closed glance in my direction. "Thank you for this food, and for our health, and for the law, which protects us, and most of all, for the gift of being alive. Amen."

We ate in silence. Occasionally, my auntie would volunteer some information about the eBay collection habits of Southern widows, or Tim would tell a riveting water installation story, but my dad looked even less interested than I was. We'd almost made it through the meal before he casually dropped a bomb.

"Tim, I forgot to tell you." He spoke through a mouthful of Jell-O. "We've been talking to Dad's agent, Mr. Volpe, if you remember him, and—I think we're going to do a preferred text edition of *A World Away.*"

The room was silent.

I looked up from my plate. "You're going to do what?"

"I think it's time." My father addressed me like I was an active land mine. "To do an author's preferred text version. A rerelease, for all the die-hard fans."

All the adults at the table nodded in unison like bobbleheads, as if it made perfect sense. *A World Away* was my grandfather's only novel, and it was a classic. It had won every award a book can win: a Pulitzer Prize, a National Book Award, been a *New York Times* bestseller, and more. It was mandatory reading for almost every high school junior in America. One time, Tom Hanks said in an interview that it was his favorite book. Tom Fucking Hanks.

"The account is pretty dry, even after this year's royalties, and . . . and Richard managed to recapture the copyright, so he says we'd get good money for it, in advance. It'd be enough to take care of us for a long time, maybe even life. He says publishers'll be lining up left and right, especially after all the press and the rumors and everything when Dad . . . left."

I swallowed my response. That was how we spoke of my grandfather's disappearance and death now: abstract generalities, whatever would end the conversation the fastest. My dad avoided it, maybe because he felt guilty about not looking for him, or maybe he didn't care anymore. The confusion had burned in a small corner of my stomach for five years, but not in my dad's. He seemed content to bury his with my grandfather.

"Does he have any preferred text?" Tim asked, excited for the opportunity to stroke his mustache. "I didn't think any of us had ever seen him write anything."

My father was cavalier and careful to avoid my stare. "Ah, I'm sure he's got some notes or something sitting around."

"Please," Karen mumbled. "He didn't even write his own grocery lists."

I squeezed my ring under the table. I hated it when they talked about him like this, even though I knew they were probably right. I'd never seen him write anything either, despite how often people outside our family wanted me to tell them that I had. I remembered all of us sitting around the television once, watching a PBS special on my grandfather's life. They interviewed expert after so-called expert, each one more certain than the last that Arthur Louis Pullman was in the process of finishing his literary masterpiece, while behind me, he was finishing a masterpiece that he called "a bottle of Jack Daniel's."

I wanted them to be right. But I knew they weren't.

"Well, then we'll make some up," my father said, shrugging again. "It's an anniversary edition. People are gonna buy it either way."

My stomach turned over.

It would make money. My grandfather's agent was right; Americans had a fetish for gossip and controversy, especially when the stories involved people going crazy, and people dying. The rumors around his death would probably drive the asking price way, way up.

But I also knew my grandfather, and he would be clawing at the top of his casket if he heard they were going to republish an "author's preferred text" version. It wasn't the first time it had been discussed, and each time, he'd shot it down. It was about his honor. He didn't want to pretend an old thing was a new thing just so he could make more money. He didn't want corporate influences to bastardize his art for profit. And I understood that, even if my dad didn't.

"He'd hate that," I said.

My father's fork stalled midair. "I'm sorry. I didn't realize you were appointed to represent my father's interests."

"I just remember last time when you tried to do this, and he called it 'corporate bullshit.' He said he'd rather die than republish the same book just so people will buy it again."

"Well, he is dead now. So."

"That doesn't mean you get to just trample all over his grave—"

"For God's sake, Arthur, would you quit pretending like he actually had some attachment to that book? I lived with him my whole life, and I don't think he remembered what he wrote it about! Have you even read it?"

I grimaced. "Not all the way, but—"

"Well, let me fill you in. It's a story of forbidden love, and adventure, and tragedy. And all the Arthur Louis Pullman I knew ever did was watch baseball and read the Bible."

"Not when he was younger—"

"*Yes*, when he was younger! Do you know what he did when he was younger? He worked on a railroad, and he drank. Never even left California—he was writing out of his ass!"

"So?"

"So stop acting like there's some pretend integrity at stake here! We're his family, we own the copyright now, we'll do with it what we want. God knows we earned it—"

"*Earned* it? How did you *earn* it? It was *his* book."

"Living with him! Caring for him! My whole life, I had to sit there and watch him lose his mind, then cater to his insanity! Do you have any idea what it's like to have to take care of someone that crazy—"

"Arthur." Auntie Karen was glaring at him, not me.

He took a deep breath. "I'm sorry, Arty. . . . I love my father. I just . . . I love you guys more. I want to take care of you. Of us. And with the account getting low, and this therapy stuff, your legal fees . . ."

"Yeah, right." I twisted the ring on my hand. "You didn't even go look for him when he ran away."

My dad sighed. "That's not true, and you know it. We looked everywhere he could possibly have been. Everywhere he'd ever been. We couldn't predict he'd turn up in Ohio."

"Except he did."

"Yes." I could tell my dad was measuring his temper, trying to give me teaspoons. "Yes, he did."

"Didn't you ever wonder *why* he went there? Or how? Or something?"

He shook his head. "I never tried to figure out what was going on in that man's head. I never cared to know."

"He was your father—"

"No. No, not those last years. That man was not my father."

We went back to eating in silence, my dad and I both staring at our plates in disgust.

"It'll be good, Arty," Uncle Tim said, ignoring the tension. "All the new attention on the book . . . might be able to use it to get laid."

The adults at the table groaned.

"I'm serious! I mean, your mother was an English teacher when she met—"

My father laughed and flung a napkin in his direction, and it was the end of the conversation.

5.

MY FATHER LEFT almost immediately after dinner. He tried to apologize. He told me he was trying his best, and that he still wasn't sure how to be a parent sometimes, and I told him it was okay, because I didn't care anymore.

As soon as he was out the door, my uncle led me to a ladder in the far corner of the room, up to the loft attic. "Here's where you're setting up camp. We've just taken to calling it 'the Arthur Room.' You know the family's had this cabin since the—"

"Gold rush, yeah, I know."

"Well, they used to tell us your grandfather was born up here. That's why it was his favorite spot, back when he owned the place. Then your father used to stay up there all the time when he'd come visit, and now you're receiving the torch. Next in a long line of Arthurs."

I examined the room at the top of the ladder. It didn't take long—it was about the size of my bedroom at home, but the slanted roof meant most of the ceiling was too low even for walking. Cut out of the slanted roof was a large, circular window that looked west over the lake. The remaining light from the sun was painting the water purple as it set behind us.

"Best view of Donner you'll find in any of these cabins," he told me. "We'd know. We've checked."

The only furniture was a nightstand next to the bed and a desk underneath the window, facing out. There was a single book in the room, on the nightstand: *Birds of Tahoe*. Next to it, a pamphlet for weekly church activities.

"Sorry," Tim said. "Your auntie is, well, you know."

I dropped it into the trash bin next to the desk and scanned the photos: mostly my aunt and uncle at various spots around Truckee, skiing, boating, drinking wine. On the far end was a small, rectangular frame. As soon as I picked it up, I felt a lump in my throat.

Uncle Tim saw it in my hands. "It's, uh . . . that's the last picture we got of him, actually."

It was my whole family, squinting into the sun, most of us half smiling at whatever stranger had been asked to take the photo. My face looked excited, although I can't imagine I had any reason to be. We were standing on the Truckee platform where my auntie had picked me up earlier that day. Somehow lost in the middle, surrounded by the family he had built and wearing what had become his signature confused squint, was my grandfather, Arthur Louis Pullman the First.

"When did we take this?" I asked.

"It was the morning you all rode up here to drop him off.

Five years ago, the day he . . . took off."

I looked closer at the photo, to the digital clock on the platform behind us. It read April 27. It was the last day I'd ever seen my grandfather.

I ran my thumb over it. "I don't, uh, I don't remember taking it. I feel bad, I wish I would have—"

"Don't." He cut me off. "There was no way to know." He swallowed. "We all feel bad, but there was no way to know."

I didn't say anything. It didn't sound like he was really talking to me.

It was strange, looking at my grandfather in the last moment of his life ever captured. He was a calm person, expressionless and almost cold. But in this photo, he was the opposite. His face was alive; he looked scared and intense. He looked like there was someone, or something, he was trying to avoid.

"He hated most photos, but God, he loved that one," my uncle said. "We got it developed right away, and he just stared at it. For hours, sitting right there." He nodded to the small folding chair where I sat. "Sometimes I would think he was trying to remember who we were, then sometimes I think he knew and . . . and I guess it was just his way of spending a little more time with us."

I nodded. "During those last few months, I hardly . . . I mean—"

"He wasn't well, Arthur. You know what they call Alzheimer's? 'The long good-bye.' We get to remember them how we choose." He waited a moment while I stared at the photo.

"You've gotta go easy on your dad, kid," he said finally, nodding to the frame in my hands. "He's still not right with all of this. He misses him, he does. It's just . . . it was a complicated relationship."

"Yeah." I flipped the photo over, and taped to the back was a newspaper clipping cut from the *Chicago Tribune*. My grandfather's photo was enormous, a smiling black-and-white portrait from long before I was born.

"What's this?"

"His obituary," my uncle said. "The best one, at least. Fit for a king. Actually, I'm pretty sure even kings don't get this many column inches when they die."

"Who was Sal Hamilton?" I asked, reading the byline.

"Closest thing Dad had to a biographer. As in, he actually knew this guy. This's gotta be one of the best articles anybody ever wrote about him."

"How'd he know him?"

Uncle Tim shrugged. "I don't know. I doubt Dad even remembered. One of his many mysteries."

6.

A FINAL MYSTERY FROM ONE OF AMERICA'S
MOST CAPTIVATING STORYTELLERS

BY SAL HAMILTON

CHICAGO, IL. MAY 5, 2010—Perhaps one of the most culturally heartbreaking events we've been forced to become familiar with in our country this century has been the passing of our literary icons. Yesterday, this routine tragedy came to us as anything but routine and claimed one of our most beloved. Arthur Louis Pullman, author of the modern classic *A World Away*, passed away, tragically and mysteriously, in a Kent, Ohio, hospital.

His wife, Josephine Pullman, passed away in 2005. He is survived by his sons, Arthur Jr. and Timothy.

The death was announced by Mr. Pullman's long-time literary agent and friend, Richard Volpe, who'd cited a long-developing degenerative brain disease as the cause of death. "We have no reason to believe there were any extraordinary circumstances surrounding his death, other than the extraordinary manner in which he lived. [Mr. Pullman] has been battling illness for the better part of his life, and the only explanation for his passing is that he must have decided it was finally time to move on from this form and go see what else was out there for him."

While all evidence sides with this conclusion, Mr. Pullman still left a few unanswered questions for his family and literary communities at large surrounding the location and events leading up to his passing. A week prior to his death in Kent, Ohio, Mr. Pullman was reportedly staying for an extended period with his son Tim Pullman at his cabin in Truckee, California, 2,300 miles away. The events of that week, the manner in which he traveled those 2,300 miles, and his reasons why are all, at this point, unknown.

Presently, his family and law enforcement have chosen not to speculate on any of these questions. "His life was miraculous and his death was natural, and that's all that matters to us," his son Arthur Pullman Jr. said in a statement issued to the press. "We ask that, like my father asked so many times, our privacy be respected."

While it was not well publicized during his life, recent statements are making clear that Mr. Pullman's later years were marred by early onset Alzheimer's, a neurodegenerative disorder that affects over five million Americans. In his statement, Mr. Pullman's son continued, "Throughout his longtime struggle with this disease, his brilliance and spirit never wavered, and we hope that he can be an inspiration to others out there struggling with early-onset Alzheimer's and all forms of dementia."

A World Away, Mr. Pullman's first and only published novel, was first printed in 1975, when the author was 25. Tilda Pullman, his mother, said her son wrote the novel after moving back to live with her at age 20. Commercially, it was an instant success, developing a cult following among teenagers of the post-antiwar era. It took less than two months to become a certified bestseller, and that success has been reborn with every new generation; the book still sells nearly 50,000 copies a year.

His book, argued to be among the best of its literary generation, follows a young protagonist, Jeffery Colton, on a cross-country journey to reclaim a lost something. Literary experts, high school English classes, and strangers on bus rides have long debated the novel's cryptic and noncommittal description of the object of the narrator's quest—in different sections called "an empire," a "her," a "Him," "the Great," and many more. Critics have often heralded Pullman's detailed handling of Jeffery's psychosis, observing what it says about the human compulsion for desire, and how that compulsion evolves as we achieve those things. In the novel's final line, Jeffery remarks, "I have become all that I want, and for that, I am the one thing I will never understand."

The writing style of the novel has become, in and of itself, subject for literary study. An early review written by Tomas Cornish of the *New Yorker* called Pullman "the degenerate son of Kerouac, the quicker cousin of Whitman, and the only one of them that could ever tell a real story." His usually plot-heavy and focused prose is spattered with abstract moments and poetic musing, frequently highlighted by grammatical touches such as scorning capital letters and replacing the word "and" with ampersands (&). When asked once whether he felt that the different, seemingly competing styles were indicative of some kind of split-personality writing, he remarked, "You show me an author who's got just one trick, I'll show you his blank piece of paper, and my thing will be more interesting."

After the publication of *A World Away* in 1975, Mr. Pullman began his lifelong hiatus from formal literary publication and the public eye. He met Josephine Webb just prior to the novel's release and they were married three months later at a private ceremony in Northern California. Retreating to seclusion immediately, they purchased a home in Palo Alto, where he spent the remainder of his life.

He made his scorn of public attention well-known. Mr. Volpe has confirmed that Pullman had a long-standing objection to any proposed interviews, stories, fan mail, or connection with his literary audience in general. This aversion did little to reduce the outside world's attempts to connect with Mr. Pullman, and rather added to his mystique. It has long been believed that Mr. Pullman spent his thirty-five years in seclusion writing what would become his most representative work, or body of work. Other rumors go further still, suggesting Pullman's connection to a collection of unpublished works from America's greatest writers, himself included, but these theories offer very little explanation beyond the naming of the seemingly mythical collection: "the Great Library."

Arthur Louis Pullman was born in 1950 and raised in Truckee, California, the son of a hotel chambermaid. A child of California through and through, he wouldn't leave the state until he was an adult. At age 14, he began working for the Pacific Railroad Company, laying tracks across the blossoming Bay Area of San Francisco. After several stints of employment, he enrolled briefly in the National Guard, but never made it past his training in the Bay Area. His transition to writing, as with the majority of his life, is not well documented. When asked about her husband by a reporter in public, Josephine Pullman said, "My husband is a private man."

While these stories and his forbidden history may paint a portrait of Mr. Pullman as a cold, bitter recluse, those who were close with him maintain the opposite to be true. After meeting him at a function for this newspaper forty years ago, I described him in a letter as "warm and inviting; the sort of kindness that extends beyond formality and into real understanding. . . . To speak with [Mr. Pullman] is to speak with yourself as you wish you were."

This is the Arthur Louis Pullman that I knew, and the one that I will always remember him to be. The literary revolution and subsequent youth culture movement that he inspired are a testament to the seminal nature of his work, his character, and his reading of humanity, all of which will rightfully be remembered as among the best in the English language.

As Lou Thurman, political writer and contributor to this newspaper, said, "At the end of his life, a man's story is written in the words he never said." Almost as compelling as the stories Mr. Pullman wrote are the holes in his own story that he left behind.

Whether these holes are ever filled and understood, Mr. Pullman will forever be remembered for his incredible ability to captivate and inspire.

7.

I KNOW WHAT it's like to not feel anything.

It's overwhelming light. It starts at a single spot and spreads outward, so fast that the real world burns in its wake until there's nothing but light. It's the white-hot flashbulb in the space behind the bridge of your nose and between your eyes. It's the inch of empty air between your skin and everything else that exists.

At a certain point, your body stops negotiating with pain and becomes it. It's liberating; you lose the control and the consciousness and all the parts that make you human, and let your body—the vicious, instinctual animal it has always been—make all the decisions. You think nothing. You feel nothing. You are nothing. Nothing but light.

The room was dark and the house was quiet. My auntie and uncle had gone to sleep seven hours ago, at 9:00 p.m., like Truckee people do. But the moon was reflecting off the lake, through the window, too bright for me to think about sleeping. I reached the end of my Twitter timeline, so I checked again, then again, and again. Each time: *No New Tweets*. No one posts on Twitter at 4:30 a.m. No one does anything at 4:30 a.m., unless they're on meth, or me.

This kind of night had become a routine. And at 4:30 a.m., after I'd passed the point of no return on an all-nighter, I remembered what it was like to think about Kaitlin.

Dr. Sandoval told me that when that happened, I should journal, like I used to have to when I was a kid. I told him that was because I gave a shit what my dad thought when I was a kid, and I don't anymore.

I disagree with the basic premise of journaling for the same reason that I disagree with the basic premise of therapy: because feelings are supposed to be the one thing we just *do*. Because you can plan and prepare and schedule every other little detail of your tiny life, but feelings are supposed to be the disruption to that. They're not supposed to be documented and studied in a journal, then calculated by some guy in an intentionally nonthreatening sweater vest. If you're forced to identify your feelings, then what the fuck is even the point?

But the therapy was court-mandated, so I had to do it if I ever wanted to see Kaitlin again.

I was thinking about Kaitlin. I could still see her with perfect clarity, radiating outward from the prosecution bench of the superior court of Palo Alto, her skin pale and hair flawlessly brown, just long enough to tickle her shoulders, wearing a white tennis skirt and smiling forward, away from me. I'd tried to tell her I was better. She didn't look at me.

I cycled through the other tricks Dr. Sandoval had given me. "I'm getting better," I told myself. I stared at my cast, fixating on the physical pain in my hand. He thought physical pain like that would put the emotional pain in perspective. But having perspective made me think about Kaitlin. My hand made me think about Kaitlin.

Pain made me think about Kaitlin.

"I'd never felt so scared in my entire life," she was telling the judge, but she wasn't in the courtroom anymore. She was lying on the bed next to me. "He doesn't realize he can't control himself, but when he gets angry, it's like there's this little switch in him that flips, and he goes crazy." Her voice was light and airy and inviting, like a pop star's. "He expects too much from me." She looked directly into my face. "You expect too much from me," and she rolled over, away from me.

"No, I don't!" I pleaded, just like I used to shout at her, but I shouldn't have shouted because it always made things worse.

"You're not getting better!" she told me without rolling over. "You look all quiet, and hopeless, and hide behind your little *I hate the world and the world hates me* routine, but that's how you manipulate people."

"I'm not trying to manipulate you!"

"You get angry, and you can't control yourself—"

"I'm not trying to be angry!" I couldn't help myself, I couldn't let her think I was dangerous; surely she could see the irony of a "protective order." I was the one who protected her. "I'm not trying to be anything, I just want to be with you!"

"He needs me too much," she said on my bed and in the hospital and in the courtroom and forever buried in my ear, deeper than I could reach so I could never get it out. "You need me too much."

I know what it's like to not feel anything.

It's overwhelming light.

At a certain point, your body stops negotiating with pain, and becomes it. When you don't feel anything, you're not a person anymore. Nothing you do can help you, nothing can hurt you, so you submit yourself to it.

Most of the time, it puts you to sleep, stopping your nerves from vibrating so your body shuts down. But sometimes, it wakes you up. Your body knows it must survive so it lashes out at the nothingness. You still hear everything—*I'm sorry, Arthur—you need me too much—do you have any idea what it's like to have to take care of someone that crazy?*—from the tiny little spot where the light exploded, so your body goes after it, unafraid of pain or consequence, because when you aren't a person anymore, what do you have to lose? Violence is the only way to ensure survival.

Anyone who shouts *control yourself* always forgets that part; it's not me steering the ship anymore. It's my body, the primal creature it's always been, doing what it must do to survive.

The sound of the chair crashing reminded me where I was. When I looked to the far side of the bed, Kaitlin had disappeared, leaving twisted sheets in her place. I listened breathlessly for a few moments, but no sound came from downstairs.

A dozen photo frames were shattered at my feet, and their stray glass was catching moonlight and throwing it around the room. My grandfather's last photo sat in the center, on top of a book, cracked only slightly at the center, directly across his face.

I set it in the middle of the desk and left the rest on the floor.

You need me too much.

I picked *Birds of Tahoe* off the floor and began to flip through it, desperate for something else to think about.

The American robin, a small, forest-dwelling bird, had a brick-red breast and a yellow beak, and Kaitlin had a friend named Robin who she used to be friends with at elementary school in—

The hairy woodpecker is a long-billed bird that can be identified by the white stripe down its back and the kind of bird name that would make Kaitlin laugh in public, the kind of laugh that made us exchange a look like we always did when someone inadvertently made a penis joke and didn't—

I scanned the table of contents for something that wouldn't make me think about her.

Dark-eyed junco, dark eyes just like hers.

Canada goose, native to her favorite country, Canada.

The western tanager—

Page forty-seven. I remembered my grandfather telling me a story about them once, about how they were a sign of good luck, or how some guy pretended they were. I flipped page after page, as fast as I could, past all the Kaitlin birds, trying to ignore them and failing, creasing over page forty-six—

A folded piece of paper fell out of the book and fluttered softly to the floor.

I almost didn't see it, but it caught some light from the window halfway down.

It landed amid the glass.

It was thin, folded neatly, almost shimmering in the orange light from the window and the reflective shards around it.

I leaned to pick it up, and noticed the faded inverse of an address on the outer sheet:

S E KOPEK

17 C H ST

E , DA

As I unfolded the page further, it became two pages, fighting back, the creases firm as if they hadn't been touched in years, frayed on the edges. They had been ripped out of something.

The page was covered in black pen that had dulled with age. The handwriting was a familiar cursive, but sloppy, as if written in a hurry.

I slumped into the folding chair in front of the desk, and read.

april 27, the 2010

dask wooden cold lite

lite

off the photo of family

arthur timothy arthur

lite

from the lake

jagged line burning orange lite

into blackness

mountains & mountains of trees, mountains of
jagged line horizon
i always felt there was some Greater love waiting for me
just around the bend of the orange horizon
i'm learning now that the world is a circle
& what i thought is ahead of me is actually behind
but my eyes are open
& i can see that i'm coming up on it again

& i feel Great purpose.
& i feel

arthur timothy arthur
hand to desk pen shaking lite
lite
off waves, reflections of lite
they've long since forgotten us
but they're just waves
& what were they ever but reflections of lite?
what were any of us ever but reflections of lite?

i'm called to a voice i don't remember
in a language i invented & have since forgotten
lite, too bright to see its source

chevys & greyhounds & zephyrs
you & me & them

lite from the orange sky
there are clouds ahead
& i hear trumpets & angals in your voice
calling to me
finding
peace in forgotten wars
homes in foreclosed jungles
saints in slums of missions
sinners in sanctuaries of church street
hope in forests of elko
safety in mecca.
chaos in cold, wet veins of ch
lou & sal's tribute.
a true, Great purpose

great
jeffery arthur
shaking hand to desk ring
we are eternal, we're together
& we always have been

photograph
of family
arthur & timothy & arthur
& lite
too bright to see its source
in the morning

i will listen
in the morning
i'll be once again aboard my zephyr
full speed to elko
full speed to you

—*arthur louis pullman*

8.

I READ EVERY word on the page, then read them again, more slowly. By the third time through, I could hear my grandfather speaking behind me.

His voice rolled slowly out of his chest to fill every corner of the room, deciding every word as he went, placing each one carefully on top of the last. I imagined him sitting at the desk, eyes fixed out the window, but he wasn't with me; he was out there, with the waves and mountains and burning orange light.

"We're together," he tells me. "And we always have been."

I caught my breath, and the gravity of what I held in my hands found me.

My grandfather had written again.

The diary or poem or whatever it was had been dated five

years ago, April 27, 2010. It was the day of that final photo, the day he had disappeared, the first night of the last week of his life. It was the closest thing we'd ever found to an answer or an explanation.

I closed my eyes and clutched the pages, remembering the most important detail of all: he hadn't left this out to be found. He had tucked it into a specific book, on a specific page, regarding a specific story he once told his grandson, about a boy who receives a sign from the divine and sets out after it.

My grandfather had wanted me to read this. He had left a clue.

He was next to me, hunched over, looking out across the desk and the photos and over the lake. I could hear him breathing, the wood bending every time he shifted his frame. I could see his old, trembling hand pushing to apply enough pressure to form the cursive on the page. Getting lost, getting confused, repeating himself, starting sentences and abandoning them. With Alzheimer's, clarity came in waves. Waves that lasted long enough for him to write, but not long enough to make any sense.

What did he want me to find?

I flipped the page over, remembering the faded letters on the other side.

S E KOPEK

17 C H ST

E , DA

"It's a name," I said. *S* something *E*. She? Or see? Or Sue?

That had to be it. Sue Kopek.

The line below it looked like an address. 17 *C* something *H* Street . . .

The sanctuaries of Church Street, I heard him write, and I smiled to myself. It was almost too obvious to notice. 17 Church Street. Sue Kopek at 17 Church Street.

The smile only lasted ten seconds. It was still nothing: a name, a street address, and an obscure poem that did nothing for me if I didn't understand it. The address was meaningless without a city. The clue was meaningless without any context.

I read it again, heard my grandfather's voice louder.

Dask wooden cold. He was sitting where I sat.

Jagged line burning orange lite. He was staring out the window, looking at the same horizon that I was, cut along the tops of the mountains, the color of the sun exploding behind them.

You and me and them. Who was he talking about?

On chevys and greyhounds and zephyrs; forests of elko, safety in mecca. Those were all proper nouns; places and things that sounded almost fictional, and in a small way, familiar.

chaos in cold, wet veins of ch. It was an incomplete word; he'd lost the thought halfway through.

We're together & we have always been. Who's together?

Lite too bright to see its source. My excitement slowly eroded into frustration.

It was nonsense. It read like the poetic insanity of a man lost inside of his own brain for too many years. The harder I tried to put the pieces together, the fewer pieces I found.

I saw him again, sitting next to me, the pen frozen in his hand, and this time, I remembered the look that had likely been on his face as he wrote: blank, warped with permanent confusion, squinting as if staring into a "light too bright to see its source." No one in my family had seen him write in forty years, and this was why. With his illness, it was impossible; not to form the words, but to make them mean anything. I could read along with his train of thought as he lost it, distracted by the world around him—the light outside on the lake, the crucifix-shaped bars across the window, the photograph of our family . . .

Photograph of family, he had written. He had been looking at the framed photo on the desk, the photo that my uncle said he'd spent hours with.

I picked it up, the only photo on the desk. My breathing slowed as I ran my thumb over it, studying it once more. Why this picture? What was he looking for?

I realized where I'd seen the words before.

One was plastered along the side of the train behind us. The 6 train, the California Zephyr. It was the name of the train.

And next to it, reflected in the train's window, was the digital screen at the station, displaying its next three destinations:

Reno.

Winnemucca.

And Elko, Nevada.

9.

May 16, 2010

Dear Journal,

    My grandfather's funeral was today.

    I think there should be a rule that says you can't talk about how someone died at his funeral. You are there to remember his whole life, and you don't have very much time. Nobody wants to remember him dying. That's the worst part.

    My grandfather was alive for more than sixty years but all anybody wants to talk about is the last week.

    Most people there didn't look very sad. Most of them just stood by the food table and shook their heads and pointed at the giant cardboard poster of his book that someone put next to his casket. My grandfather would have hated that they put it there.

    That's another thing. We all started calling him "Grandfather" rather than "Grandpa," because I think we forgot all the reasons why we ever called him Grandpa in the first place.

    My father just stared forward the whole time at nothing. And my uncle Tim tried to make a bunch of jokes about how my grandfather always took the top of the toilet off, like nobody told him that we were all there because he died.

My grandfather's agent, Mr. Volpe, spoke, and said these nice things about him, like how he was "brilliant" and "aware" and "ferociously creative." Which doesn't make any sense because usually Mr. Volpe just called him a "senile old mindfuck."

Me: Dad, how come Mr. Volpe is being so nice?

Dad: That's what people do at funerals.

Me: But that's not what he said when he was alive.

Dad: Doesn't matter how he lived. If he died, it's a tragedy. Everybody's forgiven in death.

Me: But that doesn't make any sense.

Dad: Well, neither did your grandfather.

My father was the only one who did a good job of speaking. He told a story that his grandmother had told him, about how when my grandfather was writing, he used to take a piece of paper and start ripping it up into little shreds, like a nervous habit. He said that my grandfather's life was like that, and now we all get to have a little shred of his paper to carry with us.

Except my dad and me never got any shreds of paper. Because he stopped doing that before we were born. So we didn't have much to keep with us.

All I could think about was the last conversation I ever had with my grandfather. In my head, I played it over and over again. I wish we could have talked about anything else.

Grandfather: No mortal has ever seen God, but millions of people believe in him. Do you know why that is?

He answered his own question, but I don't remember what it was. I was preparing my comeback.

Me: Doesn't it seem cocky that we have to always refer to him as "Lord, our God, Ruler of the Universe"?

Grandfather: It's good for people to remember that someone is in charge.

Me: He's not doing a very good job. What about all the violence in the world? Natural disaster? Disease?

Grandfather: He loved us enough to allow us mistakes.

Me: What about the earthquake in Haiti? Was that a mistake? Because thousands of people died—

Grandfather: If it was easy to believe in him, it wouldn't be faith.

Me: You can believe in giant rat overlords, that doesn't—

Grandfather: Enough, Jeffery. I'm finished with this.

Me: Arthur. You're talking to Arthur.

Grandfather: That's enough.

Me: Whatever you say, Grandpa.

After that, his face went blank again, and he asked where to find his own bathroom.

I get that people that love God like to walk by faith, not by sight, but sometimes I wish they would just keep their eyes open.

I think I'm going to stop writing in you for a while. I don't feel very many emotions, and I've been seeing Kaitlin a lot, so I don't think I'm going to have much time for it.

I hope you're not upset, but honestly, I don't even know who I'm supposed to be writing to in this thing anyway.

No more later,

Arthur Louis Pullman the Third

10.

I SAT FROZEN, watching the sun come up.

The clue was placed exactly where he knew I'd find it. The address was inked to the back with just enough information. Elko, Nevada, matched the city line perfectly. The train, his Zephyr, was exactly how my grandfather would have gotten there. And the next one left from the Truckee Amtrak station in just over an hour.

I couldn't imagine what he'd want me to find, but I didn't hesitate. I threw everything into my backpack as quickly as I could. My clothes—black T-shirts and a gray Oakland A's hoodie. My cell phone charger. My wallet. My grandfather's clue. I slid the photo from its frame and folded it into my pocket. I pulled the church activities bulletin from the trash.

My whole body surged with excitement. If my grandfather had spent the last week of his life with someone, then maybe they'd know why his body ended up in Ohio. Maybe they could explain what all this writing meant. Maybe they could explain why people made up so many rumors about him.

Breathlessly, I backed down the ladder and into the living room.

For five years, I'd wanted answers. The week of my grandfather's disappearance had haunted me since I was thirteen. Back then, I'd blamed myself for not finding him when he left, but as I got older and understood the situation more, I realized it wasn't my fault; it was my dad's.

I paused for a moment and stared out over the deck.

Might have to let that one go, his voice echoed. Just like he let my mom go. Just like he let his own life go. Just like he let my grandfather go.

This was my dad's problem. He'd never even entertained the idea that there might be something he was missing, or something more to the story, or some piece of the world that wasn't in his immediate line of vision. But my grandfather wouldn't have let it go. This was my chance to go where his son couldn't, and succeed where he had failed.

I slipped past the door, and out into the early morning fog. The air was thick. I knew the road back to the train station; it was one of the only roads in Truckee. I jogged alongside it, ducking into the tall grass ditch every time I saw headlights.

There was nothing keeping me in Truckee. As it stood, my life story read like a miserable, failed attempt, no different from my uncle's or my father's or anyone else's in my family. In the fog in front of me, I watched it play out like a slide show, all the hallmarks of that failure: the letter from UCLA telling me I'd failed my scholarship, my teachers telling me I'd failed high school, the yellow cast around my failed hand, Kaitlin's face telling me I'd failed our relationship, and the judge telling me I'd failed my one chance to be able to see her again.

But my grandfather had been extraordinary, and I could be a

part of that. And people would notice. Kaitlin would notice. Of course she would notice. She'd always told me to do something, and now I was.

My jog became a run, and it didn't stop until I reached the window of the station.

"Just you today, buddy?" the attendant asked as I approached, and I nodded.

I surveyed the area while she ran the emergency credit card my father had given me.

"Arthur Louis Pullman?" The attendant's face was frozen white in the morning fog.

"Yeah?"

She smiled. "Popular name around here, pal."

"Really?"

"Sure." She stood up. "You look like you're running away from something."

"What . . ." I hadn't considered the word yet, but I wasn't a runaway. I was eighteen, I was allowed to be wherever I wanted to be. "No, I, uh. I'm not."

"It's okay," she said. "I'm not telling anybody. We get a lot of runaways."

"You do?"

"Sure; only real way to get away anymore. Everybody here's running from something."

"Why?"

"Well, I imagine the hardest part of running away is staying gone, but that's not so hard here." She handed my ticket back. "The train can't turn around."

PART TWO.

elko.

1.

april 28, the 2010.

some days
i wake up in a place i have ban a thausand times
& have naver seen before

cold plane cold nothing fence line
giant machine
warped speed into blackness
& i am standing in the nathing of it all

some days
are too familiar to understand why
some days
my life is a story i've told a thausand times
& some days
the story moves backwards

cold cemant in forgotten town,
broken man to broken sign

arthur some days streets lites men woman man

some days i
ask myself who i am
& i wonder if anyone around me
could answer that quastion

lights color breath golden
streets shining
& i am sitting in the nathing of it all

some days i am nathing but reflex,
a trampoline soul sending right back
unburdened by my influence

some days i am without
my humanness
becoming the shirt on my back
worn shoes on my feet

but even those days
i feel you
every day
i know you're there

—*arthur louis pullman*

2.

SMALL DROPLETS OF rain started to pelt the windows as I felt my way to the back of the Zephyr. The sky was dark with heavy clouds; the lights of the cabin flickered.

It didn't surprise me that my grandfather chose the train for his escape. When he turned up in Ohio, that was the one speculation we all agreed on. The train was as much a part of my family's DNA as he was—my great-grandfather helped build it, my grandfather helped maintain it, and now my dad and I were among the last people still using it. Every school trip, every family vacation when I was a kid, every summer to tennis camp with Mason—every time, we used the Amtrak, even though every trip took two or three or ten times as long as the world's slowest airplane.

But really, I didn't mind it. For all the traditions I hated—the Christmas photos in matching button-ups, the cabin, the ham loaf and mandarin orange Jell-O—the train I could tolerate. Something about it did feel nostalgic, and valuable, and possible. *The train can't turn around*, she'd said.

I could understand my grandfather's awe. There was a time in his life when the possibility of the train had to feel otherworldly, like a magic carpet ride to a far-off kingdom called Cincinnati. The Amtrak was the blood in the veins of an adolescent and growing country. But now, it looked more like an abandoned amusement park. The exterior was cold, gray, bulky, and uninviting. The chairs were ripped, logo paint chipped, and the rough, Braille-like plastic on the walls had been smoothed down from years and years of children sliding their hands along it for balance.

It wasn't a ghost town today. For whatever reason, the train headed east from Truckee was packed. Old couples read newspapers, families watched *Kung Fu Panda* on first-generation iPads, and Amish people stared at the backs of the seats in front of them. The only empty seats—one of which belonged to me—had become beds, or terrains for children's action figures. When I reached the back of the train, I turned around and began to feel my way forward, holding tightly to the plastic seats on both sides and stumbling as the train banked around the bends of the mountains.

"You're not even going to tell anyone where you're going?"

The voice came from nowhere, light and airy and inviting and seductive and dangerous, cutting through the low rumble of the tracks. I took a measured breath to balance myself against it.

"You're just going to go?" Kaitlin walked in front of me, beckoning me forward, like always.

"I'll tell them once I get there."

"Arthur, don't do this. You don't even realize—"

"I thought you'd be happy for me."

"Why would I be happy for you?"

"Because I'm *doing* something."

"The only thing you're *doing* is manipulating people."

"No, I'm proving that—"

"Proving that you're not getting better. Arthur, you can't be out here by yourself."

"Well, that's weird, because I am."

"You're not hearing me." She waved her hand, her ring, in front of my face. "This is what you do. You don't even realize that you're out of control."

"Well, you're not even—"

My voice caught in my throat as the door slid open to the observation car, and Kaitlin disappeared with it. There was only one other person reading in a booth at the opposite end—a girl.

She had short brown hair, carelessly layered all around her head, bobbing and curling at the bottom. Her skin was light brown but looked almost gold in the yellow light of the observation car. A black beanie was propped up on the top of her head, and she had small holes in her earlobes, the gauges Kaitlin had always wanted but never gotten.

Without intending it, I'd stopped my progress toward the snack area, too busy noticing her to move. She looked sad, like she was disappointed in the book, or so busy considering what she was reading she couldn't be bothered to think about what her face was doing. One of her fingers bounced on the page, keeping time as she read. I had to know what she was reading, or why she was sitting there alone this early in the morning, but I couldn't ask. She was too confident and cool for the train, and definitely too confident and cool to talk to—

She looked up from her book. It was too abrupt, I couldn't look away in time, and our eyes locked. The harder I tried to break it, the worse it got, and instead of avoiding her gaze, I doubled down and stared straight back into it. She raised her eyebrows, so I raised mine. She squinted, so I squinted. She must have decided I was tweaking, or looking past her, because she lowered her head back into the book, and I ducked down the stairs, away from her, squeezing my finger for letting myself think about another girl.

My ring always helped me remember. "Promise rings," Kaitlin told me when she gave them to me, lying backward, her body curling perfectly into mine, her ass pushing intentionally against my upper thigh, staring out the window above the headboard. "Kaitlin," I tried to correct her. "We've had sex. You can't promise your virginity to someone after you've already had sex with them, it doesn't work like that," but that wasn't what she meant. "No, idiot, I know," and I remember distinctly that she'd smiled down at her hands, because the image is burned into my brain. "Promising everything else, though. Promising . . . each other." I had smiled, too, and I slid the ring onto my finger. It hadn't come off for four years. But recent events had forced it to switch hands.

There were only a few bodies around the snack car: a twenty-something man in the corner, an attendant perched on a stool, and a mess of hair and dirty cloth curled over itself and slumped against the back of the only booth. I took my seat across from the homeless man. He smelled faintly of dog.

I couldn't sleep through the smell, so I sat awake, alternating between studying the rain-soaked Northern California mountains and studying the patrons of the train as they came down to buy their Snickers bars and cans of Coke and tiny plastic bottles of cheap wine.

I pulled my grandfather's clue from my pocket and read it again several times.

Homes in foreclosed jungles, saints in slums of missions, sinners in sanctuaries of church street, hope in forests of elko, safety in mecca, chaos in cold, wet veins of ch, lou & sal's tribute, a true, Great purpose.

It felt like an evolution of places and things, like reading a map in text. If I was right, and there was something "in sanctuaries of Church Street," and that was "in the forests of Elko," then I'd decoded two of the pieces, but now the puzzle stretched out in both directions. Did I miss something in the "slums of missions"? Should I be looking for something in Mecca?

I approached the snack counter, placing a Snickers bar in front of the balding attendant. "Three fifty," he instructed, his eyes fixed on the journal in my hand. I gave him my card and he turned around to swipe it.

"Hey," I asked casually. "You don't happen to know if there's a city called Mecca in the United States, do you?"

The man in the corner looked up.

"I'm sure there is," the attendant said. "S E K-O-P-E-K . . ." He read from the back of the journal. "That's gotta be Sue, then, right? Sue Cow-pek?"

"That's nothing," I said too quickly, crumpling the page into my pocket.

He raised an eyebrow. "You know we don't know each other, right?"

"What? I mean, yeah, I know."

"Okay." The bottom of the attendant's stool scraped the floor as he leaned forward. "So why lie to me?"

"No, it's just—it's just kind of private. Something my grand-father gave me. It doesn't matter."

The attendant wasn't convinced. "And that's why you're going to Elko? Gramps gave you an address?"

I nodded.

"Well, you wanna know what I think?"

I didn't.

"I don't think he wrote that address."

"What do you mean?"

"Lemme see it." He motioned to the counter.

My better judgment told me to return to my seat, but he looked harmless. I smoothed it on the counter in front of him, holding the edges in place with my hands.

"Can I hold it?"

Slowly, I removed my hands. He held it up to the light, turn-ing it over several times before landing on the address.

"Yep." He pointed. "He didn't write that."

"What do you mean?"

The man in the corner leaned forward from his booth. "Yeah, man, that's inverted. Must have bled through from another page, probably an envelope. Look, you can kinda see the postmark."

"There you go," the attendant said, beaming. "Mystery solved. Won't even charge you for it."

I stared at the inverted address. It took them no time at all to notice, but they must have been right. Why else would the address be positioned so strangely on the page? Why else would there be curved lines above it? Why would the handwriting be different? Because it wasn't his. He hadn't written the address for himself. Sue Kopek had written to him.

"So who's the woman?"

"I'm sorry?" I looked up.

"Sue Cow-pek?"

I paused. "I—I don't know."

Hearing someone else ask it, the way his tongue dove when he said the word *woman*, the image of my grandfather blurred. I hadn't thought to make guesses about *why* he might have spent the last week of his life with a *woman*. "I don't know," I repeated to myself, but my imagination filled in the obvious possibilities. A bitter taste tickled underneath my tongue as I saw my grandfather rushing to Elko, away from me, away from the memory of my grandmother, into the arms of a *woman*. I wondered how they'd met, how long they'd been sending letters.

"Seems important," he said casually. "If he had a little lady in Elko—"

"I don't think my grandfather would do that."

"Same goes for everyone. Don't mean they don't do it."

"Well, I actually mean it. My grandfather wouldn't—couldn't."

"Just saying, that's what everybody—"

"Stop." I pulled the journal off the counter. "Please stop."

He watched me cautiously as I fell back into my booth.

I distinctly remembered the same argument—"everyone says they would never, until they have the opportunity"—from Mason, on one of those afternoons when all three of us, Kaitlin included, were stuck inside the afternoon shift at Jesus Crust, the Christian-themed pizza place where we worked. For hours, we'd all stand there, trying to catch straws in each other's mouths and trying to figure out why some people cheat and how they do it. I said I would never. Kaitlin said she would never. Mason said we just didn't get it.

How long had my grandfather been hiding his writing from us, just to send it to her? I thought harder about the journal—*full speed to Elko, full speed to you.* It would make too much sense. I had a sudden urge to rip the page from my pocket and tear it apart.

3.

INCOMING CALL: AUNTIE Karen.

My phone buzzed hard against the table, inches from my head. I must have slept, because when my eyes opened, the doors of the train were open, the sound of rain blasting through the train like a stereo searching for a signal. The digital clock above the attendant's booth read 8:30 a.m.

"Auntie Karen—"

"Arthur!" Her voice was like a smoke detector, short sentences coming in loud, intermittent blasts. "Where are you? What's going on?"

"Yeah, I'm fine, I'm—"

"Tim and I are worried sick, Arthur! Are you feeling okay? There's broken glass everywhere up here. Did something go wrong? Where are you?"

I pulled the flyer out of my backpack. "I'm, uh, I'm at the church."

"The church?"

"They were having a camping trip, so I went down and signed up." I heard the man in the corner laugh, so I whispered. "You guys weren't awake yet, so . . . I just walked."

"Arthur! The church? That's two miles!"

"You don't have to apologize, I like walking. It wasn't that cold."

"Arthur, Tim makes that drive every morning! He could have dropped you off!"

I slid the bulletin out of my backpack. "I know, but I had to get down there in time for the, uh, the camping trip. From the activities thing you left for me, remember?"

"I thought you said— You decided to go on the camping trip?"

"Uh-huh."

She was silent for a moment, probably weighing the bullshit I'd given her to see if she was willing to buy it. "I wish you would have told us you were leaving."

I could barely hear her. The doors of the train were still open, and the rain seemed to get louder as we sat there. Above us, there were footsteps, loud ones, and voices moving through the observation car.

"I'll be back in a couple days—"

"Arthur! A couple days? We've—"

"I can't really hear you—" The sounds upstairs intensified. I thought I heard something crash. "I'll call you later, okay?"

"Arthur, we still haven't—" I shoved the phone to my chest and ended the call as there was another shuffle of bags upstairs and a louder crackling sound, less like rain on the metallic siding of the train and more like an actual stereo. "What do you think is going on?" I asked, but the attendant didn't seem to care. I sat up in my booth, and down the stairs came two pairs of wet, black boots.

I hadn't thought about the police. There was no way they could be here for me. There was no way Auntie Karen had told anyone I was missing already. There was no way the police would care. Still, I shrank as far back into my booth as I could.

The policemen that entered the car looked more like soldiers. Bulletproof vests, extra belts for ammunition, and it looked like one of them had two Tasers—in case the first Taser wasn't enough. One of them chewed gum methodically. We made eye contact, and I shriveled.

But it wasn't me they were interested in. The chewing gum officer tapped the booth in front of the homeless man and he slowly rolled his face up off his hands. His features were nearly indistinguishable from the gray hair around them. "How long you been on this train?" the officer asked.

"Been on the train. San Francisco." His *S*'s whistled.

"Where's your ticket?"

The man didn't move.

"If you can't produce a ticket or valid identification, I'm going to have to write you a ticket and ask you to exit the train."

The man's eyes flickered out into the rain.

"Twenty more seconds and you're trespassing."

"I got my ID," the man said.

"Well, let's see it." The old man didn't move, so the officer reached for his jacket, pulling it off his body and trying to locate the pockets. The old man tried to grab his jacket back, but the other officer swatted his hands away. He made a noise like a whimper.

"Y'all seriously doing this?"

The man in the corner had set his book down and was holding his place with his finger. He leaned forward, speaking directly to the officers. He couldn't have been much older than me, maybe in his midtwenties, but there was no panic or smallness to his face. He looked relieved, almost smiling. He had pale brown skin and thick hair twisted into curls on the top of his head.

"Jesus, alright. Tell them you don't consent to a search."

The old man shook his head. "I—I don't. No search."

The officer rolled his eyes. "We're well past that point."

"Reasonable suspicion of what?" the man in the corner asked.

"If he doesn't have a ticket—"

"State law doesn't require an Amtrak ticket, they're a private company. Did somebody ask y'all to search the train?"

"It's theft of—"

"Not until Amtrak says it is. Right now, he hasn't done anything."

I tried to stare at nothing, especially not the police officers. The man in the corner was fearless, but I couldn't understand how. He was black, and he was speaking his mind to two fully armed white police officers in Nevada. I'd seen this viral video too many times to know how the story ended.

With a conscious glance to the corner, the officer flipped the jacket and continued searching, but before he got his hand out of the first pocket, the man in the corner drew himself upward. "And now you're searching him without consent." He was tall— much taller than both officers. They turned to face him, but he didn't give an inch, smiling down. This was already enough to be seen as aggressive. If the officers decided to hurt him, they would call it self-defense. I shrank farther back into my booth, praying he'd sit back down.

But he didn't. He reached to the table and lifted a physical ticket. "Oh, I found it. See, he's on until Denver."

The officer didn't even look at it. "Alright, where's your ticket?"

"Upstairs."

"We'll need to see that."

This made him smile across his whole face. His teeth were bright white. "I don't know. I don't really feel like searching for it, and seeing as there's no power of law to compel me to do so . . . I think I'll stay."

The officer chewed at him a few times. I could see the restraint muscles working in his face and arms and throat, holding him to his spot on the ground and keeping him from ripping the man's throat out. "Okay." He rapped the table in front of the old man again. "You got an ID proving you're . . . Jack Thompson?"

"He already told you, he doesn't consent to a search. You guys gonna pretend to be suspicious of a real law? Or you wanna maybe leave my man alone?"

Twice, the officer chewing gum looked *Jack Thompson* up

and down, and twice, they glanced back to the man in the booth, but eventually, they handed the ticket back. "Not worth it," one mumbled, and they nodded to the attendant as they disappeared up the stairs. I breathed for the first time.

Two minutes later, the doors closed out the sound of the rain, the old man curled back up on his booth, Jack reopened his book, and the train moved again, without a word.

"Jesus," I offered, to no reaction. "Fucking cops, right? I thought for a second they were gonna . . ." No one even looked up.

Mason would have gone crazy if he'd been there to see it. He loved watching people in charge get put in their place, especially white people. His entire Facebook feed was viral videos of conspiracy theories, or people getting told off on television. Mason acted like all forms of authority were somehow a direct affront to him. Teachers, politicians, parents, our bosses at Jesus Crust. Jesus Christ himself was probably a dictator in Mason's anarcho-reality.

But now I couldn't even tell Mason about it. And if I did, he wouldn't believe me.

"What were they doing on the train, anyway?" I asked Jack more directly.

"It's late in the month," Jack answered after a moment. He didn't look up from his book. "They've gotta fill quotas, and they know they'll find petty offenders on the train. Drug charges, theft of service, that kind of stuff."

"Fucking assholes."

"They're just trying to keep their jobs."

I kept looking at Jack, even though he hadn't once looked up. "Still . . . pretty inhuman."

"They treat people as inhuman because they're forced to work for profit." He flipped another page. "Cops are not the enemy."

"Who's the enemy?"

He shrugged. "Profit. Capital. Corporation. Oligarchy. Systems of power that serve inequality. American government, basically."

The train climbed upward out of Reno, toward the high desert, and the rain against the window got sparse. Mason would have *really* liked this guy, so matter-of-fact about his conspiracy that it almost sounded true. "Exactly, dude," Mason would've added after every sentence. "This is exactly what I've been telling you about." The problem with Mason was that he couldn't understand his own existential contradiction—he lived in Palo Alto. His parents designed software. He wore Gucci shoes to prom and got a credit card when he was sixteen. If capitalism was an evil empire, Mason was going to school, driving his car, and buying his clothes on the Death Star.

"I guess," I said. "But those guys didn't have to choose to be cops. Kinda everybody's fault; they're *our* government, and, you know, corporations."

Jack looked up at me. He nodded slowly. He set his book down on the table and smiled. Every movement he made was gentle. "What's your name?"

"Arthur," I said.

"Okay, Arthur. Let's hear your logic."

"I mean, we decided to care about money. So we made them rich. Like . . . you still buy cheap T-shirts"—I motioned to his chest—"even though you probably understand the T-shirt's only cheap because it's basically made by a slave. If we wanted that kind of stuff to stop, we could just stop buying their shit. But we don't. And we won't."

Jack must have been surprised, because he smiled again, brighter and wider and more curiously. Just like with the police officers, as his expression got friendlier, he got more intimidating. The wider he smiled, the more he showed his teeth.

"Spoken like someone privileged enough to be cynical. My friends and I"—he nodded vaguely up the stairs—"we don't really have time to lick wounds, but I get it. Much easier to blame the oppressed than the oppressor. Tell me, though, where do you think we learned the love of money? And more importantly—maybe the only important question—how do we unlearn it?"

I shook my head. "Good questions, I guess."

"Really, I wanna know what you think. You've clearly devoted some time to considering how dire the human situation is; I assume you're just as interested as everyone else in keeping us alive and free. How do we fix it? How do we get better?"

"We don't. I think we accept it."

I expected a reaction, but Jack was measured. He nodded and looked down into his book for a few moments. "Wouldn't change your life much, would it? You'd still get to ride your train. Buy your shoes"—he motioned to my Jordans—"have your dinner, your car, your family, your opportunities, your life.

"Let me give you an alternative, though, for the sake of the other ninety-nine percent of people. Maybe, instead of things staying the way they are, the greater public consciousness unites over a desire for equality. A few small organizations and powerful individuals lead an awakened majority to seize their power. They exert their will over the existing structures. The system crumbles. The world rebuilds."

It was silent for a moment. "What the fuck are you talking about?"

"Fixing things. Getting better. Marx already wrote the script. Capitalism creates oligarchy, the system starts to collapse inward on itself, and the only option left is class warfare."

"Wait, what?"

Jack smiled.

"Are you insane? You think the lower class is gonna . . . go to war? That would never happen."

"It's already happening."

"Except not literal warfare? You're talking about petty crimes and T-shirt manufacturing; it's not life and death, like real war."

Jack snorted, almost laughed.

"What?"

"Look, no offense. I'm sure you're a really great guy. But the only people who think this isn't as serious as life and death are the people who have the luxury of not seeing people dying. People are dying. Just not people who look like you."

"So we all get pitchforks, or—"

"You're saying it's impossible. I'm telling you it's inevitable. You don't even have to care—I'm sure your life is really nice right now. I'm just telling you, we're at the white-hot center of a revolution. You might want to consider whose side you're on before the buildings start falling."

It sounded almost like a warning. Jack had again drawn himself to his full height, six terrifying feet and a few terrifying inches, and stared me into the corner of the booth. He threw a five-dollar bill onto the counter and nodded to the man sleeping. "Give him a coffee and a sandwich when he wakes up," he said, and he turned up the stairs. He took them two at a time, not saying good-bye on his way out.

"Jesus." I turned to the snack car attendant, who was smiling down into the Snickers bars. "Did you hear all that?"

"Oh, I sure did. Heard the same thing many, many times on this train."

"What's his problem?"

The attendant looked at me sideways. "*His* problem?"

4.

"ALRIGHTY, FOLKS, BAGS are packed, doors are closed, and we are pushing off for our next stop, Elko, Nevada.

"Some of the crew has asked me to remind you that not every stop is an opportunity to step out of the train and stretch your—do I have to say stretch your legs? Or can we just be adults about this and point the finger at the smokers?

"Look, I know how much you all love your cigarettes, trust me, but we can't have violent rebellions starting at the exit doors at every stop just so you all can try to get a quick puff. And we can't have you opening the windows while we're moving, because that's stupid for a hundred different reasons. Once we shut those doors, they are closed for good. These are nonnegotiable policies. We don't make the rules, they're handed down from the powers that be, and I'm not talking about God here, I'm talking about the Amtrak Oversight Committee, or as we like to call them, Satan.

"You can smoke in Elko, ya filthy animals. That's all, from your brilliant and loyal conductor."

5.

IF I HADN'T broken my hand, and lost my scholarship, and ruined my chance to go to UCLA, I'd probably have been preparing at that exact moment. I'd be in the home furnishings section of Target with my dad, talking about which trash basket design would work best in a dorm room, or what towel set would make me look the most like a Bruin. I'd be working out with Coach Shelby, or falling into the rhythm of my reps from the Match Mate—the pop of the machine, the punishment of the racket, the recoil of the impact against my arm, the whiz of the ball over the net, and the next ball immediately lining up for its chance. I'd feel strong and safe and at home.

Instead, I was in the back of a cab in Elko, Nevada.

"Gold," the cabdriver responded when I asked what people in town were there for.

"I didn't know people were still looking for gold."

"Everyone's looking for gold, boss. We just find more of it out here."

Elko itself was a mountain town. The downtown area was dominated by two enormous casino hotels, surrounded by a few local bars.

The town thinned as we drove. Streetlights grew fewer and farther apart until there were none, and the casinos' marquees disappeared below us as the road climbed. The only light came from an almost-full moon. "This part of town's mostly abandoned," he told me. "Everybody's living over on the west side now. These houses aren't really worth shit." I felt the sudden need to reach for my seat belt, but it was broken, lying useless across the middle seat.

A few moments later, he turned onto a lonely street that disappeared straight up the mountain. There was trash lining the gutters, and the broken street sign was half hidden behind a willow tree: Church Street.

"Can you pull past it a bit?" I asked with bitter saliva in my mouth. The houses looked like they belonged to angry Nevada men with guns and dogs.

"Whatever you say, boss."

I watched house numbers go by, each more decrepit than the last: 27 Church Street . . . 21 Church Street . . .

"You sure that's where you wanna go, boss?"

I swallowed.

Seventeen Church Street was abandoned. There was no car outside, no light on the porch, and the grass in front had shriveled into patches of weeds and dirt. The house was large, on a huge plot of land, adorned with dead bushes and two enormous willow trees. Several massive pillars held up a balcony in the front of the house, above a wraparound deck. In its day, it might have been elegant, nearly a mansion, but its day was long gone.

"That's the address," I said. "Can you keep the car running up here? If there's no one home, I guess . . . I guess you can just take me back to the train station."

"Sure thing, boss."

It was cold outside, the kind that grips every part of your body and doesn't let go. I pulled the hood of my sweatshirt up over my head and walked up the broken concrete walkway. Branches from the willow tree flung upward in front of me in the wind, like they were trying to hide the house.

The closer I got, the surer I was that it was deserted. No human could live like this. The windows were haphazardly boarded, and there were tree branches and remnants of old storms across the lawn. I wondered if this was the same house that my grandfather had found. I wondered if he'd even made it this far.

A few stray drops of rain found my face as I reached the door. I pulled open the outer screen and knocked.

"What is it you're looking for?" Mason's voice cut through the wind.

"Some kind of clue."

"In there?" Mason covered his eyes to look through the window. "Here's an important *what if*—what if she died in there?"

"She didn't die in there."

"You think the person who lived here *didn't* die in this house? You know if she is dead, you're the first suspect."

"I'd be able to smell it." I tried knocking again, slamming on the front door as hard as I could, but nothing happened.

"What if you find her, and you accidentally spit or come or something and your DNA is on—"

"How would I accidentally come?"

"Maybe she was super hot—"

"Jesus, Mason."

"Still," he said, leaning against the siding. There was a ring on his left hand, and he rapped it against the old wood. "Will you at least tell me what brought you here?"

"No, I won't."

"Arthur, I understand why you're—"

"Then good."

"But we've known each other ten years, and that was one—"

"Mason. We're fine."

I tried knocking again, slamming on the front door as hard as I could, but nothing happened.

"It doesn't have to be like this."

I knocked again, even harder, almost breaking the wood.

Mason watched. "I think . . . you're expecting too much."

"I'm not expecting anything." The handle was barely clinging to chipped wood around it, and without much effort, it clicked and let the door fall open.

"I'm sorry, Arthur." No sound came from inside the house, but the wind outside threatened to pull up several boards from the porch around me.

I ignored him. The air inside was stale, like it had been circulating inside for years. It was dark, but the moonlight showed rough outlines of what waited inside.

It was full of clutter. There were at least thirty old wooden chairs, haphazardly set around the room. Paintings were spread at random, and a table in the back was piled high with junk. Behind that were dozens of boxes. I motioned inside to no one. "Look, it's a junk house. People throw their trash in here because they know eventually the city will deal with it. No dead people."

But the wind didn't answer.

I went to slam the door, but before I did, I froze, noticing something on my hand. The hair was sticking up, ever so slightly. Small goose bumps were forming. The air inside the house was warm. I leaned my whole body inside to confirm. It was at least twenty degrees warmer. Someone was keeping the heat on.

I slipped in the door.

It felt like diving into a cave, the only light a narrow beam coming from my cell phone flashlight. There were two tables pushed against the back wall, behind the clusters of chairs, with a dozen boxes piled on top of them. I opened one—it was old records: Led Zeppelin; Crosby, Stills, Nash & Young; Simon & Garfunkel. They looked used, like someone had bought them for their record player, not just decorative living room props. Another box contained clothes, old, tough fabrics of dresses and dress shirts that I couldn't imagine anyone wearing. There was another box of plain cloth T-shirts, with old designs for businesses, like THE WATERING HOLE and BIG RAY'S SALOON. Yet another was small paintings and a collection of horseshoes. Several boxes were filled entirely to the brim with books.

I wandered through an open doorway into a kitchen. The clutter wasn't just confined to the living room—the whole house seemed full. The kitchen table was covered with appliances: old microwaves and blenders and the occasional power tool. Turning to the far window, my flashlight found another stack of books, and on the very top was a shiny new hardcover with a colored pencil sketch of a wooden shack, set against a gray-purple sky and light green corn. The title text was in light red along the bottom: *A World Away by Arthur Louis Pullman.*

I reached for it and behind me, someone laughed.

I spun around.

"Mason?" I called out tentatively, shooting the flashlight around the kitchen.

"Kaitlin?" But the house said nothing.

I backed into the hallway. I couldn't see any light, but over the sound of my own breathing, I thought I heard muffled laughter.

I snuck my way down the hallway, shining a light into every open door. There was a bathroom that was so rusted over, the sink had collapsed into itself. In a hallway closet, there were no clothes, but an enormous stack of *Chicago Tribunes* that must have dated back forty years. I picked one up, and in the address section in the bottom right corner, it read: Susanne Kopek, 17 Church Street, Elko, Nevada. I swallowed hard and placed it back on the top of the pile.

As I neared the end of the hallway, the laughter got louder. I could hear it: not just one person, a group of people.

"Kaitlin, don't do this to me," I called again to the silence of another hallway.

I waited. At the end, there was flickering light coming out from under the only door.

The reality of finding someone, or multiple someones, caught up to me. What if it wasn't Sue Kopek?

I inched toward the door. There was a clock hanging in the hallway; its ticking was the loudest noise in my ears. I synchronized myself with it: *tick-tick-tick-step, tick-tick-tick-step.* I reached the door and clicked the handle open.

The smell rushed out, like a refrigerator of spoiled food. The laughter was coming from a small, old television set in the corner, the kind that received its signal from a built-in antenna, and on the screen, a black-and-white program was fading in and out of static. As I pushed the door open farther, I noticed the small windows were covered in tinfoil, blocking any potential light from reaching the room. There was a rotting chest of drawers, a bed with a floral spread on top, and an old woman in a nightgown gingerly sliding down off it.

Her frail body tensed when she heard the door. She didn't turn around, her face glued to the far wall, her body halfway between the bed and the floor. One of her bony hands clutched the bedspread.

"Sue?" I asked.

She turned. Her face was wrinkled in confusion. She stared at me for a few seconds as if I was a ghost, and then, abruptly, the confusion melted. She had to cough a few times before she could produce words, but when she did, her voice was delicate:

"Oh, heavens, it's just you. Hello, Arthur."

6.

May 2, 2010

Dear Journal,

My grandpa still hasn't come home and it's been five days. I think my parents have decided that he's probably dead. But I still jump every time I hear the phone.

I have to walk through the garage and the backyard to get to the kitchen, so I don't have to see his room or his chair in the living room.

I thought about praying, or at least reading his favorite part of the Bible, but I couldn't find it.

I had a dream last night where he came home and said, "Just kidding! I was testing you, and you passed. I don't even have early-onset Alzheimer's or dementia or any neurodegenerative diseases! I'm just your same old regular grandpa. What time do the A's play?"

But I know he wouldn't. He would come home and say, "Who

are you? What is it you're looking for?" and I'd tell him, and he'd
say, "Arthur, that's a great name," and then twenty seconds later,
he'd ask me again, "Who are you? What is it you're looking for?"

I think my biggest fear is that we'll never find out what
happened, and then people will just forget he's even missing, and
in five years my dad will say, "Hey, remember Grandpa?" and
everyone will go, "Oh yeah, whatever happened to him?" and I
won't remember him either.

At least people will still read his book for another—well, people
actually don't even really read books anymore. Hopefully it gets
made into a movie, and hopefully they make it 3D.

That's all for now. More later,
Arthur Louis Pullman the Third

7.

FOR A MOMENT, I couldn't form words. My heart slowed to
a near stop, and every beat felt too loud in my chest, shattering
the stale air in the room.

I could tell it had been a long time since Sue Kopek—if this
was Sue Kopek—had left her bed. She tried several times to
prepare herself to drop to the floor, but her body disagreed.

"Stupid feet," I heard her mutter.

"How do you know who I am?"

In the low light, I couldn't read her expression exactly, but it didn't look like fear or surprise.

"You boys were supposed to be back last week," she said, her voice parched and dry.

"Me? What boys?"

She didn't react to the question. Instead, she looked around the room, her voice fluttering. "Tell me, where's Orlo? And Jeffery?"

"I don't—I don't know who those people are."

"Well, heavens." She watched her hands run across the sheets. "You said you were all coming back together. I thought you were going to be late."

"Who was supposed to be coming back with, with who?" I asked. I stepped farther into the room and felt woozy in its warmth. "Late for what?"

A floorboard creaked under my sneaker, and Sue's eyes shot up from her hand to my face. Her eyes were wide. "Oh heavens, it's just you! Hello, Arthur."

"Yeah, I, I know. I'm sorry, how do you know me?"

"You boys were supposed to be back last week," she said. "Tell me, where's Orlo? And Jeffery?"

I took several quick steps back, hoping to escape the room's warm and warped reality. "Who do you think is here with me?" I asked.

She shrugged, and again she was distracted by the roses and carnations sewn into her bedsheets. It reminded me of Kaitlin's drunken nonchalance, the way she pretended to care about something else when she couldn't be bothered to answer a question.

"How do you know who I am?" I asked again, more insistently.

She looked up as if she couldn't believe that I existed. "Well, heavens, Arthur. You boys were supposed to be back last week."

Outside, we heard a crack of thunder, followed by a slow, building drum line of raindrops on the roof. There was almost nothing in the room, beyond a small TV set, a bed, and a large pile of ceramic trays, the kind that charity organizations used to bring meals to the elderly.

"Tell me, where's Orlo? And Jeffery?" she asked for the third time. Her voice was soft and whimsical, and she lay back against the headboard, her head rolling around gently.

"I don't—I don't know who Orlo is. Or Jeffery."

"Arthur."

"Yes?"

She froze and swallowed before speaking. "You boys were supposed to be back last week."

"Sue."

Her eyes stayed fixed on me. "Yes?"

"Who do you think is with me?"

She didn't respond, so I took a step toward her.

"Who do you think I am?"

Her hand clutched the sheet.

"How do we know each other?"

I took another step.

"I—I need to go to sleep, I'm sorry, Arthur," she said, and her body slid down, disappearing underneath the blanket.

"Sue, I need you—"

"You know where the upstairs room is."

She pulled the blanket up, trying to escape me beneath her covers.

"Sue, tell me how you know who I am!" The frustration of ten hours on the train poured out.

I watched her face shift like the rounded ridge of a puzzle piece snapping into place. I was close enough now to recognize the look: unbothered, vacant, with more questions than answers. There was a perpetual surprise written into her eyebrows and the tops of her cheeks.

It was the same look my grandfather used to give me every time he lost track of a conversation and started over. My father called it "the reset." It was the worst, most crippling progression of Alzheimer's.

Old age was getting the best of Sue Kopek's brain, and her resets were dangerously close.

"Tell me," she asked. "Where's Orlo? Or Jeffery?"

I nodded, swallowing the cocktail of pity and frustration. "I don't know Orlo, Sue, but I need you to tell me who he is."

"Oh, don't be silly," she whispered, and turned over to face the far wall.

"Sue, please," I pleaded to the back of her head. "My, my grandfather passed away, a few years ago, his name was Arthur

Louis Pullman, and I think he came here, during the last week he was alive, and I'm just trying to understand why. Please, if you hear me at all, tell me how you knew that I was his grandson. Tell me why you wrote him a letter."

I stared at her in silence, but she didn't respond or roll over. If she ever had answers for me, they were long forgotten.

I turned to make my way upstairs. As I reached the door, her voice stopped me. "Arthur?" It was frail, cracking in the middle of my name.

"Yeah?"

"Please take his napkin. I don't need it anymore."

"Whose napkin? Orlo?"

"Please take it." She nodded toward the bedside table. "I don't need it anymore." I had to squint to see it, but on her bedside table was a crumpled-up used tissue.

I shuddered at her attachment and continued out the door.

As it clicked shut, I remembered the cabdriver. I ran back outside, flinging the door open and launching myself out into the pouring rain. I was drenched by the time I hit the end of the porch, my hair washed and my hoodie soaked through and clinging to my body. The cab was gone.

There were no signs of life within walking distance, and if I was going to make the train back, I had three hours to walk it, through the bitter-cold rain. I slouched back into Sue Kopek's abandoned mansion.

In the living room, I found a cotton dress in one of the boxes that I used to dry my hair, then collapsed onto one of the couches. The splattering of rain against the old roof melted into white background noise and it was quiet in the house. Off the vaulted ceilings and through the crowded hallways, I could hear the echoes of Sue's voice.

Oh, it's just you, Arthur.

Sue Kopek must have thought I was my grandfather. It didn't matter that I didn't look like him, that he was an old man and I was a teenager; if her Alzheimer's was forcing her to relive a moment in which she was waiting for Arthur and I walked through the door, I was Arthur. Alzheimer's did that—skewed the details to make every moment feel like reliving a memory. To Sue, I had become a character in those memories that had become her reality.

But as I ran the cotton dress through my hair once more to dry it, I realized what that meant: I *was* my grandfather. If I could figure out what she was reliving, I could figure out what my grandfather was doing here, and what happened that was so significant that it had frozen her in time.

I began to pick back through the house. I remembered the copy of *A World Away* on the kitchen table. It was still glossy and new, and the binding was rigid, like most books before they're read. I flipped through a few pages and they stuck together in chunks. Whoever received this book had set it down and never touched it again. I opened to the dedication page, hoping there would be an inscription, but there was nothing. Just the book's original dedication:

for great purpose.—A.L.P.

I sighed. Another meaningless abstraction from the great Arthur Louis Fucking Pullman.

I climbed carefully to the second floor and pushed doors open at random. Sue had mentioned a room upstairs, but most of the rooms were empty. I tried to use one of the toilets, but there was no water in it.

At the end of hallway, there was one door left open, a shallow light streaming out of it from the moon.

I crept toward it, aware of how terrifyingly large this house was in the middle of the night. The old light fixtures and chandeliers hanging from the ceiling were covered in cobwebs. Candleholders jutted into the middle of the hallway, holding more wax than candle.

I peeked around the corner. The window was covered in splatters, the residue of large raindrops, hundreds more streaking it every minute. It was the only bedroom, other than Sue's, that wasn't empty. There was a single mattress, directly in the center of the hardwood floor, with a blanket and pillow on top.

Next to the mattress, cleanly gathered, was a pile of tiny, ripped shards of paper.

My grandfather had been here.

My brain kicked into overdrive. This was exactly what my father had described in his funeral speech, five years ago. Shreds of paper my grandfather left behind. I overturned the mattress and rifled through the pillow and blanket. There was nothing.

I tried to think, but my brain was clouded with exhaustion

and frustration. The paper was left behind to be discovered, like he wanted me to know he was writing, like he'd left a clue. I ran back through the kitchen and dug into the boxes of books and loose paper, searching for something with my grandfather's scrawl.

I thought about the first poem, the "you" that he had been writing toward. Was it Sue Kopek? If it was, he would have been writing for her, and likely would have left it for her. It made sense, if that's who he was writing to, but the only things I'd seen in Sue's room were the television, the trays of old food, and—

The napkin. She had made such a big deal about the napkin, *his napkin.*

I made my way back to her room, the door groaning as I pushed it open. I tiptoed across the room, careful to avoid any loose floorboards, and snatched the napkin off the bedside table.

What she had called a napkin wasn't a napkin at all—it was a crumpled piece of thick notebook paper with ink markings on the inside of it.

I turned to leave, but something caught my eye—the stack of paper, innocently set on the bedside table, wasn't just paper: it was envelopes, small and stocky. I leaned closer; below them, barely visible, was a page of handwritten addresses. Halfway down, I recognized the Truckee address and recoiled, the wood beneath my heels grinding together in a slow creak.

Sue Kopek rolled over in her bed and my heart flew upward into my throat: her eyes were wide-open.

Her chest rose and fell steadily, as if she was asleep, and her face was expressionless, but her eyelids were pulled back as far as they'd go, leaving her eyes white and glowing. I gaped at her for a moment; it was impossible to look away from her terrifying stare. Quietly, she whispered, "You said you were coming back together."

Without thinking, I ran. I didn't care about the door behind me slamming. I took off up the stairs. I didn't stop until I reached the far bedroom and slammed that door as well. I hurled myself onto the mattress and froze, listening for signs that I had been followed.

I did nothing but breathe and listen. But the house was silent, save the soft moan of old wood.

One finger at a time, I opened my hand around the crumpled notebook paper and spread it in front of me. The moon lit the page—it was the same cursive, my grandfather's writing.

april 28, the 2010.

pillar porch ceiling mattress singing all in baxes
her castle
& we were jasters
moon through window, made of
built on
love
arthur
some days are cold nathingness

i feel us moving through it
speeches in your living room,
dreaming on your floor
songs with words that fill to the ceilings
who were we then?
where did

cold window lite from moon
i know cold
i know leaving
i know empty
i know sickness & health
i know temporary
& she knows them too

she waits here for us,
in empty boxes broken bells
in songs that still echo in the ceilings
in ruins of
a castle lite from the moon

she waits,
& we went
& never returned

but she knows the curious rush
to smell

see
touch
to know but not remember

to love
hurt
cry out
for history that doesn't exist

but for the lite from the moon

felt but not seen
held but not understood
shrunk like threads
of oft-worn cotton
her head & mine,
a diary of time forgotten.

—*arthur louis pullman*

8.

IT WAS PAST midnight when I set my grandfather's clue down on the floor next to the ripped shreds of paper and collapsed onto the mattress.

I understood more and less. He'd been on this "mattress," writing to the light from the "moon through window." Was this the castle? He kept referring to Sue as "she"—if not her, who was he writing to? Why was she waiting, and who didn't come back? Orlo and Jeffery? Or my grandfather?

The date was April 28, the second day he was missing. I wondered how long he'd stayed before moving on. I needed to know where he'd gone next.

The poem did make one thing clear: I was right about Sue's brain. She was fighting the same battle my grandfather had fought at the end of his life, and even my grandfather could tell. I could understand her as I understood him: as a victim of the unstoppable march of age. My frustration with her was buried in pity.

But it gave me an advantage: I knew how to speak to my grandfather. When he was stuck in a reset, or clearly reliving some other experience, we'd learned to play along, hoping that instead of confusing him more, we might jar loose new information. If Sue was stuck five years ago, waiting for him to show up, I had to feed her imagined reality. I had to become my grandfather.

9.

I TAKE MY last big breath at the same spot that I always take my last big breath.

The nose of the Camaro breaks mile marker 29, and I inhale. The window's down and air is rushing at me much faster than I can take it in, and I'm tasting every invisible piece of it. The air out here is sweeter, uncorrupted by the smell of San Francisco, and now my whole body is full of it. I'm 90 percent air and 10 percent right foot.

Fourth gear.

The crest of the mountain is ahead of me and the sun is breaking over it and I'm hurtling toward it. The wheels of the Camaro, the TSW Nurburgring five-hundred-dollar customs, are gripping the road and throwing it behind them. There are no cars on the road. There are no clouds in the sky. There are no spots on my window. There are no thoughts on my mind. There are no speed limits in Portola Valley.

Fifth gear.

I hit the top of the mountain, or it hits me, and the world opens below. It's like the Land Before Time, with one single road guiding me slightly to the right, and I know it like I know how to wake up in the morning. Narrow slopes on either side of the asphalt disappear into darkness. I could close my eyes but I won't because to miss this would be to miss heaven opening right in front of me. It's the perfect curve for maximum velocity. It will throw me forward, downhill inertia meets centripetal-force inertia meets the engine of the Chevy Camaro. God-made energy multiplied by man-made acceleration, as I shift into—

Sixth gear.

I spin the wheel and the energy of the curve pulls me toward the center of the circle, toward the center of the Earth. The frame shakes as the air rushes in and the speed takes over and I'm no longer mortal, no longer bound by physics and reality, I am a creature of adrenaline. Adrenaline, pumping so fast that I can see it, hear it, taste it, touch it, feel it in my head and my heart, and my foot pushes farther, the curve behind me, nothing but downhill asphalt in front of me until—

There's someone in the road.

Brown hair and pale skin, shining in the Portola Valley sun.

I slam on the brake but the brake does nothing.

The speedometer is broken. There are no speed limits in Portola Valley.

There is no decision; I can't hit her. Adrenaline jerks the wheel to the right. One inch. Two inches. Six inches.

The Camaro crashes into the barrier. The frame of the vehicle crunches but the momentum is too much, the speed is too fast. I'm flying into darkness.

My seat belt wraps and collapses my stomach. It forces out everything that was inside of me. All the precious air that I saved was gone.

Five more belts wrap around me. The ring squeezes my finger tighter.

I'm trapped to my seat, immovable beneath the belt and watching in real time as the front of the car connects with the side of the mountain and collapses the steering wheel to my throat.

The back right bumper is next, then the left, the frame snapping and sending metal rods and black leather and bucket seats flying around me, circling my head.

I'm still fully conscious as the car hits water.

I didn't know there was a lake here. For all the times I'd driven this road, I never looked far enough into the valley to see the water below. Immediately, I'm under the surface. It's cold and lifeless and dark and empty and unending, extending infinitely in every direction. I'm trapped. I want to fight it but I don't, my hands too pinned, the pressure too great, the belt too tight, my chest too empty. My eyes are stinging, but I won't close them, because to miss this would be to miss heaven opening right in front of me. There is no air under the water. There is no part of my body that I can move. All I can do is feel; adrenaline, rushing through every vein and vessel, begging me to jerk my arms, to twist my torso, to reach for the window, to shatter the glass, but I don't.

There's a light coming from the surface. As I look up I can see her outline through the water; pale skin and brown hair, shimmering against the Portola Valley sky.

10.

I WOKE UP gasping for air. My eyes shot open but my torso remained still, paralyzed on the mattress. I wasn't underwater. I wasn't in my Camaro.

Lifting my head, I pieced reality back together. The room was empty but for the mattress I was lying on, the shreds of paper on the floor, and the clue I clutched in my right hand. Light was finding its way through the enormous window, throwing shadows against the wall. I fell back and closed my eyes.

From outside the door, I heard a crash and my brain revved to life—someone else was in Sue's house. I rolled off the mattress and stumbled to my feet.

"Hey!" I shouted, staggering out of the room. "Get out of—"

I choked on the end of my sentence when I reached the top of the stairs.

Sue Kopek, the night before too weak to even support herself on her own feet, was standing triumphantly in her living room like a statue in a storm, surrounded by a mess of folding chairs.

"Arthur!" She looked up at me, almost excited. "You boys were supposed to be back last week."

I swallowed hard. Her physical strength had returned; her memory, of course, had not. "Sorry," I said, taking small steps. "The train was late."

"Well, where's Orlo? Or Jeffery?"

"They're coming, too. Just running a little behind."

"Isn't that just like Jeffery? On our last day, of all days."

New information hit me like a blast of cold air to the face. It was her last day with Jeffery. It was a start.

But she had already lost where we were, disappeared into a box of records and reemerged as a carbon copy of the Sue that I had first discovered.

"Arthur!" she said. "You boys were supposed to be back last week."

This time, I was in character. "Well, we were running late. But Jeffery'll be here any minute, probably just in time."

"Good," she said.

I inched closer. "What time does he need to be here for us to . . . uh . . ."

She didn't complete my sentence.

"For the, uh . . ."

She didn't seem to hear me, instead mumbling to herself as she pushed chairs around.

"Where is Jeffery going?" I asked again.

She pulled her head back and blinked several times. "Arthur!" she exclaimed. "Don't sneak around like that."

I slunk back toward the kitchen and tried again, but it was the same result. Again and again and again, I asked what was happening, and she refused to answer.

The question became our brick wall. She just didn't know the answer. Of course she didn't. This was exactly what memory loss did to people: took away the most important parts.

I helped her pack and unpack boxes, pushing and prodding as gently as I could for more information, but our conversation became more and more sparse, and eventually she stopped talking.

I noticed that she seemed to move in practiced circles around the room, straightening the chairs, creating a narrow aisle through the center, then shifting them back into clusters. The scuffs on the floor beneath them were etched into the floor; these chairs had made the same movements hundreds of times over. Every time I brought a box forward from the tables, she carried it back, ensuring the chairs stayed unoccupied, mumbling something about keeping them out of the way. Occasionally she'd go upstairs, walk into one of the bedrooms, nod at all the walls, and then return to the living room. Her behavior was patterned, but the pattern was meaningless.

I checked my phone constantly—the train that returned to Truckee left in two hours, the one that continued east in two and a half. I had no reason to be on either of them, and even less reason to stay.

In the middle of the day, the doorbell rang and I hid, unsure of how to explain to the police what I was doing in an old woman's house, but there was no one there, just three prepackaged meals left sitting on the porch for her. She stopped and ate in silence. In her kitchen, I found a few bags of nuts that became my late lunch.

As the sun began to slant through the kitchen window, I found a small collection of photos buried beneath some records. There weren't many, and the few in the box didn't tell me much. They either contained people I didn't recognize or were too old and yellowing to make out any faces at all.

Underneath all the frames, stuck up against the cardboard, there was a single print. It was yellow, one of the oldest in the box, fraying at its edges.

It featured a young woman, smiling, with thick brown curls and a beautiful, flowery dress. She stood in the middle of the street, next to a man with thin glasses and a plain face, wearing a polo shirt that looked about two sizes too small. In her hands, she held a small bundle of blankets—a child.

My stomach lurched. There wasn't a feature on her face that looked the same, but I knew it was Sue Kopek. And the man . . . he was familiar. He wore my grandfather's glasses. But his chin was too round, his eyes too close. I flipped the photo over and on the back, in faded pencil, was written:

Orlo and Susanne Kopek and baby Jeffery. Green River, UT.

Underneath, in shaky block handwriting, with a black pen not yet old enough to begin fading, another hand has scribbled:

the nite he was born

home

It was like I had reset, like I was looking at her world again for the first time.

Orlo was her husband.

They had a son, Jeffery.

This was their home.

And five years ago, my grandfather had come back with her husband and son. He said they were coming back together.

All the details and circumstances surrounding her life and pieces of it that she was reliving felt somehow different and new. I studied the room again with fresh eyes, noting the details that had been too obvious to notice before: the living room packed full of boxes, the upstairs bedroom cleaned out, but her room perfectly intact.

My heart leapt into my chest.

For the first time, I looked past Sue Kopek, to the experience she was reliving. This wasn't a house condemned, and it wasn't a room full of trash. This was the result of five years of one woman reliving the same moment, waiting for the same thing.

"Where is he moving?" I offered, and I extended the photo toward her.

She dropped the book in her hands. Her expression went first to confusion, then to fear, toward me and toward the picture, then finally, it melted away into a smile that I hadn't seen yet, free of uncertainty or frustration. She took it from me, her hands shaking, and held the photograph to her face, like she was trying to get closer to the people inside of it.

"Home." She pulled back, nodding toward her hands. "He's moving home."

My eyes widened and I saw the full picture in front of me, spread across her living room.

Orlo and Susanne Kopek and baby Jeffery . . .

Green River, Utah.

"To Green River?"

For ten seconds, Sue didn't move, her eyes glued to the photo. I feared I'd lost her, but slowly, she began to nod. "Green River," she said.

The picture became clear. Her son was moving, and for whatever reason, my grandfather had come to be a part of it. I felt a surge of excitement that I hadn't in months, lighting up parts of my chest that I had forgotten existed. My search didn't stop here. There was another city. My grandfather had continued on with her husband and son . . .

I shuddered as I realized why she was stuck in this moment, what must have been so significant that it froze her in time, and why she was alone in this enormous house. They'd gone to Green River, and never come back.

Slowly, Sue cleared her throat and lifted her head back to me. "You boys were supposed to be back last week," she said. "Where were you?"

My brain flashed a bright white blank. "Oh, uh, we, we were, the train was—"

"You said you were coming back." She dropped the photo

and began to move toward me, her hands shaking. Her face was unfamiliar, her eyebrows angled and lips pursed. "You said you'd be back in a week."

I clambered backward, knocking over a folding chair and a box full of encyclopedias, but Sue didn't notice. She moved faster toward me, spitting words in my direction. Her eyes were white and glossy, just as they had been the night before, this time with anger.

"I'm not, I, I didn't—"

"And I waited, and I waited, and I waited!" She was shrieking now, volume shredding her frail voice. "You were supposed to take care of him!" Desperately, I prayed for a reset, but she moved faster toward me. "You boys were supposed to be back last week!"

I turned for the stairs and ran, hurdling them two at a time, around the corner and into the bedroom.

"You boys were supposed to come back together!" she screamed after me. "You were supposed to take care of him!" and I slammed the door.

My thumbs rushed around my iPhone screen—Green River, Utah, was three stops ahead on the California Zephyr and the train left at 7:45 p.m.—in forty-five minutes. I had to be on it. I flew around the room, putting on a fresh T-shirt and calling the cab from the night before.

"Somebody was home, eh, boss?" he asked. "Or is it your house now?"

With my bag repacked, the clue from the night before tucked

in a side pocket, I inched slowly downstairs, checking around the corner for Sue. Several more boxes had been shoved over, and the contents were strewn across the floor. She sat in the middle, on her knees, surrounded by a small ocean of her possessions.

I walked the stairs carefully, step by step, waiting for her to turn on me and begin shouting again, but her eyes were closed. She was shaking softly, fresh tears on her cheeks.

I stopped as I reached the door. The pit in my stomach had returned, but this time, it was specific: guilt. Her sadness was like a weight in the room, a weight that I was responsible for.

I turned back to face her. "Sue, I, I know you don't, you don't really know who I am, or I'm not who you think I am . . . but I know that you knew my grandfather, and . . . and I, I think we both know he deserves better than what he got. And I don't know where your son or your husband went, b–but I'm gonna go figure it out. For me, and for you now, too. And I know you don't understand what I'm saying now, and even when I come back here you're not going to understand it . . . but you deserve answers. We both do. So I'm gonna go get them."

She didn't react. Her face stayed frozen, an empty silence I knew well. I hung my head and pushed open the door.

"Arthur."

Her voice didn't crack. I paused, ready for her to tell me one last time that I was a week late.

But she didn't.

She pushed herself to her feet and glided across the room. Her face was focused and intense and purposeful, staring straight into me like she meant it. For a moment, I'd have sworn she knew everything: who I was, where I was going, what I was looking for. She grabbed me by my sweatshirt and looked straight into my eyes.

"Go on now," she whispered. "Go get him back."

11.

I HELD MY breath as the cab sped across town. The train was scheduled to depart in eighteen minutes, and the next train for Green River wouldn't be for another day, which meant twenty-four more hours in Elko. I couldn't keep up with my lie to my auntie Karen.

I tried to piece my grandfather's story together, but it felt like I knew less than I had before, and I couldn't fully form the questions in my head; they were clouded by the image of Sue Kopek crying on her living room floor.

There's a popular thought experiment called Schrödinger's cat, where a physicist—who was probably also a sociopath—put a regular cat into a box, treated it with radiation, then showed people and said that until the box was opened, the cat was both alive *and* dead.

We hit four red lights, one after another. Nine minutes until the train left.

His point was, if you don't see it, then you can't know, and if you can't know, then nothing is true, so everything is true. It makes sense—truth is subjective; there's no such thing as "reality," only what we think we *know* to be reality.

But the real value of any thought experiment, the real question he was asking, I think, is: What if it was your cat? Would you open the box? If you don't, you maintain the possibility that the cat could still be alive. If you do, and you confirm the cat's dead, then you're the one who killed the cat. Would you rather live with miserable truth, or blissful ignorance?

I asked if the cab could go faster, and the driver told me I didn't want to fuck with the cops in Elko, boss. Seven minutes to the train.

My brain went back to the still frame of Sue, collapsed on the floor of her abandoned home, her life in ruins around her. When I arrived in Elko, she was waiting happily, certain that her husband and son would be home soon. I was the one who had made her painfully aware they wouldn't be. Whether she would forget it soon or not, I had forced her to remember that she was all alone. I opened the box. I killed her cat.

The train became visible, resting on the tracks, as we crested the hill before the station. It was scheduled to leave in two minutes.

I imagined it was me. Would I want to know? I wouldn't, I decided. I'm okay with feeling unresolved, or confused, because there's no way that's as bad as feeling miserable. I'd frame the box and eat breakfast every day with my maybe-cat. Even if it was fake, I'd want to live in the world that I made for myself.

We entered the parking lot the moment my phone switched over to 7:45 p.m.

The train began to shake with activity. "Fuck! Just drop me here!" I shouted at the driver, a hundred yards from the doors, where the attendants were pulling in the stepping stools. I launched myself from the cab but my shirt was jerked backward.

"Hey!" the driver shouted. "You've gotta pay me, asshole."

I fumbled with my card, the whistle of the train blowing, my fingers shaking, the world spinning dangerously fast. "Alright," he said to the authorizing screen. "Go."

I sprinted recklessly across the open concrete toward the platform, my backpack swinging clumsily behind me and slamming against my back with every step. I tore across the asphalt to where the train whistle was sounding.

"Wait!" I tried to shout, but it was too late. No one was listening. The coach door slammed in front of me.

I reached the concrete as the brakes released, the train settling backward before starting to move. Amtrak had a strict policy of never reopening the doors once they'd shut. I knew it because they reminded us every time we stepped out of the train.

I pounded the window in front of me, hoping the impact would jar it loose or pop the handle. It didn't. "Wait! Open the door!" My reflection in the window disappeared as the train moved forward.

I kept up with it, pounding the glass all along the way. It

started with a walk, the train lazily dragging itself out of the station at five miles per hour. I leapt from the platform to keep up, weeds and brush whipping against my legs as my jog became a run, the train picking up speed too quickly. The window was just above my eye level and I had to jump to see inside. Still I pounded, cast and hand against the glass, screaming from outside the train, "Someone open this! Don't leave me here!"

Out of the bathroom door, the girl with the beanie from last night's train passed in front of the window. Either I was imagining her, or she'd somehow changed trains on the same schedule I had. I gave the window one hard smack to grab her attention, and she turned and leapt backward, panic on her face. I jumped and motioned toward the window release, my eyes begging her to open it.

She stood for a moment, still. "Please," I mouthed as I jumped again, fatigue beginning to push down on me. I must have looked adequately desperate, because when I jumped again, she was throwing her body into the bright red emergency lever that released the window.

Her tiny frame was pushing upward as hard as she could, but the lever wouldn't budge. I waved, but she couldn't see me; the train moved too quickly, fifteen, twenty miles per hour. I pounded and jumped, and the girl looked up at me, her face froze in confusion. Frantically, I motioned, *Down! Down!*

The realization hit her, squarely, like a cast against a window. In one motion, she grabbed the red lever and yanked it down toward the floor. The window swung open, warm air from inside the train rushing out. A surge of adrenaline burned hot in my blood and shot through my body. I launched myself at the train, clutching the metal bar above the window with my right hand and pulling upward into the square frame. From the shoulder, I swung my useless left arm around into it and felt the nerve endings explode with pain as she grabbed it and pulled. I ran my legs up the side, transferring my weight over the window ledge, and with one final push off the siding, my balance shifted, and I toppled into the train car, landing with a thud.

PART THREE.

green river.

THE GIRL WITH the beanie shoved me off and ran to slam the window closed, the red lever clicking back into place, and spun on me. But before she could open her mouth, another door swung open and an Amtrak attendant burst in.

"What the hell was that!" He painted the walls around us with saliva. "Which one of you opened that window?"

My left hand was burning from bracing my fall to the ground. The razor-sharp edges of my nerves—hundreds of them—tickled the inside of my skin, sending waves of pain down each of my fingers and up my arms.

"Somebody start talking!" But neither of us did. "You know, I can kick both of you off this train."

The attendant looked at me, the girl looked at the attendant, and I closed my eyes, counting the seconds until I passed out.

"There was a man," she offered slowly, word by word. "He was trying . . . to smoke a cigarette, and . . . we told him . . . that he should leave."

"Some man conveniently left you two standing here while he made a break for it?" The attendant made a show of sniffing the air. "Does smell a bit like cigarettes, doesn't it, buddy?"

I looked away, shy and scared and screaming inside with pain. This was not my moment to be courageous and take the fall for her. This was my moment to huddle on the floor.

"Are we sure it wasn't you who opened the window to smoke?" he spat at her.

On the ground, her purse was open, and I made a quick decision.

She shook her head. "No, no, it . . . wasn't me. I don't do that stuff." Again, she spoke slowly, driving home every consonant with an Indian tilt.

"You don't smoke cigarettes?" Her eyes flickered to her bag, and the attendant's followed. "So if I check this purse here, I won't find any cigarettes? Or something else?"

"No. Not at all."

He snatched the bag. "I'd hate to find some evidence that you were lying."

We both held our breath as he rifled through it. I tried to catch her eye but she was focused on the search and seizure, breathing heavily through her nose. A few items popped out and fell to the floor as he dug—some eye makeup, a few tampons, a book called *Compassion*.

After turning the bag over, the attendant held it back to her. The blood behind his face was starting to saturate his cheeks. "What'd you do with them?"

I found my voice. "She, uh, she clearly wasn't the one smoking, so unless you want me to, to tell someone about your illegal search of her personal property, I'd stop *harassing* her."

He got the message. He could only hold on to her gaze for a few seconds before stepping backward. "If I find out it was either of you who opened that window," he warned us, "I'm going to enjoy kicking both of you off this train." He left us in silence.

It was a long minute before we spoke, both of us expecting the attendant to burst back in.

But he didn't. My heart settled to a normal pace for the first time in fifteen minutes. When we finally made eye contact, she was the first to speak.

"Well?" Something about her voice was very different.

"Well, uh, what?"

"You just jump onto a moving train, then?" It had completely transformed. It was light, quick, proper, and dripping with a beautifully British accent. I smiled. She hadn't wanted to seem recognizable, so she'd disguised the most unique trait she had: her accent. "Are you here to rob us? Or are you just an idiot?"

I couldn't tell if it was a joke, or real anger, or even some form of aggressive pity, but she wasn't smiling. "No. I just . . . really, really hate Nevada."

"Well, you're a bit dramatic, if you ask me," she said, her eyes now scanning the floor. "And you nearly got me thrown off the train, if not for a fucking miracle . . . I have no idea what—"

"What happened to your cigarettes?" I asked, pulling them from behind my back.

Her mouth bent to an almost-smile. "Well, that was clever. Thank you."

My chest warmed up. I wished Kaitlin could have seen this

conversation now. After four years with her, talking to other girls had become impossibly foreign, but here I was, making it look easy.

I studied the floor with her, afraid the eye contact would ruin it. "I'm not the one who faked an accent. That was smart."

I saw her reflection in the window, smiling for the first time. "What's your name?"

"Arthur." I extended my non-broken hand.

"Hello, Arthur. Mara." She accepted my hand and I held hers for a moment too long. "What happened to your hand?"

"Oh, um, an accident."

"'Oh, um'—very cryptic," she said, and without warning, she dropped my hand. "Well, Arthur. It was very nice meeting you, but please don't do that to me again."

"What, uh—" My mouth sputtered into a sentence before my brain could catch up. I wanted to say something to keep the conversation going, but I knew the cause was already lost. It would need to be something interesting, something about her, something observational, something smart—

"You know cigarettes are gonna kill you, right?"

Mara was already somewhere else. Of course she was. I slumped up into the nearly empty coach cabin, moving slowly so it didn't seem like I was chasing after her.

Kaitlin was right on cue.

"You should warn her." Her tiny frame slouched against the seat next to me, pretending not to care.

I smiled a little, because I could tell that she did care. "Warn her about what?"

She ignored the question, examining her fingernails. "Do you even know what you're looking for?"

"Yes." I reclined in my seat. "Green River."

"Great. And when you get there?"

My stomach twisted. She was right; the train stopped in Green River at 4:00 a.m., and I didn't even have a starting place, but I ignored it. "What do you mean, I should warn her?"

"It's nothing. I'm just saying, to be fair to her."

"Warn her about what?"

"About you."

"About me what?"

"Everything."

"What do you—"

"That you're not stable. That you have pretend conversations with people. That you get angry and your little switch flips and you go crazy. That you tried—"

"That's not true."

"Yes, it is. All of that is true. You're just too embarrassed to admit it."

"Well, it doesn't matter! I'm never going to see her again. Does that make you happy?"

The seat was empty.

2.

april 28, the 2010.

engine groan,
stars & invisible mountains in
infanite darkness,
i can see nothing so i hear everything.
arthur
wheels skid & scream & callide
just as thay have for dacades
the natural world whistles
as it has for centuries.

hard blue seat
gray plastic
i try to sleep, the only true piece
but you burn behind my eyes
i know i won't find piece until i find you.
or you find me.

i ask where we are,

& no one can answer
stop asking, thay say.

so i wander
train shakes gray plastic
& step by step,
i teach myself again how to walk,
walking for lite,
searching for you.

—*arthur louis pullman*

3.

INCOMING CALL: DAD.

"Hey, buddy, your uncle Tim called. He said you were going out and camping, by Donner? Which is great, Arty, it really . . . it really is. But . . . look, they said they haven't seen you since Monday. That's almost two days, and we're really . . . we're supposed to be keeping a better eye on you than that. And it would be one thing if Tim was with you, but I don't think I can be comfortable with you spending another night camping with these people I don't know. It's almost nine already, and—and I don't know, Arty. I'm trying to give you your space here, and if camping's making you happy then I'm happy, but—I just can't be comfortable with it."

"They're really great people, Dad," I said, whispering into the phone. "They're all church people. And they're all A's fans, too."

"That's great. And I'm glad you had your night with them, but two nights is too many with people I don't know."

I knew that I should feel panicked, so far from where I said I was and moving so fast in the opposite direction, and a good son would be remorseful, especially after listening to him tie himself in knots trying to sound calm and reasonable, but all I felt was annoyed.

"I can't spend my whole adult life with just people you know, Dad."

He was silent for a long minute. "Can I at least talk to the counselor or leader or whatever?"

"He's asleep. They have to be up early for a worship service."

"On a Thursday?"

"They're *really* religious."

He paused again. "Okay, buddy. I have to ask. Is this—this whole camping-by-the-lake thing—does it have anything to do with our conversation the other night? I know we got a little carried away, and I don't—I don't want you thinking I don't respect your opinion."

"No, it's fine. I'm over it."

"You understand why this money will be—"

"Dad, I don't want to talk about this again."

"I know, but I still don't like this implication that I'm some-how a danger to your grandfather, or that you have some kind of moral high ground—"

"Dad. Please."

"Arthur, we have to—" I heard him change his mind. "I want to give you all of the freedom in the world, Arthur, but you and I both understand why that can't exactly happen. I want you to do what you want, but . . . I don't know that we can count on you to make those kinds of decisions right now."

I let the line be silent for sixty seconds, counting trees that passed out the window.

"Okay, buddy." He gave up. "If this is going to help you feel good about things, then okay. But this is your last night camp-ing, alright? Tomorrow morning, you go straight back to the cabin and you spend some time with your auntie and uncle, okay?"

"Sure thing, Dad." I hung up.

I leaned back into my seat—that was it; the end of the rope, the 0:00 point of the lie.

If I turned around in Green River, I might be able to make it back in time to keep my lie intact. But what did I have to go back to, anyway? My laundry list of huge misses? My bedroom full of photos of people who had all moved on with their lives and were too scared of me to bring me with them? A best friend I couldn't speak to anymore? A girlfriend who I legally couldn't see? A year of nothing, no college, no girlfriend, no tennis, just my dad, silently pitying me? At least the train kept me away from that, but the train wouldn't last. Eventually we'd reach the end of the tracks, and that world would catch up to this one. Unless I could find a reason to keep moving forward, every moment was just delaying the inevitable collapse.

4.

"*GOOD EVENING, FOLKS, it's that time of the night. The snack car's closing, the lights are dimming, and that means we're signing off for the evening. Closing time; you don't have to go home, but you can't stay here. Actually, you can. Actually, you have to—this train's not stopping until Salt Lake.*

"*Any insomniacs with us on the Zephyr this evening, you can stare into the infinite darkness outside your window and know that I'm boldly leading you through some of the most beautiful territory that you'll never be able to see. We do ask that if you are awake during these midnight hours, you kindly make your way to the observation cars, lest one of our sleeping passengers wake up and try to throw you from the train. I am not screwing around, these people are serious about their sleep.*

"*If you're leaving us in Salt Lake City or Green River, an attendant will be around to wake you when your stop is approaching. If not, we'll be back with the good news at seven a.m. tomorrow morning with the first call for breakfast and the breaking of the new dawn.*

"That's all for tonight. In the immortal words of Dylan Thomas, 'Do not go gentle into that good night, rage, rage against the dying of the light' . . . and in the words of our own Chester Sayer, if you are going into that good night, go gentle with Tums, available at your local food and beverage car.

"Good night and good luck. That's all, from your brilliant and loyal conductor."

5.

I'M CRESTING INTO the Portola Valley dive. The wind is behind me, just like it always is, and the sun is rippling across the valley, just like it always is, and I'm hitting maximum acceleration as I reach the top of the hill, just like I always do. This is the part where the dive gets interesting, where the simplicity ends and the skill takes over, where the car demands the most of its driver, where the average motorist would pull off to the side of the road, take a picture from the scenic overlook, and then proceed with caution, but I proceed entirely without caution.

The nose of the car tilts, the downhill begins, and the natural speed urges the wheels to spin faster. I've taken the perfect angle, clinging to the outside of the road before—

The process freezes. My brain slows. My hands start to

doubt me. My foot wanders toward the brake—this has never happened before. I know this road; why should I doubt where I'm going? I slow down against my own will, fighting my intuition. I scream at my foot to return to the accelerator, but it doesn't answer. It continues to brake gradually, naturally, until the car is stopped, one hundred yards over the dive. I'm perched like a bird, the car a perfect forty-five-degree angle with the ground. There's no sound at all, inside or out of the vehicle. I have no control over the car or my own feet. I can't move at all.

Without being pulled, five seat belts slither out from below the seat and across my chest.

The silence ends with the sound of collision. I lurch forward, metal snapping and twisting all around me as another car, an enormous car, a semitruck, collides with the back of the Camaro. We're back in motion, sliding toward the edge, the cliff, the fall, the water below, the colder water below that. I can't see the face of the other driver, I can't control the movement of the car; I can't bring myself to fight the seat belts. I'm completely still.

Exhaust starts to form around the car, boxed in by invisible walls, and warning signs scream at me. Twenty feet from the edge, the car begins to shake; not a full vibration, like the result of prolonged and aggressive friction between the wheels and the road, but an unnatural shake, an explosive shake; the entire car being jerked up, and down, and up and down, my body convulsing with it against the seat, up, and down, and up and down, limp and floundering, my swinging forward, and back, and forward and back, and forward and—

6.

MY HEAD SLAMMED against the back of the seat.

"Jesus!" A face swam into focus in front of me, warm hands on my shoulders, shaking me. "Wake up!"

The features crystallized. Soft, wide eyes. A tiny nose. Light brown skin. Short, bobbed brown hair.

"Jesus fucking Christ. Are you alright?" Mara's face was electrified in confusion, as were the seven faces behind her.

I sat up quickly, orienting myself by the swirling balls of colors jumping around in front of me. It was still ink-black outside, but my yellow overhead light was on. My chest was pumping. My left hand was aching. It throbbed worse than it had when I fell asleep, and didn't stop when I folded the cast over.

"Yeah, what's, uh . . . what's going on?"

"You were screaming in your sleep," Mara said. "Really loud. We all thought you were getting murdered or something."

I looked behind me. The entire coach car was awake and glaring in my direction.

"I, uh, I'm sorry. Sorry, everybody. I get weird dreams."

"No shit," Mara muttered. The crowd behind her began to drift back toward their seats.

"Thanks for that." I swallowed. "I'll, uh, I'm just gonna—"

"Yeah, like hell you're going back to sleep. These people wanted to kill you."

"What time is it?"

"Two o'clock in the morning."

She was still crouched in front of me, and I could feel her arm against my leg. "Look, at least go sit in the observation car, okay?" she whispered. "That way, I can stop you if you go Lady Macbeth on us again."

It looked like she wanted me to follow her, so I did, not entirely convinced she wasn't in my head, another dream uprooting the first. She sat in the same booth I'd seen her in the night before, and she didn't look upset about me being around, so I fell into the open booth across the aisle from her.

"You were here last night," I said, my voice still groggy with sleep. "I saw you."

"That *was* you on a different train and everything. You're lucky I stopped in Reno." She smiled, and I knew it was really happening. Dreams were never this vivid. "And where is your final destination, *Arthur*?" She strung out my name, her accent squashing the first *r* so it sounded more like *author*. "And why are you lying to your poor father about it?"

"You heard—"

"Yeah, and you should probably know, you're a shit liar. You stuttered the whole time. I could've watched you have that conversation at a church camp or whatever and I still wouldn't have believed you."

"Well, he did," I said, trying to wipe the sleep from my eyes. "He still has no idea I'm out here."

Mara had been folding a napkin on the table in front of her, forward and backward, and she paused. "Probably better that way, right?"

"Where are you from?"

"Somerset, outside Bristol. England?"

I nodded. "And your dad . . ."

"Also doesn't know where I am. I left a few years ago—"

"How old are you?"

She side-eyed me. "Nineteen?"

"You ran away from home when you were *seventeen*?"

"Sixteen, yeah, but my sister basically raised me, and she was living in America already, so I just followed her."

"What about your mom?"

"Left when I was four." She'd resumed folding the napkin, over and over so it stacked up like a tiny paper building.

"Where does your dad think you are?" I asked.

"Right now?" She smiled devilishly. "Australian boarding school. Or the Italian military. Or dating an American celebrity."

I squinted.

"I send lots of postcards," she said, and held up a glossy photo of a ranch in Reno, Nevada. "From all over the country, too. I figure it's fun then, for him to try and put it all together, right?" She flipped it over. "'Dear Dad. Howdy from the American West. No one rides horses anymore, but that hasn't stopped me in my search for gold. Prospecting, they call it. I've got a lucky streak in me yet. Your daughter, Mara.'"

Mara's smile was a kind that I wasn't used to. It was bold and honest; it crept its way onto every line of her face, filling them with an understandable warmth and an impossible mystery at the same time. It gave me a strange, inclusive feeling, like everything she said was an inside joke, and the rest of the world was trying desperately to figure it out, but I was on the inside. At least I thought I was.

"So are you going somewhere specific, then?" she asked. "Or are you just running away?"

"I'm—" My tongue lurched, but I caught it. A small part of me wanted to try to impress her, but it was the stupidest, most impulsive part. "I guess both. I'm . . . trying to find something."

"You know," she said, cocking her head, "noncommittal and cryptic is really only interesting for so long, right?"

"Right. I guess I'm going to Green River," I committed.

"You know, I was hoping to explore Green River. Maybe if the train gets in early enough—"

"Maybe you could help me," I said, before I could stop myself. She buried her face away from me toward the window, probably avoiding me.

We both watched as a man in a black jacket, clearly drunk, stumbled from the dining car to coach. Three times, he looked back at Mara, and she rolled her eyes.

"What about you?" I asked. "Why are you here? Unless you really are . . . dating an American celebrity."

"Well, no," she laughed. Her accent was music to me. "Not yet. I have a job, in Denver. And I get to travel sometimes, so I'll sneak off and go study your protest history."

"Protest history?"

"Anti-Vietnam, Haight-Ashbury, the Summer of Love? My sister used to be really into it, traveling around the US and whatnot, so she gave me this amazing list of secret little spots that used to be important." She didn't make eye contact when she spoke, like she was always looking past me to the more interesting thing just beyond me. "It's spectacular. If there's one thing Americans are good at, it's getting pissed off at yourselves for fucking things up. I find it . . . confusing and beautiful."

Mara tried asking a few questions of me, so I told her about my Camaro, and Palo Alto, and everything that didn't involve Kaitlin, or Mason, or my dad, or my restraining order, or my cast, or my life in general. Three times, she reminded me that I hadn't actually told her anything about myself, but I knew it was better that way. Eventually, her head slipped to the table and her eyes closed. I didn't want to risk sleeping again, so I sat up, staring out the window and watching the nothing fly by.

No one knew where I was. I could've been dead for hours, and no one would have noticed. I thought about texting Kaitlin, telling her I was okay, and I was in Nevada, and I was doing something, but I knew my number was probably blocked, and it wasn't attention she'd give to me anyway. My stomach turned thinking about it, how I'd had to start competing for her attention when she used to give it to me so willingly. When we were sophomores, I never had to tell her when I had a tennis match but she'd be there anyway, the only one cheering whenever I *lost* the first point in a set, because she'd "always root for love." She'd bring me orange Gatorade and drive home with me, she'd tell my dad how great I'd been, she'd stay until we both fell asleep. She always wanted to know where I was and what I was doing. Now that I was out in the world by myself, and no one knew where I was or what I was doing, it was hard to imagine anybody ever caring about me like that again.

The train ran forty-five minutes early into Green River. Mara's head was still lying against the table, unmoving, and I thought about shaking her awake. She'd said she wanted to explore Green River; maybe I'd be doing her a favor. Then again, maybe she just wanted the sleep, and I'd be overeager and annoying. Also, again, there was Kaitlin. I shouldn't have wanted Mara's help. I should have wanted to see Kaitlin.

I didn't have to. Mara rolled over and her eyes opened to me standing over her. I didn't say anything, just stared back, watching her blink the world back into her view. "Arthur," she said, almost as if announcing it. "We have a little time, yeah?"

"Um—yeah." I didn't have to say anything more. She rolled out of the booth, and before I could move, she was leading me off the train.

7.

THE SKY IN Green River was a perfect and resolute black, dark enough for stars but starting to illuminate the streaks of clouds and the street around us.

"All that depressing fluorescent California light dies before it gets out here." Mara's neck was tipped back, taking in the whole sky. "You only really find this kind of sky in the middle of absolute *nothing.* This is what the stars are supposed to look like." She was right, they were incredibly bright, as if in higher resolution than the ones in California. Streaks of light shot down over a large plateau in the distance. "Heat lightning," Mara explained. "They get storms in the mountains up north, and you can see the lightning from here."

"How do you know so much about Utah?"

She shrugged. "Read about it, mostly poetry. There's an old Beat generation bar here; they used to write about Green River all the time. My sister went a couple times. Ah!" She pointed upward. "Shooting star, right there. Nothing insignificant about that, is there? Go on, have a wish, make it a good one."

We continued walking in silence.

"I do this thing," I started slowly, "where, whenever I see a shooting star, I pretend it's a planet that sustained life for millions of years, but then one day got too hot, and it burned up and streaked across the galaxy, and all of its life-forms died."

Mara stopped walking. "Why the fuck would you do that?"

"I think it's kind of nice to know that one day, our whole planet, and everybody that ever is or was here, is gonna burn up and disappear, and all that's going to be left of us is one single, insignificant streak across some other planet's sky. Makes this"—I gestured around us—"all of this, what's happening right now, feel a little more important, you know?"

Mara considered it. "I think . . ." She chose her words cautiously. "I'm beginning to understand why you might have woken up screaming."

I smiled. "I don't know. There are one hundred billion galaxies in the observable universe, and I'm a tiny, fractional, and insignificant part of one of them. I think it's . . . confusing and beautiful."

We kept walking, down one street, then back on another sidewalk. The town was eerily empty, even for the middle of the night. I scanned for signs of my grandfather, but none showed up. We were the only life in Green River, Utah, and it looked as though we had been for a long time. On the first block, there were four businesses that had been looted or burned down. The sign for Frank's Pizza had snapped at its center and was crookedly wedged against the roof. Even the frames of the buildings looked slouched, like they got together and decided it was time to all give up. On the side of one of the abandoned buildings closest to the train, someone had spray-painted a stencil reading

"YOU ARE HERE, FOR A GREAT PURPOSE." *Maybe*, I thought, *but we're the only ones.*

"So, any particular reason you're sad?" Mara pulled a pack of Marlboro 27s from her bag. "Or are you just a sad kind of person?"

"What, what do you mean?"

Her hand cupped the flame. "I hope that's not offensive. Just thought I'd ask."

"I'm not that sad of a person."

The paper sparked. "Looking at the ground, lying to your dad, running away on trains and whatnot. Most sad people I know, that's pretty standard behavior. You've just told me shooting stars remind you that we're all gonna die someday." She exhaled. It wasn't a cigarette. The smell was thicker, staler, stickier, more obvious. It was marijuana. She offered it to me. "And what is it with your car, then?"

I rejected it. "It's a Camaro."

"I'm sorry?"

"It's a kind of car."

"Right, yeah, whatever, I'm sure, it's a big, super, war gun car, or whatever." She inhaled delicately. "You keep talking about it. Even in your sleep. What's that about?"

"Oh." I swallowed. "It's nothing."

"There it is again! 'It's nothing,' 'it's not a big deal'—what is it with you and this idea that nothing is significant?"

I rolled my eyes. "Well, we can't all be . . . chill, and happy all the time."

"I'm not chill, ever. Or that happy, really. But at least I'm trying, you know?" She stopped to examine a telephone pole. "At least I'm talking about it." She pulled out her phone and used the flashlight to inspect it; it was splintering and covered in half-assed graffiti.

"What are you doing?" I asked.

"I don't know. I don't even know what I'm trying to find." She studied it a moment longer, then walked back in my direction. "And you still haven't told me what *you're* looking for."

"My grandfather," I told her, wincing as I felt the information slip away from me. "That's what I'm trying to find."

"He's missing?"

"Well, no. He's dead."

Her eyes widened. "You're trying to find his body?"

"No." I tripped over the details. "He died a while ago. Five years ago. He just . . . he traveled before he died. And I'm trying to figure out where he might have gone."

I could see her breath in the cold. "Why do you think he came to Green River?"

"He had pretty severe dementia, so . . . really, it could have been anything."

Mara kept her eyes in my direction as she processed this information. She had a perfect processing face. Behind the crescent creases at the tops of her cheeks, still flushed red from sleep, I could see tiny gears turning in my direction, tiny brain people holding tiny conferences with a tiny version of my face on a PowerPoint on the wall, trying to understand and communicate with me. Most people didn't look at other people like this. Most people didn't look at me like this.

"And why are you so insistent about this?"

"What?"

"Running away from home, just to check up on where your grandfather went five years ago?"

"I, well . . . I guess because everybody, in my family, and . . . everybody remembers him for running away. And I think he deserves better than that."

She frowned. "Very interesting."

"'Very interesting' meaning 'stop talking now,'" I said.

"No." Mara looked at me and squeezed her face to the center. "Very interesting meaning very interesting."

"Oh."

"Jesus, you've gotta stop doing that."

"Doing what?"

"That thing where you assume everything I say is sarcasm, or that you know everything about me because you saw a movie with a quirky Indian-British girl once."

"Afraid you're going to be exposed as quirky and British?"

"No," she said seriously. "It's just a terrible way to get to know somebody, pretending like you already do."

We turned, and the largest sign on the street pulled my head upward toward it. I felt a wave of familiarity wash over me, a smell or a sound or just a feeling, a silent and unconscious déjà vu. I shuddered, remembering the logo from the shirt in Elko reading "BIG RAY'S SALOON."

"That's it!" I pointed, suddenly sure of myself, as if I'd been pulled to it by my grandfather.

"Yes." Mara's eyes widened. "That *is* it. That's the one Leila told me to—"

"Leila?"

"My sister."

"Why would she—"

"There's people in there!" Mara was covering her eyes against the glass.

I tried to piece together what it meant; the T-shirt at Sue Kopek's house, the history Mara was searching for, the bar still open at four in the morning. "Hold on, I don't know if we wanna—"

Mara pushed the door open before I could finish.

8.

THE BAR WAS dark inside, lit only by candles on the center of tables and a few lamps in the corners. I counted twelve people, maybe more hidden by shadows. There was a low conversational hum in the room, voices mumbling in incomprehensible unison. The door slid shut, and a few eyes flickered toward us, then quickly back to their candles and their conversations, undisturbed by the two underage patrons of the bar.

"Is this it?" she whispered.

"I don't know."

"What was his name? Your grandfather?"

"Arthur." I could feel eyes on me, intensely judging, like drops of cold water against my skin, but when I scanned the room, no faces were looking my direction. "But he would have been with two men, Orlo and Jeffery."

"Right. We'll split up, then."

"Why?"

She smirked. "No one's going to talk to a girl that's got a guy with her, are they?" Before I could open my mouth to respond, she had slipped into the darkness.

I studied the people seated around the candles—almost entirely men, in T-shirts and overalls, hunched over the tables, staring scornfully at each other. It was a strange time to see anyone at a bar, let alone this many people. I tried to listen in on the conversations, but their voices didn't carry to me. The noise died immediately.

I drifted along the outside of the room, studying the walls. They were covered in old photos and drawings, crooked and chaotic and stretching from the floor to the ceiling, into and out of every crevice and corner. A single candle lit each wall, light dancing over the faces in the frames.

I couldn't understand what I was looking at. There were paintings, drawings, pencil sketches of people, places, and things, but nothing to unite them or make sense of them. The photos were seemingly pulled from different eras and image qualities, some in bright color, others fraying grayscale. The only common thread between the photos were the eyes of the subjects—the longer I stared at them, the more intensely they seemed to study me back.

A clock somewhere deep in the room counted off sixty seconds as I stared at the wall of photos. I noticed a pattern in the way they were hung, sloping inward, drawing toward a black-and-white image hung in the center by a string, a man standing on the Green River street I'd just walked. He was wearing a ruffled white shirt and squinting into the sun, his face electrified by confusion.

I stared into it, and I saw myself staring back. It was a photo of me.

"Hey there, pal, can I help you with something?"

I turned and stumbled backward. The bartender was seated on a stool by the register, looking at me with one eye. I imagined he was trying to guess my age. In front of him, an enormous figure hunched over the bar.

"I'm, I'm sorry. Are, uh—are—where are we?"

He looked around, confused. "We're at a bar."

I nodded.

"You coming through on the train?"

I nodded again.

"Where you headed?"

"Um . . ." I shifted my weight. "I'm not sure yet."

"Salt Lake, then?"

"Um, yeah."

"How come guys like you are always so ashamed to admit they've got Mormon girlfriends? Trust me, buddy," he said, standing up to fill a drink order, "I get it."

I almost laughed. "Uh, no. Not that at all."

"Good. That's smart. Work here forty years, and you see a lot of men go down like that. I always say, Try all you want, gettin' these religious girls to love ya, but can I give you five cents' worth of advice?"

I shrugged again, unsure if he was even still talking to me.

"She will always love God." He looked me dead on. "And you will *never* be God."

I smiled at the floor. "I have no interest in being anyone's God."

"Smart kid."

Across the bar, Mara had taken a seat next to an older man in a camouflage jacket, sipping a full glass of beer.

"Is there something I can help you with?" the bartender asked. "You know, this is a bar." He must have seen me watching Mara, because he added, "You look troubled." I knew I was, and I hated myself for it. She was a girl I barely knew, with a man five times her age, but unwelcome jealousy pulled my eyes toward her, noting every smile and sideways glance.

"Are, uh, um—" I forced my attention back to the bartender and sputtered the first question that hit my lips. "Are you Big Ray?"

He smiled slowly. "Naw, kid. I'm Ray, but not Big Ray. Big Ray's not around anymore."

"Not around . . . today?"

"Or tomorrow, or any day. He's dead."

My stomach curled. "I'm, uh, I'm sorry."

"Well, unless somehow *you* are fifty years of cigarettes and steady drinking, then you ain't what killed him," the living Ray said. "No point in feeling sorry."

"Did you know him?" I asked, already sure of the answer.

"Good question." He set down the glass. "How well do y'ever really *know* your father?"

I nodded. "When'd he die?"

Ray looked me over curiously, unafraid of eye contact. "Who are you anyway?"

"I'm Arthur."

"Okay, Arthur." He spent another long moment watching me, before tapping the bar. "Pete'll know. Hey, Pete, when'd Ray die?"

I looked at the man who was hunkered over the bar; his eyes were closed, a full beer untouched in front of him. He was old, very old. He was also incredibly tan, but I couldn't tell if it was natural, or if his skin had just been punished by so many years in the sun that it was starting to resemble tree bark. He moved slowly, and looked so brittle, like the Earth was starting to reclaim him, piece by piece, on the bar stool where he sat.

"January 15, 2012," he rumbled back without moving.

"And the bar, it's been here since . . . ?" I asked, and Pete was silent.

"You gotta ask him questions," Ray instructed. "He doesn't

like talking much, so you gotta be direct. Pete, when was the bar founded?"

"1941."

"See, man's a goddamn encyclopedia," Ray said, leaning over the counter. "Never forgot anything as long as he lived. Hey, Pete, how many homers'd Willie Mays hit in 1975?"

"Mays retired in '73."

"How many homers all-time?"

"660."

"Goddamn encyclopedia," Little Ray whispered, and walked back across the bar to fill an empty glass with beer, somehow sitting in front of Mara. She winked at me, then returned to the man next to her.

I sat next to Pete in silence for several minutes. If I listened close enough, I could hear him breathing. His eyes were still glued shut. "How long have you been here?" I asked.

"Four p.m."

"No, I mean in Green River." He didn't respond, so I repeated, "How long have you been in Green River?"

"Since 1941."

"Do you see the people that come into the bar?"

"Some of them."

"Would you remember someone if they came in?"

"Some of them."

I turned back to the photos. "What's with the pictures in here?"

Pete didn't answer.

"I'm sorry, uh, why are the photos in here, so, strange?" He remained silent. "Do you not wanna talk about it?"

"No."

"Why not?"

He sat up, his movement like a mountain deliberately shifting to a new permanent position. His eyes stayed buried. "Because I'm not here to enlighten anybody with talking. All you people, all you do is talk, and talk, and fuckin' talk. Could hear the whole world if you'd shut up for a second." He took a long, wheezing breath. "They're photos. That's all."

I felt tiny sitting next to him, but something about the way his eyes stayed closed was comforting. I swallowed and set a more direct course. "Were you in this bar five years ago?"

"Yes."

"Would you remember meeting someone if you did meet them?"

"Yes."

I looked around the bar, checking to make sure Pete was the only one listening. My heart raced. "Five years ago . . . did you meet a man named Arthur Louis Pullman?"

I held my breath. The dead air of the bar felt heavy on me, as if pressing me into my seat.

"No," Pete said finally.

"He was helping someone move here. Orlo and Jeffery were their names." He didn't move. "Is it possible they came in here and you weren't here?"

"No. I'm always here."

"Maybe you just didn't meet him?"

"I meet everyone who comes into this bar."

"But is it possible you didn't?"

He grunted. "Talk, and talk, and fucking talk."

The air shattered around me. If he hadn't stopped here five years ago, he must have gone somewhere else. Maybe he never made it to Green River in the first place. Maybe he never meant to.

I didn't say anything to Pete as I got up from the bar. I walked a circle around my seat, considering where I was, caught between the train forward and the train home.

Without thinking, I wound my way back around to the door, staring at the photos on the wall. I replayed my conversation with Pete in my head, trying to make the timeline make sense. He hadn't been here five years ago. Pete met everyone that came into the bar, but he'd never met my grandfath—

No, that wasn't what he said. That wasn't what I'd asked. I thought about my grandfather's first poem: *we are eternal, we're together . . . & we always have been.*

My eyes froze on the photo in the center of the wall. It wasn't a hallucination . . . it just wasn't me.

"Pete."

He grunted.

"I'm sorry to bother you, but—"

"Y'already are."

"But you said my grandfather, Arthur Pullman, you didn't meet him five years ago?"

"I told you already. No."

I swallowed and stared directly at his shadow. "Did you *see* him in here five years ago?"

Pete didn't move.

"Did you meet him before that?"

I noticed Ray staring at me from across the bar, cautiously.

Pete opened his eyes, and for the first time, he looked human. They were blue, soft pools of life in the middle of his hard, frozen face. He looked at me like he was noticing everything there was to notice, and when he finally spoke, his voice was low and unwavering, shaking the organs in my chest. "Tell me something, kid. Do you have any idea what you're doing here?"

I reached into my pocket. In front of him, I set down the photo of my family, my grandfather's final recorded moment. "I'm just trying to understand."

Pete studied the photo silently before closing his eyes once more. "Well, at least somebody knows." He took a sip of his beer. "Ray," he called. "Get him the story."

Ray moved quickly toward us. "All due respect, Pete—" Pete slid the photo toward him.

Ray's eyes shot back and forth between the child in the picture and my face across the bar. Feature by feature, his anger melted into disbelief. "He's had grandkids? Arty had fucking *grandkids*?"

Arty. I'd never heard anyone call my grandfather Arty. "You knew my grandfather?"

"Yes," Ray answered, followed by a slower yes from Pete.

"When did he come in?" I asked. "April 29, 2010?" My voice met my heart rate.

"You're gonna have to be more specific," Ray said, now holding the photo to his face.

"Why?"

"Because," Pete grunted. "Arthur Louis Pullman stopped here eighteen times."

"I, I don't—my grandfather never left California."

"Well." Pete's voice was slow and steady. "He sure as hell wasn't your grandfather then."

"He wasn't my grandfather . . ."

Pete didn't answer.

"When did you meet Arthur Louis Pullman?"

"August 15, 1967."

I shook my head violently. "That would have been over forty years ago."

"Yep." Ray nodded. "Straight from the goddamn encyclopedia."

It was as if time had slowed down.

I wanted to scream back at him, *No! You don't understand! My grandfather wasn't*— but I didn't have an end to the sentence. I knew nothing about his life before I was born. No one in my family did, and by the time that I was old enough to have a conversation with him, he was well on his way to forgetting. We didn't talk about the past at my house, because to him, it didn't exist.

And that was the piece I'd been missing, too obvious to even consider. No one in my family knew anything about his early life, but if he'd been here before, if he'd done this before, it meant there were parts of that early life that were important. If he'd come to Green River before his book, before his wife, before his disease began to claim his brain, and returned before his death, then there must have been something here he was looking for.

He was reliving. He was reliving a trip, a moment in time, a life that my family knew nothing about. All of my confusion, my doubt, my excitement, my questions, and my stress multiplied and began to collide behind my eyes, as every image of my grandfather became too large to comprehend.

I wanted to throw up.

Ray sensed my uneasiness.

"But, I mean, maybe it's a different one, kid." He took a few steps backward. From the wooden cupboard, he produced a crumpled stack of paper, hand-tied together by string. "He's your gramps. You'd sure as hell know better than a bunch of geezers like us. Still," he said, dropping the pages in front of me. "You'd better have a read."

A date was scratched into the top, my grandfather's cursive, too irrational for reality, but too perfect for coincidence.

April 29 . . . the 1970.

april 29, the 1970.

the green river bandit.

the sun was still high over the great west plateau when we
burst in the door & bellied up to a local stool at a local bar
because in towns like this the time of day was a secondary
concern to the temperature of the beer & the temperature of
the beer was cold.

in towns like this, the future had come & gone. the march of
industry had plowed through & left the streets forgotten, a
series of storefronts & promises now broken & decaying in its
wake.
first it was the gold,
then it was the train,
next it was the missile,
& one by one, they found a town more remote, an area more
plentiful, a people more desperate.

& now, in towns like this, the only reason to stay was to cling
to the rubble they called history.

the man behind the bar, the name on the cracked sign out
front, placed two beers in front of us & echoed the misery
that rang throughout the canyon.
'no business,' he said, & we nodded.
'no money,' he said, & we nodded.
'no hope,' he said, & we kept our heads steady.

'we bring some of that,' jeff told him, cause jeff was quick to warmth. & the man behind the bar laughed. 'your two beers ain't doin' shit to solve our business problem.' 'no,' jeff told him, 'but a little hope might.'

& when he talked, people listened. they knew his reputation because reputations were the only thing that mattered in this part of the world & his reputation was good. the soldier of the slum town, they called him. robin hood of the run-down bar.

'when i look at you, i see a town that's seen too much. i see a town that was promised life & then left for death, run down to its last dollar,' & people listened. 'but i also see a people either too strong or too stupid to say die & the truth is i never knew the difference.'

every eye in the room watched as he hoisted the glass of beer to his lips because when he drank he meant it.

'we live in a world with systems of equality,' he said, & the people listened. 'but when the equality ain't working, the system loses its power.'

he lit a cigarette & the smoke trickled into the air, wispy & thin, acrobating all around itself the way cigarette smoke has a tendency to do.

'we live in a world of order,' he said, & the people listened.

'but when order ain't working, the only remaining option is chaos.'

chaos. the word rang through the local bar like a gunshot, the invitation they'd been waiting for, their seats scuffing the ground as their asses slid forward so their ears could get half an inch closer to his mouth.

'you got some kind of plan?' the man behind the bar said. 'or are you just gonna sit there blowin' smoke?'

& he blew some smoke from his cigarette, taking his time because when he smoked a cigarette, he meant it.

'the gold in the hills of nevada makes its way to the penthouses of new york,' he said. '& there's only one way to get it there,' & he nodded to an approaching train, its steam rising, wispy & thin, acrobating all around itself the way engine steam has a tendency to do.

'aw, you're so full of shit you can taste it,' the man behind the bar said, & boos followed like he knew they would, because hopeless begets hopeless & misery loves when its friends come along drinking.

'look,' he said, & they did. 'i think you got two options in this world, & only one of them's a choice. you die, or you live. you accept your fate, or you rebel against it.'

& the men of the bar were silent like he knew they would be,
because no matter how thick your skin or how wide the barrel of your gun, we all bow our heads when we stand before
the Great inevitable.

'we make our stand at midnight,' he said. 'we'll see who's
standing with us.'

& he finished his beer & he ashed his cigarette & he slammed
the door on his way out because when he made a point,
he meant it.

in towns like this, the future had come & gone. in towns like
this, the only reason to stay was to cling to the rubble they
called history.

under the blanket of night, every man from the run-down bar
gathered around their robin hood, including the man behind
the bar who said 'shit' every time the wind whistled, because
arrogance is most often a mask for cowardice.

'i've seen a cardinal,' he told me.
& i smiled. 'the night is ours.'

to the rest, he barked orders & marched the men to the
tracks, &

when the train came steam-shooting, metal-whistling into
the canyon,
the men made their charge.

& i ran alongside him,
horse legs pumping,
hooves & grunts & wheels against tracks,
breathing life into the cold night in the forgotten town.
& it was cold,
but people were desperate,
& for a moment i'd have sworn,
i saw robin hood smile.

'fire!' he screamed & 'fire!' they did, & bullets bounced off
the hinge like sparks.
& the train shot steam, because it knew robbery.
& 'fire!' they did again,
but the hinge got stronger.

tenth mile, quarter mile, half mile,
the horses began to offer their resignations,
& the well of bullets ran dry,
the night began to thicken,
wet with rain & red with the blood of near-misses,
& the well of hope began to run dry,
so he made his move.

atop his horse,

alongside the train,
next to the fields,
outside the town,
he gave himself up, because to be a hero is to sacrifice.
& for a moment, i'd have sworn,
i saw robin hood smile.

'fire!' he shouted.
& he launched himself at the hinge, & he timed it just right,
& he landed with a thud,
& he swung down the butt of his rifle & the crack was deaf-
ening.
& the hinge gave way,
& the rear cars were left behind,
away from the penthouses of new york,
as the world went marching on.

a town with no hope got their gold.
& they all cheered & they gathered & they celebrated
their hero,
'robin hood of the run-down bar.'
& he pictured their getaway to mecca,
their hideaway at melbourne,
the golden sun shining on the faces of the golden,
& he smiled.

'open it,'

they said,
'let us see our prize!'

& with the rifle that freed the cars,
he shot the lock
& opened the door
& they all cheered.
& then they all stopped.

because the gold in the hills of nevada makes its way to the
penthouses of new york
along the same route that the fertilizer of nevada makes its
way to the grasslands of virginia.

& sometimes what shines like gold,
is actually shit.

—*arthur louis pullman*

9.

NEITHER OF THEM said anything to me as I finished.

It was him; the penmanship and formatting were unmistakable. The part that didn't make sense with the story of his life—or at least the version that I was told—was the date. April 29, 1970, was five years before his novel was published. According to my family, he was building railroads in California, never leaving the state, not writing cowboy fiction in a bar in Utah.

But if he'd stopped into the bar in 2010, he'd done it on the forty-year anniversary of the writing of this story, to the day.

Confusion like hot air burned my face, woozy and light. I thought of my father—he must have known something about this. If my grandfather had been running around the country, surely those were the kind of stories he would have told his son. How had no one ever told me?

The worst part was that it all did sound almost familiar. The story, the storytelling, the cardinal, the gold—tiny pieces of it showed up in fragmented images I had in my head of time with my grandfather before his disease worsened and I gave up on understanding him. They were all there, pieces of moments I almost remembered, but had let myself forget.

But it wasn't there for no reason; I hadn't found this place for no reason. The clue, I realized, must be hidden somewhere inside of it. That's why he'd led me to this bar. The forty-year-old story would tell me where to go. *The penthouses of New York* and *the grasslands of Virginia* didn't make sense—he wouldn't have had time to travel there and back to Ohio, and besides, it's not where the characters would have gone. If he was the narrator of the story, he'd be making a "hideaway at Melbourne," or . . .

A word from the first clue struck me: *safety in mecca*.

When I looked up from the story, Little Ray was walking across the bar with a burger and fries. "Kind of a depressing ending, huh?" He set them in front of me. "I always thought it was a bit dramatic, but shit, writers'll be writers."

I nodded to the burger, distracted. "I'm vegetarian."

"Not in Green River, you're not." He pushed it over to me, and I smelled it in my stomach, empty but for three days of old nuts and Snickers bars. Hating myself, I ate.

"So how is ol' Arty?" Ray asked. "Still so full of shit he can taste it?"

"He's dead." Hamburger spilled out the sides of my mouth.

Ray hung his head. Even Pete shuffled at the information. I saw Ray open his mouth to protest, but thought better of it, and instead smiled into a glass of whiskey he'd set in front of himself. He pushed one in my direction. "Peaceful sleep's not the end of night," he said, tilting it toward me. "By morning we'll dance with the angels of light."

The words rang in my ears, warm and familiar as I drank. "Who said that?"

Ray smiled as he hit the bottom of his glass. "Just now? I did."

Ray's silent memorial lasted another two minutes. He poured another drink. He drank it. He opened his mouth to speak. Again, he gave up, and turned his back to me.

Mara had moved to a table in the corner, surrounded by three older men, and somehow still looked comfortable. It was reckless, but she didn't look nervous. She looked almost like she was having fun.

I waited until Ray drifted back across the bar before turning to face Pete. "Pete, I don't wanna bother you—"

"Y'already are."

I composed myself, trying to pick off the most gnawing curiosities drumming inside of my skull. "Do you know what my grandfather was doing here?"

"What's anybody doing anywhere? Trying to get somewhere else."

I slid the story toward him. "Do you know what he means by 'Mecca'?"

Pete cleared what sounded like years of phlegm from his throat. "Mecca of the Midwest is Denver."

My heart leapt. Denver. He'd make his way to a hideout in Denver. It fit my grandfather's progress perfectly. The story *was* a clue, and that was the solution. My trip didn't have to end tonight.

I fought to keep my pulse down. "What about my grandma?"

I asked. "When did you meet her?"

"'S a lot of questions."

I shifted in my seat. With his eyes closed, it was impossible to tell if he was angry or just making an observation.

"No," he said. "Never met no grandma. Guess I didn't know it was like that."

"What about Orlo Kopek? Did you ever meet him?"

"Yes." Pete sighed. "I did."

My fingers started tingling with excitement. "Do you know where he is now?"

"I do."

"Where is he now?"

"Elgin Cemetery, out on Hastings."

The roller coaster inside my chest swung around into an enormous dip. There it was again, the sorrow of realizing that someone I didn't know, someone I needed, had passed on. But sorrow morphed to curiosity, and I asked, "When did he die?"

Pete grunted again. "September 15, 1974."

A familiar beanie head bobbed over the bar. I saw Ray speaking to her, and Mara's full-scale charm offensive in response. Naturally, she drew every eye along the bar, hanging up over it, balancing on her elbows. Ray glanced nervously back toward me and they both caught me staring.

"I have to go," Mara mouthed, gesturing to her wrist where a watch might have been, then outside. I glanced down at my cell phone: it was 3:55. The train left in five minutes. "Come say good-bye?"

I nodded and stepped back from the bar.

"Hold on." Ray stopped me. "One thing I'm confused about. If Arty died five years ago . . . what're you looking for?"

He asked loud enough that several tables at the bar noticed, looking up at me. I rolled the question around my head, the door standing behind me, the story sitting in front of me. "I'm just trying to understand."

Ray seemed satisfied by the answer. "Well, thank God," he muttered. "What's it they say? Mystery's only a mystery if someone's still tryin' to solve it?"

"That's right," I whispered, and with one glance back up at Ray, I snatched the string-bound pages off the table and took off for the door.

If someone behind me shouted about me stealing their Arthur Louis Pullman story, they did it after I was already out onto Green River Street, sprinting toward the train. Mara started after me, letting off an excited cry. "What did you get!" she shrieked, her footsteps directly behind mine on the abandoned street. "Why are you going back to the train?" I didn't answer, and we sprinted back to the platform.

10.

april 29, the 2010.

i can hear hooves,

the grunts of wheel against tracks,
in towns like this,
there's only history.

the only life is,
the son of the name on the bar.

he tells me of his passions,
the wild love affairs of his dreams
the mundane almost-affairs that he wakes to find.
with men like this, love never comes easy,
not for lack of wanting but for wanting too much.

he tells me he's fallen ill over a church girl
& i tell him it's best to cure his sickness immediately.
'she'll always love God,' i say,

'& you will never be God.'
for the better, we decide, as we'd make shit Gods.

he asks me of love,
i tell him all i know.
love is & always has been a mystery,
but a mystery we've signed our lives away to solving.
he asks what would happen if we ever stopped.

'a mystery,' i tell him,
'is only a mystery if someone is trying to solve it.'

i pray you never stop looking

—*arthur louis pullman*

PART FOUR.

denver.

1.

april 30, the 1970.

*"As we crossed the Colorado-Utah border I saw God in the sky
in the form of huge gold sunburning clouds above the desert that
seemed to point a finger at me and say, 'Pass here and go on,
you're on the road to heaven.'"*

jack said that, & for all his failures, i don't know that he'd
ever said anything more true.
we are on the road to heaven.
i always felt there was some Greater love waiting for me just
around the bend of the orange horizon.
i can hear the trumpets sounding from the fast-approaching
mountains to let us know that we're finally free, finally far
enough away from everything behind us that it doesn't have
to be a part of us anymore. i always love this moment because
of that, & i think you do too.

i can see it written in your face, sun-splattered, my great
angel in the window, as we've taken the entire cabin over, our

congregation holding worship in the observation—
55 miles per hour—
4 feet above the earth—
men & women dancing, 6 hours becoming forever & never,
everything & nothing at the same time, time expanding &
contracting, as we cross the colorado-utah border.

orlo pours me a drink, 'do you really think this'll happen?'
& duke answers for me, 'of course it will,' duke is sure, 'it has
to,' duke is arrogant, 'the truth is on our side,' duke is right
& the truth righteous, & the truth is never arrogant, but orlo
doubts, 'what if it doesn't?'
'then up the waterfall,' i tell them. 'up the waterfall we shout.'

& you look on through all of this, sun-splattered, my great
angel in the window, & we smile in secret like the world is
just one big laugh, no worry & doubt, just one big joke we tell
each other, over & over again, every single day. a joke that
only we know.

i always love the moment where the desert gives way to the
mountains, because it reminds me that the highest peaks are
borne of the lowest valleys,
that the radical only exists in proximity to the mundane,
because life can only be viewed relative to its opposite.

i always love the pull of the train, the immovable & unstoppable engine of life.

i always love the moment when my stomach turns with nerves
& excitement & energy, the great anticipation of a greater
life. this morning, my stomach is turning twice as fast,
because i'm moving full speed to mecca, full speed with you.

the world will tell us we're wrong,
& the evils will speak their certainties,
& your mother will be furious,

but those things don't have to be a part of us anymore,
because we're on the road to heaven.

& from the fast-approaching mountains, i hear angels calling
in your voice, telling me,
this road gets steeper
& the curves get sharper
& the tread on our tires will wear down thinner than the skin
on our fingertips,
but just so long as we keep going,
we'll find ourselves in paradise.

—*arthur louis pullman*

2.

WE FLUNG OURSELVES, panting, back into Mara's booth in the observation car and stared at the door behind us. No one had followed us.

"What in the fuck was that?" She stared at the pages in my hands. "What did you steal?"

I toyed again with the information in my head, finally deciding, "Nothing."

"Arthur," she said, lurching back, reverberating through the empty car. "First you jump onto a moving train, then you steal something from a bar, and you've made me an unwilling accomplice in both!" She was angry. Her face was almost unrecognizable behind the expression, the same red spots above her cheeks, but this time everything was sharp and unforgiving.

"I'm sorry," I sputtered. "I'm sorry, I didn't mean to involve you in any—"

"I don't care about that," she said. "I care about you not telling me what I'm involved in."

I didn't know how to respond, so I didn't.

"Well?"

I swallowed, still certain that anything more that I told

her would find a way to hurt me later. It was the same lesson I'd learned, in hundreds of different forms, time and time again—when you tell someone something, then they have it, for good. And they can use it for whatever they want. Regardless of whether it hurts you, regardless of their intention, regardless of whether they're your best friend or your girlfriend—the more you give to someone, the less you have of yourself. And if you give too much, you end up with nothing.

Mara hadn't flinched, convinced she could outlast me.

"Look," I said, "I'm sure you don't have to worry about this, because people like doing things for girls like you, but people like me can't exactly—"

"Girls like me, people like you—what the fuck are you talking about? What world do you live in? More importantly"—she didn't lower her voice—"who do you think I am? What are you afraid I'm going to do if I have this super-top-secret information from you?"

I didn't say anything, but silently rushed to imagine the ways she could hurt me.

"You know it's not a weakness, right?" she asked. "Being honest with someone? It might feel good."

I swallowed again.

"Or." She shrugged. "You could go back to not telling me things, and just do that somewhere else, far away from my booth."

No part of this would get less complicated by involving another person. No clue would become easier to find if Mara knew what I was looking for. The journals would still be obscure, and his past would still be beyond my reach. But Mara was sitting right there, and if I wanted her to stay . . .

"He left my family," I said. "Five years ago, my grandfather left my family, and we never saw him again. No one knows what happened to him. He just went missing, and then we found his body a week later."

She didn't move.

"Three days ago, I found a clue that he left behind for me, in a house where he used to live, and it led me to Nevada. I met a woman that knew him, and she told me . . . well, she kind of told me that he went to Green River. And I just found out that he used to go to that bar, the one we were just in, even though no one in my family thought he had ever left California." I paused. "He had Alzheimer's, so most of my family assumed he was just wandering, but I think he was doing it on purpose."

"What do you mean on purpose?"

"Alzheimer's breaks down brain functions one by one— short-term memory, then language, then decision-making, then mood control—but long-term memory is the furthest back, so it stays buried. Then when an Alzheimer's patient starts struggling to understand their senses and what's really going on around them, the long-term memories start to become their reality. Like, Jewish nursing homes in the last fifteen years started noticing Alzheimer's patients hiding food and ducking nurses, because in their heads, they were back in concentration camps, reliving the Holocaust. It's called episodic reliving. At the end of their lives, people with Alzheimer's basically live inside of their strongest memories."

"And you think . . ."

"That's what my grandfather was doing, yeah. I think he was reliving a trip he used to make all the time when he was younger, and I think he was leaving me clues to find him—I mean, find where he went, and what he was doing, and why." I let the information sit, hearing it aloud myself for the first time. "Also, I learned that he liked whiskey, a lot. But I guess I kind of knew that."

I braced myself for the recoil and instant regret, but it never came. The muscles of Mara's face were frozen, and she was staring at her finger as it traced figure eights around a napkin on the table, but she didn't tell me it was stupid, and she didn't sigh like she was disappointed. She just kept staring, processing, creasing her forehead. "When was he making the trip, you said?" she asked, finally.

"When he was my age. I think, like . . . the late sixties? The seventies?"

"San Francisco to Denver and back?"

"Yeah. I mean, from what I can tell. I just know he stopped in Green River a lot."

The edges of her lips flickered as she looked up from the napkin on the table. "Your grandpa was a hippie."

My eyes narrowed.

"Summer of Love and whatnot? Anti-Vietnam protests? You know, that glorious protest history I was talking about?"

"Yeah, I mean, I know about that." I tried to speak confidently. "I just don't really get what that has to do with my grandpa."

I hadn't planned to say it, but it was my first time calling him "grandpa" since he'd passed away. I felt a rush of closeness to him, followed by a reminder that he was dead now, and he always would be.

"Well," she said, leaning forward, "in the sixties and early seventies, loads of young people were running back and forth between San Francisco and the rest of the United States for protests and rallies and it became sort of a rite of passage, you know. Make your way to the great west, make your way back, burn a flag, the whole anti-Vietnam bit. And most of them were on Greyhound buses or hitchhiking or whatnot, but loads of them took the train as well. And this route is iconic for that. The Zephyr train has been around since the forties. Allen Ginsberg probably had sex with a male prostitute right where you're sitting."

I shifted uncomfortably in my seat, trying to picture my grandfather and a male prostitute burning a flag together. I didn't know much about my grandfather's early life, and I couldn't picture him young.

But Mara knew what she was talking about. "This was a very serious youth movement in your country, and there were a lot of people talking about it." She was incredulous. "Like, all of the best writing from that era. Did you never have to read any of that? Kerouac? Ginsberg? Thompson? Pullman, for God's sake?"

My head shot up and she noticed.

"No" was the answer to the question. I'd never read any of those, save the SparkNotes of my grandfather's, but from what I could remember, none of it had anything to do with a train, or protesting, or hippies, or anything she was talking about.

"What? Why are you looking at me like that?"

I ignored the question. "Have, uh, have you read those authors?" I placed my hand over my backpack.

"Yes, in excess. And I'm not even from your country." She sounded increasingly agitated. "Really, for all the shit your lot talks about your *star-spangled pride*, you really seem keen on forgetting the only parts of your history that don't involve killing people."

Again, I ignored her. "So you've read Arthur Pullman?"

"Yes, *A World Away*, twice. Which I suspect is two more times than you've—"

"That's who I'm looking for."

Her brow wrinkled. "Who?"

"Arthur Louis Pullman." I pulled the journal entries from my backpack and laid them on the table between us.

"I'm not sure I understand what you mean."

I nodded to the clues. "That's my grandfather. That's who I'm looking for."

She didn't say anything right away, biting her bottom lip. "So when you say your name is Arthur," she began slowly, "you mean to say—your name—it's actually Arthur . . . Pullman?"

"The Third."

She looked from the clues to me, then back to the clues, still biting her lip. "And when—you say he's writing to you—you mean—"

I smiled and pushed the clues in her direction. "Read, in this order."

As she began reading, the only thing I could think about was my uncle's joke: *Maybe you could use the book to get laid.* The notion that a girl might be impressed by my relation to an old author seemed much less ridiculous now as I watched Mara's eyes shoot back and forth across the page. Her finger bounced as she read, just like before, and she smiled expectantly at the pages, unflinching. Occasionally she'd mutter under her breath, "Brilliant," or "God, what a fucking genius." Between every entry, she'd look up at me expectantly, like I was going to tell her it was a dream or a well-executed and elaborate practical joke. But I shrugged.

Out the window, the mountains of Colorado sped by us, snow-capped and white, occasionally giving way to the all-consuming blackness of a tunnel. When the train was built through this area—they told us over the intercom—it had been impossible to get over the peaks, until they discovered that they could use dynamite as an unnatural solution to God's natural blockades. Out in the open, we could see skiers making their way down the mountains, rivers gushing around the base, fighting bends and turns as if drawn in by a sloppy child with a pencil. But in the tunnels, we couldn't see anything, not even each other.

"Oh, you're going to share them with this girl?"

I flinched with terror. Kaitlin had taken the seat next to Mara in the booth across from me. "This girl you barely know? With the gross accent?"

"Yes," I said. Kaitlin looked upset; Mara looked up. "Nothing, sorry."

"Well, great idea, Arthur. When she *robs* you and leaves you for dead, don't come crying to—"

"Arthur." Mara's eyes were still closed, gears again turning behind her forehead. "I'd like to help you in your search." It sounded like she'd been rehearsing the words.

"Oh God!" Kaitlin shouted. "Who does this girl think she is? No, Jesus, Arthur, tell her no."

She was right. "I'm sorry, Mara—"

Mara raised her hand to stop me. "Let me rephrase. I *can* help you in your search. And it would be very wise of you to take my assistance."

"'I *can* help you in your search—'" Kaitlin mocked her accent, poorly.

"Look, Mara, I don't know you. And there's a girl—"

"Let me ask you something," Mara interrupted me. "You're on your way to Denver, right? Because this says Mecca, and I'm assuming you've figured that out?"

"How did you—"

"Once you get there, what is your plan?"

Both of them looked at me expectantly. I didn't have an answer but my mouth started moving anyway. "Um, I guess, I'll go, to . . . I guess I don't know yet. But I'm sure I'll figure it out."

"Well, looks like you've got about eight hours to 'figure it out.'"

I didn't respond but I knew she was right. Systems were crashing in my head.

"Or." Mara's voice warmed. "You could let me help you in your search."

"'So we can both be lost together!'" Kaitlin got up and started walking around. "'And then when we don't find anything, we can just fuck each other and take turns taking shits on pictures of your ruddy old girlfriend!'"

I looked up at both of them, rubbing my temples. I had read once that doing that helped stimulate brain activity but it wasn't helping. "How would you being there solve that problem?"

Kaitlin rolled her eyes away from me and Mara met my gaze. "Because I know where to go."

"How?" Kaitlin spat at her.

"How?" I whispered.

She motioned to the short story from Green River. "He says it in there. Not that difficult, really. Just have to know what you're looking for."

"She's lying," Kaitlin said. "I know what it looks like when a girl lies. This girl is lying."

The train flew through a tunnel and both of them disappeared.

I took several deep breaths, one of Dr. Sandoval's strategies for helping me think. "I don't know." Mara reached out and placed her small, real hand over mine on the table. It wasn't warm or soft, really, but it shot electricity up my arm and into my spine. Kaitlin noticed, and I pulled my hand back.

"Arthur, don't," Kaitlin warned.

"I have to," I told her.

Mara looked confused. "You—have to?"

"Think about it, Arthur." I could feel Kaitlin's breath against my ear as she glared at Mara. "What's in this for her?"

"What's in this for you?" I asked. "Why would you want to help?"

Mara looked taken aback. "Because it's really fucking interesting! I've already told you, I love this part of history. My sister and I—it's like our whole lives. Your grandpa is a very important person to me. What're the odds I meet his grandson? And have an opportunity to help him?"

I felt myself almost smile. Kaitlin noticed.

"What are you gonna do to her, Arthur?" She rounded on me. "What happens when you lose control of yourself?"

I took a deep breath and turned back to Mara. "Okay. Where do we go?"

"MAH-RAH!" Kaitlin groaned as Mara sat back down in the booth. "SOME RANDOM BITCH NAMED MAH-RAH! ARTHUR BETRAYED ME FOR MAH-RAH!"

Mah-rah snatched the story from Green River and flipped to the third page. "You don't know it, buddy," she said. "But you've just made the best decision of your life."

I could feel the weight of the exact opposite to be true, but when she looked up from the page, our eyes locked, and Kaitlin disappeared.

"See, right there." She pointed to a line on the third page.

"'Their hideaway at Melbourne'—that's where you're headed."

"Melbourne is in Australia—"

"Yes, my cunning solution is that your grandfather took a train to Australia, because I'm really quite a moron. No"—she hammered her finger down on the section again—"not *in* Melbourne. See how he says '*at* Melbourne'? It's not the city, it's a place."

I followed her finger along the page. "You think Melbourne is the name of a place?"

"No, I *know* Melbourne is the name of a place. The Melbourne Youth Hostel. It's been around for ages, very popular with this youth movement we've been discussing."

I reread the section a few times. She was right; he had very clearly used the word *in* when he was describing his presence in the town and *at* when he described their hideout *at* Melbourne.

The train flew through a short tunnel, a ten-second blackout.

"I'm not wrong," she assured me.

"How did you figure that out so fast?"

"My sister used to—well, because, I know things."

I sat in silence, still staring at the section of my grandfather's story where he revealed his next stop, wondering if there was anything else that was that subtle that I'd missed in the first entries.

"There's one more thing, Arthur," Mara said, slowly and more hesitantly. "I don't know that you fully appreciate what you have here."

I almost rolled my eyes. "No, I, I think I've read them enough times. All I've done for the last three days is, uh, is read these things. I don't think there's any way I'm missing something."

"No, I mean in general. Arthur Lou—your grandfather—he hasn't been published in a long time. Since his novel, forty years ago. Do you know that?"

This time I actually rolled my eyes.

"Okay, well, then as I'm sure you know, people still talk about him, a lot," she continued. "What he was doing, why he never published again. It's all very mysterious. And I've heard— obviously you'll know better than I will—but I've heard that he never wrote at home. There's nothing more that the family— you—keep secret? Am I right?"

I nodded.

"Right." She smoothed over the Green River story. "So you realize, then, what you have?"

"Something he wrote me?"

She took a deep breath. "You are now in the sole possession of the only known pieces of his writing since then." She held up the clues. "You have with you three unpublished works by Arthur Louis Pullman, written a week prior to his very, very *famous* death. There are people who have been dreaming about this for forty years. People take this very, very seriously. People will pay . . ." She didn't even finish the sentence.

"You're saying . . . they're worth a lot of money?"

"They're worth a lot of a lot of things, yes. I mean, a lot of money means different things to different people. Do you have a yacht?"

I shook my head.

"Do you have a private jet?"

I shook my head again.

"Then yes, to you, these are probably worth a *lot* of money."

The train went black as we disappeared into a tunnel.

3.

"GOOD PEOPLE OF the California Zephyr! Wander no more, for we are arriving at our Mile-High Mecca!

"For lots of you, this is your final destination and we'll be saying ourselves a teary good-bye. We know you'll all be eager to bulldoze out of the exit, but we'd ask that you keep in mind that, intentional or not, killing an Amtrak attendant is a federal offense, so stay back until the light turns green, speed racers. I promise you Denver will still be there, just as glorious and golden, if you take the extra thirty seconds to let everyone off safely.

"Those of you staying aboard with us, on through the starry night and into Nebraska, you'll have about ninety minutes to drink in the Colorado air before we say good night, Denver, and good morning, Nebraska.

"This stop does require me to reverse the train into the station, so anyone curious, feel free to check the window for a master class in train operation. That's all, from your brilliant and loyal conductor."

4.

I WAS ON the platform at Union Station in Denver when my father called me for the second time. The air was chilly and my fingers trembled against the iPhone screen.

"Arthur, this has to stop now," he started before the phone hit my ear. "You said you'd keep in touch and no one's heard from you since last night. You said you'd go back to your auntie and uncle's, but no one's seen you. You said you were by the lake but—well, I don't know what to believe."

"Hey to you, too, Dad." Mara heard me and my face burned red.

"Do you have anything you want to tell me?"

"Yeah, actually," I said, thumbing through the clues in my backpack. "I had a question I wanted to ask you."

"What?"

I squeezed my ring. "Did Grandpa ever, when he was younger . . . is there any reason he would've gone back and forth across the country? Like, before you were born?"

Mara leaned close, trying to hear his side of the call, the cold mist of our breath tangling in front of us.

"Did he . . . what? I'm sorry, Arthur, I don't understand what this has to do—"

"Did he ever say anything about Green River, Utah? Or Elko, Nevada?" I asked.

"No. Your grandfather lived his whole life in California."

"Maybe he didn't tell you—"

"Arthur, what are you asking?"

"I'm just, I'm trying to figure out some stuff about Grandpa's life." There it was again, Grandpa instead of Grandfather. The word hollowed out my stomach.

"Stop doing this," he commanded.

"Doing what?"

"Stop trying to guilt me into forgetting about the fact that you've disappeared for three days without calling or telling any of us where you are. I'm not just going to drop it because I feel bad about raising my voice at you the other night!"

Mara sensed it was a conversation she no longer wanted to be a part of and wandered away across the station.

"I told you yesterday, I want to give you all the freedom in the world, and let you find your way, but you can't keep using it as an excuse to manipulate us, Arthur. Our pity isn't a free pass for you to be inconsiderate. In fact, in light of everything that's happened, it's *more* important that you listen to us now. So give me one good reason why I shouldn't drive up to Truckee right now to come find you and bring you home."

I could taste bitter anger in my mouth. *Manipulate us*—like me not following his rules made me an inherently shitty person. *Pity*—as if he was some kind of all-star dad for feeling bad for me. *Inconsiderate*—like my life was required to be lived in accordance with his wishes.

"Well, Dad, be my guest. Because I'm not in Truckee." I took a deep breath. "And I haven't been for three days. I'm in Denver."

I pulled the phone back from my ear, but he didn't explode. "Denver? You're in Denver?" He sounded angry, but strangely only half surprised, like he was pretending to be. "Arthur, what the hell do you think you're doing in Denver?"

"I told you, I'm trying to figure out some stuff about Grandpa."

"And you think you're going to somehow find that in Denver? And you think the best way—"

Mara was getting directions from a man in a navy-blue suit across the station. She was laughing as he pointed at a map and I felt a familiar burn in my chest. The same burn I'd felt when I saw Kaitlin with the guys in her AP History class, teachers that helped her, even her cousins. I should have believed her when she said they didn't really like her and been okay with it, but I had hated it. I saw Mason in the navy-blue suit, mouthing "I'm sorry, Arthur" as he giggled with Mara over the map. I wanted to run across the station and slap the map out of his hand and the grin off his face.

My dad was still shouting. "—some bullshit about your grandfather—"

"Yeah," I cut him off. "I think I'm going to find out some more about his life here. The last week."

"And you think that's in Denver?"

"I know it is."

"Arthur," he spat. "Let me save you some trouble. He died. That's what happened. That's what always happens."

"Not good enough."

"Arthur, please. I don't know what you know, or what you think you know, about my father, but it's not worth it. I spent years, *years* trying, and you know what I found? Nothing. A shitload of angry, soulless nothing. Until I realized there was nothing to find. He wasn't a tortured genius, and he wasn't hiding some elaborate secret. He was a cynical, demented old man. And he died. And that's all."

As my father spoke, I unfolded the photo from my pocket. It was starting to crease in the center, directly down the middle of my grandfather's face, splitting him into two halves. On one side, my father, his brother, and his brother's wife, all tired faces and sunken shoulders. On the other was me, for whatever reason alive with energy, and behind me, the train.

"I'm sorry, Dad."

"What?"

"I'm sorry that you had to convince yourself he was a shitty person just so that you would feel okay exploiting him because you never did anything worthwhile in your own life."

"Arthur—"

"But just because you gave up on him doesn't mean I'm going to."

"Arthur!"

"I'm going to hang up now."

"You know that if you do, we're going to have to do a full search, right?" I couldn't tell if he was warning me or threatening me. "We'll make you a missing person. Police and everything, across the country. And they'll have to find you and *bring* you home, kicking and screaming."

I wanted to scream, but I held myself to spitting. "Really? Because it seems like the last time someone in this family ran away—"

"Don't do this to me, Arthur. Not you, too."

"—no one went looking for him! No police, I doubt he even got this fucking lip-service phone call."

"He was an adult—"

"So am I!"

"No, you're not! And my father was out of his mind—"

"Not good enough." I slammed my finger down on the screen to end the call.

Mara looked only partially interested in my rage as she danced back toward me, a postcard in her hands.

"Dear Dad," she pretended to write on the back with her gloves. "Hello from Denver. Met the grandson of a literary legend today." She smiled up at me. "Not quite as cool as it sounds. All the same, thanks for never bothering me with angry phone calls or tracing my cell phone or anything."

I laughed. "Tracing your cell phone?"

"Yes," she said. "Your dad's probably doing it right now."

I almost laughed again, but choked on it, remembering how casual my father had been when I told him how far I was from where I was supposed to be. He should have screamed, but he had to force himself to be surprised.

"You've got, like, six different kinds of GPS on that thing.

You could get walking directions to the nearest strip club in fifteen seconds, you think they can't figure out where you are?"

I spun my cell phone end over end in my hand. She was right. The search would be over before it even started. It might be almost over.

"If you're going to make a daring getaway from your parents," she said, "you might as well do it properly."

"Okay." I nodded. "How?"

"You can't turn it off, if that's what you're asking."

"Then what do I do?"

Her face lit up. Without a word, she snatched my phone out of my hand and strolled casually across the platform to a line of people waiting to board a bus labeled Express Arrow. She snuck in behind a man with a plaid backpack and, without drawing any attention to herself, slipped it into his backpack pocket and walked away, whistling.

"See, life is better untethered," she said, close enough to almost kiss me, before turning to check the train counter. "Your parents will be looking for you in . . . Billings, Montana."

I stood in stunned silence, watching the man with my phone board the Express Arrow. I thought about running after him, begging for my phone back, apologizing and explaining the miscommunication. But as I turned, Mara smiled at me, and it seemed like a good idea, if only because it was *her* idea.

"Come on now," she whispered, and she grabbed my hand and pulled me down a Denver side street and into the cold, snow-blown afternoon.

5.

IN THE LAST hour of the train ride, I had briefed Mara on every step of the journey so far, from finding the first clue in *Birds of Tahoe* to Sue Kopek's abandoned mansion. By the time I finished, she had already pulled out her own small Moleskine journal and made the following chart:

WHAT WE KNOW
- APRIL 27 TRUCKEE, CA TO STAY WITH TIM, HIS SON
- APRIL 28 ELKO, NV TO SEE SUE KOPEK(?)
- APRIL 29 GREEN RIVER, UT TO VISIT BIG RAY'S SALOON / TO MOVE SUE?
- APRIL 30 DENVER, CO TO STAY AT THE MELBOURNE?
- MAY 1 ??????
- MAY 2 ??????
- MAY 3 ??????
- MAY 4 OHIO???

She'd noticed that the stops so far were about equal distances apart, which at the very least lent some consistency to the confusion. If the timeline and train schedule held, that would place him at the end of the train route, Chicago, the day before his death. But there were no trains from Chicago directly to the part of Ohio where he had died, so the theory wasn't without flaw.

We'd talked tirelessly through the earlier journals, testing them against her impressive knowledge of the sixties and seventies. We agreed that *chaos in the cold, wet veins of ch—* was likely about Chicago; she said *Lou and Sal's tribute* sounded like a statue she was familiar with.

"It's not like we know nothing," she said as we cut across a parking lot. Outside the station, it was already dark, the faint snowfall only visible in the small radius of light surrounding the streetlamps and windows. "It seems to me that the most crucial bit would be to figure why he went to these places, if there is a reason."

"I mean, we do know why. Kind of."

"Do we?"

"Because he'd done it before. He's probably taking the exact trip he used to take all the time."

She didn't look at me, her eyes fixed forward on the street signs ahead of us. "Right, so we need to figure out why he decided to repeat the trip, in his old age."

"And that starts," I said, "with why he used to make it in the first place."

"And perhaps the most important question of all," she added. "Why he stopped."

Mara walked briskly, her feet never leaving the ground for long, her head down as if it was pulling her forward. Her beanie was still flirting dangerously with the possibility of falling off the back of her skull, but never did.

"Something else is bothering me," I said without thinking. "You know Sue, the woman in the mansion—"

"Yes, I know."

"When she was talking to me, she talked directly to me. Like, 'you,' 'Oh, Arthur, it's just you.' But then when she was talking about my grandfather's napkin, or poem or whatever, she called it '*his* napkin.'"

"So?"

"So, if she thought we were the same person, shouldn't it have been 'your napkin'?"

Mara considered it for a moment. "She also thought it was a napkin, not a poem, and couldn't get past five sentences with you. So I don't think you're going to get very far trying to derive some sort of meaning from this woman's syntax."

I nodded. "Well, then hopefully, you're not wrong about this place."

"I'm not."

"Then hopefully his clue is easy to find."

Mara drew a sharp, noticeably frustrated breath.

"What?"

"It's just, that word you use, *clue*."

"What about it?"

She didn't answer right away, and we continued walking, fewer and fewer cars passing us as we got farther from downtown Denver.

"Let me ask you a question." She interrupted the silence. "Do you think there's something at the end of this? Some prize or musical number or . . . something?"

"Yeah." I nodded, eyes fixed on my feet.

"And what do you think it is?" she asked.

Light snow crunched beneath our feet. "Answers," I said with a small nod, but she didn't respond, so I added, "I don't know. Something."

She inhaled slowly. "Have you entertained the possibility that maybe—I don't know—there's not?"

"Not really, no."

"I think that perhaps you should." She spoke slower than usual. I could tell she was being careful about offending me. "It's spectacular, either way, finding these journals. But I think it might help to consider that maybe this isn't . . . intentional. If he had Alzheimer's, he might have . . ."

"Have what?" I tried to listen, to imagine that there wasn't a purpose to the writing my grandfather was leaving behind, but it didn't make sense. "He might have accidentally stumbled back to a bunch of places he'd been before?" I could feel the temperature of my voice rising without trying.

"Yes, *accidentally.*"

"And left clues behind, at every single place, that told me where to go next? *That* would be an insane coincidence."

"Or"—Mara matched my volume—"a behavior pattern that's consistent with the symptoms of Alzheimer's and dementia."

"Look." I shook my head. "I don't know what kind of game you're trying to play—"

"Game?"

"Yeah, your angle or—"

"There it is again! Stop doing that!"

"Doing what?"

"Assuming you know everything about me! Assuming everything everyone does is conniving or self-interested or something. Not everyone's got a motive. I just—" She stopped herself again. "I just want you to be careful."

"Of what?"

"I just don't want you to get lost in believing there's going to be something there for you, or to be heartbroken if there's not. I don't want you to do something you'll regret."

I winced. "Then what are you doing here?"

Mara walked for a block without saying anything. "Your grandpa's book was very important to my sister, and to me, and to all of the people around us. She built a whole life around his ideas, so if there's more writing to be found—regardless of whether he knew what he was writing or not—that's the answer, to me." She didn't look at me. "It's just important, that's all." With that, she decided the conversation was over.

We walked without talking for several minutes. On the corner of two streets that looked exactly like the streets we'd just passed, she pulled out another joint and lit it. I stopped as we passed a bookstore, the large glass window in front covered with images of bright red birds.

"Why are you stopping?" she asked.

"Nothing," I said, studying the birds. "Tanagers."

I watched her for a few moments. She smoked quickly, nervously, barely exhaling in time for the paper to hit her lips again. She kept shooting glances left and right without slowing her motion, like she wasn't checking where to go so much as checking to make sure she noticed everything.

"Why are you walking so fast?"

She stopped and nodded across the street. "Because I know where to go."

The buildings on the other side of Larimer Street were all attached, a series of redbrick storefronts, battered and decaying from snowfall. The windows of the shops were either boarded up or displaying mannequins, abandoned and naked in empty stores. We'd been walking for so long that we were outside the city center and into abandoned Denver, where there were no signs of life other than parking lots; old, industrial factories; and an old, black awning, on which white stenciled letters now read:

THE M LBOURNE YO TH HOSTE

"Quick, here first," Mara whispered, and before I could protest, she was flicking her joint onto the street and pulling me through a door behind us.

I turned into an old mini-mart that had clearly missed its last few shipments of—everything. A man sat behind the counter, flipping through a magazine. He barely looked up as we entered and the bell on the door chimed.

Mara pulled a crumpled ten-dollar bill from her pocket. "Alright, go buy something," she said, and nodded toward the register. I reached my hand for the cash, but she didn't give it to me.

"Buy what?"

"Anything. Buy yourself some cigarettes. It'll help." Before I could ask what it would help with, she had disappeared behind a display of Hostess snack cakes.

I approached the counter and the man didn't move, his face still buried in what looked like a *Maxim* magazine.

"Excuse me?"

"Yeah," he said without looking up.

"Um, can I get . . ." I scanned behind the register. "A pack of those orange . . . cigarettes. American . . . Splits? Spirits? And a lighter, I guess."

"Ten dollars," he said without pushing any buttons on the register. I handed him cash and he tossed them to me. I picked a plain black lighter and I walked out.

Kaitlin would've killed me if she'd seen me smoking. Both of her grandparents had been lifelong smokers, and both had paid the price for it. Once, she saw Mason with a cigarette and almost tackled it out of his mouth. I guess she'd always cared about him like that, too.

Mara was waiting outside, a smug smile on her face. She opened her jacket, and under it was a bottle of Fireball Whisky.

"You stole that?"

"No! I paid for it. I left the money on the shelf where the whiskey used to live."

I laughed.

"Look, I'm already breaking one law in this country. I'm not about to add theft as well. Besides, we'll need this."

"For what?"

She noticed my cigarettes and smiled. "Oh, nice. American Spirits. Now you can smoke cigarettes and look like a douche, all at the same time."

"I mean, I just picked the, the one with the, the most colorful box they had, but now, now that I see they're"—on the box—"'made with one hundred percent organic tobacco,' I'm feeling good about my selection."

"I always thought that name—American Spirit—was delightfully ironic." I didn't feed her fire but she continued on her own. "Taking something notoriously deadly, dressing it up with adjectives so it doesn't look so bad, giving it a perky, patriotic name—that *is* kind of the American spirit, isn't it?"

I tried to think of a joke to respond with as we reached the hostel, but I couldn't think of any British insults that weren't three hundred years too late. "I've gotta say," I tried, "your anti-Americanism is—"

"Kinda getting you riled up a bit, is it?" She winked and pushed open the door.

The inside of the Melbourne International Youth Hostel was about as impressive as the outside. The entryway was an all-white room containing nothing but an IKEA floor lamp and a desk in the center. Behind it sat an old man with bright white hair clinging to the sides of his head, and a collection of keys, all hanging from screws in the wall.

"We'd like a private room for the evening, please," Mara said. My ears perked when I heard the words *private room*, but it was followed quickly by a smack in the back of the head, Kaitlin reminding me that she was still there and was still watching and that I was still expected to be faithful.

"Only got one bed in there, that okay?" He looked past her to me, as if I was the one that would have a problem with it.

"We'll make it work," Mara chimed.

We watched as the old man pulled out a giant, leather-bound book labeled "MELBOURNE 2001–2014 LOG." I felt bad for him as I tried to work out the math of how few customers he would have to have in order to make thirteen years fit into a single book. His log system was almost hilariously simple, like a guest book at a funeral. Date of visit, name, birth date, phone number, room number, and a box for checkout.

"Name and birth date," he grunted.

"Arthur Pullman," I told him, and he stared down at the log, wrinkles across his face creased. "Arthur Pullman," I repeated, louder, and he began writing.

"Should we inform him of the existence of computers?" Mara whispered.

"Thirty-one bucks. Cash only."

"My dear Arty here will be paying," Mara informed both of us. "Say, my husband and I"—she jerked her head back—"we're fairly certain his grandfather stayed here a few years ago and we're a bit curious. Is there any way we could see that logbook of yours, just to check and see?"

"Customer information is private," he mumbled.

"Even for his dear old grandfa—"

"It's private." He took the logbook off the table and handed us our key. "Have a good stay. Don't bother me."

The common area of the hostel reminded me of the basement of my parents' church. There were random pieces of furniture throughout the room; couches of assorted colors, likely gathered as second- or thirdhand donations, looking far too comfy to be safe from disease. Each wall had a different type of wallpaper that was chipped or fraying, as if twenty years ago, four different interior designers had finished their respective walls and said, "Fuck it."

Mara marched across it with purpose, her head down. I stopped, realizing, "Hey! Room six is over here," but she kept going. "Mara, our room is—"

She spun around and her facial expression stopped my sentence. She wasn't smiling or being playful. She was almost timid and totally focused. "Right, then, Arthur, it's time I tell you something. I haven't been entirely truthful with you."

Without clarifying, she continued across the room and I followed, a few steps behind. "Okay," I asked, heart starting to race my footsteps. "What do you have to tell me?"

She stopped abruptly in front of the farthest door in the farthest corner, ROOM 16: DORMITORY. "I know this place because I've been here before. Several times, actually."

My heart pounded inside my head. I smelled smoke, and from behind the door, I heard muffled voices.

"Wait, what? Why?"

Without answering, she tapped lightly on the door, a very specific rhythm:

knock, knock-knock, knock knock, knock

The voices behind the door went silent. Smoke slid under the tiny crack in the bottom of the door. Mara closed her eyes, either concentrating or trying to avoid mine. The pulsing in my head got louder.

"Mara, what's going on?" I asked, but she didn't answer, just swayed back and forth.

In an instant, I noticed how silent and deserted the hostel was, how remote its location was, and how little I knew about it, or the girl that had led me here. My eyes searched for an escape, increasingly aware that I might need one, but the windows were all boarded. My only hope was a dead sprint back across the open room and out into the wide-open, run-down inner city of Denver.

The door opened hesitantly. What felt like a silent eternity came to an end with the clattering of the lock chain behind the door tightening.

There was a face in the darkness behind the door, but I couldn't make out any of its features.

"What do you serve?" its voice asked.

I looked to Mara frantically and she didn't react. I wondered if she wanted me to answer—what do I serve? God? The devil? This fucking British girl?

But she didn't expect me to answer. Her eyes opened calmly and met mine.

"I serve a Great Purpose," she whispered, and from behind the door, I heard the latch slide off.

PART FIVE.

the great purpose.

may 1, the 1970.

we've reached our hideaway at melbourne, for what must be
the hundredth time; but this time, it's all new again.

our feet know where to go when our minds do not, as if
they've been biblically trained. we're walking, not by sight or
information or instruction, but by faith in the feet themselves.
this building's warmth will forever stay unfamiliar, foreign
now & then; i feel my body outside itself, looking in.
some days i'm the passenger; some days i'm the captain; &
some days, i let chemicals steer the ship.

it's the same routine. every time we gather for these holy
meetings in the back of unholy buildings, we remind ourselves of our birthright to a Great purpose, our desperate
search for the Greater love, & this time, i'm certain we're
close to it. closer than we've ever been.

but this time, it's all new again. it all feels different, greater,
because this time, we stand in the face of greater evils, at

the bottom of their waterfalls.
we know what they look & sound like; we know who they
are, unambiguously killing our brothers, trying desperately
to kill our spirits.
this time, we have an answer, or so everyone is convinced.

so we worship at the altar of chemical alteration,
baptize ourselves in liquor & perfume,
drink the ideas of many
in communities of few,
preparing to converge on the grandest, most central
stations,
congregations of the damned.
we're the gods we pray to,
we're the righteous truth,
& we doubt nothing.

we stand in the face of the great evils,
& this time, we've brought a Greater purpose.
this time, we will be heard.

or so everyone is convinced.
but in my heart, i fear the evil may be too great.
i fear the evil may already be among us, inside of each of us.
i fear we may have lost our better intentions to our lesser desires.
i fear the worst.

—*arthur louis pullman*

2.

A CLOUD OF smoke rolled from behind the door and disappeared, thin and wispy, into the open air of the common room. I lost Mara in it as she launched herself through the door, her brown hair bobbing and disappearing into the haze.

I could hear voices, soft and low, too many piling on top of each other to hear any single one. Batting smoke from my eyes, I picked the spot I thought I'd seen Mara and walked blindly forward, step after step after cautious step after—

My foot connected with a mass on the ground. It was dense and lively, the *thud* of fiber against fiber, and the hair on the back of my neck stood up. I'd kicked a pair of tattered blue jeans, with legs in them. I'd kicked a body.

"Whoa, easy," the body said slowly, and it tumbled over, away from my foot and back into the abyss.

I couldn't tell if it was smoke or my overwhelming confusion but the room was less visible from the inside, only stray fragments of light catching pieces of color to interrupt the unending gray around me. "Close it!" a voice shouted loud and clear over the tunnel of steady conversational noise. The door was my only source of light and my only way out. "Close it!" and I slammed it shut. The room was dark.

Music was playing, a familiar beat with a familiar jazz melody on top, piano climbs played soft and loose, a trumpet and an 808 kick drum that thumped against my spine. I knew the voice—"Fuck Your Ethnicity," Kendrick Lamar. The room slowed down to the swing from the bass and drums; it was as if he commanded the smoke with his voice through the speakers.

My pupils contracted and adjusted, clinging to the bits of detail they could find, and as my hands cleared the smoke around me, I began to put together the room I had walked into.

There were people, and they were everywhere. Too many to count, spread across the floor, seated at rows of tables along the walls, or lounging across one of the eight dormitory-style bunk beds pushed into the corners. The only people not hunched over laptops were hunched over in conversation, every face glowing electric, MacBook blue.

The first faces I found were young; they caught the low light and radiated in it, men and women, somewhere between their late teens and twenties, from what I could tell. Their colors were dark; intentional and interesting, in long T-shirts and tight jeans and crop tops and baggy sweaters. There were older faces, too, people I guessed to be nearly forty; less frequent, less noticeable, but very present, almost like they were fixtures of the room themselves.

The room seemed to get bigger the farther I walked into it. It was pulsating, waves of sound breaking over me every measure when the sub drop landed. I couldn't believe they could concentrate with the music so loud and the room so dark, but they did. Some people laughed, others clouded up the air with smoke, most stared intensely at the screen in front of them.

My head was spinning.

"Arthur!" I found Mara's beanie in between two bunk beds, surrounded by three men in long white scarves. "Come here. Don't linger, you weirdo."

I had to step over three people on my way to her, trying to smile but mostly focusing on remaining conscious. I could feel the stares of strangers around the room. I was sure I could hear Mara apologizing for me.

"Lucas, Marcus, Jack, this"—she turned to present me as I approached—"is Arthur. Arthur, meet Lucas, Marcus"—she stopped and smiled—"and Jack."

"Wait—"

The man closest to Mara's left towered over her, tall enough to watch me approach from above her head. His mouth fell open as I came into the light.

"I know you." Jack Thompson, the anarchist from the corner of the train, reached a hand out to grab me by the shoulder. "I *know* you! What're you doing here?" he asked loudly. He wore a blue button-up hanging over tight gray jeans, and a white scarf around his neck, embroidered with some kind of fist symbol with green flowers that I didn't recognize. "What's he *doing* here?" He turned his attention to Mara before I could respond.

"This is Arthur Pull—"

"What *are* we doing here?" I asked to interrupt. "Where the hell are we?"

All four of them heard me, but none responded.

"Mara?"

Jack continued speaking to her, and right past me. "He doesn't know? I literally met this kid on the train the other day!"

"No! I don't—"

"Relax." She put her hand against my shoulder. "He's important," she whispered to Jack, but it sounded like an apology. I couldn't stop myself from watching him watch her. "Let me introduce him to the room. You'll understand."

"Mara, I can't let just anybody speak to the room, and besides, this kid is . . . not one of us."

I watched them have a conversation without speaking: Mara pleading, Jack hesitating, Mara assuring, Jack agreeing. Finally, Jack turned to me, his right hand finding mine. "Bygones, brother. Bye and gone. Maybe you're more on it than I thought. I appreciate you showing up."

Before I could tell him I didn't know what he meant, he paused the music, and the conversation in the room halted. My eyes had fully adjusted, and without the mystique of smoke and darkness, the room was much less intimidating. There were too many people; it was hot and cramped and the bins of trash in the corner overflowed. Everyone was dressed comfortably, not fashionably, and many of them looked like they hadn't slept. Across all the screens I could see were coding programs I didn't recognize.

"Movement." Jack's voice was soft, but carried to every

corner. He must have been the leader, the way everyone looked at him. "We got a new presence."

"Hello, everyone. I'm Mara, Leila's sister, in case you've forgotten." Mara's ever-present poise made her perfectly comfortable with this kind of attention. "She certainly always was more of the one in the family for speeches, but I'll do my best." The room laughed.

When she spoke again, it was louder and more deliberate. With this many eyes on her, her voice sounded revolutionary.

"The greatest movements of human history are experiments in truth. Movements in which the righteous few are compelled against their powerful oppressors, not because what they're doing seems easy or even possible, but because they understand that they are closer to the righteous, the almighty . . . the truth. And when you're closer to that kind of truth, then you are, undoubtedly, closer to the spirit. In movements of truth such as this, there's no room for doubt."

Nodding and drinking and light applause around the room.

"The trouble, of course, is that proper reason dictates we must question every truth, including our own. Only a foolish man is certain of anything, and true intellect is the ability to doubt. What an impossible paradox the universe offers: to know what is right, we must doubt what is right. Fortunately, the universe has created one, and only one, precarious way of validating truth: it sends a sign."

Word after unquestioned word, the Mara I knew grew, to a bigger, emboldened version. She stared her audience in the face as she spoke, rather than looking past them.

"Before Moses could free the Israelites from their oppression in Egypt, he was visited by the great truth, coming to him in the form of a burning bush, a message from the divine that his path was true. The story of every great movement is littered with examples of this: people reaching for what is holy, and what is holy reaching back.

"The trail to any great revolution must be marked by these signs, these mitzvahs, these hallmarks of either great fate or great coincidence, whichever one you put your faith in. Without them, the truth remains questionable. But with them, a movement becomes a revolution.

"I speak to you all directly now—your purpose is great, your path is righteous, you are closer to the truth than the powers that oppress you, and today, I can prove it. Today, I bring you a sign."

The room was so silent you could hear the old wood in the walls bending. Every face in the room was reaching toward her, expectantly. Mara, the revolutionary. Mara, the leader. Mara, turning to look directly at me.

"His name is Arthur," she said.

Fifty-some faces turned to me.

If there were ever a moment that I was so overwhelmed by fear and self-consciousness that I'd lose control of my bowels and shit where I stood, it would have been that one. I clenched my stomach, but nearly fainted under the weight of her introduction. She was talking about me. I was the burning bush.

The room felt twice as hot and I became suddenly aware of every line on my face, every spot on my hoodie, every out-of-place curl in my uncombed hair. They could see the sweat forming on my forehead, the uncomfortable bend of my smile. I could feel eyes burning holes into my chest.

"Arthur." There was Mara's face, a calm in the storm. "Tell them who your grandfather is."

I almost choked on spit before speaking. "Hello, I, uh, I'm, my name is Arthur." Stares intensified. I looked to her for help.

"And—" She spoke for me. "Your grandfather is . . ."

My eyes widened; I tried to jerk my head in a quick shake, to let her know there was no way in hell I was telling a room full of people that my grandpa was—

"Arthur Louis Pullman." She spoke for me.

I heard every tick of every wristwatch in the room. No one raised a bottle or even a cigarette, they just sat staring, every pair of eyes begging for an explanation. I tried to concentrate on sinking into the floor beneath my feet.

"I'm sorry." Jack's voice came from behind me. "Arthur Louis—*the* Arthur Louis Pullman?"

Mara nodded.

"*Our* Arthur Louis Pullman?" Jack asked, and I twisted to face him, several minutes behind the conversation—*their* Arthur Louis Pullman?

"Mara, I appreciate the dramatics, but the odds . . . I mean, do you have any kind of proof, or—"

"Arthur, show him the photo."

I didn't, right away. I clutched it to my thigh inside my pocket, trying to catch up but running circles in my head instead. I looked from Jack to Mara, back to Jack, and then to Mara once more, painfully aware of the mob of strangers waiting silently in just-visible darkness. She didn't waver in her expression, but nodded to where my hand twisted in my pocket. I did as she asked.

For a full minute, Jack inspected it, glancing up occasionally, comparing the wide-eyed, full-haired eighth grader in the photo to the unwashed and sullen eighteen-year-old in front of him.

Finally, he raised his head and whispered, "Jesus Christ. You're his fucking grandson."

The room burst into wild and frenzied applause. I half smiled, unsure of what I had done to be so celebrated. "Someone get these kids some chemicals!" someone hollered over the noise of Kendrick Lamar firing up the speakers once more, and a cup was thrust into my hand, a suspicious silver carbonated mix that smelled a lot more like liquor than it did like Sprite. It was a mess of celebration. People swarmed around me, my drink spilling onto several black shirts.

"What is this?" I shouted over the noise at Mara. "Why am I a . . . bush?"

"You didn't tell him?" Jack stepped between us, raising his own red Solo cup to avoid having it knocked out of his hand. "He really doesn't know *anything*?"

A beautiful blonde girl in black sweatpants and a tattered

pink sweater grabbed my arm. "He gave you his name?" Her face was less than a foot from my own.

"Uh, yeah. I mean, he, I guess he, like, gave it to my dad and, then, my dad gave it to me."

She swayed into me, her hands against my chest for support. "Wow." Her breath was warm cigarettes against my cheek. I imagined it was Kaitlin's breath against my cheek and I wiggled away from her.

"Would you like some answers?" Mara pulled my arm, delighted, watching me. "Or are you rather enjoying being a mitzvah?"

"Answers," I said, and she yanked me through the crowd to a quieter, smaller dormitory room through a door on the back wall. Jack was already waiting.

"Why didn't you tell me that when we met?" Jack addressed me, then turned to Mara. "How'd you find him? How'd you even know he existed?"

"He found me." Mara sat cross-legged on a lone desk. "I told you, it was a sign."

"Well, whatever it was, it's . . . incredible. Leila and I looked it up once, early on. We knew this kid existed but all we could find about him was some tennis shit?" Jack glanced over to me every few seconds in the low light, reading and judging and cataloging every line of my face and muscle on my body. "And you're sure we can trust him?"

Mara smiled. "I'm sure. He's truthful. Sometimes, he wakes up screaming."

I burned red but Jack smiled. "Good." And for the first time, he addressed me straight on, clasping my shoulder with a long, muscular arm, close enough for me to smell him. "Then you're fucked in the head. Just like the rest of us."

"I don't have any idea what any of you are talking about," I confessed.

Jack lit a cigarette and exhaled, the smoke lingering in front of his face. "So you know nothing about who we are?" He pointed to Mara. "Who she is? Who her sister is?"

I shook my head.

"Who your grandfather is?"

I hesitated, but shook my head again.

"Wow. Well, then this is gonna require a little history lesson. You might wanna sit."

Jack was casual, effortlessly charming with a cigarette. I pulled out my American Spirits and tried to casually, effortlessly light my own to distract from the circus in my chest. I couldn't get the flame on the lighter to stay on long enough to spark the paper.

Jack cleared his throat. "Does the Freak Power Party mean anything to you?"

I shook my head and tried not to notice his disappointment.

Jack drew his own lighter and held it up to my cigarette for me. "Alright, well, then I guess we'll start there.

"In 1967, the world was ending. It was the height of the Vietnam War and political corruption was a fucking epidemic in the United States. So Hunter S. Thompson—one of the best social justice journalists of the time, I'm sure you've heard of him"—I nodded, pretending I had—"decided to start a political, social movement. He observed how colossally fucked America was by its government, and decided Americans needed not just a new political alternative, but a new *kind* of political alternative. Something totally grassroots, completely outside the establishment."

He began to walk back and forth, spinning to address the opposite wall every time he ran out of space. "He found Aspen, Colorado, a tiny city with a bunch of people who didn't really give a shit about politics, and set up shop. The idea was to find all the disenfranchised people that the rest of the political world had forgotten about, and get them out to vote for his party— Freak Power. Two candidates on the ballot—Joe Edwards for mayor, Thompson himself running for sheriff. He united the addicts, the bikers, the criminals, the immigrants—the 'Heads,' as he called them—and he turned them into a voting bloc. It was all satire—I mean, the fucking *name* of it was Freak Power—but he wanted to prove that when you unite the people that nobody else cares about, there's a hell of a lot more of us than them."

"So this is—"

"Hold on. Still a lot left." Jack was pacing faster. "After a few setbacks, as the election got closer, Hunter realized they were going to lose. He wrote a letter to Jann Wenner at *Rolling Stone*, saying, The outlook here is grim . . . I trust you see my problem in timing and magnitude . . . but the sheriff's gig is just a small part of the overall plot. He had realized that losing meant the whole movement wasn't going to have the impact he wanted; it was actually going to have the opposite. People would think, well, if you can't even win Aspen, what hope is there for everybody else? He realized that solutions couldn't come from within the existing framework. So he started work on something much, much more important.

"In 1967, under the guise of the Freak Power Party and in the room where we're standing now, he formed a separate organization. A secret one. He personally sought out the best social justice writers at the time, and trained them into a small army of—well, honestly the best word to describe it is prophets. Then he sent them out, city to city, to speak to young people, get them fired up and pissed off, and then teach them to revolt. You gotta remember, protesting hadn't really kicked off in America yet. Sure, some people had started, but it was all disconnected, so the papers could just write it off like some fringe movement. Everybody was too scared of Nixon.

"The result was *hysteria*. Protest exploded across the country; Savio and the Summer of Love, Days of Rage in Chicago, Ohio riots—all of it coming from the same underground group of fifteen writers. Their photos are everywhere, their fingerprints are all over the newspaper stories, but nobody ever figured out a fucking *thing*. They had to keep it a secret, because they knew if Nixon got word of something like that, he'd stomp it out at its source. This was the sixties and seventies; people were getting killed for much less. And the magnitude of it, I mean—these were the protests that ended the Vietnam War, and it was all set into motion by fifteen guys. By one fucking brilliant idea. Hunter S. Thompson, Duke, he was the real leader of it all, but he knew he couldn't stand too close to it. People knew him. So to run the operation on the ground, he brought in a kid, a seventeen-year-old he met at a protest in San Francisco. Fresh, excited, a little sheltered, but brilliant. You know who that was?"

The words caught in my throat. "My grandpa."

Mara nodded. "Arthur Louis Pullman. The United States's glorious human protest history. It was the most significant political movement in American since 1776, and it's all still a secret."

I looked back and forth between them. "So that makes you guys—"

"We're that movement, 2.0," Jack took over. "After ALP—sorry, after your grandfather—after he . . . died"—he paused, waiting for me to react, but I didn't—"a few of us in a forum online started talking about how the organization needed a resurgence. So me and this girl Leila—Mara's sister—we built our own group of writers, and musicians, and journalists, and computer technicians, and lawyers, ten times the size of the original. We got the room back—they were trying to close this place, and we convinced them to stay open, just for us—we gathered everyone together in Denver; now this, that you're standing right in the fucking middle of, is the reclaiming of that ideology."

My head spun. "But there's no draft, or even war, really—"

"Oh, yes, there fucking is." I remembered our conversation from the train, his insistence that America was engaged in, or about to engage in, some kind of all-out class warfare. "There's a corporate ruling class that controls everything that happens in this country," he continued. "They control politics, they control the media, they control public resources, and if you don't realize it, then they're fucking controlling you, too. And they're sitting in penthouses and private planes, drinking twenty-thousand-dollar bottles of champagne while they watch the world burn."

"You mean like . . . corporations?"

"Don't just say it like it's some sophomore thesis paper!" Jack was pacing wilder than ever. I could feel why he was the leader. He was so intensely excited, so passionately hateful, that he couldn't hold himself in one place while he spoke. "This isn't abstract! These are real people, with real obsessions, with their hands around every ballsack in Washington, DC, muscling them into cutting welfare while one in five kids is going hungry, and ignoring emissions while half the species on Earth are dying out. Everyone knows it's fucked up, everyone knows that politicians are puppets for corporations, everyone knows the Earth is being destroyed, and somebody needs to stand up and say, 'Hey, fuck you, we're not going to take this anymore. We're the people, and we want our power back.'"

"Okay. So you're going to . . . protest?"

Jack shook his head. "Nope, not us. I mean, we've been there, we've had a presence everywhere, but those are coming from people's real, organic anger. We're here to channel that. The original Great Purpose plan wouldn't have the same effect today, so we've had to get more . . . pragmatic."

I started to notice the charts and graphs all around the room: maps of political districts, polling data for positions I didn't recognize, and names that meant nothing to me. It was obsessive, printed documents with scribbling all over them, chalkboards so hastily rewritten that their old messages still snuck through.

"This part was actually Mara's sister's idea. Do you know what the second most politically powerful office in the country is, behind the president?" He didn't wait for an answer. "A mayor. There are about two hundred American cities where mayors have functionally unchecked authority—they can legislate through local ordinance, build a government of their choosing through appointments, veto any proposal, even reassign federal government funds. After that, it's a city manager. After that, city councillor. Local politics is where shit actually gets done. That's what we need to take back.

"So we've recruited some candidates—super-progressive, anticapitalist candidates—to run in local elections, in conservative cities across America. Thirty-three city managers, forty-five city councillors, and fifteen mayors."

He pointed to a table on the wall; cities in one column, political offices in another, names in the last. I recognized one name from the list. Next to CARSON CITY, NEVADA, the name MARA BHATT.

I turned to her, seated on top of the only desk in the room, half her face hiding behind a shadow. "But they're gonna lose—"

"You'd think. But that's where the real work of what we do comes in. America's current political system infrastructure was built by the people who still maintain and control it—the old and wealthy. It's discouraging, but it also means their voting systems are as archaic as their candidates. This is where youth has its advantages. Those people out there—" He motioned back toward the main room. "Half of them are computer engineers, and they're really, *really* fucking good. They've built programs that live within directory computers and voting machines, then automatically register voters, contact those voters about their ballots, and submit them, without actual physical interaction. And in the process, *maybe* our candidate gets supported. *Maybe* that's what all of these people would want anyway. *Maybe* the city accidentally does what it's wanted to do since the start of this oligarchy shit show."

"You're rigging elections?"

"No," Jack snapped. "We're suggesting something people already want. The other side has been weaponizing voter suppression since the birth of America. It's about time somebody weaponized voter turnout. You couldn't do it on a presidential level, because there's too much scrutiny, but who's gonna give a shit about a local election? In most cases, we're talking about a couple hundred votes making the difference. We're gonna turn power in America's cities over to the people who will actually protect them."

"But how— They don't even live in these places. How could she even be the mayor if—"

"Arthur." He stopped me. "You're coming in at, like, step nine of a ten-step resistance. Every one of those problems has been solved. We're already on the moon. Enjoy it."

"Okay." The engine in my head was still processing. "Okay. So this is the new Freak Power Party? Or . . ."

"No, Freak Power was the diversion. We're the more important part. We're the ones spreading the ideas, inciting the riots, inspiring the masses."

"And what's that called?"

Jack smiled and pointed toward the far wall, directly opposite the door. I couldn't believe I hadn't noticed it: expertly painted across the wall, above a fireplace, was the symbol from Jack's scarf, a fist holding a small, green branch, and two bold, enormous words:

GREAT PURPOSE.

3.

april 30, the 2010.

feet step on the concrete
mecca & melbourne
arthur
following my feet

through cold concrete step,
but i keep faith in my feet
buildings of an old man,
melbourne & unfamiliar warmth
my body outside itself
looking in
arthur.
some days

i feel our unwavering spirits
in cold buildings, soft couch,
color & more lite from the window, large
17D our
liquor perfume smoke & music
if i could speak to tham naw;
i would say give this up,
this is not what you think it is
you are not what you think you are,

i doubted nathing than.
but naw i am nathing but doubt.

—*arthur louis pullman*

4.

I CROSSED THE room to where the words were etched across the wall, the dedication of my grandfather's book hidden in plain sight. Reaching for it felt like reaching for him. But I couldn't tell if he was reaching back.

"How do you know all of this?" I spun on Jack. "How do you know that my grandfather . . ." I paused to gather the question. "I mean, I, I lived with him. My father was his son. And we didn't know about any of this. What makes you so sure he was here?"

The corners of his mouth curled in a smile. "Well, for starters, he told us himself."

He kicked the bottom of the wall. Far below the GREAT PURPOSE logo, there were twenty to thirty names, all in bold, capital letters. The wallpaper around them was chipped, making it clear that this part of the wall had been there the longest. The ink was fading, but on the top of the first column of names, I could still make out the first six that I recognized:

ERNEST BANKS

HUNTER S. THOMPSON

ORLO KOPEK

JONATHAN LEWIS

JEFFERY KOPEK

ARTHUR LOUIS PULLMAN

I leaned down and traced them with my finger. My grandfather had written his name. I returned to Jack's level. "Okay, how did *you* know, though?"

"What do you mean?"

"How did *you* know about this? This room, my grandpa . . . who told you?"

Light from the fire danced on his face as he smiled. "You're not the only one here with royal blood," he said, and from his pocket, he pulled a small, metallic object. He danced it between his fingers. "It's a stamp. A Gonzo fist, for Gonzo himself, except instead of holding peyote, it's holding an olive branch. This was their logo, *their* stamp. There's only one in the world, saved only for Great Purpose documents. And it used to belong to my birth father."

He reached for my hand, raising it in front of his face and lightly stamping the back of it. He blew on it to dry the ink: dark, black, the symbol directly in the center.

"Jack . . . Thompson." I read the names on the wall. "You're his grandson?"

"His son." He smiled at me. "Thompson and Pullman, reincarnate. The prodigal sons, together, right where it all started. Only the Purpose is stronger this time." He motioned to the other room. "There's some serious influence out there. And these people—they're serious. This isn't just something we do.

This is who we are. This is our religion."

I nodded. *And that makes our families the gods,* I thought. *Which would make us—*

"Jesus Christ!" a shout came from the other room, and a boy with dark hair entered. "Jack, if we're gonna try to grab Greenberg at the DataFirst building itself, we're gonna need someone *in* the building to follow him out, and Kade doesn't—" He stopped when he saw me. He couldn't have been much older than me, with a hairless chin and sunken eyes.

"Kade's afraid of a little camera time?"

The boy nodded and I whipped my head back and forth between them. *Grabbing Greenberg* didn't sound like something you would do to a voting machine.

"Tell him I'll do it myself," Jack nearly shouted, speaking to someone outside the room as well. "And I'll wear a shirt that says, 'You loaned money to slave owners two hundred years ago, and the only difference now is you cut out the middleman'!"

The boy shook his head and left. I tried to get Mara's attention, but her eyes were fixed on the floor.

When the boy was out of earshot, I mumbled, "I thought you guys were just—"

"DataFirst holds forty-five percent of the information for America's short-term, unsecured loans—the payday ones that fuck over poor people. Two weeks ago, they agreed to sell their collections information to law enforcement, as if these people's lives weren't fucked enough. So we're gonna borrow their CEO for a day or two." Jack was smirking proudly, but he could sense my uneasiness. "Look, we're not here to hurt anybody. He's gonna be fed, he'll have a place to sleep—pretty fucking luxurious prison, when you consider the crimes." He could tell I wasn't sold, and Mara wasn't backing him up. "We're just trying to fight this thing with every weapon we have. Fear is a weapon. Your grandpa helped halt the march of imperialism in this country because he wasn't afraid to put his own body in the way. It's about time somebody did the same."

"But . . . you're not going to kill anybody?"

"No." Jack smiled. "We're just gonna show them that we could."

The boy reentered. "He's pretty serious, he doesn't—"

"Shut up." Jack lit a cigarette. "I'll be right back." The room outside parted like the Red Sea, and Jack disappeared into it.

Some moments, I'm certain I can feel the rotation of the Earth twice as fast, like the horizontal axis of what's normal and expected and intended is visibly shifting in front of me, and try as I may to reorient my brain to it, it stays inches ahead of me, ensuring that the whole world is off-kilter and impossible to grasp. As I stared out across the tops of the heads of the room full of Great Purpose revolutionaries, I felt the axis speeding up.

I turned my confusion to Mara. "They're gonna kidnap somebody?"

"Yeah." She looked over the graphs on the walls. "That part was Jack's idea, not my sister's. He says it's totally nonviolent, but . . . I don't know."

I stared at her but she wouldn't meet my eyes. "When did you decide to bring me here?"

"I mean," she said, smiling down at our feet, "I was coming here either way. But you were a nice addition."

"Why didn't you tell me?"

"And ruin this surprise?"

"This is your idea of a surprise?"

"It's not every day you get to tell someone they're part of a royal bloodline." She patted me on the back playfully. "Besides, if I told you what this was, we wouldn't be here. And these people can *really* help."

"But that doesn't—" I stopped, replaying the chance encounter of our meeting. "You found me."

"I didn't."

"You tracked me down. You knew I'd be on the train, and you—"

"Arthur, you ran into me on two separate trains. You leapt into the car and landed on me." I could feel her slowly, intentionally moving her body closer to mine. "As much as I'd like to take credit for this, *you* found *me*." She was inches away from my face. "But it wasn't an accident. It was a sign."

I held my breath for the kiss but it never came. She walked back to the desk and gathered her coat.

"So your job . . . is to be the mayor of Carson City, Nevada?"

"Kind of cool, right? It's a promotion, basically."

"Have you ever been to Nevada?"

"Just the other day, actually."

"It's not that cool."

"I thought it was nice. Rainy."

"It's a desert."

"Good to know, seeing as I live there now." She handed me a Nevada ID. It was her photo, her name, Mara Bhatt, with an address in Carson City. It was the same face, the same smile, the same Mara, but I barely recognized her.

"What do we do now?" I asked.

"What do we do? We find his journals! We get a few of the history experts from the group together, maybe the literary ones as well, we go over the journals we have—"

"Mara."

She stopped.

"I don't want that."

"Don't want what?" Her eyes shot around the room. "Arthur, these people are experts on his life! They're *exactly* the kind of people you'd want to help. I'm handing you an army!"

"I know." I exhaled. "I know."

"Then what?"

"It's just . . . I don't know if it would be a good thing to let this get more complicated than it already is. I don't know any of these people."

"I do!"

"And I just met you yesterday, and just found out that you're . . ." I motioned to her name on the wall. "Why do you want me to tell these people so bad, anyway?"

"Because they'll care, more than anyone! And they'll help!

And I'm one of them, so please stop talking about them like we don't know them. I *am* these people."

For an uncomfortable moment, Mara and I tried to reconcile our gazes. She couldn't believe I wasn't grateful, and I couldn't believe she'd expected me to be.

"I can't lie to these people, Arthur," she said. "I can't keep this from them."

"Can we at least think about it? For, like, a night?" I nodded to the door where Jack had left.

Again, she fell silent, pretending to read the writing on the walls. "Right, then," she decided finally. "We'll tell them tomorrow. Just promise me you won't tell Jack. He'd kill me if he knew I'd kept this from him."

I nodded, unsure if it was hyperbole.

Mara handed me another cup and led me back to the common room. "You'll like these people, Arthur, I know you will. I've known them for years. My sister used to say these people were so righteous, it was like there was no telling where one person stopped and another started. Just one big, unified brain."

"Where is your sister?" I turned, but she kept pushing me. "Isn't she supposed to be in charge?"

Without an answer, Mara shoved me back into the throng of people, still mingling and celebrating. Almost immediately, she was gone into the mass of skin, and in her place was the blonde girl from earlier.

"I'm so sorry—" I tried to tell her, but she stopped me.

"It's a party." Her whole body was in a perpetual bobbing,

swaying motion. "We're celebrating—didn't you hear? Arthur Louis Pullman's grandson is here."

"I know," I said, my voice too quiet for the room. "That's me."

"Oh, cool. I'm Laura."

I took a huge swallow of the silver drink.

The night carried on like that. The music got louder. The drinks got faster, and the people melted into a single dancing, laughing organism. Occasionally I'd drift back to the image of my grandfather, young and aware, leading a secret political organization, but as the weight of the questions got too large, it felt better to let them go. The dull, obscured past became strangely unimportant in the face of the vibrant present.

I watched Jack and Mara speaking quietly to each other in the corner, laughing and scanning the room. Twice, she caught me staring at her, and twice, she poured me a new drink, toasting to "the idiot of the hour." In a few moments, I caught them arguing, Mara yelling and Jack scowling back, and inside, I beamed.

Kaitlin showed up to scold me—"You're drinking, with a bunch of people you don't know? You know how you get when you drink, Arthur!"—or to tempt me—"Wouldn't you rather be here, with me? Don't you think I'm hotter than any of these girls?"—but she never stayed long, always disappearing when Mara's face came swimming into view.

Somewhere in the middle of the mob, between my third attempt at smoking a joint full of marijuana and a group acoustic rendition of a song I didn't recognize, Jack found me again, his eyes now intense and sober.

"On the train . . ." He spoke softly but clearly, his voice cutting through the tunnel of noise. "I just remembered, you were looking at something. Some journal, or letter. What was that all about?"

I felt myself starting to sweat. "Yeah, I mean, it's—" The alcohol was tugging at my tongue, weighing it down with moisture. "It's just, uh, I's, just some, some writing." I shrugged. "'S writing."

"Writing?" Jack looked deeper into my face. "Writing . . . from who?" I felt tiny in front of him. Mara appeared behind him, her eyes widening as she watched him shift closer to me.

"Yeah's, 's just, a couple clues, 'n' things."

"That's cute, man," he said, making me feel even smaller. "Clues from who?"

"Uh, I was—uh—it's—" I said. Whoever was using my voice sounded like a child, but I didn't care. I didn't care about anything, other than wanting him to stand as far away from Mara as possible. Other than wanting to impress her, in front of him. "From my . . . grandpa. Arthur Louis Pull-Pullman," I said, and smirked at her.

Her eyes doubled in size and I immediately regretted it.

"Clues?" Jack forced his face between ours. "Your grandfather left you—he wrote? Clues? When—"

"No, not, uh, not to—just some stuff." I tried to backtrack. "Just a letter—or two, or so. I dunno."

"Can I read them? When did he write them?" Jack didn't

break eye contact. "If you're here now, following them . . . Arthur." I watched Mara's eyes triple in size. "Did he write them during the final week?" He took another step toward me. "Do you have them with you now?"

"Actually, Jack," Mara said, jumping between us, moving him backward. "There is something we need from you. The logbook, from the man at the front?"

He wasn't paying attention to her.

"Jack." I couldn't see the faces she was making at him, but I could feel her ass against my leg. "The book? Can you get it?"

His eyes searched my bright red face, digging underneath my skin to see where I was hiding the things I wasn't telling him. He knew there was more.

"Jack."

He broke his face away. "Right. Yeah, yeah, that's easy. Let me grab Lucas; we can—we can get that for you now."

"What the fuck?" Mara whispered privately to me, and we followed.

He led Mara, Lucas, and me across the common room, every few seconds glancing up, like he was afraid I might make a run for it. "Alright, kids, here's how this goes. Ernest"—he motioned to the old man—"carries that thing like a child. Lucas has a relationship with him, so Mara, you go in with him, and get what you need. If it doesn't work, Arthur and I will be your backup."

They all nodded. I swayed back and forth.

"Why wou—wouldn't I—go—" I tried to fight the words out of my mouth.

Jack's eyes rolled. "Keep it together in there, Pullman Three," and he nodded to Lucas and Mara.

Jack and I sat alone outside the door in silence. I couldn't figure out why we were alone, why he wouldn't want me going into the room with them, other than the obvious reason—he wanted to be alone with me.

"What was he like?" Jack asked.

"Huh?"

"Your grandpa." He didn't turn toward me.

"I, I didn't read the book. I dun, dunno what's so special for you guys. He didn't—"

"No, I mean what was he like, as a person?"

"Oh, I dun, I dunno. Forgetful. Kind'uh, kinda angry. It'as . . . mostly Alzheimer's, toward the end. He didn't talk much, jus', uh, repeated himself a lot. He was, he was never writing, if tha's, that's what you think. It's nothin' like that."

A bell rang somewhere outside one of the windows.

"He's . . . he's always readin' the Bible, 'n' . . . 'n' baseball, a lot. He remembered lotsa . . . quotes from books."

Jack still didn't answer, so I returned the question.

"What's it like, growin' up with, with a Hunter, Hunter Thompson for, for a dad?" I waited, then repeated, "What's it, what's it—"

"I never met him," Jack said.

I didn't know what to say so I focused on breathing.

"It was an accident, and he was pretty old, so . . . He sent me letters, though. Jesus," he said, turning abruptly toward the door. "What the fuck is going on in there?" He peeked through the glass before mumbling, "For fuck's sake," and shoving it open himself.

I watched through the window as the scene played itself out like a silent movie. Jack burst into the room, and everyone turned. From beneath his button-up, tucked into the back of his jeans, Jack pulled out a small black handgun. He held it directly at the old man, who shriveled behind the desk and shoved the book forward. Jack shouted several times, towering over the man's submission. Mara and Lucas both stared at the floor. The quick movement forced the contents of my stomach to slosh around on top of each other so I collapsed against a wall, burying my mouth in my right arm and waiting for it to pass.

Jack looked back to the window, nodding that I should come in, so I did.

Mara already had the book open. "2010 . . . what's the date?"

"Ap—Ap—" I took a huge breath. "April 30, 2010," I muttered, then returned to covering my mouth.

Mara began flying through pages, whispering to herself as she went. "2008 . . . no . . . 2011 . . . back, 2010 . . . June . . . May . . ."

"What's—what's it say?" I asked.

I couldn't stop looking at the old man. His eyes were half the size of his head, and they hadn't moved from the barrel of Jack's gun, still fixed between his eyebrows. I'd never seen a gun in real life. On television, they looked so fake, like toys, like all they were was the action they represented, and they could do nothing more than produce a loud *BANG*. This close, I could

arm, stabilizing me. "Let's go," Mara said. "Lots to discover."

"Where's Jack?" I mumbled, letting my eyelids bounce open enough to walk forward.

"This doesn't belong to him," she said, pulling me forward toward Room 17D.

5.

THE ROOM WAS lit by a single fluorescent bulb hanging directly over the bed. I collapsed onto the bed and tried reopening my eyes. The world was slow motion, and the light dripped outward in every direction, illuminating my periphery and bringing the world into focus.

The room was plain, cream-colored, with wallpaper that frayed in the corners. The bed had stiff gray sheets that smelled like I imagined the blouse on a corpse might. I turned to the left. An old alarm clock, covered in dust, read 3:45.

Mara offered me a paper cup filled with water. I'd never been so glad for sink water. "Okay, what do we expect to find here?"

I looked around the room. There weren't many hiding places. The bed, a bedside table, and a lamp. "I don't know. Something. He had to have left something."

"Arthur, it's been cleaned. Even if he left something, it's probably not here anymore."

I nodded gently, trying and failing not to disturb my throbbing head.

"It was five years ago," she continued. "Even if he wanted to, *how* would he leave something? Hide it? Behind the wallpaper? I mean it—this might take more than just me and you to search."

Neither of us spoke for a long while. Every movement I made reminded me of a different kind of pain I was in. I tried to decide between more sleep, more water, or more booze.

"Is it possible," I asked, "we got the wrong room or something? Maybe 17D is code for something else?"

"Why would any other room be any different?" Her face was serious. "I'm being honest, Arthur, I think we may need some help, or at least another opinion—"

"Mara." I stopped her.

"Come on."

I waited a long moment. "Did you know Jack never met Hunter Thomas?"

"Thompson, and yes, I knew that. His birth mother just told him who his father was, and even her—she's in an institution, so . . . so I don't know. He didn't take the name until a few years ago. It's all a bit strange."

"Well, my grandpa was real," I assured her, although I didn't know why.

"Right," she said. "So figure out where he went."

I closed my eyes and saw my grandfather in the room, lying on the bed, staring at the four plain walls, breathing the old air, writing and reliving and stumbling back into his old habits. I hoped he had less pain than I did, but realistically, he probably had much, much more.

"There was no shredded paper anywhere?"

Mara shook her head.

"Anything in the Bible?"

Mara shook her head.

I motioned toward one of the two doors in the room. "Is that a bathroom?"

Mara nodded.

"Is there a toilet?"

"Yes?"

I closed my eyes. "Could you check the plumbing for me?"

"No, absolutely not."

"Come on, Mara, just see if it's running properly."

"Do I look like a plumber? How would I even know if it was—"

"Mara, shut up and look in the top of the toilet."

Mara stared at me for a moment before dragging herself off the bed and into the bathroom. I heard the clinking porcelain as she removed the top. "Yeah, looks like a toilet from—" Mara screamed. There was a loud clanging as the top of the toilet connected with the base and then the floor.

A moment later, her head popped back into the room. "There's a paper! There's a fucking paper, taped to the top of this toilet! How did you know that was going to be there?"

I half smiled as Mara skipped back into the room. "My

grandpa used to take the tops off people's toilets. Every single time. Sometimes he'd do it to every toilet in the house. My dad would get so pissed."

"And why was that? Was he a plumber in a half-remembered life, searching for the perfect toilet drain?"

I shook my head against the pillow.

"Then what do you think he was doing?"

It hurt to swallow, but I smiled through it. "Looking for clues."

She looked at me, surveying the fractured pieces of a new puzzle, then smiled, like she'd found a few pieces that fit together and was starting to see the picture on the box more clearly. "Alright, then, Sherlock. Read it."

I folded it open.

"Aloud," she insisted, and bounced onto the bed next to me, slouching at the same angle, the back of her neck against my pillow. She closed her eyes, and I stared at her, her face too close for me to think about anything else.

Her eyes opened again. "Well? Are you going to . . ."

I looked down at the page. Her eyelids fluttered shut once more, and I read aloud.

april 30, the 2010.

i first felt you
at thirty secands old.
i was intraduced to the world
& you were thare,

color & breath & warmth

growing up was
growing towards you,
pieces of you in every word.
learning the language just so i could speak it for you,
learning words just so they could fall short with you.
color & breath & warmth
arthur

i felt you in
our souls colliding,
i was eighteen,
you a year older.
like discovery of what i'd known all along.
you were breath.
you were color.
you were warmth.
& finally you were there,

& i felt you still, when
that warmth disappeared,
the world was gray,
my breath was gone.
& words that failed me were all i had
to remember you,
to re-create you,

arthur
color & breath & warmth
& i created you
out of words that were never enough.

i've written
this dream,
this room,
this great,
this love,
a thaosand times,
envisioned us meeting in
life after life,
body after body.
face to face finally
when all the words have failed.

but this morning,
i woke up a million miles from you
familiar trumpets reminding me that i'm not what i used to
be
& angals spoke to me in your voice,

they said,
this road gets steeper,
& the curves get sharper,
& the tread on my tires will ware down

thin like the skin on my fingertips,

but if i keep going,
i'll find myself in paradise.

& i'll find you there.

—*arthur louis pullman*

6.

WHEN I RETURNED my eyes to Mara's, there were tears beneath hers. "Shut up," she said, wiping them. "It was really nice, okay? I'm allowed to be a little emotional."

"Yeah," I said.

"Did you not like it?" Her voice still watery from the drops under her eyes.

"No, it's, it's really nice, but I . . . I don't, I just don't really notice anything right away, as far as, like, a clue is concerned—"

"Oh, shut up about that for a second!" She smacked me in the arm. "Just enjoy the poem! I mean, can you even imagine? Someone writing about you like that? That kind of love? Your grandmother was a lucky woman."

I felt a lump in my throat. "Yeah, maybe."

"'Yeah, maybe'?"

"It's just that he says, 'I was eighteen and you a year older.'"

"So?"

"So he didn't meet my grandmother until he was twenty-five."

"Oh."

"So this means there was another woman. That he was writing to."

We sat in silence, the alarm clock ticking to let us know that it was now 4:00 a.m. Mara sat up and spoke properly.

"'The best way to know God is to love many things.'"

"Oscar Wilde?"

"Close. Vincent van Gogh."

"He cut off his own ear."

"Okay, but—"

"For love—"

"Yes, but—"

"—of many things."

Mara's face was close to my own. Six inches of air separated us, both our cheeks against the shared pillow. The dim overhead light was painting the room yellow and her skin a soft gold. I'd never looked so closely into her face, but I realized now that it was all perfectly placed: her small eyebrows and small ears and small lips. Her eyes glowed green in their frame and flashed around the room. Down the bed, up to the ceiling, out the window, and finally resting on me, reaching directly into mine.

"Okay." She leaned her face toward mine and kissed me, softly, quickly, before I could react. "Read it again."

And so I read.

7.

January 5, 2010

Dear Journal,

Our house almost burned down today. Some of it did, so now we're at a hotel.

My whole family hates my grandpa except for me. My dad isn't talking to him and he's not talking at all, of course. So the only sound in our hotel room is the A's game. I haven't decided if I hate him or not. I don't know how I feel about him.

Let me explain.

Everyone in my family says that my grandpa needs help. Ever since my grandma died, he just walks around the house looking for things and never finds any of them. And if you ask him what he's looking for he raises his hands and says "don't bother." I don't think he means to be mean but sometimes it feels like it.

Every day, he makes himself a sandwich and most days, he just walks away and leaves it in the kitchen. Some days he leaves it on his desk, or on the toilet. It doesn't really bother me; I think it's pretty funny.

Yesterday, he wanted to make himself soup. But he didn't know how to make it, or where to find the broth, so he gave up after step one.

The problem is, step one was turning on the burners of the stove. That's why I'm writing from a hotel room right now.

My dad told me that the difference between a good person who does bad things and a plain old bad person is that the good person feels sorry about the things they did, and the bad person doesn't understand that they were bad. He said my grandpa didn't feel sorry about almost burning our house down. He said my grandpa was mad at everyone else for making the house so confusing.

I can't tell if he's actually not sorry, or if he just forgot he was supposed to be.

Either way, that's not why no one is talking to each other. That's because of what happened afterward.

My grandpa is a little rich. He made a lot of money for writing a book that everyone loves—everyone except for me, I tried to read it and it was too boring. Maybe I'll try harder when I have to read it for school, but probably not. My dad figured that because my grandpa burned down the kitchen, he should pay for a new one. So he went into my grandpa's bank account.

And that's when everything got really bad.

My dad never screams in front of me, but he did today. I guess my grandpa had been taking money from the account and my dad was screaming about it. Even while my grandma was alive, he was writing checks for "thousands of dollars a year," my dad said. He said it wasn't illegal, technically, because it was my grandpa's money, but he'd been secretly spending it for so long that it had "driven us into the ground."

And now that we're in the ground, I guess we don't know what we are going to do next. My dad said we should do a new version of the book but my grandpa said it was "bullshit." My dad said that my grandpa was being a "stubborn old man," and my grandpa didn't say anything. My dad said that if my grandpa "really cared about us" he'd do it, but my grandpa just turned on the A's pregame show.

I'm sure my dad will figure it out, but for now, everyone hates my grandpa, for burning down our kitchen and driving our family into the ground and not caring about us at all.

Except me, I don't know how I feel.

More later,

Arthur Louis Pullman the Third

8.

I FELT THE whole world before I saw it that morning.

First, light from the open window, stinging my eyelids, welcoming them to existence again. I kept my eyes closed, not ready for the world and all its brightness.

Then, pain, icy hot, directly behind my forehead. My face was burning, and after raising a shaky hand to feel its temperature, I left it resting above my nose, too exhausted to move. There was nothing in my body at all.

I was a thousand miles from home and my father had no idea where I was.

I was sleeping on the cold, hard bed of a hostel, occupied by a secret society that worshipped a man that I most vividly remembered for forgetting his sandwiches and drinking whiskey. But I was unintentionally engaged in my own form of worship, stringing together bread crumbs he had left behind in an attempt to understand him.

And I did understand him, at least better than I had before, at least enough to clarify what I really didn't know about him: What was he reliving, and why? Why had he stopped doing it in the first place? Where was he going and why did he end up in Ohio? Why did no one in my family know anything about it? Why was this all a secret?

Behind my eyelids, I saw him in Room 17D, gathering whatever he carried and preparing to make his way back out into the uninviting world. His view of the future from 17D must have been a bleak one, and I wondered what had compelled him forward, why he hadn't just decided that this spot, this bed, was as good as any to lie down in and die.

But that answer was the easiest of all. It was written into the poem from last night, and every poem. There was something there for him, a "great purpose," a "greater love," an "angel," a "paradise," a "you" that he was chasing, and it kept pulling him forward, train after train and city after city. I wondered how much of his life had been spent in search of it, whatever it was. Whoever she was.

And then I remembered why I was waking up, and why I would continue forward. Because for the first time, when I thought about searching for something, it wasn't Kaitlin's face that popped into my head. It was Mara's.

I could see her even before opening my eyes, perfect and delicate and small, lying next to me, sharing the same pillow, facing me, not turned away as Kaitlin always had been. The future from Room 17D didn't look bleak with her in it. For me, I knew what that meant—it meant that I was ready. It meant there was a reason for waking up. So I did, and I opened my eyes.

But Mara was gone.

9.

MARA WASN'T IN the bathroom, so I checked the hallway, the common area, the entryway. They were all deserted.

I rapped on the door to Room 16, the dormitory, several times. It took what had to have been a hundred knocks before someone answered, the door still latched. Through the narrow opening, I recognized half of Lucas's face.

He yawned, wiping sleep from his eyes.

"Hey, is, uh, is Mara in there?"

He shook his head, expressionless. "Naw, man, no one's here," he mumbled, and went to slam the door.

"Wait!"

He held it open.

"She's Indian, short, she's got a little—"

"Yeah, I know who Mara is, dude. She's not in here."

He moved to close the door and again, I pushed back against the latch. The recoil force knocked me backward. "No!" I shouted. "I, uh, I serve a Great Purpose! I know the whole, the whole thing."

"Dude, I get it." He lazily shook his head. "But everybody left this morning, on the train."

"Where'd they go?"

"Yeah," he said, wiping his face again. "We kinda have this policy—'if he wanted you to know, he would've taken you with'."

I didn't respond. I trembled, my knees threatening to give. Lucas must have sensed my panic, because he slid off the latch, and opened the door.

He wasn't lying. There were three male bodies sleeping on the bunk beds, one that I recognized from the night before, and the rest of the room was empty but for the cigarette butts, Solo cups, and remaining bottles of liquor. No Laura, no Jack, no Great Purpose, no Mara.

Lucas shrugged again. "See, all gone." He slammed the door shut.

I felt empty as I dragged myself across the deserted common room, weighing possibilities. Maybe she'd gone to our original room, number 6, so she could have a full bed to herself. Maybe she'd gone to get us breakfast, or coffee, and would be back any minute. Either way, there was no way she would have given up, not with so many clues left to solve. She wouldn't abandon the clues that we already had. Those had to mean something to—

A bead of sweat formed on my forehead and I started moving faster toward 17D. *I don't know that you fully appreciate what you have here*, I could hear her saying. *There are people who will pay a lot of money for this.* I was at a near run when I burst into our room. The tiniest, most silent part of my brain expected her to be sitting on the bed, waiting, with a McDonald's breakfast sandwich and a half smile on her face. The whole rest of me knew she wouldn't be.

The rest of me was right. The room was empty and colder than it had been the night before. I sprang toward my backpack, ripped it open, and found my clothes, my toothbrush . . . and nothing else. All four of my grandfather's clues were gone.

My brain fought to think of scenarios that didn't involve Mara stealing from me, didn't require her to be the person I didn't want her to be. I tried to give her every excuse. She went to make photocopies. She hid them so no one else could steal them from me.

But the more I invented, the more ridiculous they all became. The only one that made sense was the obvious one: I had been lied to, led on, and cheated. She had used me, preyed on my social discomfort, and made me feel like a god so her job would be easier. Thinking about how willingly I'd let her in and followed her, how eagerly I'd drugged myself and given her a getaway, how happily she'd been giggling with Jack the night before, made me want to drive my car off a bridge and into a lake. I had been played, plain and simple, right from the first minute, and now I had nothing.

I wondered if Great Purpose was even real.

I wondered if the Sharpie on the wall had been written there that morning.

I wondered if her name was actually Mara.

I know what it's like to not feel anything. The light from the lamp spread and began to burn the real world around it.

I let myself be consumed by it. My hands, arms, and legs began to tingle as they lost feeling.

Mara's face swam in and out of the nothingness; her head was on the pillow and the pillow needed to suffer; her body leaned against the shelf and I needed it gone; the lamp and its light were a threat to my survival and I was stronger than they were. My body took over, limbs swinging blindly, grabbing, pulling, ripping, throwing, screaming, grunting, begging for everything to go away but it didn't. I submitted, my nerves waking up on their own.

I left the room with my backpack, speed-walking out the door with my head down, and the light followed. I was sure the man at the front desk glared at me, but I didn't stop to apologize, I didn't stop to look, I couldn't see him anyway.

A rush of cold air bit my face; miserable, hopeless, stinging, perfect cold; it wasn't my face, it was my body's. It dragged me street by miserable street, stirring into the sting of the wind and the rush of the traffic, into the street and into the cars around me.

"Arthur, you're okay, buddy, but you've gotta slow down." Mason jogged to keep up, so I sped up to get past him. "Just take one deep breath."

Mason always did this, tried to lie to me when things went wrong. I'd come home fuming, furious about Kaitlin and all the ways she tried to make me jealous, and Mason would remind me that frustration was part of the process of learning to love someone. Then he'd asked me a hundred questions—what she'd said, how she'd said it, and what I thought she wanted—to mine for information. Of course he didn't want me to feel better, he just wanted to know what I knew. Just like Mara.

I opened my mouth, let the air chill my lungs until my chest was burning, then slammed my left fist against it as many times as I could. I stretched my left hand underneath the cast and it burned like the day I'd broken it, perfect, melting, all familiar, the physical, unnatural crunch of bone against bone channeling all the hurt into one emotionless spot, voices in my ears, screaming—

"It doesn't have to be like this." Mason was trying to make his voice sound calm but I could tell that he was panicking, I could always tell when I was making him panic. "We can beat this, we've done this before."

I found myself on another row of abandoned buildings, shops that had closed and boarded up their windows, shops that decided it wasn't even worth it to keep on trying—and I saw birds flying across glass one hundred yards in front of me.

"Just slow down and tell me about it." Mason tried to grab

my shoulder but I shrugged him off. "Talk to me."

"Tell you what?"

"What's going on, why you're walking this fast, why you keep hitting yourself like that, all of it. You can tell me about whatever." Mason wasn't letting me get him out of my sightline. "Tell me about what just happened, what you guys are fighting about. I swear it will feel better, it always does."

I stopped to pant, my breath materializing in front of me, and stared at him.

"What, do you think I'm gonna talk to her about it?" His face didn't flinch. "You can trust me, Arthur."

I began to move forward, quickly, again, away from him; as I passed an interstate, a Camaro sped by in the HOV lane, begging me to smash the windows, yank the driver out by his shirt, throw him against the sidewalk, and go speeding off into the mountains of Colorado, get up over a hill, somewhere where I couldn't see anything behind me. and fly recklessly into and out of the world ahead of me.

"She's not worth this, man," Mason shouted. "She told me it was okay."

"Fuck you!" I shouted back, screaming at the light, the brick wall it became, closing in around me, faster and faster, the ring on my finger choking me, the wall closing in on me, and I felt myself needing to do something I'd regret, needing to break out of it to survive, overwhelming light streaming from the window next to me—

I stopped and stared up into it. Tiny red birds, a dozen

western tanagers, fluttered over the name, BAULD BOOKS, chipping off the top of my glass. I'd found my way back to the bookstore from the night before, following the birds. The light shrank back into its source.

This kind of bookstore made no sense in the modern world. Each book looked older than the last, barely qualifying as "used" books, unorganized and piled high on top of each other on both sides of the store, split by a center line. One side was FICTION. The other, NONFICTION.

I could feel my body inside of my skin again, my left hand trembling uncontrollably, my chest and face swollen with pain, my skin bitten with frostbite.

An old shop owner emerged from the back. The only hair he had left clung to either side of his wrinkled scalp, a tiny forest into which the legs of his glasses disappeared. "What can I do you for there, bud?"

"Just looking," I muttered.

"Well, if you're looking for anything specific, you'll probably need my help to find it." He leaned against the back wall.

"What's with the birds?"

"It's from a book," he said. "One of our favorites—"

"Why don't you have a filing system? Like every other bookstore?"

"Got one, right here," he said, and lightly tapped his skull with two fingers.

I held up a book, *A Moveable Feast* by Ernest Hemingway. "This is a memoir. It belongs in the nonfiction section."

I tossed it across the line and the man laughed. "Yeah, according to him."

"Well, he'd be the authority."

"Far as I'm concerned, a man's history of himself's usually a hell of a lot more fiction than it is fact."

"No," I said.

"Just 'cause someone says it happened—"

I reached for another nonfiction book and waved it at him. "No, because it actually *did* happen. In his past, that's what non-fiction *is*."

"Eh." The old man shrugged. "That's the thing about the past, kid. It's really just the fiction we all decided is true."

I turned back to the fiction section.

For five minutes, he watched as I pulled books from random stacks, thumbed through the first page, then tossed them off into a different stack. Even as I assaulted his "filing system," he kept smiling.

"How do you even keep this place open?" I asked.

"I'm sorry?"

"I mean, business-wise. Do you have a lot of customers? Did I come in at a bad time?"

The man didn't give me a fight. He chuckled and shook his head. "No, I suppose not."

"Do you have *any* books written, I don't know, in the last ten years?"

"No, I suppose not."

"Then how do you stay open?"

He shrugged and continued to smile. "Life finds a way."

"There's a word for *meth lab* I've never heard before."

He stopped smiling, crossing his arms sternly. "What is it you need, kid?"

"Just looking." My eyes found a display in the back of the fiction section. There were three paperback novels, their covers bent and faded, but with a colored-pencil wooden shack and gray-purple sky still visible.

"You have identified our prized possession." The old man walked straight past me and grabbed the first copy of *A World Away*. He turned it over and over in his hands. "Signed by the author and everything. We got a couple signed copies a few years back, sold 'em, and that's what's kept the doors open."

The words caught me across the jaw. "Signed by . . . Arthur Louis Pullman?"

He rocked the book gently in his arms. "Life finds a way."

"How did you . . . I mean, how did he sign them? How'd you get them?"

"That's the million-dollar question, isn't it? You wouldn't believe me if I told you."

I didn't say anything, just watched him watch the book. It was strange, how closely people held something my grandfather had let go of so long ago. I'd never seen anyone look at my grandfather that way. The old man handed it to me, and I sat back onto a stack of books directly in the center of the room, straddling the line between fiction and nonfiction, unsure of which side was which and where I belonged.

The old man trembled as he told the story. "He just wandered in here, same as you. Poor bastard. Looked cold as hell, kept writing in some little journal, saying his name over and over again, 'Arthur, Arthur.' I ask him, 'What are you looking for, buddy?' You know, thinkin' there's some old folks' home I'll have to track down. But I go to help him and I see in his book, he's got it written down, *A World Away*, so I say, 'Oh, yeah sure, we got a couple of those, let me find 'em.' And when I grab it, I see the picture on the back, and, and I don't know, I just knew it. Granted, guy on the back here looks like a kid, kinda like you, actually, but . . . I could just tell. I thought, This is the guy! And he's got his ID on him; sure enough, Arthur Louis Pullman. All he says the whole time is 'I gotta get on the train.' So I say sure, I'll take him, if he doesn't mind signing some books on the way. He spent most of the drive just writing in this little journal, not paying much attention to me, but when I gave him the books, sure enough, he signed them."

I swallowed. The coincidence felt too great. I started to feel sick to my stomach.

"Did you see anything else in the journal?" I asked quietly, my eyes running back and forth across the cover of the book.

He shook his head. "Nothing. He didn't want me reading it, that's for sure. Just caught a glimpse."

The book felt light in my hands, like it might break if I squeezed it too tightly.

"He even wrote a little inscription." The words choked on the way out of his mouth. "Here I was, mumbling on like an idiot, about the store, about money, about all this bull hickey, and he doesn't say a goddamn thing, just writes two words into every book. And those two words, that's all it took. Changed my life."

The corners of the paperback were hopelessly bent and there were stains on what remained of the front jacket. It had been read so many times that the book fell open, the binding of the book trained to reveal the title page with my grandfather's signature and two words of his hesitant cursive:

keep going.

PART SIX.

mccook.

1.

may 1, the 1970.

i am nothing but a mosaic of the people i've met & the things they've carried.

the woman across the aisle has a one-way ticket & she is rapidly moving life to life. she's imagined herself a place called indiana where her three children will be happier & is leading them without hesitation or doubt or fear. their names are not names in the traditional sense, they are affirmations of the love that created them.
treasure.
precious.
beautiful, the youngest, rushing around the car with heaven on her fingers. she does not care that we are older or that we do not look like her or that perhaps we look dangerous. she's so young that she's not yet been taught how to not love. she instead runs to touch our faces, filled with the joy & curiosity that is our basic nature. she is a self-fulfilling prophecy,

& i am her beautiful eyes.

the man next to us is unable to stand up, unable to walk, unable to think. he is covered by his own jacket, shivering cold, because he left all of his warmth on the doorstep of a woman who could not return it. he's imagined himself a place called new york where joanna doesn't exist, but he's had to sedate himself with the bottle in his pocket just to take the first step away from her.
he has to begin every day by asking himself questions, is it worth it?
should i start over?
& whiskey answers for him, so long as he never leaves it. he says it's the worst thing that's ever happened to him, but it's the only thing that's ever loved him. he wouldn't even know where to begin putting it back together,

& i am his broken heart.

the man outside the window stands in a field too big in a world too big for just one man. his horizon looks the same every day, gray-purple in the morning, gray-orange at night, punctured by light green corn, swaying unanimously in the only thing that changes: the wind. his hands are worn from the tools he must use to support the life he never chose, the life he was born to & will die to.
but his hands are not weak. his hands have taken the blisters

& turned them into calluses. his hands have grown stronger
with pain.

every day, at 7:30 a.m., he watches the train go by, every day
waiting for the stop it will never make.

every spring he watches life begin

& every fall he watches it die

& every summer he sweats until he has nothing left

& every winter he worries & he prays

& every day he watches the train, but the train goes too fast,

& now he just waits for the end.

but he is not sad. every day he wakes in the morning to watch
the train, because he is strong where it matters. he is strong
where he holds his entire planet,

& i am his hopeful hands.

i am nothing but a mosaic of the people i've met & the things
they've carried.

—*arthur louis pullman*

2.

"GOOD MORNING, MOURNING doves! Arise and greet the new day with open arms and—and, well, honestly, don't get too excited. It's just Nebraska, and it's gonna be for a while.

"We're coming up into McCook, right on time, and with no one jumping aboard to join us, we should be off immediately, onward and upward into the new day.

"If anyone needs me, I'll be up here McCook-in' up something clever for the next stop, which is . . . Holdrege. Gonna need all the help I can get on that one.

"That's all, from your brilliant and loyal conductor."

3.

THE TRAIN RATTLED and shook me from my half coma. I hadn't been sleeping, because my eyes were open, but I couldn't remember the last time I'd moved. It had probably been hours. It might have been the entire night.

From a kiosk in the Denver Amtrak station, I'd purchased a topographical map of the United States that spread the country in front of me in soft blues and greens, fading into oranges where the plains gave way to mountains and black-dotting every city serviced by a cross-country Amtrak train. I'd drawn lines connecting all the cities I'd been to so far, measured their distances with the inside of my thumb, and then charted a course forward, circling stops that might make sense. The train was reaching the end of my next circled section, and I'd stared at the map long enough to decide that there was nothing significant to be observed from it. I might have been able to figure it out if I'd had the clue he left in Denver, but that clue, and all the others, were gone.

We were edging farther and farther into the enormous patch of sapphire blue in the center of the map—the Great Plains, as it was affectionately known. I don't know if people in the Midwest ever appreciated the supreme irony of calling their region "the Great *Plains*," like there was something great and significant about their mundanity. I don't know if people in the Midwest appreciated irony at all. The sign outside the approaching station read MCCOOK, NE, but it could have been ANYWHERE, NE; it was all the same: long, slow-sloping hills of corn underneath the same hopelessly wide sky.

For all the terrible, twisting, irreconcilable confusion, I felt strangely content watching the world pass, arriving east and departing west out of the tiny window in the back of the train where I'd sat. I'd heard a Buddhist monk on a daytime talk show once describe the work he did with death-row inmates, and how they were actually more peaceful than most people he knew who weren't awaiting their imminent death. "We're all on death row," he'd said. "They just have a schedule." I imagine it felt something like this. When you can see death in front of you; when you have a relationship with your mortality, not as a stranger, but as an acquaintance with an appointment, you can be content in whatever direction you're taking to get there.

At least I knew that this was the direction my grandfather had gone. At least I knew that I was doing what he wanted me to do. He told me himself to *keep going*, so I did. I watched the sky outside, hoping a burning planet would go streaking by.

As the train screeched and slowed to its final resting position, I saw a man outside the window, only there long enough to be a single image as we flew by. He was standing alone in a wide field of grass, visible in the low light of morning under patches of slowly melting snow, wearing faded blue jeans, a winter jacket, and an expression that I'd seen a thousand times before: mostly blank, but haunting and hopeful.

His arms were open, his hands pointed toward the track, as if he was looking for me, reaching into the train to find me. Every process in my body froze, my breathing and my blood.

It was my grandfather.

He was alive.

I sat motionless, petrified. By the time I put my face to the glass, he had disappeared into the morning mist.

I sat staring, ripped cushion and Amtrak logo where his

body had just been. Where I thought his body had just been.

It was a hallucination. Of course it was a hallucination. He couldn't have actually been there, in a field in Nebraska.

I shook the image from my head.

But still, from the resting train, the world outside looked like a world I'd seen before. The station was wooden and unimpressive. The horizon behind it was gray-purple, punctured by stalks of light green corn, swaying together in the wind. The breaks between colors blurred and softened, almost like they were drawn in . . . in colored pencil.

I had seen this image before. And the light red text around it.

It was the cover of his book.

This was *A World Away*.

The mirage became real.

I threw my backpack over my shoulder and tumbled down the stairs, past where the Amtrak attendant was preparing to close the door.

"Hey, buddy!" he shouted, snatching at my backpack as I ran past him. "We're closing the door! You can't smoke here!"

"I know!" I was already off the train and onto the platform.

"Well, this ain't your stop! And next train's not till tomorrow."

Without my commanding them, my feet moved west, back up the track.

"Do you at least have someone to pick you up?" he shouted at my back. "There's nothing here! You're headed toward a bunch of nothing right now."

I leapt off the wooden platform and onto the grass, avoiding piles of leftover snow. I was too far away to even hear the door slam.

The mist was thicker than it appeared on the train, but I pushed myself into it, faster and faster, the inner thigh threads of my jeans ripping at each other.

The train began to move, following the track east, our paths in opposite directions, and soon, it was gone.

Still I ran, mist closing around, flying in and out of my chest in breaths that became slower and slower, my legs starting to hesitate. I couldn't see directions in the mist; had I veered off? I spun, edging my way forward until—

One hundred feet ahead of me, a figure broke the fog. His outline appeared first: arms wide-open toward where the train had just been. He was real.

"Grandpa!" I called, unable to stop myself. The outline of his head turned to me, frozen; a ghost suddenly realizing mortal eyes could see him. I threw my arms out.

But he didn't move toward me. Instead, he turned his head back over his shoulder and walked in the opposite direction. "Grandpa, it's me, Arthur," I said, the words pouring out with five years' worth of force. His walk became a run, plowing forward, faster away from me. "Grandpa! What are you doing?! It's Arth—"

Without warning, he dove off into the field to his left, leaving a few shivering stalks where his brown coat had just been. I didn't hesitate, launching myself in after him.

As soon as I entered the cornfield, the world shifted dramatically. There was no mist. High leaves blocked most of the morning sun, the only light fighting its way through in tiny rays. It was cooler, and silent. Evidently cornfields felt the wind but didn't hear it, as none of the whistling could permeate their fortress. The only sound was the occasional chirp of an insect.

I inched forward. Every time I pushed a stalk out of my way, it recoiled, sharp leaves biting at my skin like the edges of paper. My eyes began to sting, and I remembered my father telling me about the pesticides used to treat the corn that rested on its leaves. My face and hands swelled. It was almost unbearable, but still I wandered, deeper and deeper into the maze.

I couldn't tell if it had been five minutes or thirty. Every direction I looked, I saw nothing, just stalks and leaves and darkness on an infinite loop.

"Arthur, what you're talking about is a hallucination," Dr. Sandoval said, sitting atop his high-backed orange chair in a clearing. "When you're fixated on someone, you project them into the world. Those conversations you're having, they're not real."

"This one was real." I stopped moving. "I saw him." Dr. Sandoval shook his head and wrote something on the pad in front of him. "What are you writing?"

"You see people exactly as you remember them. You don't think it's strange that they're always wearing the same clothes? Or that they always say the same things in conversation?"

"He was here," I panted, turning in circles. "I saw him.

Hallucinations don't run away from me."

"You have to ask yourself, Arthur. This false remembering, these dreams—what are they protecting you from? What is it you're running from?"

"This one wasn't false, I *saw* him standing—"

"You're doing it again."

"Doing what?"

"You're avoiding the question. You're hiding from yourself. You're using cynicism as a means of forgetting—"

"No, I'm not!" I twisted again, hurling dirt in his direction, and it fell softly to the ground.

Next to where he had just been sitting, ten feet from me, several stalks rustled. I took off after the noise, leaping over low, fallen stalks and throwing my elbows in front of my face to guard it from the assault of leaves. More stalks were moving; someone was in front of me, a trail I could follow, a person shoving their way through the corn.

The sounds of crashing got louder as he moved faster ahead of me. I watched the corn movement take an abrupt turn and I dove to my left to head him off. But the turn was too violent, my movement too sharp, and my feet caught a discarded stalk on the ground, yanked it out from under me. I flew forward, and as I fell, a brown coat appeared out of the mess of stalks and leaves. Without intending to, my body struck its side and we tumbled to the ground, stalks falling with us.

And again, the world was silent.

"Grandpa?" I whispered. Neither of us moved.

In the soft streaks of light that fought their way through the corn, his face appeared for the first time. It was firmly wrinkled, more than it ever had been, the skin having fought five more years of gravity. His hair, full when he'd left, was now gone entirely. His lips were cracked and caked with dirt.

But his eyes were shining like mirrors, just as they always had been.

Tears hit my eyes before I could stop them. I squeezed my face and choked the words out. "Why did, you, why didn't, anybody, tell me . . . Why are you alive?"

"Arthur." His voice was higher than I expected.

"Why didn't you tell me?"

When I opened my eyes, he was blurry in front of me, and the image started to change. It wasn't his skin. It wasn't his hair. It wasn't his voice.

"Tell you what?" He nursed his right arm. "Why are you here?"

I trembled. "You're not him." I couldn't stop staring at him like he was a ghost, even though I now realized he wasn't. "You're . . . you're . . ."

"Henry." He nodded.

And again, the mirage became real.

4.

MY GREAT-UNCLE HENRY and I barely spoke as I followed him out of the cornfield, across the train tracks, through the melting snow, and toward his rusted pickup truck, parked on a nearby service road.

"You can stay with me," he'd told me. "I've got a couch. Next train's tomorrow." I thanked him, and he let the conversation die, turned the dial on the hissing and popping of the AM radio, something about the price of corn and the cold front coming in.

It was unnerving how much he looked like my grandfather, even in his posture. He curled back against the driver's seat with the same slouch, wide shoulders hunched forward, seeming to permanently occupy it the way that my grandfather had become a part of his living room chair.

Even when my grandpa was alive, my family hardly ever spoke of Henry. I'd never met him. He'd never come out to visit, and the only times anyone brought up going to Nebraska, it was treated as a punishment. Henry himself was only mentioned in passing, in general condemnation of the Midwest: *Don't go to the firing range, Arthur; wouldn't want you to end up a red-state maniac like your grandpa's brother, Henry.*

But he was a living relic of my grandpa.

"Why haven't I ever met you before?" I broke our silence as his old, red Chevy bumped and bounced along the gravel. He shrugged but didn't answer, almost as if the question had been a meaningless pop of the AM radio. "You never came out to visit us or anything."

The tracks disappeared in the rearview mirror and the whole world became corn, stretching wider in every direction the farther we drove, reaching up over each horizon. If you lived surrounded by this, it would be easy to believe that there was nothing else in the world, like the Earth dropped off into the galaxy once you reached the end of each field. Maybe that's why people in this part of the country never left.

"Did you ever want to?" I asked, and for a third time, he shrugged, finally mumbling, "It's a long way."

"I know," I said. "It's just crazy that after all this time, and hearing about you since I was a kid, the only way for me to meet you is to just randomly see . . ." I stopped, remembering how I'd seen him: not randomly, but waiting, standing outside the train—the exact train that I was on. "Wait."

He shifted in his seat.

"What were you doing at the train?"

"Just waiting."

"For me?" I asked. He didn't answer.

"What were you going to do if I didn't get off the train?" He didn't answer.

"Did someone tell you I was going to be there?" Again, he didn't answer, and this time reached for the dial of the radio to drown me out.

"You don't have to lie to me," I said, turning it back down. "How did you know that I was going to be on that train? Did my dad tell you? Did he ask you to come get me?"

Henry snorted.

"Answer me!" I almost shouted, and he slammed on the brake. He turned to look at me with his entire frame, shoulders and chest rotating ninety degrees to the passenger seat, and studied me with the same expression. "I haven't spoken to your damn father in fifteen years. You think I run his errands?"

I felt tiny in front of him. "So . . . you just happened to be there?"

He stared for another moment before turning back to the wheel, back to the road, and pressing the gas once more. "I guess so."

We didn't speak again until we arrived at his house.

It was a single-story shack, the roof slanted from left to right, built on a plot of land cut out from the cornfields around it. There was some farm equipment scattered across the lawn, buried in grass so tall, it must not have moved in years. Inside, blue pastel wallpaper was chipping to reveal the plaster behind, and a tweed couch and coffee table were the only fixtures in the living room. Three books were set on the table—the Bible, *Birds of Nebraska*, and an old copy of *A World Away*—and a thick stack of *Chicago Tribune*s sat beneath it. "Mmm,"

Henry noised when we got inside, nodding to the kitchen, an invitation to eat. Without another word, he slipped out to the barn.

Clinging to the refrigerator was our family's most recent Christmas card. I hated them, all of them, a totally meaningless exercise in pretend normalcy. I remembered laughing one year when my grandfather had asked my mother, "Do you think I'll look less miserable wearing a button-up shirt?" Next to the fridge, a phone was mounted to the wall.

I only knew two numbers—the first that I'd dialed over a hundred times and could plug in without thinking—five five five, one five eight, five six five seven—but the voice on the other end would be Mason's. And I'd think of all the times that I'd called him and he'd answered and told me the things I needed to hear at the time, and I'd realize how all of those times were bullshit, and how he was using them to get close enough to steal the one thing that was important to me, and I knew that now. *I'm sorry, Arthur.* Fuck you, Mason.

The other number was Kaitlin's—five five five, one five eight, three three five three. "You need to be taken care of," I heard her say. "You need me too much," and I could see her at the kitchen table, legs crossed toward me, leaning forward to expose enough of her chest to make me think about it. She nodded toward the phone.

"Are you mental?" From across the room came a voice that wasn't Kaitlin's; it was Mara, perched coolly on the edge of the tweed couch, running her hand over my great-uncle's old radio. Seeing her split my head in pain. She made me want to call Kaitlin more. "Just don't do something you'll regret," Mara warned me.

"You need to be taken care of," Kaitlin cooed. I looked back out the sink window at my great-uncle, sprinkling food down on the heads of a dozen chickens that ran around him in excitement. I knew chickens didn't feel any emotional attachment, but watching them scurry around Henry like tiny planets in his orbit, I wondered if he knew something chicken scientists didn't yet. He wasn't paying any attention, so I found the old plastic receiver in my right hand, raised it to my ear—

But there was no dial tone. I slammed it back on the base, and Mara and Kaitlin disappeared.

I fixed myself some toast, and as I ate, I pulled open the cupboards. Most were empty, with nothing indicating that my grandpa had ever been here. In the final cupboard, closest to the back door, I found a collection of envelopes, formal-looking letters addressed to Henry Pullman. I thumbed through them. On the top was a letter dated February 1969, from the First Bank of McCook:

> Mr. Pullman,
> We regret to inform you that, given the last twelve months' missed payments, your property has entered foreclosure proceedings. The overdue balance of your property mortgage now totals $458.12; please remit this payment to the bank in the next ten (10) business days or we will be forced to . . .

But there were no foreclosure signs, nothing at all to indicate that we were on the property illegally. I wondered if this was from a previous property, or if the bank had forgiven the balance.

I picked up the letter below it, this one from the same bank in October 1974.

Mr. Pullman,

We regret to inform you that, given the last eighteen months' missed payments, your property has entered foreclosure proceedings. The overdue balance of your property mortgage now totals $865.76; please remit this payment . . .

On like this, the letters continued, telling the story of my great-uncle's battle with the bank. One from 1977, another from 1980, 1982, 1987, when the bank changed their formatting of foreclosure notices, 1991, 1995, 1999, 2002, a long break before another notice in 2010, and the most recent, a letter from two months ago, indicating that he now owed over $22,000.

I looked back out the window, where he'd moved from chickens to pigs. He sat perched on the fence behind their trough, watching them eat, occasionally slapping one on the side. He smiled at them, and they seemed to smile back, "happier than a pig in shit," an expression my grandpa had used.

Returning the letters to the cupboard, I wandered to the living room, collapsing on the tweed couch. It was uncomfortable, itchy almost, and the only blanket was a wool quilt about half the length of my body. Still, I wrapped myself up in it and toppled over.

I pulled *Birds of Nebraska* off the table and thumbed through it, but there were no tanagers in Nebraska, and no signs that my grandpa had ever touched the book.

5.

IT WAS EVENING when I opened my eyes to the clanging of a single pan on the stove. Night had set in over Nebraska and the only light for miles was coming from Henry's kitchen. Other than that, the house, the yard, the fields, the whole state was going dark.

Finally, my head felt normal; my twenty-four-hour headache had eased and my temples no longer felt like they were slamming together to the cadence of a Kendrick Lamar beat.

When I came around the corner, Henry nodded to the table without speaking. He had set two places, one with his only fork and only plate, overflowing with too many scrambled eggs, eight pieces of toast, and three glasses of milk. I sat, and he brought the pan to the table for himself, drinking from a full gallon. I must have been his first company in years.

"Easy." He stopped me as I picked up my fork. "No manners in California?"

He bowed his head, cupping his hands and closing his eyes, and, to be polite, just as I always had, I did the same and half shut my eyes, watching as he spoke slowly and directly to God.

"Thank you, Lord God, and Jesus," he said, his voice softer, almost as if he was nervous to have their audience. "Thank you for the Earth. Which gives me what I need. Thank you for the corn. And for the eggs. For the pigs and chickens, and all their blessings. Thank you for the prairie. Thank you for Nebraska. Thank you for my mom. Hope you're taking care of her. Thank you for my home. For the sunset in the evening. And for the train in the morning. I live this life for you. Amen."

I pursed my lips. This was the problem with religion— other than a few animals in a shitty barn and $22,000 in debt, Henry had nothing, but the idea that it was given to him by God made him content to live this muted half existence. My grandfather had always done the same with his illness, reading the Bible and living in accordance with it as though God had given him the divine gift, and not the horrible burden, of memory loss.

We ate in silence. I wanted to ask about my grandpa, about the times he'd stopped here, about his last trip, but Henry didn't give me a single chance. He never lifted his head from his pan, shoveling eggs from pan to fork to mouth at twice my speed, then washing them away with quick sips from the gallon bottle. When the eggs had dwindled to nothing, he leaned back on his stool, sighed loudly, and spoke before I could.

"Why are you here?" Both of his hands were resting atop his

stomach, a small gut protruding below the brown coat that he wore even inside.

It was a surprisingly complicated question. "I'm taking the train route that he used to take," I decided.

"He?"

I swallowed. "My grandfather? Your brother."

"Huh." He used his tongue to clean some loose egg off his teeth and turned to look out the window behind me. His body shifted, but his expression didn't change. He gave nothing away. Just like my grandpa.

"I was actually wondering—"

"Why you doing that?"

"Why am I . . . retracing his train route? I . . . I guess I'm hoping it might help me to learn more about him. I'm trying to understand more. About his life."

"Huh."

"Do you mind . . ." I took a deep breath and decided to test the waters. "Do you mind if I ask you about some places I've been? Just to see if you know any more about them?" He didn't say no, so I continued. "Well, first, I went to Elko, and I met Sue Kopek. Do you know her?" He didn't react. "And Green River, with Big Ray's—"

Henry exhaled sharply and loudly again, like the snort of a pig. "Sorry to disappoint," he said. "Don't know much 'bout my brother."

I set my fork down. The way he ignored the questions reminded me of my grandpa as well, except Henry wasn't battling memory loss.

"He did stay here, didn't he?" I asked.

"Once. In forty years."

I knew the answer before I asked, "Five years ago?"

He shrugged.

"But he used to come here more often, right? He used to stop here—"

"That was a long time ago."

"Every couple of weeks, right, in the sixties, or seventies? He was coming through all the time? Because the place I stopped in Green River said he used to stop every couple of weeks, so I'm assuming his train route was—"

"That was a long time ago." Henry began to clear the table, an excuse to walk away from me.

"Why did he stop?"

Henry paused at the sink. Night had fallen completely and he was looking at nothing, but I followed his gaze anyway. The barn, the grass, the corn, the prairie, the pigs and chickens and cats, his whole life was out there, but it was invisible in the dark. His face was empty, the flickering light of the stove bouncing off the soft white porcelain of the sink, lighting his features from below, blank and unquestioning, desperately vacant, just like the brother he seemed eager to forget.

I changed course. "What was he . . . like? As a person?"

Again, Henry grunted to deflect the question. "You'd know better than I would."

"Not really," I said, and it surprised Henry. "His disease was pretty bad by the time I was old enough to talk to him. Most of my life, he . . . he wasn't himself."

Henry took another long pause, leaning himself against the sink, before asking, "How'd you know that?"

"What?"

"How'd you know that wasn't himself?" He swayed back up to his full height. "How'd you know that wasn't just him?"

"Because, I——" I dead-ended, again. "He couldn't have been. He must have been different. When he was younger? When he had more of his brain? When he wrote the book?"

"Never read the book," Henry mumbled.

"Me neither."

"Some family we are."

It hurt to look across the room at him.

He returned to the table and slouched onto the stool, his entire frame collapsing onto it like sinking into the dirt. It reminded me of the way he'd stood in front of the train that morning, his hands outstretched as if there was no separation between the grass and the soil and the snow and wind and the edges of his skin, like he'd been there so long that he was a part of that world and it was a part of him.

I'd envisioned this moment in my head before, but with my grandpa. Henry spoke as my grandpa, moved as my grandpa, ignored questions the way my grandpa had, stared forward with the same unflinching, unexplainable nothingness as my grandpa, carried on his shoulders the weight of an entire, unexamined life like my grandpa, and yet here in front of me, there was nothing to reconcile them. If they had ever had a life together, Henry had left it behind.

But that didn't stop me from pushing forward in frustration.

"What about when you were growing up? Didn't you do anything then? What was he like?"

He ignored me.

"Can you at least tell me what he was like? Before the disease?"

Henry didn't respond and my frustration finally boiled over.

"Jesus Christ! What happened between you two?"

Glacially, he curled upward, sitting at his full height.

"No," he said slowly. "We did not talk. And if we did, it does not matter now. I'm sorry to disappoint," he said, sucking down a deep breath and turning to face me, "but other than the direction we slithered into the world, my brother and I got nothing in common. I didn't see him then. I don't see him now. And if you use the Lord's name in vain one more time, you will be sleeping on the side of County Road 15. And begging, *begging* for His mercy."

From where I sat, the stove lamp was directly behind his head, casting light out around the outline of his face, sliding down all of his wrinkles. I didn't hear the threat. I didn't hear his anger. But I heard him, loud and clear. He said *now*. I swallowed softly and spoke softer. "Why were you at the train this morning, Henry?"

"Told you. Waiting."

"For what?"

The house groaned in the wind, its aged foundation pushing and pulling as the prairie tried to bring it down. "Just don't wanna miss him."

My heart collapsed into the very bottom of my stomach.

No one had told Henry that his brother had died.

He looked up, and I felt the crushing weight of his sadness. I saw him holding it, his arms spread, face calmly examining every window of the train, just as he had today, every day, for how long? Five years? Ten years? Forty years?

Neither of us spoke for ten minutes. I listened to the sound of his stool rocking against the wood, not a soul around for it to reverberate off of. He stared, unmoving, at the center of the table. Three times, I opened my mouth to tell what had happened, but no sound came out.

Finally, he looked back up at me. "When you see him, tell him I'm still waiting."

I swallowed. "Of course," I whispered. "I . . . of course."

Without speaking, he pushed his stool out and stood up from the table, disappearing into the living room.

I sat alone at the table and watched the doorway where Henry had just left.

There must have been a moment in his life when he'd wanted more than this. Maybe he'd been married, maybe there were friends that had come and gone, maybe my grandpa's trips through had given him a life more than the one he was living now, but he couldn't have been this alone all along. I wondered what had led him to this point, driving to the train every day to watch for a man he must have known by now was never coming back. I couldn't imagine the mistakes he must have made to get himself here, or how often they must have replayed themselves across his empty existence. I couldn't imagine the way that regret must pile up upon itself after decades in isolation. No wonder he continued talking to God. Even if God had abandoned him.

Unless this was what he wanted. Maybe he liked the chickens, and the eggs they gave him, and the single plate he used to eat them, and the giant fields of corn that insulated him from the rest of the world. It was hard to imagine, but there was purpose here, a different kind of purpose, and comfort, and meaning. There were things that relied on Henry, and Henry relied on them, and that was all that it had to be; the circle of life could be that small and uncomplicated. Maybe the life my grandpa had lived wasn't the life he'd wanted.

Or maybe this was the life my grandpa would have wanted as well, if he hadn't accidentally ended up with a family. Maybe I was the thing that got between my grandpa and living Henry's perfectly isolated life.

Henry came back through the doorway with a newspaper clipping.

"This is his," he said. "He had it last time."

Henry must have understood the significance of what he was handing me, because my grandfather had cut it out of a newspaper and circled it several times, especially the byline, a name I recognized from the logbook in Denver. I could feel my heartbeat creeping into my throat as I read:

OMAHA: THE ANTIPOLITICAL HUB OF THE MIDDLE UNITED STATES.

BY LOU THURMAN

MAY 1, 1970—Resiliency! In the
good people of the Midwest, afraid to

see their country sold to the highest
bidder, when the currency being traded
is young lives, poor lives, black lives!

From the Midwest they see the full
portrait of America, or whatever that
means. The Midwest brand of
compassion extends to all people,
regardless of creed, color, or
pocketbook; the Midwest brand of
compassion is what will end this war!

From the Midwest will come the
revolution, the revolutionaries already
sharpening their pitchforks of
nonviolence, readying cannon blasts of
ideas, a conversational protest.

Join us, Tuesday, May 2, in the back
room of the old Westwood Library, to
speak softly of revolution, and prepare
our rally cry!

"You finished?" Henry asked, and I nodded, still gaping at
the clue.

Without a doubt, this had been left for me. I don't know what
clue I'd missed in Denver, but he'd wanted me here. And Omaha

was only four train stops away.

"Did he tell you?" I asked. "To leave this for me?"

Henry took the newspaper clipping back. "Didn't say nothing."

I nodded, feeling my chest swell with affection for Henry. "I've found some journals," I told him. "Some stuff he'd written, during that last—uh, the trip he made, five years ago. Since the book."

"Okay."

"I don't have them now, but I can show them to you when I get them back. I think you'd really like them."

"No, thank you."

It wasn't rude, but Henry was uninterested. "It's just, because we all thought he never wrote again, I figured you might wanna read . . . I don't know. It might help."

Henry squinted at me. "Never wrote again?"

"Yeah, after the book. When he got . . . the disease, you know? He stopped writing altogether. Except these journals."

Henry stared at me for another moment, then got up from the table and left. If he was upset, he'd hidden it, but it wouldn't be hard; his face revealed almost nothing.

I sat in silence in the kitchen for five minutes, poring back over the newspaper clipping. The back room of a library would be easy to find, almost too easy. Again, I'd be looking in plain, public sight for a clue placed five years earlier, but a library was the perfect place. Bibles, encyclopedias, books my grandpa had talked about—all of them could serve as a secret language that only he and I spoke. And there were rumors about my grandpa and libraries—the Great Library. I wondered if the Westwood had anything to do with it.

When Henry returned, he dropped a thick stack of envelopes in front of me. He didn't sit, instead fixing his eyes over my shoulder on the creased and ripping paper.

"What is this?" I asked, but he didn't respond.

Carefully, I pulled the first envelope open. The paper was old and the ink was disappearing, but I recognized the handwriting.

february 15, the 1968.

dear henry,

heavy hearts this month—not sure if she's written you, but mum's getting sick. if you've anything you'd like me to pass along, i'd be happy to bring it my next trip through. coming in from omaha next month, i'll see you at the tracks, as always.

feels like i've been around the world & back this year already. this mum thing might be a nice chance to take a break from it all. don't know if that will ever be possible though—the more i learn of the world, the more i realize it needs help, & i'm afraid i may spend every day to my death going hoarse shouting up at waterfalls from the bottom, begging them to reverse their course. ah well, this is the life i've chosen & the life i love.

jeffery sends all his love, & duke; everybody out here does. what a fantastic bunch we've put together. you'd love them.
hope this year's crop has been plentiful. i've been watching the weather reports & they said lots of rain in nebraska. i hope you've been doing our dance, & if it's not helping your crops, i trust it's helping your soul. even ugly shits like us deserve to dance.

by the way—the old bastard saw his shadow. as you know, i'm a man of my word, so i'll honor our agreement until the day i die. the check's enclosed. tell those blowhards at the bank they're going to have to work a lot harder if they want to take what's ours.

—your brother, arthur

There was a small photograph enclosed: identical teenagers, holding each other up, both of them leaning forward against the railing of the McCook station, a train track stretching off into the horizon behind them.

There were dozens of envelopes, postmarked through five years ago.

"He wrote you?" I asked.

"We had a bet."

I looked up.

"Punxsutawney Phil." For the first time, it looked like Henry might almost be smiling. "The groundhog. Every time he sees his shadow, I get a thousand dollars."

I traced back through the letter: *the old bastard saw his shadow.* "And if he doesn't?"

"Well." Henry looked out the window behind me. "My broth—Arty didn't want no thousand dollars from me."

"What did he want?"

Then Henry smiled fully. It was foreign on his face, and the wrinkles tried to resist. "A poem. Son of a bitch. Said it was worth more than money."

All of it made sense—the foreclosure notices in Henry's kitchen, my father's fury at discovering my grandpa had been sending thousands of dollars away in random checks—all for a bet about a groundhog. All of it told a story of a grandpa I didn't recognize.

"I know he don't remember much," Henry continued. "I seen it. Couldn't barely remember my name." Henry blinked several times at the envelopes. "But he wrote. Every year, he sent that letter. Always remembered the goddamned bet."

He gave one firm inhale, as if to suck the words back in, and disappeared into a small door in the corner of the kitchen. I didn't see him for the rest of the night.

The house was full of loose boards that snapped around, creaking and groaning. All night, rain drummed against the outside walls in a pattern that became musical and comforting, soft percussion to complement the wind's howl.

I sat awake at the table, listening to the sounds of Nebraska, reading the letters my grandfather had sent to Henry over their forty years apart. It was a story I'd watched my whole life but had never truly been told. The story of my grandfather, the slow progression of his life, and, tied inextricably to it, the progression of his illness.

The second letter, dated *april 25, the 1970*, was as inspired as the first, shimmering with clarity and tales of recent adventures, as if they'd just seen each other. I'd never heard my grandfather speak like that, but the characters were all recently familiar, and another year brought "another shadow, & another goddamn check for your brilliant & loyal groundhog."

After that, the letters started changing. Starting with *march 2, the 1971*, the awareness and information stopped, coming only in waves that broke and scattered into sections of chaos. They read like his clues—the only details were cryptic, the stories had no beginnings or endings, and the writing itself seemed to pain him to the point of difficulty. Even the rules of grammar escaped him. *still can't, place pain*, he wrote in one, *writing & sometimes it makes me forget but usually just makes me remember.*

After a few years, he seemed to stop trying altogether. The letters became short and cordial, no more than a few sentences reminding Henry that he was still in California. The most important details of his life came and went in small paragraphs, his pivotal moments covered like basic details in a plot summary. When he met my grandmother, on *march 21, the 1975,* it received two sentences: *i've met a woman, josephine. she's very lovely, & we're marrying in a few weeks.*

Often, I could trace a hint of remorse for the life he'd given up, or at least a yearning to understand. *why, when i think of nebraska, am i filled to sorrow,* he wrote in 2002. *why can't i bring myself to the thought?*

The letters grew shorter and shorter. The final letter, dated in 2010, was a single sentence, four words long: *i've seen my shadow.*

In the yellow light of the single bulb above me, I read through them again, and again, and again. They confirmed everything I thought I had learned, and nothing more. They fell short of even telling the story of his life, missing so many significant moments it was as if my grandpa himself hadn't been there.

And still, they came. Every time the "bastard groundhog" saw his shadow, Henry received his check.

One letter broke the pattern. In only one letter, in one specific year, did he seem to rediscover clarity. It was the final letter I found, out of order and stuck to the bottom, its postmark softly fading off the front: March 16, 1997.

march 16, the 1997.

dear henry,

writing to you with so much joy in my heart

i can feel it, like a little joyous tumor—my son has just
had a son of his own.

he named him arthur,
plagiarizing bastard.
but still it doesn't feel like i deserve to have my name
on such a beautiful piece of creation.

when he opened his eyes, i saw the world again for the
first time. he looked at me & i saw myself in his eyes
as everything i wanted to be for him. everything was
possible again.

i thought i knew & understood love in an old life. as it
turns out, i had no idea.

check's enclosed.

—your brother, arthur

6.

THE 7:00 A.M. sun gleamed off the tracks in front of Henry and me, casting a sharp beam of light into our eyes. I didn't need to ask him to bring me to the train in the morning; he was already up and scraping the ice off his truck by the time I got outside.

Through every moment I'd ever spent with him, from our best trips together up to Truckee to the worst arguments, I couldn't remember a time when my grandpa seemed truly happy I was there. We didn't talk like that in my house, him especially. He didn't say "I love you," not because he didn't appreciate the semantic value of it, but because I don't think he knew whether he loved me or not. After all, the only things he seemed to love were his incorruptible concepts, like Jesus, like Dickens, like baseball; the things that could never let him down or leave him or die.

My existence seemed to only matter to him in pieces: on good days, I was two ears to hear whatever he felt like talking about; on bad days, I was a mouth, full of unholy and inappropriate words. Either way, I existed in proximity to his needs. It was inconceivable that something as small as me could affect something as large as him.

But I was wrong, and the proof was tucked into my back-pack. On the day of my birth, he had loved me, he had wanted me, he had needed me; I was his sign that everything was possible again. This single letter rewrote the story of our thirteen years together. I pictured the silent moments, but they weren't indifference; they were exploding with unexpressed sentiment. The terrible moments and nasty conversations weren't anger, they were just a disease, getting in the way of his relationship with a grandson that he loved, that he wanted, that he needed.

And now he wanted me to keep going. He needed me to find him.

"Few minutes late this morning," Henry grumbled from the driver's seat, leaning forward to examine the west end of the train tracks.

I'd considered telling him his brother was gone, but every time, the image of Sue Kopek collapsed on her living room floor came swimming back into view, the cat in the box and the value of not knowing, and I decided not to. Henry needed the train in the morning.

So instead, we listened to the rumble of the truck, the pop of the radio, the steady recycling of our breath, and a few moments after seven, the California Zephyr came pouring over the horizon. Henry trudged across the melting snow in the ditch, over the tracks, and took his place beside the train, eyes closed, arms raised, hair blowing across his face as the train pushed wind over it, his body rumbling like it was him, not the Zephyr, shaking and shuddering down the tracks. A smile curled across his face.

I followed him out, but by the time the train reached us, he'd forgotten I was there. Patting his back lightly, I turned and walked across the grass to the platform. "Thank you," I whispered under the roar of the train. He didn't hear me and didn't need to. I didn't look back.

Today's attendant had a mustache. "Getting on in McCook, that's rare, kid!" I dragged myself through the door and up into the nearly empty coach car. As the train pulled away from the station, I sped up, almost running to the back window.

Henry was still planted firmly in the grass, the same warm air rushing over him and leaving him behind.

Every morning, the train arrived, and with it came a new day that would be exactly the same as the last. With every train that passed, he was twenty-four hours further from his brother and twenty-four hours closer to God. And he couldn't stop it or slow it down. It was true for me as well; with every day, I was further from the time we'd spent together and closer to the myth he'd left, fact writing itself into fiction as even "I love you" came five years too late.

But that was everyone, I realized. As sure as the sun rising over it, the train ran, day after day, year after year, an immovable and unstoppable force across the country,

past my auntie and uncle, who watched it and wished it was better,

past Sue Kopek, who watched it and wished it wouldn't forget her, past the men in Green River, who watched it and wished it would leave them alone,

past Mara, who watched it and wished it would take her somewhere far away,

and past Henry, who watched it and wished it would turn around.

But it never did.

Still, he fixed himself like a statue, sacrificed himself to it, standing in the exact spot he'd stood for forty years; calloused hands reaching, weathered face smiling toward the train as it sped too quickly away from him.

And I knew that tomorrow morning, and the morning after that, and every morning after that, he would be in the same spot, feeling the same rush he'd felt for decades, with an immovable and unstoppable faith that as long as he waited patiently, one day, he and his brother would be reunited.

PART SEVEN.

omaha.

1.

may 2, the 1970.

so begins the grand march; the righteous rally, close to either
the beginning or the end.

omaha is a city with a pulse; a city where they see the full
portrait of america; resiliency. we met in secret on hollowed
grounds, our holy temple of diversion.
far & wide, we spread our message of revolution, & from far
& wide, they came, flooding our false temple,
& now the false temple begs to be made true; full of heads,
who am i to call it empty?

we built this Great library to be our Great diversion, & now it
begs again for truth,
duke tells me it will be fine; that we were destined for this &
we're merely answering the call.
i tell him i have my doubts, but duke tells me this is weakness.

what is the virtue of doubt? if exploration is the engine of

discovery; & questions are the engine of answers; is not doubt
the engine of truth?
which would make not doubt, but certainty, its opposite.
the world knows no shackles so rigid & unforgiving as
certainty. for certainty leaves no room for debate, or for
questions, or the delicate nuance of fact-and-fiction.

duke is certain. i have my doubts.
to duke, we are gods, but to me, we only act like them,
& it makes me wonder:

at what point does the misdirection become the direction?
at what point does the fiction become the fact?
at what point does a believed lie become the truth?
who are we, ourselves or the people we pretend to be?
who are you,
& who am i?

—*arthur louis pullman*

2.

STEPPING OFF THE platform in Omaha, everything felt
uneasy, like a million eyes were fixed on my chest. I could feel
something terrible, but whatever it was, it stayed just beyond

my periphery. I walked with my hood up, reminding myself that if the panic was in my head, so was the calm.

The Westwood Library was an enormous building in the middle of an average neighborhood, like it had been placed by an arrow thrown drunkenly at a map and left there to rot. There were four resolute stone pillars in the front, two slanted staircases leading to the front door on either side of a slanted fountain that still spewed water despite the cold. Inside, there were three floors of wall-to-wall books. Banners celebrating the most illustrious authors and their readers hung from the ceiling like championship titles in a basketball arena—Charles Dickens, William Shakespeare, F. Scott Fitzgerald, J. D. Salinger, and, sure enough, a black-and-white portrait that showed my grandfather in his early twenties, clinging one-handed to the railing of a train: the Arthur Louis Pullman that Henry knew and I had never met.

"Excuse me, sir." The librarian at the front desk had noticed me scanning the room. "Anything in particular I can help you with?" She didn't look like the librarians of California; she was young, round, and very pretty, curls bouncing on the sides of her face to frame a small-lipped smile.

"I, oh, I, uh, I'm looking for, for a book."

She had enormous boobs.

"Well, we've got a few of those," she said. "Three million, in fact."

"What about, uh . . ." I motioned to my grandfather's banner. "Him?"

"Oh, Arthur Louis Pullman is one of our favorites." Her face lit with excitement. "And if you're a fan, you're in luck. This is truly the *best* possible place."

"I don't know about that," I said under my breath.

"The whole place is designed like a maze." She shuffled her heels as she led me up the stairs, weaving in and out of aisles of books. "You know how they say you can get lost in a good book? Well, here, we think you should get lost in three million! As for Arthur Louis Pullman, we've got a display—a shrine, really—over here. It even has a couple of first-edition copies of his book, signed and everything."

I wasn't surprised anymore.

"I'm a *huge* Pullman fan. I think I know everything there is to know about him. Not sure if you're familiar with the story, but they say he was working on a masterpiece for forty years before he died, and there's a copy hidden in a vault in the basement of his mansion in California."

"It's not really a mansion."

"What?"

"I said, uh, wouldn't that be amazing?"

"I certainly think so. But then again, I've also heard that he was torturing his family while he wrote it, psychologically, you know? Keeping them as slaves in his basement, like test subjects. And if that's the case, I don't know if I'd want to read it."

"I think I'd want to read it more."

"Either way"—she ignored me—"at least we have this." Like a game show model, she gestured to a glass case at the end of an aisle with a few photos, the obituary from the *Chicago*

Tribune, and three signed first-edition copies of *A World Away*. My grandfather had been generous.

"This is great, thank you so much . . ." I looked for her name tag.

"Suzy."

We both noticed how blatantly I was staring at her chest. "Arthur."

"Great name. Let me know if you need anything else, okay, Arthur?" And she walked back to the front of the library.

Nothing in the display looked out of place, or like it had been touched for years. None of the books had any marking or insignia or difference to indicate a clue. I considered cracking the display open and looking through them. It wouldn't be difficult; it was the same kind of security that guarded condoms at grocery stores, not like stealing the Declaration of Independence or anything, and even Nicolas Cage could do that. I leaned close to study the glass, and in the reflective glass surface, a bright yellow image flashed past behind me. I turned, hands up, adrenaline protecting me from—

A small child, holding a Curious George book, running from his mother to the water fountain behind me.

I steadied my pulse and made my way toward the back wall. The library was almost too big, too many rows of books for any single person to take in. I found myself in the classic literature section, surrounded by all the books my grandfather had always talked about. Every title, I remembered by his reaction.

A Tale of Two Cities? "Genius! Thing's a goddamned masterpiece."

Tom Sawyer? "Bullshit! Twain couldn't write his way out of a left turn."

A World Away? "Eh, that one might be worth a read."

I circled the aisles on the first floor three times before moving up the stairs. There were doors all along the back wall, but clearly marked, and no back room: "Staff Only," "Surplus," "Supplies," "Men's," "Women's." None of them looked like the birthplace for a revolution.

"Find what you were looking for?" Without realizing it, I'd made my way through the entire library and was standing where I'd started, in front of Suzy's desk. "Shouldn't be hard, he only wrote one."

"Oh, no, I guess I, I haven't," I said, and her brow furrowed. "I haven't really been looking all, all that closely."

"Alright, then tell me," she said, lowering her voice. "What is it that you're really looking for?"

I took a small step back. "I'm, I'm looking for your back room," I said, and immediately regretted it.

She gaped at me, her cheeks tinting pink with disgust.

"No, I, I mean, not like that, not a back room . . ."

"I'm sorry," she said, quick and cold. "This library doesn't have a back room."

"No, I just, I read this newspaper article about it, and I'm pretty sure—"

"Well, I'm sorry, but you must be thinking of somewhere else."

Five days ago, I'd have walked for the door without looking

back. Five days ago, I'd have sat outside the library, helplessly replaying the interaction and hopelessly lamenting my failed experiment. But I was five days and two thousand miles from all of that.

I took two steps toward her. "Can I ask you a question? And you promise you'll answer it honestly?"

She nodded.

"What is it you serve?" Her face flushed red again. She wrung her hands nervously, staring down into the desk. "Because I serve a Great Purpose."

Her eyes flickered, a few quick blinks, glances around the room. "Okay," she muttered. "Now you answer my question. Arthur what?"

"I'm sorry?"

"Who are you?" She swallowed. "Arthur what?"

I nodded to the banner, to the photo of my grandpa fearlessly hanging off the train.

"Well, if you must use the bathroom"—she spoke at twice her normal volume—"I suggest you do it quickly." She slid a key over the counter in my direction and whispered, "Second floor, end of the hallway by the religion section. Through a door labeled 'Surplus.' It's your first door on the right. It's labeled 'Great Surplus.' I know it's not clever or anything, but—"

"It's perfect."

I raced upstairs.

The door labeled "Surplus" was directly across from my grandpa's display. It was at the end of a small hallway, which led into another small entryway with two doors, one without a door, full of mops and brooms, and the other, "Great Surplus." The key fit perfectly. With one last glance around the deserted entryway, I pushed it open.

The smell hit me before I entered the room. It was musty and recycled, the smell of books that had existed long beyond when they were intended to. The air in the room was stale, cold, unaffected by air-conditioning or human breath. As I edged around the corner, I felt out of place, like I was an intruder on holy ground; Alice entering Wonderland.

But the room itself was a masterpiece.

The ceilings were vaulted to make room for all the books, three of the four walls covered with shelves that ran all the way up to the top; gray, black, brown, and maroon bindings. Two pulpits stood in command at the head of the room, displaying a dictionary and a Bible. An old fire stove sat between them, its chimney funneled out the back of the building. Light streamed in from a small square window about six feet off the ground, low and dim, interrupted by the rough texture of the glass. In the center of the room was an oak table with only one thing on it: a tiny pile of shredded paper.

I felt the weight of once-ridiculous rumors materializing in front of me. I felt my grandpa.

I was standing in the Great Library.

My heart raced faster with every detail I took in. I moved in circles beneath the books. I breathed the leftover air my grandfather and his prophets had left behind, the ideas and words and legend that had once shared this room. I slid my hand along the table, my fingertips brushing the smooth wood finish. I ended at the Bible, a bright red, sixth-edition King James, on display like an untouchable truth, watching over the room from on high. I recognized the book and chapter—Corinthians 2, Chapter 5—the mark of my grandfather. In black block letters across the top, penmanship I didn't recognize had written, *No mortal has ever seen God.*

I swallowed. It was *his* verse. All of this was left here for me.

I turned the banner, hung from the ceiling, covering the only wall without books; the banner that let me know I was exactly where I needed to be.

GREAT PURPOSE, it read. There was a bird painted onto the corner—a tanager, I was sure.

I could see Mara, apologizing for abandoning me, begging to be around me again, drowning in regret.

I could see Jack, watching the news on TV, how crazy it would make him that there was a Great Library, and how furious he would be that he wasn't a part of the discovery of it. "I guess you can just pay to visit the museum like everybody else," I told the air in front of me.

I could see Kaitlin, watching the news on television and rushing to call me.

I approached the banner, wondering if I should bow before it. I touched the bottom lightly, and behind me, the door slammed shut.

3.

THE CEILINGS WERE so high in the Great Library that every decibel of sound chased outward, with so much space to fill that it kept making noise long after the noise should have ended; deep echoes, shooting back off the books as if coming off the walls of a canyon.

The slam of the door. Echo.

Three slow footsteps. Echo, echo, echo.

I didn't move, silencing my breathing.

Out of the corner of my eye I could see the poker for the stove, hanging sheathed like a medieval weapon against the black metal fireplace. I inched toward it, craning my neck to get a look at the figure in the doorway, but it was too dark.

I acted first. Without waiting for them to emerge, I leapt for the poker, grasping it firmly and attempting to draw it like a sword. I pulled it, swinging my arm forward, but the sharp end caught and hooked the log rack next to it, and as I pulled, the whole apparatus came crashing with it; the brush, the shovel, and the rack itself clattered to the floor, covered in so much dust that a cloud rose and formed around me. I was a magician who failed to disappear.

Falling metal against hard linoleum floor. Echo.

From the doorway, Mara burst out laughing.

"You really are very intimidating, you know that?" She looked the same as before she'd left, and now entirely different in front of me. Her voice, her accent, her demeanor; the exact images I remembered, now painted in a bright red. The tiny light in the room shot outward across my field of vision. Anger flushed through every vein and vessel in my body, swelling up in my chest and pushing outward. I swallowed it silently.

"You're also just about the easiest person in the world to track down." She wandered around to the far end of the table. "Seriously, I wait for exactly one train at one station, and now here we are." She was avoiding my eyes, or I was avoiding hers. "Although I am impressed you found this place so fast—it took Leila *years*."

My heart sank, and she must have noticed my face slip.

"Oh, no. You thought—no, I'm sorry, this isn't the Great Library or whatever." I hated the pity in her voice. "No, it's a total bust. All history books and encyclopedias. We looked through the whole thing. Does look like it ought to be something, though, right? That's why they did it, Leila thought. A Great Diversion."

I clenched the chair in front of me, chips of splintered wood pushing painfully into my right hand, but I could barely feel them.

"Arthur—"

"Why are you here?" I asked, tempered and timed and so

slow that it gathered some of the gravel from the lowest register of my voice.

"Right." She pursed her lips and nodded. "I apologize for the French exit. I realize that must have felt—abrupt. And not good."

I fought back the pain in my chest, numbing it by squeezing my left hand underneath the cast and my right hand against the breaks in the wood.

"I understand it may not have made sense to you right away, but I hope you can understand the position I was in; I had to show them. There was no other way to. And now"—she gestured to the room—"here we are. They sent me to watch for you, but I'm doing the opposite. I want to help you. A double cross, they call it. And I swear I can prove to you I'm in earnest."

She moved toward me, now just ten feet of noticeable silence between us, and surveyed me, up and down and back again, my unkempt hair and my clenched fists and cheeks, bright red from the blood bursting behind them. "Are you alright, Arthur?"

"You left."

Echo.

"Yes. I know, and I'm so sorry. But I had to."

My body pulsed, firing into my legs, my voice taking over. "You didn't say anything to me. You didn't leave a note, or something . . . or anything." I tried to fight the light backward from swallowing my vision, tried to take even breaths so I didn't explode, but I could feel the tips of my fingers going numb against the wood.

"Arthur, I don't—"

"No." My whole body shook as my breath shuddered.

She pursed her lips.

"You abandoned me." My tongue slapped the back of my teeth, clicking with every word. My face was red with rage. "And now you're back . . . because you realized you needed me. Right?"

Mara stared intently back, looking entirely unsorry, almost like she thought I was kidding, the way her mouth hung slightly open. "Arthur, I understand this reaction, but it had to happen like this—"

"Because that's what you do." My voice was soft but it didn't feel small; it swallowed hers, echo and all. "Because that's who you are."

Mara's eyebrows sharpened, then softened as she took a breath. "I don't think you realize how serious this is to them—to *him*. When you told him about the journals, he demanded them. Not asked, *demanded*. If I hadn't taken them, they would have done it themselves, and hurt you in the process. And I told you who they were, and I told you who I was, and you chose to involve me in this—"

"I *chose* to?"

"You told me about the journals—"

"You forced me to tell you."

"No I did not."

"You manipulated me. You said I had to explain everything to you or get the fuck away from you—"

"Which means I gave you the option to leave! And you chose to stay, and to involve me, even after you knew who I worked for. I'm not sure where you think this implied loyalty is coming from, but these people—my sister—that was my life, Arthur. And I told you that. Unambiguously."

"I said I didn't want to share them, and you said okay, then you—"

"I said you didn't have to share them *yet*. And I told you not to tell Jack the other night. And you did. Willingly. You put me in an impossible position."

"That doesn't—"

"Also." I could see Mara's finger twitching on the chair in front of her. "For the record, I *am* here now. I don't think you've even yet seriously considered how fucking difficult that is, for me to be here. I left a group that I've worked with for three years, just to help you. All the danger you're in right now, I just put that on me, too, because I want to help you. But you wouldn't consider that, would you? Because it wouldn't fit right with the monster you've made me in your head, would it?"

"Then why leave?" I'd lost control of my volume. "If they mean so fucking much to you?"

"Because they're not—he's not . . . they're not what they used to be."

I shook my head, slowly, careful not to look at her face. "They're not going to find anything."

Mara didn't react. "They know that. They're not looking for clues anymore. They're looking for you."

I didn't say anything, counting the seconds until she gave up on me again and left.

"I can help you, Arthur, but pushing me out of here—"

"I don't want your help."

"This isn't helping anyone, least of all you."

"Well, you're not helping me either."

"Arthur—"

"We're done, Mara."

"It won't take them long, you know, to find you—"

"I really, *really* don't want to hear it."

"They don't think he has Alzheimer's."

Echo.

Neither of us said anything. The room came back into focus, then out again. She stared at me but I didn't meet her gaze.

"What?" I couldn't feel myself forming the word, only heard its echo.

"They don't think that your grandfather has Alzheimer's, or dementia, or anything at all." She leaned forward over the table, her face intense and angry. "They think it's a ruse. They think his writing is too complicated for someone with his condition. They had a doctor look at it and everything, and—and . . . they think he was faking the whole thing. Pretending to be sick, just to hide the secret library."

Our eyes met for the first time and the contact surprised both of us.

"But they're serious, Arthur," she continued, looking back down at the table. "They're really serious. They think it exists, and they, they think they're destined to find it. Not just that they can; they think they're chosen, on a mission from God, or something. And anything that gets in the way of Jack finding it, he'll . . . God, I don't know what he'll do. And I just thought you should know." She paused. "And I'm sorry. I didn't mean to upset you."

I didn't say anything. The silence was punishing her, but the words in my head were sprinting closer together, then farther apart from each other, too fast for me to grab on to more than one to form a sentence.

Finally, two collided. Two she had just said. Two that I could repeat.

"*Had* Alzheimer's," I whispered.

She brought her elbow to her face. "What?" she asked into her sleeve.

"You said '*has* Alzheimer's.' You mean, he *had* Alzheimer's."

Her head shook beneath her arm. "No," she whispered. "They think it was *all* fake." I felt the foundation of the library shake beneath our feet. "They think he's alive."

Echo.

4.

March 3, 2007

Dear Journal,

Sometimes I think that my grandpa is faking every time he talks about forgetting stuff, and actually, he can remember better than anybody.

He does forget some stuff.

He makes sandwiches and forgets them in the kitchen almost every day.

Sometimes he starts working on a toilet, then forgets and just leaves it like that.

He calls me "Jeffery" sometimes, even though my name is Arthur, which he should be able to remember, because it's his name, too.

But sometimes I forget that stuff, too.

He can always remember books. It all started when I was telling him about my Tom Sawyer *project for school.*

Me: Have you read Tom Sawyer*?*

Grandpa: Bull$#&*, Twain couldn't write his way out of a left turn.

Me: I have to write a journal on what I think is the best part of

Tom Sawyer *and what it means.*

    Grandpa: That is easy.

    Me: No, it is not! How is it easy?

    Grandpa: Because I know the best part of Tom Sawyer.

"the elastic heart of youth cannot be compressed into one constrained shape long at a time."

    (He said he would write it in my journal for me. That is his handwriting, not mine. I don't write in cursive.)

    Me: What does it mean?

    Grandpa: I can't tell you.

    Me: Why?

    Grandpa: Because that's the mystery. You have to figure it out yourself.

    He just told me he could do it for any book! Which I don't believe (because if he can't remember sandwiches, why would he be able to remember books?). But we're going to try.

    Me: A Tale of Two Cities.

    Grandpa:

"a wonderful fact to reflect upon, that every human creature is constituted to be that profound secret and mystery to every other."

    Me: The Great Gatsby.

    Grandpa:

"i was within and without. simultaneously enchanted and repelled by the inexhaustible variety of life."

    Me: The Bible.

    Grandpa:

~~*"for all of the*~~

He thought about it for a long time and I think he forgot what we were doing, because when I asked if he had an answer he got mad and now I have to go to soccer. I guess I fooled him.

More later,

Arthur Louis Pullman the Third

"for our light and momentary troubles are achieving for us an eternal glory that far outweighs them all.

so we fix our eyes not on what is seen, but on what is unseen, since what is seen is temporary, but what is unseen is eternal."

better luck next time.

—grandpa

5.

I SLUMPED INTO a chair at the head of the table. The Great Diversion room had the distinct feeling of being closed off from not just the rest of the library but the rest of the world. The little sound and light that made it in from outside were muted and unnoticeable. The air in the room didn't belong out there; the rest of the world didn't belong in here. I didn't belong in here. The table between us was a million miles long, Mara's voice a million miles away.

"It's ridiculous, right? He couldn't be alive, could he? I mean, he would have at least told his family, right? He couldn't have been faking that whole time . . . could he? You knew him better than that, didn't you?"

"He's dead," I breathed, as if giving the words a place in the room would help me see them better, but it didn't.

Mara saw straight through them. "Arthur. How well did you really know your grandfather?"

I stared past her, counting books on the bottom shelf across from us, fully aware that she was watching me and waiting for something.

Eventually, out of focus, her dark figure began to bob toward the door, then stopped after a few steps.

"When I asked Jack why he wanted to find this so badly he said, 'We deserve this.' And when I asked you, you said, '*He* deserves this.' That's what Leila would say. That's why I came back. For her."

"That sounds like bullshit," I said.

"What?"

"That sounds like bullshit."

She took a few steps closer to me.

"I know what you're running away from, by the way. I looked you up. You were in court three weeks before I met you."

I closed my eyes to hide, letting myself be somewhere,

anywhere else. Driving. I was driving. I could see the inside windshield of my Camaro, and the road in front of me.

"Hitting your girlfriend? Attacking your best friend in a courtroom? A restraining order?"

I was driving the Portola Valley Dive, taking the curves hard at 120—

"That's your reason for being all cryptic, not wanting to talk about yourself, wanting to get the fuck away from California?"

—shifting into sixth gear on the straightaway, the speedometer hitting 160. My shoulders were pinned back by inescapable acceleration.

"Let me guess what happened. You did something that you would never do because you felt like you *had* to do it, and then you regretted it immediately after. Does that sound right?"

I could feel the g-force energy, screaming forward, pulling me toward the center of the Earth, pumping me full of the most addictive substance that exists: adrenaline.

"If *Kaitlin Lewis* was here right now, is that what you would tell her?"

Kaitlin's name brought me back. The road, the car, the escape disappeared. I wasn't driving. I was in the library with Mara.

"I know what that's like, Arthur. But I think maybe . . . it's time you start acknowledging the worst parts of yourself, rather than pretending they're not a part of you. Rather than putting that shit onto everybody else."

I hadn't noticed that she'd made her way back to the table and dropped a page in front of me. "There. That's all they want,

and I want you to have it. What does that do for your trust?"
I pulled my eyes from the bookshelf and saw my grandfather's penmanship scrawled inside the fold, with new ink on top of it: a tiny black fist, threatening me. "Sorry about the stamp; Jack put it on all of them."

She stood still for another moment. "Say something."

"Giving something back after you failed isn't noble," I whispered. "It's cowardice. It doesn't earn you trust, it earns you pity."

She turned up her nose. "Better to live as a coward than to die as a hero."

"You have that expression backward."

"I know. And that's exactly why I came back." She paused. "I hope you find what you're looking for, Arthur."

She walked quickly out the door without looking back.

I felt a headache tickling the sides of my brain, everything behind my eyes crashing and colliding. I took three deep breaths. I didn't know how to do anything else.

The page she'd left behind was the first journal, from the cabin in Truckee.

i'm called to a voice i don't remember
in a language i invented & have since forgotten
lite, too bright to see its source

"He's dead," I told the empty room. "They sent us his . . ."

The room didn't respond. It swallowed the words and sent them shooting away from me.

For thirteen years, his illness had pushed my family to every conceivable breaking point. For thirteen years, we'd given him every care and comfort, excused every mishap, fought to understand every absurd behavior. For thirteen years, we'd given up our lives for him, only for him to abandon us in the end.

But I hadn't been without my doubts. He *had* remembered things I was certain he'd forget. His clues *were* filled with complex thoughts, more complex than I would have ever thought he was capable of. He *had* made a clean break, disappearing without questions or a search and never coming back, without telling any of us.

Unless he was telling me now.

6.

AFTER TWENTY MINUTES of nothing, I pulled myself up from the table and took the small red King James Bible from the shelf.

I thumbed through it. It reminded me of the one my grandfather had carried with him everywhere. In the last few years of his life, it had become an extension of his body. He read it constantly, retreating into it whenever he was lost or confused as if it was some kind of map. And the tiny little text—full of its irrational and outdated stories, its lessons handed down from an all-knowing leader, its psalms and chants and quotables—took over and became his memory.

There was no inscription in the front of the Bible. I shook it, but there was nothing tucked into the pages. I turned it over, moving on to the next set of shelves, but before I could feel for anything else, a drone of sirens came pouring in from outside the library walls.

I pulled a chair to the room's only window, smashing my face to the circular glass. On the street below, there were police cars gathering, throwing red and blue around the neighborhood. Loud footsteps and shouting voices came from outside the room as the officers took over the building.

I sat in the stillness of the back room for ten seconds. No one knew I was here, other than Mara and Suzy, but neither had reason to call the police. Even if my father did know I was here, he couldn't have called this kind of siege on me. Some other criminal must have led a police chase here, thinking the library was the last place they'd expect. Still, I tucked the Bible into my pocket and rushed to—

"I'm learning now that the world is a circle. And what I thought was behind me . . . was actually ahead."

Jack slammed the wooden door shut behind him, and the voices outside disappeared. His white scarf seemed to glow, perfectly visible in the low light. He paced slowly around the table. "I was hoping I was going to find you here. Or rather, you were going to find us."

I shook with nervous anger, but he didn't notice.

"It's cool, right? I mean, they had it built for Great Purpose, specifically. Meetings, recruiting for protests, all of it. Thompson and Pullman—Duke and Arty—heading the room, leading the revolutionaries into battle.

"Here's what's funny, though: when the organization disappeared, they kept the room secret. Still here, obviously, and still gets maintenance, but nobody uses it. Forty-five years. Why do you think they would do that?"

He wanted me to answer, but I didn't.

"The library says it's for historical purposes, but don't people usually like to *show off* their history?" He examined the banner. "Not lock it up and keep it a secret? And sure, they let us use it now—I can be *very* convincing—but what about the forty years before that? Why were they keeping it here . . . if there wasn't something—someone—they were waiting for?"

I took three deep breaths, glaring into his grin. "You stole from me."

His smile didn't break. "Well, that's based on a narrow understanding of possession, Arthur."

My face twisted further.

"Look . . . I don't want you to have any bad feelings about this, so let me explain as best I can: we're the closest thing there's ever been to a new Great Purpose. We've got the same buildings, the same ideas . . ." He motioned to himself. "The same leader. And that's exactly what our fathers—grandfathers—wanted."

He stopped, ten feet and an oak table between us. "Isn't it? I mean, during his final week, he went to all the Great Purpose spots . . . wrote for the first time in forty years." He spun the journal on the table around. "'My eyes are open, and I can see that I'm coming up on it again. And I feel Great . . . Purpose.'" He looked up. "He was writing to restart the movement. And it's not stealing if you're taking what's already yours. I'm sorry you were put off by our way of doing things, but sometimes revolution requires . . . greater measures. For the greater good, right? The greater truth, isn't that what she said?" He glanced quickly left to right, like he thought Mara might be in the room. "I'm sure you can understand that. Either way"—I watched from the corner of my eye as he studied me—"who did you think he was writing to?"

My fists clenched at my sides, desperate to lash out at him, but the more he talked, the fewer reasons I could find. Even my anger was fading. "You're full of shit," I said.

"I'm full of shit? Why would I lie to you?" He shrugged. "You're talking like I've got some kind of self-interest here. What do you think I'm doing this for, anyway? Money? I don't get paid for this. I'm here because the world is crying out for new leaders. And I was chosen to answer that call."

He smiled up at the banner, lightly touching the bottom. "They built so much. All these libraries, and secret meeting places, and . . . diversions. And for what? Just to give up? Walk away and let the whole country fall back into ruin? I mean . . . there's gotta be more to it than that, right? That can't be it."

"I'm not afraid of you," I said, convincing myself.

He turned slowly back to me. "Good." He shrugged again,

reaching his right arm behind his back. "Don't be." He pulled the gun from his pants and slid it onto the table. "We need your help, Arthur."

I stared at it, resting between the two of us. "What?"

"We've got all of the resources, we know the history of this thing inside and out, but we don't know your grandfather like you do. And when we can find him . . . then that's it. That's the ball game. He comes back, and this is a true revolution. We could lead armies." Jack spoke so confidently, it was difficult to find reasons to doubt him. But as I fumed, focusing on the in-and-out of my breathing, I realized I had just as few reasons to believe him. With every time he said *we*, I became more and more aware that it was just him in the library with me.

"You don't wanna be on the wrong side of this, Arthur," he said.

"No."

Jack blinked deliberately. "No, you don't want to help us? Or no, you don't know your grandfather?"

"No." I stood as tall as possible. "Fuck you, you stole from me."

"Arthur. Can you really not see past that? There's a hell of a lot more at stake here than your delicate little sensibilities."

I glared back. "I've got an idea—why don't you just try to remember all of the things you learned from *your* father?"

A streak of anger ran across his face, but before he could act on it, it disappeared back into his calm. "This isn't a negotiation, Arthur. I'm not asking you. This?" He motioned outside.

"These cops? You wanna take a guess who they're looking for?"

I swallowed. "You're lying."

He gave me just enough silence to consider that he might be right. "I'm sure it's a coincidence. I'm sure they're not looking for you. There's no way someone tipped them off that there might be a fugitive in possession of stolen property here. I mean, how would I even know you were here? Other than Suzy, of course."

A wave of consequence washed over me and I swayed, suddenly woozy from the movement of the Earth. I felt the axis begin to shift, heard the footsteps and shouts louder through the wall.

"They don't know about this room," Jack said, moving dangerously close to me. "Unless I tell them about it." His eyes roamed the high ceilings. Every few seconds, I glanced at the gun on the table, but Jack hadn't looked once. "Come with us, Arthur. Let's go find your grandfather."

The thought flickered for a single second before I responded, with all the volume and resolve I could find. "No."

"No?"

"No, absolutely, fuck no." I looked down. I was closer to the gun than he was. If I made a lunge, I could grab it before he knew what was happening, but I had no plan after that. I'd never fired a gun before, and shooting someone with the police ten feet away would effectively end my life as well.

"You don't understand." I could feel Jack's temperature rising, spiking and then cooling back to his confident default setting. "This is happening with or without you." He got louder as he spoke. "We knew this was coming, and now that we've found it . . ."

"Good luck without me." I barely felt conscious as I spoke. "Looks like it's working out so far."

"You know, it may not mean anything to you, but you've got a name that means something," he said, steering into his rage, winding around the table back toward me. "You were *chosen* for this. Your grandfather was an extraordinary man, and you owe it to him to continue that. I'm giving you a chance, and I'd recommend you take it, because you do *anything* short of changing the world, and people are gonna start to wonder if you're actually an Arthur Louis Pullman." He stopped, his face hovering three feet in front of mine. "I guess maybe that's not a problem for you, though, is it? Nobody doubts your relation."

"Because my grandpa is actually my grandpa."

"Don't you—" Jack's evenness slipped, and his right arm shot up toward my neck. Before I could move either arm, he'd thrown me against a chair by the collar. "Trust me. You do *not* wanna fuck with us."

"Who's us?" I asked. "You're the only—"

He drove his hand farther into the base of my throat and I felt the air escape me. "You don't know *shit*!" he shouted into my face, and with one final twist of his knuckle, he let go.

He stumbled back a few steps, shaking his head, a smile returning to his face. I clung to the ground and Jack stared down over me with manufactured pity. "I'm sure you think it's cute, and safe," he said. "Being all cynical like that. But you're not doing shit. All you're contributing to the world is . . . nothing. The people who matter, who actually deserve their names . . ." He grabbed the gun from the table and dropped it back into his belt without finishing the thought, instead nodding to the clue. "Keep that. You deserve a souvenir. I'll tell your grandpa you say hi."

He propped the door open on his way out.

As soon as his figure disappeared, I threw my backpack over my shoulder and followed, inching around the frame and into the small hallway.

The library was chaos. Everyone else on the second floor looked terrified, huddled together out of the way of the officers. Two of them sprinted past at different intervals and I hugged myself to the wall. Lying or not, whatever the police had come to search for, they hadn't found it.

"Officers, there's a back room in that corner." The voice was Jack's. "I think I might have seen him go in there."

A pair of hands grabbed me from behind and pulled me backward into the closet.

"Idiot," Mara whispered, her breath warm against my ear.

I shook her off me, clattering over a mop bucket. "What— what are you doing? How long have you been waiting?"

We both held our breath as three officers charged past us and into the Great Purpose room.

"We don't have a whole lot of options here," she said. "Either we try to muscle out the front . . ."

"Or?"

"If we can get them out of that room, I can get them out."

I watched the officers through the open door of the meeting room, rifling through cupboards. "Why are you doing this?" I asked.

A flashlight running past threw a single streak of light across her face. She was smiling, the same terrible and impossible smile. "I told you already. This belongs to you, not them."

I watched several more officers run past, felt Mara's body against mine, considering the world in front of me and the world behind me. "Okay." I nodded.

"Are you sure that you're up for this?" she breathed.

I nodded again.

"Because you can go home, if you want. You can turn yourself in, and—"

"No. I'm not going home."

Mara swallowed. "I need you to follow me," she whispered. "And not turn around. Okay?"

Before I could move, she sprang upward and out the door, grabbing the edge of the display case as she ran, forcing it to come crashing down, glass shattering. I took off after her.

The colors around me blurred. My eyes focused on the back of Mara's head, her beanie like a blackened orb guiding me through the maze of books, diving right when she dove right, swimming in and out of displays and shelves. Behind us, there were shouts, and soon, they weren't just behind us.

All around, officers lunged for her. As we came flying around one corner, someone managed to grab ahold of her jacket, pulling her backward and slowing her forward momentum, his face focused on where she was attempting to run. Without thinking, I threw my right arm in the air, yanking a hardcover book off a display and slamming it into the back of his head. The pain forced him to recoil. He dropped the back of her jacket. Onward we flew.

Somewhere in the chaos behind me, I heard Kaitlin shouting, "You're running from the police! Who even *are* you anymore?"

But I was running too fast for her words to catch up. All the chaos was in our wake; the uncontrollable difficulty of the world stayed a step behind me. All that was inside of me was adrenaline and all that was ahead of me was Mara. I felt a near smile creep onto my face.

Mara led the chase expertly. She wound us up a far staircase to the third floor, then back down two flights into the enormous main room of the library. She ducked us through the giant mass of library patrons, shedding her hat and exploding out the other end where no officers expected her to be.

There were moments when I thought they had given up, that no one was chasing us anymore, but every time, another officer would leap out in front of us, out of the vast openness of the library, forcing us down aisle after aisle of books.

Mara wound our way back around to the "Great Surplus" door, the exact spot where the chase had begun, and froze. There were no officers in sight. Leaping over the glass, she dove into the meeting room, and I turned, searching for officers in pursuit. I couldn't see any, but I could hear them, everywhere.

"Anybody have a visual?"

"He's gotta be around here somewhere."

"Both of them, some girl was running, too."

Mara was kneeling in front of the door of the stove, her hands inside of it, and I stayed at the door.

"What the fuck are you doing?" I shouted across the room. "A fire?"

"You think she's some sort of accomplice?"

"Gotta be. You know how these people work."

I tried to sink into the door frame, away from where two officers went sprinting past, their boots crunching against the glass. The case—my grandfather's display—had shattered in front of where I was standing, and his *Tribune* obituary had slid toward me. The logo caught my eye, a crescent moon cupping the *T*, the same one that had been at the top of the article that led me to Omaha. My eyes fell to the bottom—*Lou Thurman, political writer and contributor to this newspaper*—

"Holy shit. Mara—"

I turned to her as she yanked the door off the stove. "In," she barked, gesturing to the invisibly black interior.

"What?"

She jumped in front of me, clutching a bar above the door and lowering her legs slowly into the open front grate. I watched her legs, her torso, and finally her head disappear.

"Did we get everybody evacuated yet?"

"Yep, the place is clear. Just be careful with your shot; this kid's not worth wounding an officer."

My stomach flipped—*your shot*? *Wounding an officer*? Who did they think I was?

I pulled myself up and lowered my legs into the hatch. Sure enough, there was a solid concrete step a foot below where the bottom of the stove should have been. Past it, another step, leading down into complete darkness. I lay there for ten seconds, stunned. It was an escape hatch. Great Purpose had built themselves stairs.

"Where'd that noise come from?"

"I think they went back in here!"

It was all I needed. I edged myself down the stairs, feeling with my heel for each next step, the top of Mara's head in front of me.

I counted steps as we went . . . five, six, seven . . . the world was now in total darkness; the only sound was Mara breathing behind me.

"I know where we're going," I whispered to her. "Chicago. I know where to go."

"We can't take the Zephyr tomorrow," she whispered. "Jack will know we're going east, and we'll be sitting ducks all the way to Chicago."

"We have to," I whispered back, twelve, thirteen, fourteen stairs deep, feeling upward, my hand slamming into mildew-covered concrete two feet above our heads. There was no room to stand up, only to slide. "That was the train my grandfather would have—"

"They know that!" she spat back.

Up the stairwell, we heard shouting. "There are stairs in here!"

"Then what?" I asked, and my heel connected with solid ground.

I put my hand on her waist as she felt her way through the dark. The ceiling overhead must have been five feet, just tall enough for us to rush through, heads down, hands outstretched to keep us from running into anything ahead of us.

"Then we leave tonight," she said. "A different train. One he *wouldn't* have taken." She stopped abruptly in front of me. "Tell me that's okay."

Before I could respond, my hand slammed into something wooden. There were boards, up and down the hatch, preventing us from moving forward. We could hear the police sliding down behind us.

"Does Jack know about this escape?" I asked.

"Yes."

My head pulsed with every amplified heartbeat. "So why wouldn't he be here waiting for us?"

"Because he doesn't know *you* know about it." She threw open the hatch, and crisp, fresh air from the outside world rushed in. Behind the library was a wide patch of grass, flowing directly into the backyards of neighboring houses. Over all of it, the sun was beginning to set burnt yellow. The horizon burned orange in front of us. "He doesn't know about me."

She blew past me, and I followed, away from the library, away from the police, away from Great Purpose, and back to the train.

7.

THE BACK OF the 7:55 p.m. Mid-State Cruiser from Omaha's downtown station to Chicago Union was empty.

It was a different model of train, smaller, with no observation or dining car, just a small desk for snacks at the front of the coach section. The train only ran between Omaha and Chicago, and made the trip twice every day. The station at boarding had been so quiet, with one attendant at one door taking tickets, it was as if the train snuck into Omaha itself and stole us away in the darkness.

"Looks like we're in the clear." Mara collapsed into the seat next to me and dropped a postcard with a photo of downtown Omaha in front of her, sizing it up and clicking a pen with conviction. "Just one couple, about fifteen rows ahead, and they don't look like they'd give us much of a fight."

I watched her carefully trace a British address into the "Deliver To" section and begin to doodle around the edges of the card, small stars and hearts and wavy lines connecting them. I wasn't sure how to feel about her now that she'd left and come back again, inadvertently showing me the best and worst of her.

"Dear Dad." She spoke as she wrote. "In Omaha, and I've taken up work with . . . a library conservation unit."

She smiled to herself. I was confused by her motivations, confused by her patterns and mannerisms, confused by her convictions, certain only of the mystery that surrounded her. It was a mystery she chose and reveled in, but the pieces I had discovered felt altogether incomplete and inconsistent. Why leave and then come back? Why throw something away, then risk everything to save it?

"You'd love Omaha; it's cold and wide and exceptionally American, but just dreary enough for your depressing British heart."

Looking at her, the Mara I knew felt like a postcard herself: a carefully selected image, representing a much more complicated thing; a thing so overwhelming that it preferred to be understood only by carefully edited still frames, observed at a distance.

"I've made a friend. I think you'd like him. Love, your daughter."

"Why did you come back?" I asked as she signed her name in swooping cursive. "Why help me, instead of them?"

"I told you, because you want this for your grandfather, and they want it for themselves."

"Yeah, but—you *know* them. You are them, remember? You had a future with them. And you decided to throw that away, for . . . what? Honor, or something?"

Mara turned the postcard over in her hands. "I don't know. I don't like questions like that."

I waited.

She shifted uncomfortably. "I've been with them for three years. Because of Leila, of course. I grew up with all of her ideas, and her anger, and her love of American protest culture and your grandpa and . . . she didn't fit in Somerset, neither of us did, so we were always scheming these ways to get out, or things we would do if we were in the real world. 'If you want to do something important, you've got to do something for everyone,' that was what she said. Actually I think your grandpa might have said that.

"So it seemed so obvious, three years ago, that this is what I was meant to do. Follow her to America, follow her into this big, beautiful, righteous, communal, revolutionary . . . thing. And I've stuck it out, through all of the shitty jobs, and grunt work, and relegations to Nevada, and—still, I don't think anyone ever looked at me seriously enough to think I was a real part of it.

"So when I found you, and the journals, I thought—I guess I figured it was some kind of magic that would inspire everyone again, and give us this new purpose, and it would all make sense, and I'd be the one—I know it's selfish to say out loud, but I thought I'd be the one who would be in charge of it, and get to feel good about it. Like I'd actually done something, rather than just . . . been there. But I guess I didn't really think that all the way through."

"What happened?"

"It wasn't like that." She shrugged. "Jack took them, and immediately began acting as though they were his, and they were some kind of sign to *him*. I told him I thought that I should be the one holding on to them, for safekeeping, and he said that my sister would be disgusted if she could see how selfish I was being."

"Where is your sister, anyway?" I interrupted. "Couldn't she just . . ."

Mara looked up at me, small and questioning and almost smiling.

"Oh . . . oh, right."

"Yeah." She fidgeted. "Two years ago. She tried to drive her car drunk."

I nodded for a long time, afraid to look up. "I'm sorry."

Mara shrugged, fiddling with the corners of the postcard in her hands. "It's okay. That place doesn't even feel like her anymore.

"That's the other thing. I thought your grandpa's journals might remind Jack of what we were doing this for, but they just did the opposite. Leila only wanted to inspire people to advocacy, building something for everyone, you know? Jack wants to make noise. He puts his friends' lives at risk for basically no reason, just to make people pay attention. He'll say he doesn't have anything personal to gain, and that he's just answering the call or whatever. I think he just wants to be famous."

I watched her continue to trace circles on the postcard in front of her, far away from where we were. "What do you want?"

She didn't respond right away. "I want to do something important," she said, settling on staring out the window.

I nodded again. It all made sense, the best and worst parts of her, and it made it impossible to find the animosity I felt toward her.

"Your turn," she said, turning back to me. "Kaitlin Lewis."

"Mara—"

"Did you see me save you from that library?"

I sighed. "She cheated on me. With my best friend since like kindergarten. We all worked together, I told him everything about her, and then one day—bam. She said she'd slept with somebody else, and I didn't even have to ask who it was. Turns out, it was a bunch of people, and he was just one of them. And when she told me, I lost it. I hit a wall in her room, and she said I was trying to hit her, and I guess I might as well have been, for all that I could control myself. If I couldn't stop her from fucking Mason, I couldn't really control anything."

Mara smiled, strangely satisfied. "You can't," she said. "But at least we're all gonna burn up and die someday, right?"

I pushed it—all of it, the journals and the purpose and the gun on the table—as far from my brain as possible, counting streetlights as they passed, and when tunnels came, counting graffiti. I'd always wondered about the people who drew it; was it some kind of rush, knowing you were doing something illegal? Or was it a desperate attempt at making something permanent, so they could be remembered, however faintly?

"Why does he spell words wrong?"

Mara was looking over the first clue under the narrow beam of the reading light. "See, sometimes he uses an 'a' where there shouldn't be an 'a,'" she continued, as if noticing it for the first time. "'Dask' . . . oh, look here, 'angals.' Why is that?"

"Can we not talk about this?"

"Why not?"

I shrugged.

I knew exactly why I didn't want to talk about it: talking about my grandfather meant thinking about my grandfather, and thinking about my grandfather meant thinking about whether he was alive or not, whether he'd tricked my family or not, whether he was trying to communicate with me or not. It meant letting myself entertain the kind of hope that makes possible the kind of disappointment that you don't come back from.

"Can you at least tell me why he spells the words wrong?" She shifted in her seat, pulling her legs up underneath her. "Come on, I've just told you my sister died. That doesn't buy me at least a few questions?"

"Yeah, alright." I shook my head. "It's an Alzheimer's thing."

"The letter 'a'?"

"Phonetic spelling."

"Phonetic spelling is a symptom of Alzheimer's?"

"No. Phonetic misspelling. Spelling and grammar are nuanced, and tough to hold on to when your brain stops storing information. And when your brain loses its ability to remember spellings, it chooses to write out words however they sound in your head. Which for my grandfather meant using a lot of *a*'s."

"Oh?" She turned on her seat toward me. "What about these random sentences: 'jagged line burning orange lite'?"

"It's a memory device." I turned toward her. "His doctor taught him. When he didn't understand where he was or what was going on, he was just supposed to start calling out the things that he saw, or the parts that he didn't understand. If you think it's weird on paper, try hearing it in person."

"Wait," Mara said, her fingers dancing down the page. "So do you think he really saw a greyhound? Or all these waves?"

"No, no." I winced, remembering all of the times that my family had been fooled, overly excited or extremely confused by this particular habit. "Sometimes he would see the world in metaphor. You've gotta watch out for that."

She smiled sideways at me in the window reflection, eager to test this new trick she'd learned. "Alright," she continued. "Why his name? Why does he say 'Arthur' so often?"

"Self-awareness." I heard his voice, booming out my name, my father's name, his own name, just enough to throw the entire household into confusion. "The doctor said as long as he could remember his own name, he could tether to it. He would do it at home, too, and he said—" The words caught in my throat. "He said he was just reminding himself who the, the narrator of the story was."

Mara watched me, hearing my voice break, and I carefully turned back to the window. "What about this, the date?" she asked. "Why *the* 2010? Why not just 2010? Some kind of weird contrarian thing?"

"No, he, uh, he did that on purpose."

"Why?"

I spoke to the window glass. "Because he, he said it made him remember what that number, the number of the year, what it actually means. 'The 2010th year' since Jesus, or, as far as he was concerned, since human beings started to understand what it meant to be conscious. He said before he started writing, he always wanted to remind himself that he was the product of two thousand and ten years of conscious evolution. He's a part of *the* two thousand and tenth try."

Mara was silent for a long moment. "I think," she said, slowly at first, "that he had a pretty limited scope of evolution if he thought that—"

"I know. That's just what he thought. He was . . . He liked God. A lot." I leaned my head back onto the seat and let it fall against the headrest.

"Okay. So what do you think he—"

"Mara," I said, closing my eyes. "Can we . . . can we not talk about my grandpa?"

"Just one more question?"

"Mara—"

"You do know him," she said, pursing her lips in earnest and leaning them toward me, so I couldn't forget it. "I asked you, how well you even . . . you did know him. You do know him."

I made a noise between a sigh and a grunt. "One more question."

"Do you think—your grandfather—do you think he knew how old he was? Or what year it was?"

"No," I said quietly, without looking at her. "I think he had his own world. And in that world, it was 1970, and he was twenty, and he was happy."

Mara sighed and reclined her seat, her head resting a few inches from mine. "It just seems absurd, doesn't it? To remember something for that long, even when you forget everything else? To feel something so strong that it never goes away? Like that woman, Sue, stuck saying good-bye to her husband over and over again." The train hummed under her as she spoke. "I guess we really do keep love somewhere much deeper than the rest of it, huh?"

I didn't answer, pretending to sleep, and before too long, the real thing found me.

8.

"*PARTY PEOPLE OF the Mid-State Cruiser! You may just be joining us, but we are entering what we excitedly and affectionately call 'the home stretch'!*

"*Omaha to Chicago! One single, solitary blast across the plain Great Plains of Iowa, and this nonstop steam engine will come to its final resting position in the Union Station, Windy City, Chicago,*

Illinois, United States of America! We're on time today, folks, and we intend on keeping it that way, so let's keep the stops short and the good-byes sweet—if you're off in Creston, then for God's sake, get off in Creston! We've all got places to be and mysteries to solve and worlds to conquer and it all starts . . . eight hours from now.

"We're coming up on the Nebraska border, and we've got only heaven beyond that—no, wait, excuse me, this isn't heaven, no, it's Iowa. That's all, from your brilliant and loyal conductor."

9.

May 4, 2005

Dear Journal,

I am writing in you because my grandpa and I are riding on the train.

Me: Why does he say that?

Grandpa: Why does he say what?

Me: "That is all, from your brilliant and—"

Grandpa: Because people like knowing they can trust the person in charge. They like knowing he will do a good job. God calls himself "ruler of the universe" because it makes people feel safe. They know they are being taken care of. Do you feel safe?

Me: Kind of.

Grandpa: What if he said, "That is all, from your average &
boring conductor, who does not really know how this goddamned
thing works anyway!"

I like riding on the train with Grandpa because he explains
everything to me, and he makes up a lot of funny stories that make it
less boring.

Also, he says "goddamn" in front of me and does not apologize
because he knows I'm not a kid.

He makes me sit on the inside, because he says that I am "too
desirable of a young man," and I might get snatched up. So I let him
sit on the outside.

Me: Why do we have to go to Truckee?

Grandpa: Because it's important to pay the respect.

Me: Pay the respect?

Grandpa: When someone dies, it's important for people to get
together and talk about how sad they are.

I wish he wouldn't have said that, because it reminded me of how
sad I was. I couldn't stop thinking about it. I knew that he was sad,
too.

Grandpa: Alright, one more question, then you have to go to sleep.
I thought for a long time about what I wanted my question to be.

Me: Where is Grandma gonna go now?

My grandpa didn't answer right away and I thought for a second
maybe he forgot that we were talking. Finally, he talked really quiet.

Grandpa: A peaceful sleep's not the end of night; by morning,
she'll dance with the angels of light.

Me: Who said that?

Grandpa: It was one more question.

Me: Please?

My grandpa smiled, like he was remembering something that made him really happy.

Grandpa: One of my favorite poets said that. Henry Pullman.

Me: He has the same name as us!

Grandpa: Yes he does. Now no more questions. Time for bed. That is all, from your brilliant and loyal grandpa.

I fell asleep for a long time.

I woke up only once in the middle of the night, when it was dark outside. But my grandpa wasn't asleep. He was just sitting there.

His eyes were closed, but I knew he was awake, because he was holding his hands out and facing them upward like someone was about to hand him a pile of logs.

And he was smiling at the window. And he looked at me, and he did not say anything. Just smiled.

I think he likes taking the train more than I do.

More later,

Arthur Louis Pullman the Third

PART EIGHT.

chicago.

THE AIR THROUGH the window wakes me up to fill my lungs.

There are no clouds in the California sky and there's a familiar highway in front of me, a familiar safety belt snaked around me, a familiar pedal sliding under my right foot, easing forward, my big toe propelling me closer and closer to the crest of a familiar climax, a tipping point I'd desperately missed. We break the top of the mountain and the sun swallows the frame of the front windshield, uninterrupted by clouds and shimmering off millions of invisible particles, blinding us for a moment, but we don't need that moment; we drive by faith, not by sight; we know this road.

Don't do something you'll regret—the kind of warning that only comes from those who don't understand; this kind of high doesn't come safely; this kind of life, the kind worth living, is only found dangerously close to the blade of regret.

When the world comes into focus, the dive is twice as steep as it ever was before, the highway twice as narrow, one single road, the peak of its own winding mountain surrounded by impossibly deep canyons, the bottom invisible through fog and darkness, so far below that by the time I hit the bottom, I'd be too far away for sound to carry back up to the road. I would disappear silently.

I hit the inside of the curve at maximum acceleration, only centripetal energy left to pull me forward, spinning the steering wheel sharply, wide rubber beneath me clinging to the asphalt for my life. The safety belt tightens; every organ in my body continues northeast but the vehicle veers northwest, my liver and stomach and heart slamming against the inside of my rib cage. I jerk the gear to sixth, a downhill free fall stretching ahead of me until—

There's something on the road.

Somethings: small, circular, perfectly silver, formed of invisible particles and shimmering in the Portola Valley sun.

My ring. Our rings.

I clench my teeth and drive straight over them. One, two, three, four independent explosions, each shattering the still air. I grip the wheel so hard that I feel shattering in both of my hands, bone against bone and pain shooting up my arms.

There's someone in the passenger seat.

Brown hair and pale skin, shimmering in the Portola Valley sun.

Ahead of me or behind me, through the shattered windshield, I see the bottom of the hill. There's never been a train track here before, improbably carved out of the mountains, no barriers or lights to warn oncoming traffic, an enormous train fast approaching.

The car stops. No air, no breath, no escape, no stopping the train. I lose the struggle to myself and I lie still. There's no one in the passenger seat. It's just me.

You need me too much.

There's a moment of singular and perfect clarity. I think about trying to move, but I don't. All I do is feel; adrenaline, rushing through every vein and vessel, begging me to jerk my arms, to twist my torso, to reach for the window, to shatter the glass, but I don't.

The engine lights start to flash. The smoke around me starts to become visible. I can hear my dad crying out behind me.

2.

"ARTHUR!"

The outline of Mara's face was hovering above mine. "You're doing it again."

The stray swatches of color began to clarify: blue patterned seat beneath me; soft yellow light through the window; cold gray skyline outside it.

"I'm sorry, I, I'm . . ." I sat up, still blinking. "I'm sorry."

Mara slumped back into her seat and packed her bag.

My left hand was throbbing. Gingerly, I squeezed the cast around each finger, making sure I could still feel them. "I think

I was having a nightmare," I said, my ring heavy on my finger.

"About what?" I tried to look past her, to the rest of the train compartment, but she blocked my view. "Arthur," she said. "About what?"

"Car crashes," I said slowly. "I dream I'm driving my Camaro, and then something always happens, and right before I'm about to die, I wake up."

Mara's eyebrows raised half a centimeter.

"It's weird that I'm screaming, though," I continued. "In the dream, I'm just sitting there, like I'm not even surprised by it."

"Why?"

"I don't know. It's a dream. Everything makes sense until you wake up and realize none of it made any sense."

"Has something happened while you were driving? Like, did you crash your car?"

"No. Just in dreams."

"Is it possible you actually did, but now—"

"Mara."

"Okay." Mara nodded to herself. "Okay."

I didn't feel any better about it, but at least Mara had turned her attention to staring at the fast-approaching station.

We exited the train cautiously, both of us checking around every corner and making no mention of it, like admitting our paranoia might legitimize it. I knew we were both looking for Jack.

"He does talk about Chicago in his book," Mara told me. "Just a bit, though. Nothing specific, but it's always, kind of . . .

negative. Gloomy, angry, loveless. Almost evil."

We must have looked noticeable in the boarding room of Chicago Union Station; I hadn't showered since I left home and my hair was starting to clump and stretch wildly; my hoodie and hands and face were stained with black and green, soot from the old stove and grass from the lawn behind the library, like I was starring in a low-budget community theater version of *Oliver Twist*. Mara looked basically the same as when I first saw her in the observation car, still in a black sweater and orange coat, so we walked quickly. Once we hit the main room, however, we disappeared into the crowd.

It looked nothing like the abandoned stations across the rest of Middle America. The ceiling was vaulted in a grand window arch, letting natural light through. There were people, lots of them. It was chaos, trains and buses and cars and police officers and families and hot dog vendors and people in suits everywhere.

"It's always like that, isn't it?" Mara asked from nowhere, her steps bouncing almost merrily along the crowded station.

"Like what?"

"You go all the way across the country, find all of these different people and places and twists and turns and . . . and then it turns out, the thing you were looking for, the end of the maze, was right there with you all along; you just weren't looking at it right." She nodded to my backpack, inside of it the clue, inside of it the *Lou and Sal's tribute* line that had taken six days and two thousand miles to properly materialize. "Seems like that's how it always goes."

Overnight, we had charted a walking course to the Tribune Tower, the iconic home of the *Chicago Tribune*. Mara had attempted to call them and ask about the two writers we were looking for, Lou Thurman and Sal Hamilton, but had only gotten through to their evening message machine, a robotic voice that instructed us that if we wanted to offer them some kind of information, we should call during the daytime hours, and if we wanted to report a crime, we should call the police.

"I don't think this is gonna be the end of the maze," I told her.

"No, but still," she said, her voice straining with forced optimism. "You can appreciate the sentiment."

"The sentiment that most of life is nothing more than a runaround, trying to learn the things we already know?"

"Oh, let it be," she sighed. "Not everything needs to be as hateful as you—"

The words froze in her mouth.

"As I what?" I asked. "As I'm capable of recognizing that it is? Because maybe it doesn't *need* to be, but to say it's not . . ."

Mara wasn't paying attention. Her eyes were focused above my head, unflinching. I followed her gaze to a large television screen in the corner of the station's lobby, where a reporter with golden curls and a tan pantsuit was staring dead into the camera, reading my name off the prompter.

"—grandson of famed author Arthur Louis Pullman has been missing for four days, after fleeing a relative's home in Truckee, California. Authorities involved in the search say they have witness testimony from three different states over the past week and believe he may be in possession of stolen items . . ."

As she spoke, they showed my house, shaky camera footage behind a police barricade that had been set up around our front yard. They showed my father, covering his head as he made his way to his car in our driveway. They showed Tim and Karen's house, my uncle and auntie nowhere to be found. They showed the hostel in Denver, the innkeeper confused behind his desk, refusing to show anyone his logbook. They showed the Omaha library, Suzy the librarian being interviewed. "He didn't seem dangerous—" They showed my grandfather's display and the mess we'd left behind.

It was a tour of the last week of my life, but on the TV, every stop looked cold, lifeless, and dangerous, as if they'd just been the scene of a murder.

Finally, they showed Jack, his Great Purpose scarf suspiciously absent, speaking in front of the library. "He seemed so nice when we met him, but this is just, it's inhuman. I mean, it's his own grandfather's legacy! We knew he was out of control, but it's hard to believe he was capable of *robbing us* like that."

The pit in my stomach tripled.

They ended back on the reporter at the desk, her face solemn and serious as if it was her that I'd *robbed*. "If anyone has seen Arthur Pullman, please contact authorities immediately. He is believed to be traveling and may be dangerous."

The television switched over to a pet food commercial.

"Robbing them?" I asked finally, as quietly as my rage would allow.

"Arthur—"

"I robbed . . . them?"

"Arthur, this is bad, I know, but we can't make a scene—"

"I will, I'll, I'll fucking kill him," I stuttered, louder than I meant. Every head in a fifteen-foot radius whipped around, every body stumbled away from me. I felt their stares, intense and hot against my skin, judging me, undressing me.

"Sorry, just play-acting." Mara tried to push me outside but I didn't want to move. "Practicing a little theater. Got a bit carried away, carry on."

"I'll fucking—"

"Arthur." She grabbed my wrist and squeezed. "It's a lie. You know it's a lie. I know it's a lie. Can we accept this and move past it, just for ten minutes? While we're in public?"

At that moment, I couldn't move past it. I wanted with every ounce of me to scream, to strike something, to turn a boy nearby into Jack and lash out at him with a strong right hook, planting him on the ground, jaw unhinged, his face slamming against the concrete.

But Mara was glaring at me, piercing the skin between my eyes, so I let her push me toward an exit door and out onto the Chicago street.

As soon as we were outside, the sting of the air froze my brain. It was an overwhelming city, the downtown area packed with cars humming and people yelling and buildings groaning under the constant assault of the wind. My rage boiled, but I wasn't the one to scream first.

"Jesus!" Mara bent forward over the weight of her own voice. I'd never heard her so loud. "So we've got Jack, the whole of Great Purpose, the police, and *now every citizen* in the United States, all looking for us!"

I didn't say anything, but put my head down in the direction of the Tribune Tower.

She turned it on me. "But no, we can't wait a few days until it's, you know, safe! It *has* to be today!"

"Mara," I said, spinning back on her. "Literally the only way things could be worse than the situation we're in now would be if we *didn't* do anything. There's a clue waiting for us here, and I don't know about you, but I'd rather shoot myself in the fucking head than let Jack find it before we do. So yes, it *has* to be today."

For a half hour, we walked without speaking, the wind pounding us every time we turned north. Paranoia gripped the back of my head and pulled; every body that approached us was Jack's body, only at the last moment before they passed turning back into an old woman or a grocery store clerk. We kept our heads down, constantly adding entire city blocks to the trip just to avoid parked police cars. Finally, we came over the top of a cement hill and the Chicago River stretched in front of us. To our left, a beautiful old building shot upward, spires along the sides like a skyscraping castle. The lettering on the front was bold, old, and proud:

CHICAGO TRIBUNE

I stared up into the newspaper's logo—sharp, medieval-style

lettering, the *T* in *Tribune* cupped by a crescent moon—and watched the slide show in my head of all the times I'd seen it over the past week: in the Westwood Library display and the newspapers I'd spilled across the back room; in the stack hidden behind Henry's record player; the subscription in Sue Kopek's closet; the obituary in my uncle's attic, the only one he thought was worth saving; and now, on the building in front of me.

"Alright then," Mara breathed. "I guess we go—"

Without waiting for her, I set a course for the door. I elbowed past several old men outside smoking and walked directly to the front reception desk. On either side were security checkpoints, each with two guards, scanning IDs before the elevators.

Mara grabbed me in the middle of the lobby. "Easy," she said without moving her lips. "There are police everywhere."

"These people don't watch the news. They read newspapers. They won't find out about me until tomorrow."

Mara nodded to the three televisions in the lobby, each with a different news broadcast.

"Can I help you?" the stern woman at the desk asked. The name tag that hung around her neck read CINDY.

"Yeah, I'm looking for Lou Thurman at the *Tribune*."

"Do you have an appointment?"

"No, but I need to see him."

She typed, scanned her screen, and frowned. "I'm sorry, I'm not finding anyone in our system with that name. That's T-H-U-R-M-A-N?"

I nodded, drumming angrily on the wooden desk. She retyped the name slowly, all of her fingers hovering above the keyboard but only the index fingers pressing keys. Twice she typed the name, deleted it, and started over.

"Huh," she mumbled finally. "Nothing. No one with that name."

"He doesn't work here anymore?"

"No." She looked at me over the frame of her glasses. "He's never worked here. Name's not even in the system."

Mara's hand gripped the back of my jacket, as if to keep me from flying forward. "Okay," I breathed. "Well, what about Sal Hamilton?"

Cindy didn't start typing. "I'm sorry, is there a reason for your . . . insistence? Is something wrong?"

"I'm fine," I said. "Just search the name. Please."

"You know even if he's in our system, unless you have an appointment—"

"I know, I just have to talk to Sal Hamilton, okay?"

"What'd you say?"

One of the men from outside, a short one who'd been smoking a cigarette, stopped on his way to the security checkpoint. He had more skin drooping from below his eyes than the rest of his face, and his voice was hesitant, forced out through the remaining ash of thousands of cigarettes. "You need something?"

It felt as though his physical form flickered, placed too perfectly in the lobby at the moment I needed him to be, half real and half coincidence, or half hallucination. I watched him carefully, noting the spots where his real form intersected the real world, like the scuffed brown leather of his shoes touching the floor, and the lapel of the jacket that hung in his hand brushing against the leg of the security guard.

"Are, are you Sal Hamilton?"

He examined me without expression, and I glided in his direction.

"You are."

He took a step back, his bowler hat rocking slightly as he nodded.

"I need to speak to you. It's urgent. I've been across the whole country, looking for you."

He looked past me, around the room where I knew Mara and Cindy and maybe more were watching us.

"Five years ago, a man named Arthur Louis Pullman came to—"

"I'm sorry, son." For the first time, his wrinkles animated and stiffened, worry creasing his forehead. He stumbled backward. "I don't know anything about that."

"About what?" Curiosity pulled me toward him and the guards stiffened their stances. "You knew him?"

"Look, kid, I'm not the guy you're looking for, alright?" He slid backward again, through the turnstile and toward the elevator.

"What do you mean? I just want to—"

I reached the checkpoint and both guards closed on me, their hands firmly on my chest. I caught one last glimpse of

Sal Hamilton, and he called, "Please, go bother someone else!" before disappearing into the elevator.

"Yes, I'm sorry, but now I *definitely* can't let you up there without an appointment," Cindy said, stiff and humorless. I stood for a long moment, burning holes at the spot where Sal Hamilton had just been.

"We could try the hospital," Mara offered as we returned to the front sidewalk. "Maybe see if there's something near it that . . . Still, that was so . . . What do you suppose that was all about?"

"I don't know."

"It's weird, right? Something must have happened, recently, or—there's something about it that he doesn't want to talk about. Or some*one* that he doesn't want to talk to." She spun to face me. "Do you think that means he knows where your grandfather is now?"

"My grandfather is in a box, buried in a cemetery in Palo Alto."

"You know what I mean. But if he—"

"Mara." I shook my head and we marched forward in silence, the steady and mindless pattern of step after step after step keeping my brain from thinking about the fact that the steps didn't have a direction.

"Where are you going?" she called after me.

"Walking."

"You know," Mara said, jogging to catch up with me, "we've got to talk about Jack. Now that you're calm."

"I'm not calm."

"You seem more calm."

"I'm pretending to be calm."

"Well, now that you're pretending to be calm, we should talk about how we're going to prove that you're not a criminal, and how it was *them* who stole from *us*."

I stopped in the middle of the sidewalk and Mara rocked backward to face me.

"Me," I said.

"What?"

"Me. They've stolen from *me*. You didn't find any of these, *I* did. Stop acting like I'm some kind of . . . sidekick. Or like you had anything to do with this at all, really."

Her mouth hung open with no trace of a smile. "Arthur, I don't—"

"It's fine." I turned and started walking again.

"Right," she said, catching up. "I'm sorry, slip of the tongue— they stole from *you*. That's what we have to prove."

"Why would we have to prove that?" My eyes were dead set forward, counting off block by block, the river getting bigger as we drew closer, the light at the end of the skyscraper tunnel. "They're *my* grandfather's. They have my name on them, for God's sake."

"Because the police wouldn't be this interested if they didn't have reason to believe that you had stolen something valuable. And the only reason they would think that, the only reason Jack would come forward, is if he had some way of proving that the journals belonged to him."

We walked another two blocks in silence before I slowed to a stop.

"What?"

Like a brick to the face, out of my own mouth: "The stamp."

"What?"

"He had that—" I shook with frustration. "That fucking stamp, the 'only one in the world,' remember? *His* father's, and you said he . . ." I watched Mara's eyes reach the end of my sentence before I did. "He's gonna say they're his because he's the one with the stamp. And they're gonna believe him."

I took off again away from her, my head down.

"No, we can beat that!" Mara called after. "We could say that he stamped them after he stole them from—"

"It doesn't matter."

"People will believe—"

"No! No, they won't. They have absolutely no reason to! Why would they? He's the leader of my grandfather's organization, and tall, and strong, and in control, and I'm a criminal, runaway fucking child! And every second longer that they *don't* find me, the more it looks like I'm guilty, like I actually stole something."

"Okay," Mara said, and she stopped walking. "I'm going to have a cigarette."

"I'm gonna walk," I said, and I didn't look back at her.

For three blocks, I walked alone. There were moments where it felt like I was walking in place, every step forward counteracted by the wind blowing me three steps back. The walk was the whole trip, I realized. Moving barely, slowly, painfully forward, toward what might be nothing, while the world swirled and pulled just behind me. Every time I thought I was a step closer, something knocked me back, and I realized I didn't even know what I was a step closer to. I wondered what it would be like to be back in Palo Alto, back in Kaitlin's bed, back when things made sense, and I knew why I was where I was.

I passed a small sign, with hand-placed block letters, in front of an unimpressive chapel, and I stopped.

The FIRST CHURCH OF CHRIST clung to a square lot in between a dry cleaner and a closed retail store of some kind, the water of Lake Michigan visible behind it. It wasn't immaculate and enormous, as most churches attempt to be, as all of the churches I'd visited with my grandfather had been, but instead looked like a storefront with stained-glass windows. Three bodies crouched in front of it, two in sleeping bags, one underneath a cardboard sign that read: "VETEREN, PLEASE HELP."

The sign in front read, "WE WALK BY FAITH, NOT BY SIGHT."

Without thinking, I climbed the stairs. The door to the church was unlocked, the loose handle clicking softly to open. I pushed through an entryway and as the door slid shut behind me, Chicago was gone, the click echoing through the empty sanctuary.

The atmosphere of the room felt heavy on my shoulders, exactly as I remembered every church I'd ever entered with my grandfather, and I stepped forward into it, like stepping backward in time.

I was eight years old. I was at my grandma's funeral.

The pews were old, brown wood, smooth to the touch. Burnt-orange cushions rested on every seat. Vanilla incense filled the room, a smell that I loved. I could hear the preacher saying my grandmother's name softly, my mother crying, my father coughing, the choir gently singing something in Latin, and in the second row, I could see the outline of a single figure.

"Well," it asked. "What is it you're looking for?"

3.

may 3, the 1970.

to me, chicago is something of a sickness.
it's no fault of the city itself, although the architecture does
it no favors. stone gray buildings, overlooking a stone gray
river, & my heart feels stone gray as i walk beneath them.
but seeing you will warm it up. seeing you can save even
chicago.

the waves speak to me; tell me they've forgotten me. that they never cared if you or i lived or died, was or wasn't. but they're just waves, & what were they ever but reflections of light? what were any of us but reflections of light?

i'll see sal in a moment, & i'll ask him to sound the trumpets, & he'll tell me to do it myself. whether the tribune is a friend or enemy, i've never known, but at least it's a loud one.

we've disembarked, every one of us, here finally to seize our Great purpose, & for all the plans & people, all the numbers & figures, it still feels like a faint idea, that belongs to some-one else. i feel like the main character in a stranger's dream, standing at the helm of an unlikely & irrational revolution without any idea how i got there.

this is what i wanted, right? you'll tell me i'm right. you'll remind me of the speeches in your living room; the dreams on your floor; the times i told you this is all that i want. but now i've become all that i want, & for that, i'm the one thing i will never understand.

omaha set us off with a mighty charge & a hundred heads. their pulse connected to ours & carried outward to a mass of people, waving flags & screaming revolution, propelling us

forward to be truly Great,
& you smiled like you knew i'd done something right, & i felt everything.

two hundred heads will join in chicago; you & me & them;
we'll load our chevys & greyhounds & zephyrs & march
across the midwest with a rally cry too loud to be ignored.
the idea of someone else will then be too large for any one
person, & instead will belong to the beautiful youth of a
once-beautiful country. the tide will turn, the mountains will move,
& you'll be there, joining me hand in hand.

but for now, i feel stone gray, misplaced & alone.

the curse of feeling everything,
is that you're painfully aware when you feel nothing.

—*arthur louis pullman*

4.

"GRANDPA?"

He didn't move as I approached him, a statue in the second pew, but I could feel that it was him. His hair was light gray, backlit and angelic against the hazy pulpit in front of him. The smell, the smoke, the gravity of the room, it all radiated outward from where he was sitting.

I sat across the center aisle, only red-and-blue stained-glass sun to light the visible side of his face, fixed forward on the Bible in front of us. I didn't need to look to know which book, which chapter was displayed.

"Is this real?" I asked.

He didn't move. The one eye that I could see remained closed, and I worried he'd disappear, just like Kaitlin or Mason or Dr. Sandoval, another hallucination retreating back to the wildest part of my brain.

But then he exhaled, softly and quietly, almost a laugh. "I think"—his voice was deep and slow, soft like mine but commanding like my father's, just as I remembered it—"that I'm the wrong person to ask."

My finger twitched. I tried to control my heartbeat. I didn't know how I was supposed to feel, but if it was anger or sadness, I couldn't find any.

"What are you doing here?" I asked.

"What is it you're looking for?"

I swallowed and my saliva tasted familiar, a reminder that I was still in the real world. "I was looking for you."

"Is that why you left?"

I opened my mouth but didn't answer right away, turning over his response in my head several times, trying to decide what it meant. He knew I'd run away.

"What is it you're looking for?" he repeated, louder, and I swallowed. The pew beneath me creaked as I shifted my weight toward him.

"I was looking for you," I said, the words crackling out, so much smaller and less important than his. "Why are you here?"

No answer. Soft sirens and the anonymous chirping of birds found their way through the walls, but only for a moment, before the church returned itself to complete silence.

"Why did you tell us you were dead?"

He didn't flinch.

"Does this mean that you really . . . you spent your whole life pretending . . . for what? What could be worth that?"

Silence.

The clocks around the church ticked, but time didn't move at all.

"We have to tell people you're alive," I said finally, to myself as much as to him.

A smile flickered across his lips, then disappeared.

"My parents will forgive you," I said, looking forward at stained-glass Jesus, speaking to him. "I know they will, I think they'll just—they'll be happy you're alive. Everyone will just be happy you're alive," I assured him, as though nothing had ever been more important. "People will want to interview you, but you don't have to do any of that if you don't want to. And, and my dad's trying to do the stupid rerelease of the book, but you can stop that, right away, if you want. And I guess you'll probably have to address the whole Great Purpose thing; I'm not sure if you're aware but there's a whole group of people that are, like, worshipping you. And they're chasing me now, but they won't be anymore once they find out that you're—I've got so many people for you to meet, too, you never got to meet Kaitlin. We started dating right after you died, or we thought you died, but she knows all about you, or even Mara, this girl—and Henry, I met him, he, he'll be so excited. He's been going to the train every single day, just to look for—"

"Would you like to pray with me, Arthur?"

I fell silent. He'd ignored me. He hadn't heard a word I'd said, or if he had, he didn't want to acknowledge them.

"I'm, uh . . ." I was too disappointed to calculate a polite response. "No. No, I want to talk to you."

The edges of his lips curled upward in a smile. "What's the difference?"

"Grandpa, please. We have to tell people you're alive. People need to know. I'm going to get my friend Mara, she's right outside—"

"No mortal has ever seen God," he said deliberately, ignoring me again. "Not one, not even in the Bible. And yet millions, *millions* of people believe in him. Do you know why that is?"

I sigh. "Because people walk by faith, not by—"

"Because people don't *want* to see God, Arthur. They think they do; they say they do. But deep down, they know they can't. They can't, because they know that seeing God would ruin God, because he could never be all they wanted Him to be. If they could see him, then he would be the truth. He would be a fact. And if you tell someone the fact, then you kill the fiction. Truth is the enemy of the mystery.

"So it's better if people don't see him. Better for him to exist invisibly. That way, they can just trust their own belief that someone's protecting them. That's why everybody likes the mystery. They *want* the mystery. They *want* to live inside the stories they tell themselves about the world. The truth is always much, much uglier. The *truth* is, everyone dies. In the mystery, everyone lives forever. The truth is, we're all tiny, and meaningless. In the mystery, we get to pretend we're not." He paused and shook his head. "People don't want to see God, because anything they can see is temporary. The unseen, the mystery . . . that's eternal."

From nowhere, rushing down through the still air molecules in the church, I felt a wave of inconsolable, unplaceable sadness, staring at him unmoving across the aisle from me. I'd spent the last five years—my entire life, really—wondering where he was and wishing he was there. Now he was here, right in front of me, thinking and breathing and speaking in complete sentences, but he was absent. He was more hollow than ever before.

"Did you leave clues for me to find you?" I asked, words catching in my throat.

He didn't answer, and tears pushed at the inside corners of my eyes.

"Did you want me to find you?"

He ignored the question again, now looking away from me.

"Was this a plan? The poem in the bird book and the clues to get me here? Or was that a mistake?" I was almost shouting at him, but the words ran over and off his skin like water. "Did I ruin your plan to fade away into nothing until we forgot you? Did I?" I stood up. "Tell me, because if you want me to leave you alone, I will."

Somewhere above us, a bell for the church sounded, softly.

"Tell me." His voice returned. "What is it you're looking for?"

Just like every picture in my head, he was blank and impassive, unquestioning and unquestioned. It was the third time he'd asked exactly that, automatically and without context. He wasn't better, or cured, or even faking an illness. It was a reset.

"Do you remember me, Grandpa?" I pleaded, but he gave me nothing. "Please, I just want answers. Please."

He shifted in his seat to face me, and both eyes opened. "Is that why you robbed Jack?"

My stomach tightened as the question echoed. "What do you, what do you mean? How did, Grandpa, I didn't, I didn't—"

"Is that why you ran away?" I couldn't look away from him. His eyes were colorless and cold. "Is that why you're not going back? Lying to your father and putting him through hell?" His voice boomed through the church.

"Wait. How, how did you know I—"

"Is that why you tried to hit her, Arthur?"

All of the breath I was clinging to shot out of me.

He stood, no longer mortal, towering over me with the size and strength of five men, his presence filling the church, the edges of his body blurring into the smoke, swirling around me and trapping me in, choking me. I fell to my knees before him, gasping for breath, while all around him, tiny Bibles rose from the pews, like a storm poised to roll over me.

"Answer me, Arthur!" he boomed. "What is it you're looking for?"

"I don't know," I gasped, voice wet from tears. "I just need to know why."

The Bibles fell, and the wind stopped, and my grandfather's human form became clear, retreating back to the pew where he'd been sitting. I collapsed to the floor, the breath rushing back into my lungs.

"You need it too much," he said.

I looked up from the floor. "What?"

The pitch of his voice shifted, sliding upward as he spoke and morphing with the voice that never left my head.

"You need me too much." And the sanctuary fell silent.

Behind my eyelids, colors swirled. The adrenaline that had

crested tumbled back down and I felt empty, and alone. It was all fake, I could tell now, but I could still see my hatred, bright red in every corner of my vision. Hatred for my grandpa, hatred for where I was, hatred of myself.

When I opened my eyes, there was an older man standing in front of me. He was wearing a jet-black robe, a white collar around his neck, and his gray hair was perfectly parted. He spoke quietly, like he didn't want to disturb the room around us.

"Arthur? Arthur Pullman, right?"

I blinked, trying to see more clearly who he was.

"It's okay, you—you don't know me," he said, his eyes chasing back and forth, his head twisting slightly to look behind him to the door. "I'm Father Stephenson; this is my church that you're . . . lying in."

"How did you know my name?" I asked, sitting up.

Again, he glanced back toward the door, and for the first time, the sound of Chicago permeated the church walls—sirens.

He cleared his throat. "I'm not sure if you're aware of this, Arthur, but people know that you're missing. People are looking for you, and I . . . You must forgive me."

The sirens got louder.

5.

I TORE OUT of the church as fast as my legs would allow, blinded by every terrifying thought in my head like an overwhelming stream of light, too bright to make out any of its sources, and spilled onto the street.

I couldn't feel any of it.

An insignificant blur, brown hair and a cigarette, waited—"Arthur, did you hear the"—but my body tore past it; everything about the world was violent; the color, the light, the noise, all of it was strobing inside my head, forcing my senses to throb—*what is it you're looking for?*—my body sent its energy to the weakness that surrounded it, sharing it with the too-bright world and the too-close man on the sidewalk—"Hey, buddy, what the fuck?"—but the world needed it, and my body was past it, moving faster and faster down the street, too fast to know what it was moving toward. I could see water rushing in the windows of the car, hear the beeps of the warning lights, see the exhaust climbing, and hear my father screaming.

City blocks flew by like lines on the sidewalk, but my eyes saw none of it. It was all infinite light, extending impossibly in every direction. People shouting behind it—*you need me too much*—sirens screaming around me, but my body was too far away now to be touched, flying forward and ahead of me, my eyes found the words at the end of my tunnel of noise and sound and lights—CHICAGO TRIBUNE. Voices, trying to pull my body backward—"Arthur, what in the hell are you doing?"— brown hair and a cigarette, small and frail and superior, chiding me, observing my weakness—"Stop! Arthur! Please!"—looking through my skin and into my chest where it knew it had control over me.

"Don't touch me," my voice reacted, but the words weren't mine. "Get out of my way."

Hundreds of horrible voices echoed over the blinding light, blowing out my senses—*just don't do anything you'll regret*—and from the top window my body could feel Sal's wicked eyes, mocking me over shitty coffee—*please, go bother someone else!*— and my left hand throbbed, animal instinct pushing its rage further and further to impulse, onto the body that wasn't mine anymore, through the door, and straight to the desk—"Excuse me, sir, what is it you're looking for?"—every person in the room was faceless, a blur of skin and color and identity that would never matter, but my body registered the intense heat of their judgment against my skin. My ring tightened; my left hand burned.

"Get me Sal Hamilton, now," my voice snarled.

Exploding out of the nothingness around my body was a horrible, wicked shriek I remembered—*you always do this! This is how you manipulate people!*—brown hair and pale skin, radiating outward white-hot light—*when you get angry, it's like there this little switch in you that flips and you go crazy!*—and then more laughter, this time male, Mason behind her—*she told me it was okay*—his hands all over her—*I'm sorry, Arthur*—and another male, taller and angrier—*you've got a name to protect*—and—*I didn't think he would rob us.* The stares all around me grew more intense, my skin could feel it.

"I don't need anything!" My body fought its way back across the room, stumbling away from the desk, gripping its head to stop the light, hand burning, face exploding.

There were hands on me now, tall men in uniforms—"Sir, please lower your voice"—black like Kaitlin's wall, holding my body down—*you need me too much!*—and their faces were Kaitlin's, the walls of the building around them getting closer, determined to not let me escape. *What is it you're looking for?*—my grandfather's voice, his face now floating on one of the warm bodies of black cloth around me, taunting me, shouting, over and over on an infinite loop—*you need me too much!*—and my body fought the words back, every ounce of heat and energy and despair, my arms swung and the ring on my left hand burned and they aimed at the wall behind where Kaitlin stood—

and I felt my body go limp,

and then, finally, I felt nothing at all.

6.

may 3, the 2010.

arthur in stone gray walls
with nothing,
surrounded by nothing

the curse of
feeling everything
is that you're painfully aware
when you feel nothing.

—*arthur louis pullman*

7.

"ARTHUR PULLMAN?"

"Mmm."

"You're Arthur Pullman?"

"Yeah."

"I'm here to inform you that your father has requested that, in lieu of further time in holding, you complete a psychiatric evaluation, upon which the terms of your release will be conditioned. Now, seeing as you are eighteen, you do have the right to refuse his suggestion and remain in the cell, but—and I'm speaking of my own volition here—I'd strongly suggest that you do as he requested and complete the evaluation."

"Why?"

The uniformed officer standing in the cell door in front of me shrugged. "Chairs are more comfortable in there."

I followed. I'd never been in a police station before, let alone a cell. They were terrible, built to convince you of your guilt. He led me down a series of hallways, through an oak door, to a room with two high-backed chairs, an oriental rug, and a coffee table with a plastic green plant. The illusion of comfort, rule number one in the Book of Therapeutic Bullshit.

I couldn't feel anything. It wasn't a temporary flash of numbness, or an overwhelming light, or a moment of my body taking control and operating on instinct; it was a complete and total nothing. No want, no fear, no purpose, no hope, no sadness, no happiness, nowhere to go and no reason to be there, no desperate truth or longing for answers; just a plain white emptiness where everything else used to be. I tested myself.

Arthur, your hand is healed! UCLA wants you to start practice Monday! "I guess that's fine."

Arthur, your grandfather is actually alive, he's waiting to talk to you. "That's very interesting."

Arthur, Kaitlin fucked Mason again. "Huh . . . huh."

I had become a plastic human being.

The door opened and a copy of Dr. Sandoval, this one female, and black, came through the door and sat in the chair adjacent to mine. She opened a folder on her lap and read silently. If I cared, I'd have read it upside down. Instead, I stared at the plant.

"Arthur Pullman," she announced.

Our eyes met, and I noticed another similarity with Dr. Sandoval, maybe the most noticeable—inhuman detachment in her eyes. I'd imagine it was the kind of look that only developed after years and years of looking too closely at people. It would be hard to still have faith in the species.

She leaned forward, looking me up and down, like she was checking to see if there was anything about me that wasn't in the folder. She must have decided there wasn't. "Tell me about your dreams."

"My dreams?"

She nodded.

"What about them?"

She reopened the folder. "Your therapist at home, Dr. Sandoval, said you described them as 'driving your car off a cliff, crashing into the water, and drowning.' Is that right?"

I shrugged. I didn't want her to know anything. I couldn't let her have that power over me. I knew how she would use it.

"What about your hand?" she asked.

"What about it?

"You're wearing a cast."

"I broke it."

"How?"

"By breaking it."

"Yeah, I got that part, and I'm asking *how?*"

After a moment of silence, she began speaking quickly. "A psychiatric evaluation such as this exists for me to make a determination, on behalf of the state, as to whether or not I believe that you can be released from the jail here without further risk of violence, either to yourself or to others. I make this determination based solely on what I observe. There is no second opinion, there is no appeals process, and, at this point, you've consented, so bail doesn't really do anything for you unless I say you're ready to leave." She slapped the folder. "You're not hiding anything from anyone here. This thing tells me everything I need to know. So tell me, Arthur Louis Pullman, how is it that you broke your hand?"

"I thought you had, you said you already, already had all of the answers in your, your little . . . folder." My voice was dry.

"I want you to tell me. Unless, of course"—she found a section in the folder with her finger—"'Arthur broke his hand punching a wall forcefully. The punch was thrown at Kaitlin Lewis, his girlfriend at the time.'" She looked up. "Is that really all there is to it?"

I sat still, feeling none of it. "I guess that's all."

"Why were you mad?"

"Nothing."

"Nothing?"

"It was stupid. Sometimes I get mad." I quickly added, "Back then. But not anymore."

She leaned toward me and said, as if she understood, "Is that why you tried to hit her?"

I didn't respond.

"What's that on your finger?" She noticed my thumb was twisting around my ring finger. "Let me see it."

Reluctantly, I set the ring on the table in front of us.

"A ring, huh?" She picked it up and rubbed the silver in front of me, smoothed over from having spun on my finger so many times. "It's nice," she observed, checking back on my face for a reaction but logging zero results.

"You know . . ." She set it back on the table. "I handle a lot of domestic violence cases in here," she said. "It's the most common kind of case I'm called in for. You start to recognize patterns, between these guys, and the most noticeable one is that they never seem to get why what they did might not be okay. It's always like they *had* to do it, like they were provoked, or they were just doing what anybody would've done. Some of them, they go so far as to think they're doing her a favor. 'At least now she knows not to be such a bitch,' that kind of thing."

"So?"

"So, none of those guys would blame it on themselves getting mad," she said, leaning in. "So I guess my question is, why hit the wall?"

"I guess I was mad."

"Takes a lot of force to break your hand. I'm going to bet," she said, nodding to the ring, "it wasn't your hand you were trying to break."

My eyes found the ring, still perfectly intact on the table in front of me and in every dream.

"When'd she give this to you?"

I swallowed. "Two years ago."

"And then she cheated on you."

I didn't say anything for a long moment.

She held up the folder. "She admitted to you that she had three other active sexual partners. One of them was your best friend, Mason Cromwell." I could still feel her watching my face. "Three active sexual partners is a lot for a girl with a boyfriend. Did you not know that?"

I blinked, waited a few seconds, then blinked again.

"Did you not know that, Arthur?"

"No, I mean, yeah, you . . . like you said, she, she told me."

"But when I asked you what happened with Kaitlin, you said 'nothing.' And when I asked why you were upset, you said 'it was stupid.' Do you think your girlfriend admitting to you that she has three secret sexual partners is a stupid reason to be upset?"

"I just . . . How I handled it was stupid. Getting mad, at her. At the ring. I shouldn't, I know that I shouldn't have, have gotten so mad, and I know she, she told them, it was, it was for my own good, because she, she knew I needed—she wanted me to be . . . She said I was difficult. I'm difficult. I'm not a . . . I shouldn't have punched the wall."

She let my mumbling drip into silence. Catholics always said confession made them feel relieved, forgiven, and pure, but I didn't feel any of that. Talking just reminded me of the moments I hated myself the most.

"I'm Dr. Patterson."

Her hand was extended toward me when I looked up.

"What?"

"I just realized I hadn't introduced myself. I'm Dr. Patterson, on-call specialist for the Chicago Police Department. That's why we're talking now."

"I'm Arthur."

"Arthur Louis Pullman," she said. "With the famous grandfather."

I rolled my eyes.

"I never read the book." She returned to the folder. "There's a pretty serious search out for you, now, Arthur. Police on the ground looking for you in . . . California, Denver, Omaha, and

Albuquerque, New Mexico. And now here you are in Chicago. That's a pretty wide net."

I shifted in my seat.

"You told the officers that brought you in that you were in Chicago . . . 'following clues'?" She paused, expecting me to explain, but expecting wrong. "You don't talk to many people who are looking for clues anymore. What clues?"

"I'm not crazy."

"Sure," she said, shrugging. "Me neither."

I watched her for a moment, and she stared back, unflinching, reminding me that answering the questions wasn't my choice. "My grandfather."

She held her stare for a moment, then fell into a laugh. "Fucking writers, right? I married one, terrible mistake. Everything's gotta have some kind of . . . plot. It's like the way things are just isn't enough for these people." If she expected me to laugh with her, she was wrong. "So . . . he left you clues? When?"

"He ran away from home." I shifted in my seat, trying not to think about the timeline or my failure to understand it. "A week before he died."

"Right. I remember reading about it. I'm sorry. Dementia can be very, very painful for a family. I've seen many, many children, grandchildren, try desperately to interpret . . . I'm sorry you had to go through that. It's very difficult."

I accepted her sympathy by crossing my arms.

"I'm confused, though," she continued. "Your grandfather . . . in his final days . . . struggling through what must have been severe Alzheimer's, was able to leave clues behind for you?"

I shifted in my seat. "He wrote some journals, and I followed them."

She rapped her pen a few times against the folder. "And why did you do that?"

"Do what?"

"Follow these clues? What were you looking for?"

I took a deep breath and focused only on the plant on the table, unflinching, unaffected by our conversation. I didn't have an answer.

"Did you find anything?" she asked. "Did it reveal anything about him to you?"

"When do I get to be done with this?"

Her expression froze. "I'm sorry?"

"I'm answering your questions. I've proven I'm not danger-ous. When do I get to be done?"

"Arthur, you punched a police officer." Her lips tightened. "You rioted in a secure building and started shouting at the walls in the lobby. They're not going to let you high-step out of here. We take this kind of thing seriously."

"That was a mistake," I said, trying not to remember it. "But obviously I'm sane."

I felt a confused frustration tingling in my stomach, in my left hand.

She locked her eyes onto mine. "Arthur, we're gonna talk about a few weeks ago."

"Okay. Why?"

Her round eyes became slits on her face. It was her turn not to speak.

"What?" I asked again, more frustration creeping on top of the frustration that was already resting in my stomach.

She shifted in the almost-comfortable chair, and slowly, she began to nod. "What have you been doing for, I don't know, three weeks?"

"Well, I've been on a train—"

"Before that."

"I don't know."

"Think about it."

I thought about it.

I couldn't remember much. Every day had been so similar after Kaitlin and I broke up, it was almost like they hadn't happened at all. I'd gone to the hospital for my hand, and when I returned home, there was nothing I wanted to do. I thought about applying to a few other colleges, but I guess I hadn't gotten around to that. I watched TV a lot, when I could bring myself to it, but I couldn't remember watching any more than a couple of episodes of any series on Netflix before giving up. None of them looked good. All I really remembered was spending time on my bed, looking at my hand, showering, eating, and driving.

But I couldn't tell Dr. Patterson that. "Well, I had to go in to take care of . . ." I held up my broken hand.

She nodded but didn't speak.

"I guess . . . well, I sat around my house a lot. I couldn't play tennis or anything, and Kaitlin was—well, you know. So I watched *Lost, Game of Thrones,* I got some college apps for the spring semester, and . . . I masturbated a lot? Is that the kind of honesty you were looking for?"

She shrugged.

"I guess," I continued, "I guess the only reason I'd really leave my house every day was to go driving."

"Driving? Like the dreams?"

"I mean . . . no. I didn't crash."

"Where would you drive?"

"Uh, there's a road near my house, in Portola Valley, with a big hill. I would drive that."

"Every day?"

"Every day."

She wrote something down in the folder. "Any particular reason?" she asked.

"Uh, because I like driving, I guess?"

"Why?"

"Why do I like driving?"

She nodded.

"I do—I mean, I just like it."

"What about it?"

I felt my face get hot. "I don't know, like, the thrill of it? I like . . . knowing I'm going faster than humans are supposed to go. The adrenaline. And I guess, when I'm driving, I don't think about anything else."

"And you did that every day?"

"Every single day."

"Up until you left."

"Yes," I said, swelling with discomfort.

"Nothing else happened, no days you didn't go driving?"

I shrugged. "Nope."

I was still gazing at the plant. When I looked back at her, she had set the folder on the table and was looking back at me with intense sympathy.

"Do you know what trauma is, Arthur?"

I shrugged.

"It's the way that we respond emotionally to the bad things that happen to us," she explained. "The most common effect that trauma has is a sort of . . . intentional forgetting. Our brains want to protect us, so they mask the bad experiences by remembering them as different, normal ones. That's how people are able to forget war, or death, childhood abuse, anything that scars them—they remember it as something else."

Irritated, I sat up. "And you're saying I was traumatized by Kaitlin breaking up with me? Because check your math, professor, I punched the wall *before* we broke up. We were still together. That was part of why she broke up with me at all."

Dr. Patterson shook her head. "No, that probably felt like a terrible thing, but it wasn't trauma. That you remember very clearly."

"I remember punching the wall, too!" I protested.

"I know," she said, then, more quietly, "I know."

I was starting to feel strange, like a sadness was showing up in parts of me that I couldn't get to. It was familiar, but I couldn't reach it to understand it; darkness that was too dark to see its source.

She spoke again. "Do you know what happens to our bodies right before we die? The last chemical we release?"

I shook my head.

"Adrenaline." She made direct eye contact with me. "Fight or flight. When the body thinks it's going down, it sends every bit of energy it's got, in the form of adrenaline."

"Why—why are you telling me this?" I stuttered. All around my body, I felt tingly, cold water against the back of my neck. The sadness was starting to get overwhelming, an unavoidable gravity pulling me in. I wanted to get rid of it, get away from it, but as I thought about the pain in my hand, everything just got worse. I was back in the world of my dreams, driving my car but having no control over what I was doing. I was in the lake, on the train tracks, with no desire to move, no energy to even lift my hands. "What does this have to do with anything? What are you—"

"Arthur, three weeks ago, you attempted suicide."

I blinked several times.

"You sat in your garage, in the front seat of your Camaro, you turned on the gas, and your father discovered you just in time to get you to the hospital." She paused. "You tried to kill yourself."

I stared at the plastic plant as it sat on the table.

"You haven't been able to remember it because your brain registered the adrenaline and decided you were driving. Do you remember it now?"

I didn't move.

"Think of your dreams, Arthur. Put yourself in the car."

I remembered a day, waking up and getting in my car to go drive to Portola Valley, not wanting to come back, not wanting to feel anything other than the blinding speed-high of racing down the dive.

I remembered a moment, sitting there, watching trickles of smoke starting to rush into the car like water.

I remembered a seat belt, one that felt like five, pulling impossibly tighter and choking the air out of me.

I remembered a beeping warning light on the dash, the screaming of my father behind me.

I remembered a blurring, blinding fading of everything I was feeling into nothing, the roaring silence, like adrenaline, like pain, like bright, bright light, too bright to see its source, so concentrated and overwhelming that I didn't have to think about waking up without her.

I remembered needing to move, needing to fight my way out, and deciding not to.

"Do you remember, Arthur?"

The sadness I had been searching for finally found me, and I remembered.

I began to cry. Heavy, wet, rapid tears, huge, heaving sobs, right in the police room's comfortable chair.

"Why—" I tried to ask but my throat was closed, swelled from the foreign activity. I was all feeling, nothing but the salt water leaking out of my eyes. For what could have been minutes or hours, I sobbed. When I could chance a full sentence, I sniv-eled and nearly shouted, "Why—why did you"—the words were muted, watery themselves— "why did you tell me?"

Dr. Patterson waited a moment before answering. "Because you're not the person you were three weeks ago." She paused. "It's time to remember now."

8.

MY MOUTH WAS dry and lifeless. The rest of my body felt the same.

Dr. Patterson let me sit, and left the room when I wouldn't answer questions. It wasn't that I wanted to be silent; I just couldn't will myself to speak.

The further inside myself I looked, the worse it got. It was like my brain was at the center of a hundred wrestling matches, nerve endings having it out over what I remembered and didn't remember, believed and didn't believe.

The dominant parts felt cheated and unsure of who to blame—Dr. Sandoval, or Dr. Patterson, or my dad, or Kaitlin, or Mason, or my grandpa, or myself. The weaker parts wondered if anything had actually happened—the clues, or the Great Purpose, or Mara—or if the entire last week had actually been just a vividly convoluted dream, too perfect for reality, a story I played out behind my eyelids while sitting in the front seat of the Camaro, slowly waiting for all of the thoughts to stop.

All of it looked broken. The past was a dull and fractured kaleidoscope, constantly shifting, out of focus, black and gray images. It wasn't that I wanted to be unsure, I just couldn't will myself to understand.

So I sat, the room getting darker as the sun disappeared. I could hear voices talking about me in the hallway.

"—just a confused kid, didn't mean any—"

"—stations all over the country are still getting calls—"

"—keep him here that long? We'd be—"

"—all the way to Chicago, but he insisted—"

Occasionally I'd shoot a glance across the room where I could see parts of my face in the small mirror, but the person looking back was a stranger. My hair was wild and unwashed, and my face was covered in someone else's bruises. I couldn't look for long without wanting to smash it, so I collapsed back into my hands, unmoving, wanting to be as far from myself as I possibly could.

I felt a soft hand on my shoulder, Dr. Patterson, likely to tell me it was back to the cell until they could figure out a punishment for me. Community service, jail time, thousands of dollars in fines . . . it all sounded like the same thing.

"Can we call someone for you, Arthur?" she asked.

I shook my head once.

"Okay." Dr. Patterson inhaled. "You don't have to, but we strongly suggest it. In moments like this, it helps to talk to someone who . . . who'll be honest with you."

I thought for a long moment. Kaitlin was illegal. Mason might betray me again. Mara would be angry. My auntie and uncle would keep panicking.

"You can do it, Arthur," she said. "You can talk to someone."

I sighed. "My dad," I heard myself say. "I'll talk to my dad."

Dr. Patterson moved slowly back toward the door and disappeared, leaving me alone again with the plant.

When it reopened, my father stood in her place.

"Hey, buddy." He looked exhausted and unsettled, inching toward me. He sat hesitantly in the doctor's chair. "I heard you wanted to talk to me."

"You're here."

"I had to be. We didn't know where you were, and when they called . . ." He shifted in his seat. "They thought you were in Albuquerque," he told the ring, still on the table. "Denver, Omaha, Minneapolis, Kansas . . . someone called from Miami, thought they saw you there, driving a sports car. Karen's been a mess, all of us have been. You wouldn't believe these last few days, Arthur. It's been terrible." He ran a hand through his hair. It looked like it had been just as long since he'd showered, maybe longer since he'd slept. "And all I had from you was that phone call about your grandfather? This fight to remember of you?"

"I know," I breathed. "I know."

I closed my eyes and there it was: the guilt. My father, my family were waiting for me, waiting for answers. They weren't pretending to be grieving, they were actually grieving—the real and familiar dread of losing a family member—and it was all my fault. When I opened my eyes, my dad was still looking at me.

"So?"

The lights in the room were off, and as the sun continued to disappear, it was getting difficult to see detail around the room.

I took a deep breath. "I fucked everything up." I exhaled, and took another enormous breath. "I, I ruined it. I ruined all of it. I don't know, I don't know what happened." My breathing scattered, fighting the words, fighting my throat. "I'm sorry. I'm so . . ." He didn't interrupt me and I felt more tears form under my eyes. "I thought I knew what I was doing. I, I thought I was figuring things out, and it was all gonna be okay, but . . . but it wasn't. I wasn't." And suddenly, I couldn't stop the words from tumbling out now. "I was so . . . so sure, about everything . . . and I came all the way out here, and lied, and . . . but it was wrong. I was so wrong. I don't even know what I was looking for. I don't even know . . ."

He let my sentence dissolve into wet nothing. The clock in the room ticked slowly; the sun fell farther outside the window.

"That's nothing," my dad said finally. His voice was barely loud enough to hear. "One time I almost bought a plane ticket to Australia, because I thought I heard my dad say something about *Melbourne*." I heard him smile. "But, of course, that didn't make sense. None of it ever did. Just got worse the harder I tried."

For the first time, I tried looking up into his eyes. They

weren't frustrated or judgmental. They were just looking for me.

"What'd you find?" he asked.

"Nothing," I told him, my voice beginning to dry.

"You came all the way to Chicago for nothing?"

"I was just wrong about it. All of it."

"What happened?"

I sighed. "'Just got worse the harder I tried.'"

He smiled. "Well, what got you out here?"

An image of my first night at my auntie and uncle's clicked into the kaleidoscope. "He left a little journal, on a page about western tanagers in a book in Tim's attic, so I figured it must have been a clue or something. He must have known I'd be the one to find it. But it was stupid."

He looked confused.

"Because he always had that story, about the tanager?"

He shook his head.

I sighed again. "The old Native American story or something he used to tell me, about this village that was in a drought, and they needed to get to this weird, magical river to keep them alive. But the river was through a wood, with all of these—you know, you don't realize how stupid stories like this are until you're trying to retell them when you're older."

My dad laughed and I almost smiled. "Well, try."

I swallowed. "So there was a young man in the village, the son of the chief, and they had kind of decided he was the only one strong enough to make the journey. But because he was so vital, they weren't sure if they wanted to send him out to die, because if he died, then the village was done for, for sure.

"So I guess they decided to wait for a sign from God—or the divine, or whatever they called it—to let them know whether or not they should send him into the woods, because that's the kind of people they were. And they waited and waited, and nothing happened. And the young man started to get sick, because he didn't have enough water, but they didn't want to send him, because they trusted the divine to tell them when.

"Then one day, the boy's father, the chief, came running into the village, shouting about how he'd just seen a cardinal, which, according to their superstitions, was a sign of good fortune. So they prayed, or whatever it is you do, and they sent the boy into the woods to get water.

"But after the boy left, the chief confessed—it wasn't a cardinal. It was a tanager. Which isn't lucky at all; evidently it was common in that area. And the father knew that, and still he lied, to his own son, just for the sake of trying to save his village."

My dad took it in silently, waiting for me to continue.

"So, yeah. That's the story. I don't know if the kid survived or not, but I don't think that's the point."

He didn't move. "What *is* the point, then?"

"The point is, I was wrong the whole time. I thought . . . I thought because he told me that story, he was giving me a sign, but *in* the story, the sign is fake." I got louder as I spoke. "The point is, sometimes when you think you're getting a sign, and you're actually getting lied to. It wasn't a cardinal. It was never a cardinal," I said. "It was just a fucking tanager."

I couldn't believe how strong and fast the words came out of my mouth. They hung in the air, thick and heavy like a quilt around us. My dad must have been shaken as well, because he didn't respond. Watching him, I wished I'd never left home. I wished I'd never found the clues, or followed them like I had. I wished I'd never heard the story from my grandpa, or told it again now.

"I didn't know if I was being brave or being stupid." His voice cut through the quiet. "But to tell you the truth, the more I've lived, the less I've understood the difference."

I blinked up to him.

"Arthur Louis Pullman. *A World Away*, 1975. It's not a Native American tale, Arthur; a hooker tells that story to the main character outside of a gas station." He smirked. "I *really* would've thought you'd read the book by now."

I sat back in my chair and breathed.

My dad continued. "You're not that different from your grandpa. Did you know that?"

Hearing him use the word *Grandpa* turned my insides over.

"He used to take us to church, and I didn't really get it, so one day, I asked him why everyone would believe in God, if nobody ever saw him. And he said, 'If they saw him, that would ruin it. It's the faith in the mystery—that's the part that matters.'" He paused. "Now, granted, he was a devout Christian, and you're a bloodsucking atheist—"

I accidentally smiled.

"—but you got his . . . his ability to . . ." He stopped himself and leaned toward me. "He didn't mean that sometimes you're lucky and sometimes you're not. He meant that it doesn't matter. He meant that a tanager is an invitation to be extraordinary if you just decide that it's time for you to be extraordinary." He swallowed. "And what you're doing, Arthur . . . signs, or cardinals, or answers, or not. You're chasing something you can't see, and . . . and that's more than most people ever do."

Outside, the moon was rising, and its light was spilling into the room. I hadn't realized it for the hours I'd been there, but the Chicago Police Department building was next to the lake, with no skyscrapers to obscure the view. The moon must have been incredibly bright over our heads, because while I couldn't see it, it was starting to paint the horizon line a soft orange.

"Anyway, I don't know if they told you, but someone bailed you out. I tried, but resisting arrest is expensive, and I couldn't quite . . . Either way, someone stepped in."

I sat up abruptly.

"Sounds like one of your friends from this week," my dad said, looking toward the door.

I'd been in the station so long I'd forgotten the world around me and moved on from the idea that there might be more to the trip. There was still Ohio, but who would know that? Mara?

My father stood and knocked on the door. A moment later, Dr. Patterson answered. "How're we feeling?" she asked.

"Better, I think," my dad said. I shrugged.

"You're going to be charged with misdemeanor assault," Dr. Patterson said flatly. "That's going to come with a fine and some community service time, but I've spoken with your father, and Dr. Sandoval, and we agreed. You're an adult, and . . ."

She let my father continue. "And we think you should finish going wherever it is that you're going."

My head restarted and groaned back to life, engines beginning to fire as if the gears were shifting too rapidly upward, grinding against each other to force the machine forward. I didn't know what I wanted: to go home and be done, or to go on and be frustrated again.

"You're very lucky, Arthur." Dr. Patterson still spoke as a matter of fact. "You may not be paying much attention to it now, but . . . a lot of young men don't get this many second chances."

I flashed to an image of Jack on the train, how close he had been to being apprehended for nothing.

"So," my dad said, standing to lead us out the door. "The guy's here already—"

"The guy?"

"I don't remember their names," he said. *Names.* Multiple. "But it sounds like he was a part of some organization your grandfather was in."

The room turned to ice. I felt cold water up the back of my spine, chilling realization shooting its way to my brain.

"Something plain, real normal name. Like—"

"Jack?" I said, trying to stop, but the officers kept us moving toward the door. "Was it Jack?"

"I don't know. He's waiting for you outside, I figure we'll—"

"No, Dad, I can't—" I stopped myself. If Jack was here to bail me out, I was either going to be punished or, even worse, forced to work for them, but if I told him that I didn't want to go, told him that this was an enemy, that I *had* enemies, then I'd have to go home. Or, without being bailed out, I'd have to stay in jail. And whatever was in Ohio would belong to Jack, and only Jack.

"—does that sound alright, Arthur?"

I didn't respond. The final door was in front of us, the continental divide between bad and worse. I didn't know which side was which. I held my breath as we plunged through it.

But Jack wasn't waiting for me in the lobby.

It was another man. Short, old, wearing a necktie and a bowler hat, a briefcase to his right, and a British girl to his left.

9.

MY FATHER, MARA, and Sal Hamilton watched in silence as I filled out the required bail forms before leaving the station.

Did I acknowledge that I knew or had a relationship with the person who had posted bail for me? No, not really.

Did I swear that I wasn't going to leave the state? No, couldn't really do that.

Did I know where I was going once I left? Nope, not a clue.

I signed all of them anyway.

As soon as we were out of the station, Mara tackled me to the pavement with a running, jumping hug.

"You—fucking—idiot!" she shouted into my shoulder.

Resting her feet back on the ground and pulling away from the hug, her left hand still squeezing my arm, she cocked her hand back and slapped me across the face.

"What the fuck *was* that?" she said, now completely serious. "For a solid minute there, I was actually terrified. I didn't know who that guy was. And he scared the shit out of me."

"I, uh—" I remembered every word of this conversation with Kaitlin, the one we had after I punched the wall. The conversation where she broke up with me. "I'm sorry, I, I don't know what happened, I just, I got—"

Mara didn't wait for me to finish my sentence before hugging me again.

"Everyone I know is fucked up, okay?" she whispered into my ear. "Just tell me things." She pulled back again and I noticed small tears in the corners of her eyes. "Also, thank God you're white." She wiped her eyes. "Otherwise you'd be in there for months."

I nodded to my father and Sal Hamilton waiting in silence behind us.

"Right," she said, straightening. "This is Sal Hamilton."

He stepped closer, light from the streetlamp washing over him, and for the first time, I noticed his face. It was badly bruised, a near-purple spot under his right eye that hadn't been there the day before. There were several cuts on his chin and neck and what looked like dry, caked blood on his lower lip.

"What happened to your face?"

My father leaned in to listen, and Sal looked to Mara. "Jack . . . happened," she said, clearing her throat.

"What did they do?"

"Look, I owe you an apology," Sal fumbled. "It was a big misunderstanding. There's a lotta complexity surrounding your grandpa, and I—uh—I guess I clammed up a bit." The words got caught in his throat, and when they finally came, they were soft. "You just look so goddamn much like him. Thought you mighta been a ghost or something." He spoke harshly, with traces of an Italian accent. "And this group of kids—this Jack—they've been hassling me for a couple years now, and when you came 'round—I guess I thought you mighta been a part of that."

"How did you know we weren't?"

He pointed to Mara. "She's pretty convincing, 'specially after they . . ." He ran his hand along the wounds on his face. "And it helped that she had that poem."

"Poem?" I'd forgotten my father was there.

"Yeah, he . . . well." I nodded to Mara and she pulled the journal from her pocket and handed it over. My father pulled it open and began to read. Back and forth across the page, only his eyes moved, and he concentrated intensely. I could only imagine what was happening behind his eyes, the world as he knew it expanding and contracting and changing in a way that he hated. When he finished, he started again, back up to the top of the page, finally turning to me.

"This, uh—" He coughed. "This is real?" I nodded, and without warning, he hugged me. "Okay," he whispered. "Okay," and I knew that was all he wanted to say.

"Why would they come, come and find you?" I asked Sal quietly as my father stepped back, folding the journal into his pocket.

"Well, they musta saw you come by early in the day, assumed I knew something."

Remorse came surging back and I almost doubled over, it hit me so fast. I'd put him in danger. I was responsible for his wounds.

"Well?" We all turned, surprised to hear my father speaking. "*Do* you know something?"

Sal sighed, the exhale pushing his head back, then forward, in a nod. "I think . . . I was the last person to see him alive."

I swallowed hard. "Do you know where he went next? Or how he got to Ohio?"

Sal nodded again. "I drove him."

I stared at Sal in petrified silence.

"The thing is," Mara interrupted, nodding to Sal's face. "Now they know where as well, and it's likely that they're on their way. Sal has no idea why your grandfather needed to go Ohio, he just knows where he dropped him off. So . . . it might be nothing." She turned to me, lowering her voice. "Look, Arthur. We have no reason to believe there's anything there, other than Jack, and a bunch of people who want to hurt you." My dad's eyes tripled in size. "So it's possible that going now would be running fast into a dangerous situation with little hope of finding anything. You've done more than anyone could ever have imagined. You've got something he wrote for you; no one can take that away."

They all looked to me for an answer. I looked back, jumping from Mara's stare to my father's caution to Sal's bruises.

"No."

"No what?"

"No, not good enough," I said, and I meant it. "There's gotta be something more than that."

The edges of Mara's mouth flickered upward. My father took

a deep breath, then nodded. "Tanager," he mouthed.

"Are you sure?" she asked. "Because if you said stop, we could turn around right now and go back on with our lives. No danger, no disappointment, no—"

"Mara," I interrupted, her face a foot from mine. "We're wasting time."

She smiled.

"It's almost eight," my dad said, pacing. "Does it have to be tonight?"

"Yes," the three of us said in unison.

"Why does it matter?"

"Because." Mara spoke first. "It mattered to him. He had to be in Ohio right away. So do we."

I turned to my dad. "You're coming?"

"I mean, if you, if you don't mind—I, I don't fly back until—"

"No, that's great," I said. "You might notice something." I turned to Sal. "And you?"

"No chance I'm missing this," he said. "You forget, I'm the world's leading expert on Arthur Louis Pullman." He noticed my father and me staring at him. "Maybe the third leading expert. Besides, you'll need to borrow my car."

He motioned to the back of the parking lot, where only one car sat perfectly illuminated under the streetlight.

I felt a surge through my fingers, adrenaline flaring through every vein. He was pointing to a black, 2012, 323-horsepower Chevy Camaro.

I could feel them all looking at me, but I was alone with the car. It was an exact replica of my own; I saw it on the lot the day that I bought it; I saw it in Portola Valley, diving and gripping the road; I saw it in my dream, crashing and burning down the hill; I saw it in my garage, filling with exhaust.

And now it was in front of me.

"I'll drive," I volunteered without thinking.

"No offense," Sal started, "but that's an expensive—"

"Trust me," I said. "I have to."

Sal studied me for a moment, then pulled the keys from his pocket and handed them to me.

"You sure you're up for it?" Mara asked, letting Sal and my dad crawl into the back seat.

I didn't say anything, just smiled back as I strapped myself into the cockpit and flipped on the engine.

PART NINE.

kent.

1.

AS SOON AS we exited the Chicago area and reached an open passage of Interstate 80, I slammed the accelerator of Sal Hamilton's Camaro to the floor. Mara laughed as her body was thrown against the passenger seat, inertia pushing her backward, momentum pulling her forward at sixty-five, seventy, seventy-five miles per hour. Passing streetlights threw waves of light over me, half smiling and comfortably at home behind the wheel as I shifted into fifth gear, sixth gear, whipping around a bend in the road at eighty, eighty-five, ninety miles per hour, sliding in and out around slower-moving cars like flags in a slalom ski race.

Twice, my father mentioned the speed, and twice, I winked in the rearview.

"Alright," I said. "We need to hear what happened. The whole story. Start forty years ago."

Sal leaned forward from the tiny back seat of the Camaro. "I don't know what you know," he said, wedging his torso between the two front seats. "So I'm gonna assume you know nothing."

I nodded.

"Just to give you some history of the relationship, I know your grandpops because back in the sixties, he used to be a part of this organization—sort of secret anarchy movement—called Great Purpose. You familiar?"

Mara and I nodded.

"*What?* Secret anarch—"

"Dad," I said, finding him in the rearview mirror. "I'm sorry, but there's a lot we didn't know. I'll fill you in, but we've kinda gotta move forward right now."

He looked like he might throw up.

"I mean, it wasn't anything too serious, not at first anyway. Just a bunch of kids, right around your age. This was Vietnam time, so everybody and their mother was scared shitless they were gonna get drafted, and they were starting to think maybe the government wasn't so smart sending our boys over there, but they didn't know what to do about it.

"So Arty n' them, what they'd do is, they'd find a city, go meet the people, give 'em some literature, get 'em all pissed off and excited, and they'd teach 'em how to protest. 'N 'cause it was happening in San Francisco, everyone in Washington'd just say, 'Ah, that's just San Francisco, bunch a fuckin' hippies.' But then, bam. Riot in Denver. Kids on the march in Omaha. Now people are paying attention; phony newspaper guys like me are startin' to give a shit, seems like a revolution is afoot in America. That's what your grandpa did. He started the revolution.

"And these new kids, this Jack—" He pointed to his face. "I don't know what kinda God complex they've got, or what kinda powerful shit they're smoking, callin' themselves Great Purpose and thinkin' they've got something to do with that, but it's bogus. I don't even know how they *know* about all this."

"The leader, Jack," Mara said. I smiled at how disgusted Mara sounded saying his name. "Is Hunter S. Thompson's son."

"Well . . . that makes sense, seeing as his pops was also a royal asshole. Apples and trees. So how I come into the story, how I know your grandpa, is that Arty, being smart, realized these protests were only gonna get as big as the newspapers would say they were. So he decides he needs a newspaperman, somebody with a national circulation, who'll run what he tells him to run. We get introduced at a *Rolling Stone* function, we get blackout drunk, he tells me 'bout what they're doing, and I see this could be mutually beneficial. I tell him I'll print what he wants, but only so long as he promises it's all coming to me first. So I did, and it was the best thing I ever did, too. I ended up gettin' friendly with all the guys—Arty, Johnny, Jeff and Orlo, Duke, when he wasn't off playing God—the whole gang."

I kept nodding at the familiar names.

"Now, late sixties, this thing started to really catch fire. Felt like every day there were five more spots where kids were gettin' riled up, all over; weird cities, too, startin' on their own, even without Arty saying so. Course, Arty 'n' them kept secret through all of this, didn't tell anybody who they were, so's hard to tell what was them 'n' what wasn't. People'd know there was a protest on, but nobody'd know why, or who was behind it. As you can imagine, it all started to get a little . . . mystical, you know? Lots of rumors. Crazy shit."

My dad was staring out the tiny, triangular window in the back seat, his thumb rotating slow circles around his index finger, his eyes closed and his brows creased.

"But, downside of being mysterious: people started asking questions, making connections. All of a sudden, there's rumors about these government groups looking for 'em, pro-war types, Nixon-heads, starting to figure out what's causing all the ruckus, trying to snuff 'em out. As I'm hearin' these things, I realize I'm startin' to hear from 'em less and less. At this point, I'd set Arty up direct with the editor, so he could publish without me, 'n' I wouldn't even see him when he was in town. He was printin' every couple days.

"Then all at once, it just stopped. None of us heard from 'em again. Tried a couple times to get in touch with Arty, but he was off the map. All of 'em were. Five years after that, a book comes out. Arthur Louis Pullman. Tried to get in touch then, say congrats, but I got nothing. Forty years of radio silence."

He let the blackness outside take over the car. It didn't seem right. Not with the path that he'd left behind, not with the way that he'd retraced it before his death, not with the way it tormented him throughout his life. A slow, paranoid, fearful retreat from a life of activism wasn't the kind of thing that forced reliving.

I felt my hand lift from the gearshift; Mara had picked it up, and was running her thumb down my finger. "Where's your ring?" she asked. A streetlight ran light along my hand. As I had left Dr. Patterson's office, the ring had stayed behind. I looked around, but didn't see Kaitlin anywhere. I couldn't feel her either, and my hand didn't feel broken.

All I could see was what was ahead of me out the front windshield.

"So." Sal spoke up from the back seat. "Then, 'bout five years ago, I'm sitting in my office, when I get a call from security at the front. 'Sal, there's some guy in the lobby, he's not talking, just sayin' a couple of names over and over, and one of 'em's yours. You wanna come have a look?' I say sure, come down, and who should it be but my good friend Arthur Louis Pullman, wandering like a fuckin' lost duckling. I say, 'Arty! What the hell, what're you doing in Chicago?' and he doesn't say nothing. That's when I realized he looks bad. I mean, real bad. He's not showered, his clothes are torn up good, and—God, his face. It was just . . ." He checked my father before finishing his sentence. "It was like there was nobody home. He just wasn't there."

Sal's eyes found mine in the rearview, but I knew that it wasn't me he was looking for.

"Did he have anything on him?" I asked.

Sal thought about it for a moment. "Uh, yeah. Come to think of it, he had a little red Bible he kept pulling out.

"So I bring him up to my office, and we have a little chat. Well, no, no, we don't, because he's not saying anything. I'm asking him all these questions, how's life?, how's the family?, what are you doin' in Chicago?, why are your clothes torn up?, and he doesn't answer a single one of them, just keeps looking around, like he's looking for something. Finally, out of nowhere, he asks me if *Lou's* in today."

"Lou Thurman," Mara breathed.

"Exactly. He says Lou Thurman, he's gotta talk to Lou Thurman, and that's when I knew that something was very wrong."

"He was one of your writers, right?" Mara asked. "For the *Tribune*?"

"I think my grandpa knew him," I said.

Sal nodded. "Yeah, kid, your grandpa knew Lou Thurman real well, on account of he *was* Lou Thurman. It was an alias, the one we used back when he needed something published and I was too chickenshit to say it was mine. Ar*thur Lou*is Pull*man*, rearrange that, you've got Lou Thurman. Not even that creative."

Mara squeezed my hand.

"Anyways, I got real worried. I mean, he publishes all of these articles under this fake name, and now here he is, forty years later, straight as an arrow, asking if he can talk to the guy? I tried to tell him, 'Arty, that's you! You were Lou Thurman, don'tcha remember?' But he's just not getting it, so I say, 'How about I get you some of the stuff he wrote?' and he nods. So I dig into our archives and get out all the papers from around that time." Sal slapped a cardboard box sitting next to him. "I even took 'em home for myself, just to see if there was something I was missing, but it's a lot to get through, and most of it makes no goddamn sense. Three years' worth. Arty wrote for us in secret from '67 all the way up to . . ."

"May 1970," I interjected.

"Yeah, sounds about right. But it got confusing, because they had all these articles from him saved that they kept publishing, even after anybody'd heard from him.

"Anyway, he starts reading the papers and sayin' he wishes he could talk to the guy, asking if I know him. At this point, I don't think he even knows who I am, he's just staring out the window like there's something happening out there. It starts getting dark, I start figurin' out what I'm gonna do with him, looking for you guys' number and all, and he looks up at me and says, 'Sal, ya head, can you take us to Ohio? Gotta march across the Midwest, come on, take us to Ohio.'"

I swallowed. "'Us'?"

"Yeah, kid. Us. Multiple people. God fucking knows who he thought he had with him. But I said sure, 'cause at this point I was too curious to say no. So we load up into my Camaro and I start driving him across 80. I ask him, 'Where we going, where in Ohio?' and he just says drive, says he'll know it when we see it.

"So we're driving, and he's not saying anything, just got his head buried in that Bible of his. I keep asking him questions, he keeps just acting like he doesn't hear 'em. All of a sudden, he just pokes his head up from the Bible, says, 'Take this exit,' and then it's 'Turn left here,' and then 'Turn right here,' like he's just picking streets at random, driving through all kinds of little towns.

"At this point, I'm starting to get excited, because it feels like he's got a specific place in mind, somewhere he's gotta get before he kicks it, and I'm thinking he might be leading me to . . . well." Sal lowered his voice. "There is one rumor about your grandpops I've always been a little curious about, 'bouta loada secret writing—"

"It exists?" Mara blurted.

"See, I don't know! Seems a little crazy, but the more I think about it . . . I mean, what else would make a man go so quiet for so long, if it wasn't some secret he didn't want anybody else being a part of? I'm thinking maybe he's got it hidden somewhere, and now that he's knockin' on heaven's door, he's decided it's time to go dig it up. And I'm the guy goin' with him."

The car began to shake as I slid onto rumble strips, easing around construction. "Where did he lead you?" I asked, correcting back onto the road.

Sal cleared his throat. "Uh, nowhere. I realized it after we took a couple of circles; he had no idea where we were going. He was lost . . . in the head, I'm sure you know what I mean. So somehow, we fumble our way into some city—Kent—and he says, 'Pull over, this is my stop.' And he gets out in some parking lot, and I ask him if he needs anything, or wanted me to go with him, he said no, said I'd done enough, and said thank you. And he starts walking off, and I follow for a while, but he's gettin' real agitated about me bein' there, so I give him my cell phone number, tell him to call me when he's ready, and I leave. And that was it."

The car was silent for a full mile.

"That—that was it?" My father spoke for the first time, his voice breaking midsentence.

"Yeah. That was it. I got a room in Kent, 'cause I figured he'd probably need a ride back, called in to work and all, but I didn't hear from him. Then I woke up the next morning, and the news was saying that he was dead."

More silence.

"I know it's terrible to say now, with what happened n' all . . . but I started working on his obituary that night. Before I even heard that he had passed. I just knew, you know? That Arty, he was . . . he wasn't dead, but he was gone."

For what felt like the millionth time on my trip, I imagined my grandpa pulling himself through anonymous, foreign streets that to him were a labyrinth of confusion and regret. I remembered the morning we'd found out, the crass Facebook headline that had told me before my father had, the reality of the world without him.

We sat in silence for what felt like an hour. We'd reached rural Indiana, and there were no other cars to interrupt the empty blackness of the road ahead.

"He was a great man, you know," Sal offered from nowhere, like a consolation prize. "Really good guy. Real tough . . . and—and passionate, too. Loved what he loved."

My dad exhaled loudly, sarcastically, and Sal noticed.

"What? What's that all about?"

"Great, maybe," my dad said. "But passionate? Not for most of his life. I spent forty years watching him give up on his job, his writing, on me, on my mother, on—on everything."

Sal sighed. "You gotta understand—and I can say this because I'm an old man now, and I knew him when—but you gotta understand, there's a difference between not knowing and not caring. Your dad didn't give up, he just—well, he just forgot to keep going."

My father didn't respond, and no one said anything as Indiana passed.

I wondered where he was in his head. In thirty minutes, he'd learned more about his father's history than he had in thirty years. He'd taught himself to stop asking questions by teaching himself to stop caring, and now answers were being dumped on him, answers he probably wasn't sure he even wanted anymore, answers that would just lead to more questions.

But even as resentful and dismissive as he was about it now, there must have been a time when my grandfather was great in his eyes. Even when I was a kid, I remember stories, real stories, moments when he wasn't missing in plain sight. I hoped my father had seen the man that Sal described, brilliant and passionate and loyal. I wished my father and I could have seen him in that way again, just once before he passed. I wished there was some way that twenty-year-old Arthur Louis Pullman could have been preserved—

"Wait."

Everyone looked up at me.

"Open the box of newspapers."

My dad did as I instructed. "What are we looking for?" he

asked. The kaleidoscope behind my eyes clicked into place.

"You said he asked for Lou Thurman, you gave him the articles, *then* he asked for the ride, right?"

"Uh, yeah," Sal said. "Yeah, that's right."

Mara sat up. "Why?"

"Because every newspaper I looked at had an article by Lou Thurman in it." I swallowed. "That's how he was figuring out where to go next, when he couldn't remember. He was communicating with himself. It's like he was following his own bread crumbs, forty years later. And if he found something in one of those that told him to go to Ohio, we can find it, too."

The car became a flurry of newspaper. Mara smiled at me, and I heard my dad mutter "brilliant" under his breath. I smiled, leaning into the accelerator, and we flew faster into the darkness.

2.

may 4, the 2010.

cold evening in
midwest wind like a
wandow i've seen threw before

sal's tribute,
we've been here before.
whare i lost my breath
underessed before myself
in a midwest march
a civilization baried 100 of years ago
& i hear voices in the graund,

music scream siren explode gasp
like applause
whare
perfect black & nothing nite
& i feel these theings
i feel everything & see nothing
cold evening near the

i'm crying but do not know my tears
i'm running but do not know my legs
i want so badly
to know
to bellieve
to see threw the darkness

—*arthur louis pullman*

3.

WE EXITED THE interstate at Ohio State Route 8, near Hudson. In the back seat, Sal mumbled the directions, often just seconds before we got to them. "It's harder in the dark," he complained as we corrected and recorrected, off, then on, then back off another exit ramp.

Mara was cross-legged on the passenger seat with a stack of newspapers up to her belly button, and had been scanning up and down every page with a single finger.

"Left here!"

I jerked left, the back wheels of the Camaro skidding out into the middle of an intersection, Sal flying into my father in the back seat. The rubber found the asphalt, the car shook, and I corrected us back onto Graham Road.

My father had been silent for most of the drive, pulling through copies of the *Tribune*, and announcing every time he found something that might be of interest—like the report of a protest, or the arrest of a protestor, or an article about the Vietnam War. But by the late sixties, we discovered, everything was about the war, and it was impossible to separate what might be relevant from the hundreds of other op-eds and exposés and profiles and conspiracy suggestions the *Tribune* had chosen to run.

It was strange, the way they all talked about Vietnam. It was like it was a profound part of every person writing about it, but it had become so big and mysterious that they could only talk about it in the abstract, like it was an idea. "Ever since the war," "hard to imagine with the war," "divided by the war." No one knew what to say about it, or what was really going on, and still, no person or part of American culture was unaffected by it.

I'd always believed that modern America was incapable of being wrapped up in something so all-consuming; I had figured that the ability to know everything had given us the ability to avoid everything. Thousands of poor teenagers could be dying in a jungle, and images of it could be hitting us faster and more often than ever before, but as long as they were running on a front page or a Twitter feed next to a politician's sex scandal or a Kardashian baby, we'd find ways of avoiding it. I figured being the land of the free had made it difficult to be brave.

But hearing the clips aloud, listening to the headlines as Mara shuffled through them, I realized I might be wrong. The way they talked about Nixon, about the war, about the dissent, it all was strangely reminiscent of the way people talked about the age of Twitter. Abstractions had consumed us again; every celebrity felt the need to speak on "the state of the world these days"; every institution and event had to adjust their mission to account for how "crazy things are right now." Maybe Jack wasn't so far off; maybe there was a war buried just beneath the surface of everyday American life.

"Arthur, can I ask a question?" My dad was folding another *Tribune* over neatly in his lap.

"Um, sure."

"Why are there people who want to hurt you?"

Mara and I exchanged a look. "Well," she answered. "The political group—the one your father was a part of—they've had something of a . . . resurgence, and they believe that your father is still"—I shook my head quickly to stop her—"they believe that your father left something, and they believe they are entitled to it . . . by any means necessary."

"Huh." He clicked his tongue nervously. "And these are the people who—" He pointed to Sal, who nodded. "And now these people know exactly where we're going?"

"Yes," Mara said. "And they have a gun."

"Good to know," my father said.

The streetlights got closer as we entered a town. Kent, Ohio. It looked like every Midwest town, with buildings like hand-me-downs, too big for the businesses that filled them: First National Bank of Kent, Herren-Schempp Supply, Lindy's on Main, all three-story storefronts standing like skyscrapers in the tiny town.

"Take a right—that street right there, past the bank. Keep your eyes open." Sal pointed past a digital clock that read 11:35. We were the only headlights on the road.

My dad sat up. "What are we even looking for?"

"Anything Grandpa would have noticed," I said, scanning

the area as I slowed to twenty-five miles per hour. "Anything he would have wanted us to see."

The buildings began to thin and disappear, farther from the road. A sign told us that the speed limit was fifteen miles per hour.

"Things that might have been there a long time ago, also," Mara added. "Back when he was first making this trip. He must have had a reason for coming to this spot."

Sal pointed ahead. "That was it. That's the parking lot. That's where I dropped him."

The lot was remote. A single streetlight hung over it, the only light in the area. From what I could tell, we were in a park of some kind, with wide stretches of open grass extending from all four sides of the concrete. Walkways cut across it, twisting and curving out from the lot like endless veins, disappearing into darkness. In the distance, buildings surrounded the grass, covered in dozens of perfect square windows; offices, or apartments, I imagined.

There was one other car in the lot, a Ford Explorer parked directly in the center.

"Is that his car?" I asked, but Mara didn't answer. No one said anything, and I felt our collective breath get deeper and slower as I parked next to it.

"What do you think?" Mara asked as soon as we were out of the car and watching the two older men pull themselves from the back seat. "About Sal's story?"

"What about it?"

"Do you think," she said, turning to make sure I was the only one who could hear, "that it sounds like a man with Alzheimer's?"

"Or?"

"Or . . . like a man pretending to have Alzheimer's?"

"Jesus, Mara."

"Think about it, Arthur," she said. "Really think about it. He led a car from Chicago to Ohio to exactly this spot, got out, and no one saw him again until he turned up dead the next day. *Supposedly.* Even though no one can prove that. If you were going to fake your own death, can you imagine—"

"Um, I'm sorry."

Her insistence had forced her voice too loud. My father's face hovered a few feet behind her, completely blank. "Did you say . . . faked his death?"

"No." Mara tried to recover. "No, that's—that's not what I think. That's—that's—"

"It's just this crazy theory," I said, taking a step toward him. "Some people, crazy people, they think he was faking his Alzheimer's, just so he could, I don't know, make a clean getaway, and go live in peace with some buried treasure. It's all ridiculous."

I had to strain to hear him. "They—they think he's alive?"

"Yeah, but that's just Jack. He doesn't know anything. I mean, he was *confirmed* dead, right? You saw him dead . . . right?"

With barely any movement, my dad shook his head. "No, they . . . they just sent me the ashes. I never saw him."

"Yeah, but . . ." Now it was my turn for disbelief. My dry throat cracked. "It was from a hospital. The hospital called you?"

My dad could barely speak. "I—I think so. I thought so. I don't know."

"Well." Sal leaned against the Camaro casually, like a spectator. "*Now* what are we looking for?"

Mara took charge. "We'll split up. You and I"—she pointed to Sal—"we'll each take an Arthur Louis Pullman with us. If you find anything, you text us. If you see Jack, or any of them . . ." She paused, and all four of us looked around. "Then shout."

I looked at my father. He was still reeling. I'd never seen him so unsure of himself. Our eyes locked, and he gave me a feeble smile. "At least take Sal's phone. So I can get ahold of you if . . . so I can get ahold of you."

I nodded in return, took the phone, and followed Mara to one of the concrete walkways.

"Should we really be out here in the middle of the . . ." The wind carried my father's whisper all the way to my ears, fading into silence as we moved in opposite directions.

Our footsteps felt dangerously loud, and I began to breathe in rhythm with them, in and out through my nose. The farther we walked, the more it felt like the darkness would never end, like we were on the very edge of the world, and moving past the parking lot was just moving out into the infinite nothing. Occasionally, we'd hear a noise—a branch falling, a car starting, grass colliding with grass—and Mara would jump, spin, and settle herself with a single breath.

We passed another empty parking lot, this one with no light to offer us. Past it were the buildings that had been in the distance, and we tiptoed around them, aware of all the places someone could be hiding. They were all surrounded by bushes, dressed up and professionally maintained. There were signs in front of some of the buildings, but they were too far from the sidewalk to make out in the dark.

"What is this place?" she whispered once we were a few hundred feet from the streetlight. "I can't make out what any of these buildings are. They seem . . . almost like . . ."

"I tried to kill myself."

The words were out of my mouth before I felt myself speaking.

"I'm sorry?" Mara hesitantly turned to me. "Did you say—"

"A couple weeks ago. After I punched that wall, they pulled my scholarship so I couldn't go to UCLA. And my girlfriend hated me so much that she fucked somebody else, and . . . a year ago, I remember thinking, *This is it, I've got everything I ever wanted, because I earned it,* and then all of a sudden, all of it was gone. And I didn't have anything to look forward to, or even anything to *do*; I was just . . . nobody. So I started my car, in my garage, and I-I sat there. I didn't move." I took a deep breath. "I'm on suicide watch. That's why my dad's been so weird . . . and that's why the police are so serious with me. That's why I get those dreams about . . . It's because I tried to kill myself."

The lines on her face didn't move as she listened with her mouth hanging half open.

"I, I don't really know why I just told you that. I'm sorry for, for putting that on you. It's stupid, and really, really fucking embarrassing, and, and I don't really wanna talk about it, or anything, I just . . . I guess I needed to tell somebody. To tell you. I needed to tell you. I'm sorry."

Mara studied me without moving. "Did you . . . did you want to die?"

"I didn't." I swallowed. "I don't know, I didn't decide anything. I just didn't have a reason to move."

A tremor crossed Mara's tiny face, but her expression held, fighting pity or disgust or confusion or whatever it was she was feeling.

"I don't actually send any postcards," she said finally, her voice wavering.

"What?"

"The postcards I write to my dad? They're not going to anyone. Leila used to send them, but after she died, he stopped speaking to me. Two years, and I haven't heard anything from him. I think he sees me as part of this thing, this country, or . . . this stupid, naive idealism that killed her, so . . . I just write them. And pretend like they're going to someone who would care where I am."

I watched her shift uncomfortably in front of me. She didn't look at me while she spoke, instead kicking the cracks in the concrete between us. We were the farthest we'd been from any light, but I felt like I could see her the clearest, complete with the rips in the corners of her picture-perfect postcard.

"Do you feel better? Since your . . . Are you feeling better?" she asked, using the end of her jacket sleeve to wipe her cheek clean.

"I don't really know what that means."

She nodded but didn't look away from me, so I kept going.

"I think, if I was sitting in my car right now, I would try to get out."

Without a beat or a warning or even a change of expression, Mara launched herself across the pavement and latched on to my neck, and for a moment, I was blinded by everything about her. The skin of her cheek was soft against mine, with warm life below it pulsing heat. I finally placed her smell; it was a candle, one I'd kept in my room when I was a kid, a Vanilla Wood-Fire that had burned through to the bottom in three days, but I kept relighting the recycled wax because it just smelled more and more like a fire. I could hear her nose over my right shoulder, a calm inhale and a sputtered "I'm sorry," and for a second, she was the only thing that really existed; no trains or poems or clues or coincidences, no Jacks or Sals or phone calls from parents, no hallucinations of ex-girlfriends or cars in garages, no pain or danger or shame or disappointment, because in her world, those things didn't exist; in her world, everything was ashes and vanilla and warm skin. I wasn't feeling nothing; I was feeling everything.

"We're all ruined," she whispered against my ear. "Everybody's ruined."

Sal's phone buzzed and the real world came back. Mara

uncoiled herself from my neck, but stayed a foot away. I held my shirt to block the light and read a text from my dad:

nothing here, heard voices. meet back at the car NOW. BE CAREFUL

Mara read it over my shoulder and looked back in the direction we'd come.

I shook my head. "Not yet."

She didn't protest.

We continued slowly down the walkways, now navigating between more buildings than grass.

"Over there, I see them—" the wind whispered, but I pretended I didn't hear it.

"I can hear their foosteps—" I ignored it.

"Quick, somebody get out and shoot them—"

Mara didn't react. The voices were in my head.

We turned the corner and the largest grass field yet opened in front of us. It was ink black, and looked to be in a small valley, giving way to a tall, forested hill on the other side.

"Actually," Mara said softly, "I think we're at a uni. A campus."

Across the grass field, a stone threw light in my direction, then disappeared.

Without thinking, I turned toward it, stuck on the darkness where the light had just been. Automatically, I began to walk.

"Where are you going?"

I didn't turn around.

all i remember in the whirlwind was running.
running nowhere,
running because it was the only thing i could think to do
& i knew that i wanted to be anywhere but where i was.

& i found you, & nothing else existed.
your arms were so weak in mine, your hand could barely
clasp.
you had three breaths left & you gave them all to me.

you said,
keep going.
you said,
i'll be waiting for you.

bullets are tiny.
those who fire bullets are tiny.
but you, you are big. you are so big.
you are the sun, the source of all light that i've ever seen.
you are so much bigger than today.
you are so much bigger than a bullet.
you are so much bigger than death.

some days are best left in the distant past, so far away &
behind that they can never be viewed again.
no part of today, or who i was today, will be any part of
tomorrow.

but someday, i'll make it back,
& i pray you'll still be waiting.

—*arthur louis pullman*

5.

THE KENT STATE massacre. May 4, 1970. The lives of five students were taken when the National Guard opened fire on a group of peaceful protestors, the first time in American history that the government has knowingly executed its citizens for practicing their First Amendment rights.

There was no light around us, just traces of moonlight through the trees.

The long, open quad created a funnel for wind to whistle directly to the clearing where we stood. Leaves brushed across the sign, the monument, the bell at the bottom of the hill and the statues at the top of it.

"Do you . . . do you think . . ." Mara was breathless. "This protest . . ."

I nodded.

"Five . . . five people died."

I nodded again.

"And he was there. He watched five people . . . he watched what *he did* get five people killed."

I didn't say anything.

"Do you think that's why . . . he had to come back? Because he watched someone die?"

"It wasn't just someone."

I nodded to a smaller stone behind the memorial, inscribed with the names of the deceased. The first name on the list:

Jeffery Kopek.

The weight of my grandfather's life, both hidden and apparent, his trauma and loss and loneliness and disease, crashed onto both of us. At once, it made sense.

Jeffery was the protagonist of his novel. Jeffery was the hero of his Green River short story. Jeffery Kopek was the name next to my grandpa's on the wall in Denver. Jeffery Kopek was Sue's son, for whom my grandpa had been responsible.

Jeffery Kopek had been more than a passing character in my grandpa's life. He had *been* my grandpa's life. When my grandpa wrote of great love, and great loss, great guilt and great pain, his great angel, finding what he was looking for, and letting it go, and making it back, it was Jeffery that he was writing about.

And my grandpa had watched him die.

I remembered Dr. Patterson's description of trauma: the internal forgetting, the way our brains choose to block the things they couldn't bear to remember. My grandpa hadn't just forgotten Jeffery dying; he'd forgotten Jeffery's existence, Great Purpose, his train trips, and his friends along the way. He'd forgotten everything, left it behind in a novel, and started a new life. But it never left him.

"Do you think when he said 'my great angel'—"

I nodded.

Mara sniveled loudly, holding herself together and squeezing tears back into her eyes. I put my arm around her and pulled her closer to me. She was warm, and her hair clung statically to my jacket. "'Full speed to you.' This was who he was looking for." I paused for a moment. "This is who he was writing to."

She squeezed my chest. "Are you okay?"

I thought about the question.

This was the answer I'd been searching for, and I knew, face-to-face with the monument, that it was the only answer. There wasn't a prize at the end of the maze. It hadn't been a puzzle, set up to reward me for being brave enough to follow my grandfather's clues; they hadn't even been clues. They led to nothing but a terrible realization, a cry mourning the loss of a person and a love that I could have gone my entire life without ever knowing existed.

When I thought he had been writing to me, he hadn't—he'd been writing to Jeffery. When I thought he was describing a great treasure, he wasn't—he was chasing a memory, something that was forty years behind him.

And still, I felt full.

"Because this is what he wanted," I said, and I knew it was true, whether he knew it or not. I thought about Dr. Patterson's assurance: *It's time to remember now.*

I pulled the small red Bible from Omaha from my bag and set it atop the stone memorial. Mara smiled back at me, light reflecting off one damp circle below her left eye. I looked out over the field, and imagined it flooded with students, eager to change the world. I imagined my grandpa, standing atop the hill where I stood now, looking down across the beautiful resistance that he had created; the movement that he had built. I imagined his terror and his guilt as the National Guard showed up, his steel-willed activists looking like children next to the barrels of the soldiers' guns. I imagined him screaming as the bullets began, running across the field to find Jeffery, holding him as life left him.

"I wonder if this is where he died," I said. "In the same spot where he saw Jeffery . . ." His words filled my head. *The world is a circle, and what I thought was ahead of me is actually behind . . .*

"Oh, this is too perfect."

The voice wasn't Mara's or mine.

"Okay, both of you, drop the backpack, hands on heads."

Fifteen feet behind us, Jack stood tall against the side of the hill. It was too dark to see details of his figure, but it looked like the white Great Purpose scarf was his only non-black clothing; a beanie was folded up over his forehead, just above his eyes, and his right hand fidgeted anxiously, a metallic surface catching and reflecting distant streetlights. He was holding a gun. And he was alone.

"I knew it was just gonna be the three of us." He took a few casual steps up the hill toward us. "I knew. Right when I met you, I knew." He stopped less than ten feet away. "With or without each other, we were gonna end up here together. Like a . . . sign. From the divine. Right? The prodigal sons; isn't that how the story's supposed to go?"

We were close enough to see the lines of his face, balanced and dangerously casual as his right wrist twirled and twisted absentmindedly, and his head twisted with it.

"Well, truthfully, I didn't see it *just* like this. I knew it'd be the two of us. You—" He nodded to Mara. "You're just . . . what? Yoko?" He rolled his head around to smile past me. "Was that the game? Play both of us, stick with whoever gets here faster? I mean, I trust you told our dear friend Arty here about us, right?"

He motioned toward me with the gun and I felt its impact twice: the threat of the deadly weapon in front of me; the woozy heat of jealousy from behind me. I wanted to turn my head back to her, but I couldn't take my eyes away from Jack's right hand.

"Arthur, he's lying." Mara's voice stumbled frantically from behind me. "I swear I—"

"Oh, Jesus, Mara. Relax. This isn't about you. We have more important things going on, don't we, Arthur?" He used his left hand to straighten his scarf, glanced to the monument behind us, and then found my eyes in the dark. "Where is he?"

For a moment, with the overwhelming presence of Jack and the gun, I'd forgotten where we were standing, and why we were all there. Jack still thought my grandpa was alive. My face must have broken; my eyebrows must have lifted; my cheeks must have filled with a terrified almost-laugh, because Jack's lips curled and he raised the gun to Mara's chest.

"He's dead," I told him.

"Arthur." He made a show of clicking something into place behind the trigger; removing the safety, I assumed. "Now is not the time for being shy, or cute. Where is he?"

"I'm not lying to you," I said, trying to balance my voice. "He's dead."

He paused, scratching his head with the butt of the gun, then smiled. "Do you know who Sir Kay was?" He waited for a response, but I ignored him. "Of course you don't. Don't feel bad about it; no one does." He took a step toward me. "He was a knight; sat at the Round Table; supposedly he was a legend on the battlefield. No one remembers him, though, because the most famous thing he ever did was be the last person to try removing Excalibur from the stone before King Arthur." He took another, longer step toward me. "If you think lying to me will prevent me from claiming what's mine"—he took another step—"you're wrong. If you think"—another step—"this is a negotiation, you're wrong. If you think there's any way I don't already know—"

"You couldn't figure this out?" I cut him off. It was strangely peaceful in my chest. *We're all on death row*, I thought. *Some of us just have a schedule.* "You don't get why this spot might have mattered?"

"I'm familiar with the fucking Kent State massacre. I'm Hunter S. Thompson's son, for fuck's sake." I heard the first waver in his voice, noticed the way that *fuck* had timidly slipped its way into his vocabulary. "You still don't get it. This is my whole life. You can pretend you know something about this but . . . I fully comprehend why he may have chosen this spot, I know exactly what he was doing here; the only thing—the *only* thing—you know, and I don't, is *where.*" He stared me down, but I held my ground, eye to eye on equal footing. "So tell me. Or I will shoot her. And that'll be on you, not me. I wouldn't want to have to live with that, if I were you."

I raised myself by an inch, and smiled. "Where are your friends, Jack?"

He didn't respond, but took another step.

"Supposedly righteous force," I continued. "Threatening violence against innocent people?" I jerked my head back toward the KENT STATE SHOOTING plaque. "You've gotta be able to appreciate the irony of this, right?"

This time, he didn't smile back. "I'm a patient guy, but—"

"There's nothing." I shook my head. "I told you. I've told you everything I know, actually. There's no secret hiding place, no library, no—"

"Bullshit!" It was the first time he'd raised his voice, but rather than sliding upward to a scream, it fell downward, booming across the lawn and nearly ringing the bell below us. "That's bullshit and you know it!"

"It's not bullshit. There's nothing."

He shifted the gun from Mara's chest to mine. "Say it again."

"There's nothing."

The gun shook once in his hand.

"Look." I spoke quietly. "You don't have to believe me. You can go ahead and keep looking. I hope you do, actually. Because when *you* look back in forty years and realize you wasted your entire life searching for something that was already gone, it'll actually be a *fair* punishment for you."

His eyes dropped to the ground, and the gun dropped from my chest as the wrist and elbow holding it went slack. He took a step back from me.

I took the chance to step up into him, building steam with every word. "But I'm not lying to you. There's nothing here, other than the last chapter in the story of a guy whose life was ruined"—I raised a finger and held it to his chest—"because people like you decided to answer some fucking call, for them."

Jack didn't lift his head, instead swinging it loosely back and forth, shaking. "There's more than that."

"Jack, you're wrong," Mara said.

"There's something else here—"

I felt her hand against the small of my back. "Time to let it go now."

"He left something for me," he said quietly, rolling his head around to come face-to-face with me again, and my stomach dropped.

"He . . . as in Hunter Thompson?" I could feel my strength coming back as Jack's wavered.

It was as if the color had left his skin, and the fire behind his eyes had died. "She told me, he left this for me. He wanted me to—"

"He probably wasn't even your dad, Jack."

Jack stood unraveled in front of us, an unassured and

abandoned boy where a confident man had once been, the gun dangling recklessly from his right hand, running up the side of his body, alongside the Great Purpose scarf.

A blue light scanned the field, breaking only against the outline of Jack's figure, and with it came loud voices and the slamming of car doors. My father must have seen us. Someone must have called the police.

"This is it, Jack. This is all there is."

"There was supposed to be something for me," he said, unaffected by the world closing in behind him. He stopped the gun as it reached his heart, where the Great Purpose logo, the bold, black-and-green fist of his father was embroidered, and rotated the barrel. "There was supposed to be more."

I saw what was happening a moment too late, too scared to notice his hand squeezing the handle, his finger sliding around the trigger, his eyes deciding to stop fighting back, and his face mirroring the look I'd seen on my own in every dream, the empty acceptance I wore in the driver's seat as I sank to the bottom of the lake.

I threw myself against him. I felt the ripple and recoil of the machinery as I fell forward against his arm and threw both of us backward, red exploding before my eyes as we collapsed and began to roll down the hill.

The sound of the gunshot was so loud that the rest of the sound in the world disappeared in its wake; Mara's scream was watery and distant; the sirens were inaudible. I couldn't tell what I was feeling around me, the wet leaves of the ground intertwined with the wet blood on his chest, the warmth of his body molding with the warmth of my own. He wasn't moving, and I didn't want to see what I knew was waiting for me, so I held my eyes closed and laid my head back onto the grass.

Noises began to filter back in; I heard the sirens droning up from the ground. I heard the voice of my father calling out for me. I heard the voice of my grandpa, swimming through the chaos, at once clear enough for me to understand, and finally, the ringing of the bell, reverberating across the grounds as I lay in the wet dark, the edges of my vision collapsing into blackness.

6.

THE LIGHT CAME back, just as it always does.

They told me I'd been in shock, which was why I'd just lain out-of-body in the dark. They gave me a jumbo Snickers bar and a can of regular Coke to get my blood sugar up.

We watched as Jack was loaded into an ambulance, the monitor attached to his heart letting us know that he was still breathing, and then followed in Sal Hamilton's Camaro to the hospital, stretching ourselves across the blue-green chairs of the half-lit waiting room. After a loose explanation of what had happened, Mara and I were both silent. Instead, I focused on walking, and breathing, and avoiding my father's mournful glances.

"The protest," I said finally, and all three heads looked up. "At Kent State. Jeffery, he was . . ."

I couldn't finish the sentence, but Sal shook his head. "I don't know how I didn't realize it. I mean, we heard what happened, everybody did, but I didn't know Jeffery Kopek was . . . No wonder we never heard from them again."

I leaned back in my chair. "My grandpa blocked it all out."

Sal nodded sadly. "Trauma's a hell of a drug."

"I found the article," my father said quietly, unfolding a newspaper from his back pocket. "While we were waiting for you." He slowly pulled himself across the room to drop it on the table in front of me. "It's called 'OHIO: Our Final Stand.' He sent all those kids to Ohio. He organized the protest. That's how we knew about the monument."

I nodded. "I figured something else out, too." I closed my eyes, hiding from the dim light of the room.

"What?"

"I've spent this entire time thinking that Sue Kopek was reliving my grandfather's trip to see her five years ago. But she kept asking about Orlo, and Orlo would have been long dead by then."

"Why would that—" Mara started.

"It's the same reason she kept calling me 'Arthur' and my grandpa 'him.' She didn't think I was my grandpa in his old age, she thought I was Arthur in his twenties. She wasn't reliving what happened in 2010, she was reliving when my grandpa and Jeffery and Orlo left in 1970. They were supposed to come back after the protest in Kent. And that matters, because she'd set up the placement of the chairs, sent those invitations . . ."

Mara solved the mystery before I could finish. "They were getting married. Arthur and Jeffery."

The information hung in the silence of the room, too sad to be touched. I closed my eyes, deciding I wasn't quite ready to face the world yet.

"He was gay?" Sal asked, too loud for the room.

I looked to my father. His head shook slowly, involuntary, as he stumbled, "I . . . yeah, I . . . I didn't know if he ever really loved her." He paused. "Us."

In the empty space, I thought about Kaitlin, and the moments when I'd loved her, needed her, the most; then I thought about losing her. It had been three weeks and I still felt it every time I breathed. My grandfather had buried his love, and his pain, for forty years, and built a new life on top of it. It was no wonder he'd become detached. It was no wonder he'd rushed to forget.

"He did love you guys," Sal said unconvincingly. "I just know he did."

I remembered the letter in my backpack, the one he'd written Henry on the night of my birth. "He did," I told my dad, and when I said it, I think he believed me.

"Excuse me," a nurse said, hovering in the doorway. "Are you Arthur Louis Pullman?"

"Yes," I said in unison with my father. He had returned to the corner, as far from everyone else as possible.

"We're both Arthur Louis Pullman," I said. "Do you know if . . ." I nodded toward the hallway where the ambulance had raced Jack.

"Yes," she said. "He'll be fine, it just caught his stomach. Relatively minor, considering. If you'd like to press charges, we're sending someone—"

"No," I said immediately.

"Arthur." My father sat up. "He pointed a gun at you." Sal leaned in behind him, the wounds on his face still visible.

"He doesn't need to get arrested."

"Sure he does." Sal snorted. "He should be in jail."

"Sometimes, people need to be punished," my father said. "It's good for them. It'll teach him to think twice about using a gun like that in the future. Sometimes"—he lowered his voice, below where Mara could hear it—"the only way to make people appreciate what they have is to take it away."

He was talking about Kaitlin. He was talking about the restraining order.

I thought about where I was sitting, upright and unwounded, in a hospital with my father. I wasn't in a jail cell in Chicago or Palo Alto or Albuquerque, serving time for disorderly conduct or assaulting a police officer. I thought about the closure I got to have with my grandfather, and the years I'd gotten to know him. I'd been lucky. My whole life, my whole week, I'd been lucky.

Then I thought about Jack, lying one room over in a hospital bed, without any of that. From the moment I met him, he'd been under attack. It was the police, it was corporations, it was Mara, it was me—the world challenged, and he stood his ground, fearless in his belief.

But now I didn't even know if he'd have that. He'd probably have to force himself to unlearn everything he thought he knew about his father, his path, and his place in the world. He'd probably have to create an image for his actual father, not a literary icon at all, but just a man; a man who never showed up for his son.

Jack's stamp, *his* symbol, was still permanently pressed to the top of the journals. Without his stamp, I realized, none of this would have been possible. The Melbourne Hostel would've closed before I could get there. The back room of the Omaha Library would've fallen into disrepair. Without the stamp, there would've been no reason for Mara to cross my path. Without Jack, most of my grandfather's life would still be a mystery.

"No," I said again, more resolutely. "No, he's . . . He should get a second chance."

Sal sat back down, unsure.

I heard the nurse swallow. "I actually came to talk to you about something else."

Everyone around the room shifted uncomfortably.

"My name is Mary, and I—I think I've seen you. On the news, right?" She was speaking to me quickly, as if someone might be listening. "You're the one searching for his dead grandfather?"

I nodded again, too tired to feel pride or shame or worry. "Look, if you think I stole—"

"No, not that," Mary said, and nodded several times. There wasn't enough light to read her expression, and she hovered by the door. "I—I was here, the night the ambulance brought him in. Your grandfather. I was the attending nurse. I was there when he died."

I sat up against the back of my chair. "You were? What, uh, what did he say?" I noticed she was holding a small plastic box in front of her.

She shook her head. "Almost nothing. We get a lot of people like him, you know, people who were there, at the shooting. On the anniversaries, especially. It was a traumatic event."

I nodded, and she didn't say anything, just stood swaying several feet inside of the doorway.

"Well, thank you for . . . for taking care of—"

"Arthur?" she interrupted me.

"Yeah?"

"I know it's strange to say. But I wasn't surprised when I saw you on the news."

Everyone in the room sat forward, listening.

She closed her eyes. "I always knew someone was going to come for him. He told me someone would. He said someone was waiting for him."

We didn't say anything, surrendering to the soft beeps of the hospital around us.

"Anyway, I just wanted to leave his personal effects with you. No one ever came to collect them after he died, so they've just been sitting here, waiting for you."

She set the plastic box on the coffee table in front of me and quickly left the room without a good-bye.

I smiled.

There was only one item, a single possession that he'd carried straight through until he died. I'd seen it in his hands a million times, everywhere he went. I'd seen him constantly poring back over its pages, flipping forward and backward, never sharing it, always keeping it close to his heart. Its soft, red jacket was so faded it was barely readable anymore:

King James Bible, 6th Edition, 1962.

I held it up to my dad. "Well," I said, "at least he died with what he loved."

Mara stood up, gently touching my leg. "I'm getting coffee. Take a minute with it, will you?"

Sal patted me on the shoulder as he followed. "You should read it, you know," he said of the Bible. "Might learn a thing or two."

I smirked back and watched them leave, holding up the Bible and running my hands over it. I felt close to him, as if he'd just reached through time and space to hand it to me. I thumbed the pages, feeling the creases and the surprisingly thick paper.

My dad sat down next to me and put an arm on my shoulder and smiled down at the Bible. For as important as it was to me, it must have been more important to my father.

Finding the middle, I closed my eyes and opened it, hoping it would fall perfectly on the fourth and fifth chapters of Corinthians, so I would know that my grandpa was watching.

But I didn't land on Corinthians. There was no typed text on the page; just lines and lines of scribbled cursive.

"What is that?" my father asked. "Did he . . . did he write in the Bible?"

I flipped backward, and it was more of the same. I tore through page after page of hesitant cursive, occasionally falling on ripped pages. The number of them overwhelmed me; page after page, some completely full and others with only a few lines. I opened it to the very first page . . . *april 29, the 1970.*

"It's not a Bible." I ran my hand over it. "It's a journal."

My dad looked back and forth from the Bible to me and back again, his eyes widening.

"It goes all the way back to 1970," I told him. "This trip, the one he was reliving, the one that ended in . . . He wrote the whole thing."

"He brought that Bible everywhere," my dad breathed. "He was carrying around a journal. And reading it—"

"He was rereading his own story," I said. "He was reliving the parts he forgot."

I set it on the table in front of us, closed. My dad was holding his breath, staring nervously, unsure if he wanted to open it or not, and I could understand why. It was almost too much: all the answers we'd wanted tucked neatly between two faded covers and now presented to us. What if he wasn't who we thought he was? What if we were in there? What if this changed things?

But my dad had a different question. "Where do we start?"

I swallowed and nodded and flipped it open to the last page. The final entry was dated *may 4, the 2010* . . . the day that he died.

I imagined him sitting alone at Kent State, under the bell
where I'd just been, and writing for the last time.

7.

may 4, the 2010.

i always imagined, when i died,
i'd want to think about every secand
of my life
except the one i was in.

i imagine some dying people hold tight to their memary,
view single slides of a life lived,
weigh regrets & accomplishments like stones on a scale,
polish medals & paint over scars,
in anticapation of the Great judgment.

i imagine others fret the Great transation,
realizing they're finally cornered
by the questions they spent their human lives avoiding,
consumed by a fear of heaven
& abyss & reincarnation & dirt.

but i'm not doing that.

cold bell dirt arthur,
i'm just saying my own name.

arthur.
i'm saying my own name
arthur.
& i'm reminded that i exist.

i spant sixty years watching a past that never happened.
i spant sixty years chasing a future that never came.

i spant sixty years
thinking your voice was over the mountain,
but it was with me all along.
you were here all along,
waiting,
unseen.

& now, in my final moment,
i'm here too.
finally awake,
i can finally see,
& finally,
we are eternal.

—*arthur louis pullman*

THE EPILOGUE.

time remembered.

may 6, the 2015.

there are pieces of me that i'm learning to question & parts of my past that i'm learning to rewrite. i started a journal again, without the capital letters, which feels like an appropriate tribute. maybe it is worth it to think about how you feel sometimes. maybe i could do well with the therapy. maybe it's not a weakness to give parts of yourself to other people.

"you're in an interesting position, you know?" mara told me after the police had left & the dust had settled & it was just the two of us, left with the journal my grandpa had left behind.

"i know," i said. "but i don't know what you're talking about specifically."

"there are people who believe your grandfather to be a god, & those who believe him to be a complete asshole. communities that worship him, professors that teach him, family members that despise him. you are in sole possession of the only remaining piece of his legacy, & so, it seems, you are in sole possession of this decision."

"decision?" i asked her. "what am i deciding?"

she smiled, like she'd just seen a face once loved & lost & now found once more.

"how he's remembered," she said, & the wind took over.

kent, ohio, air is crisp when the seasons start to turn, just enough chill to remind you of where you've been, & just enough sun to show you all that you have to look forward to. punxsutawney phil saw his shadow in 2015, the tricky bastard, promising six extra weeks of winter. the six weeks had turned into sixteen & kent, ohio, was just starting to look like spring.

"well, i've made my decision," i told her.

"you have?"

"his legacy is & forever shall be"—i held it up to read—"'the people he met & the things they carried.'"

she didn't understand. "i appreciate the poetry, but i'm afraid the substance is . . ."

"he wasn't writing for a big audience, & he wasn't writing in the abstract. he wasn't telling stories that he wasn't a part of. & you were right all along, he wasn't writing for me. he was writing to them.

"henry needed a companion; my grandpa wrote him one. the letters, every year, his whole life, something to look forward to, someone to believe in.

"the bar in green river needed a train full of gold, & so he wrote about it in fiction, but in reality, i'd imagine the sale of an arthur louis pullman short story could probably buy you the entire town of green river.

"& sue kopek, she . . . she needed something to help her remember who she is, & he reminded her. he wrote for those people."

"so you're giving them back, then?"

i nodded.

"every last one?"

i nodded again.

"except for the journal with dozens of additional works that doesn't really have a home other than with you."

it was my turn to smile.

i'd made that decision as well. my family needed closure; my dad needed something to help him remember the best parts of his dad. more than that, the world needed a reminder of what an incredible writer my grandfather had been, & the fortieth anniversary of *a world away* seemed like the perfect opportunity.

"you're sure?" my father had asked.

"yes, i'm sure."

"because we don't have to. i don't want to bruise the legacy he left behind."

"no, you're right," i told him. "& you were right before we found the journal, too. he deserves to be remembered."

mara & i sat for hours watching the students of kent state as we read & reread the journal entries.

"this one," i told her, holding up the poem from denver, his confession & process & understanding of love. his ode to his breath & warmth & color. "this one doesn't really have a home, because jeffery's not here to take it anymore, so . . . well, you better."

"you—you're serious about this?" i couldn't tell for sure, but as i nodded i thought i saw a glimmer of liquid in the corner of her left eye, an overwhelmed, involuntary thank-you.

on may sixth, i began rewriting the pieces of my past that i didn't want to carry with me anymore. i'm sure a day will come when i'm reminded of how reality tells the story, but for now, & for the foreseeable future, i like how i remember it better.

mara told me she was going back to denver, back to great purpose, to help them rebuild without jack. i thought she might stick around, or come back to california, & i got mad when she first told me we'd "still see each other sometimes." but i realized that mara's life is about mara, not about me, & mara needed something to chase. mara needed a place to belong, & i could be happy with sometimes.

i wrote a letter to mason from the hospital, because i was mad at myself, & he got caught in the cross fire, & no one deserves to carry the guilt of another's person's self-hatred. i'd write to kaitlin, too, but i'm not ready for that just yet. also, it's illegal.

"you know what is interesting to me?" mara had mused as she flipped page to page through my grandfather's diary of time he'd forgotten. "he made almost no grammatical errors, other than of course the blatant disregard for the rules of proper cap-italization, & other than excessive use of the letter 'a,' almost no spelling errors—"

"yeah, i think he was neurotic."

"—*except*, in this little bit here, that he wrote on his last day." she opened to *may 4, the 2010*. "look, here, he misspelled the word 'things.'"

i followed her finger to the word. she was right, he'd acciden-tally slipped an extra *e* into the word, now spelled *theings*.

"well, he was literally dying," i said. "i think we can let him off the hook. maybe his hand slipped & he didn't want to spend his final breath spell-checking his work."

"i know, i know, i know. i'm just saying, it's weird, right?"

i couldn't deny her enthusiasm for even the mundane, & so again, as it had so often, her wave washed over me. "yes, it is weird."

i didn't have anywhere i wanted to go or anywhere else that i wanted to be, so i began to read again. with my thumbs, i smoothed the creases at the edges of his pages, where his world stopped & everyone else's began. next to me, mara's head tumbled to my shoulder, asleep.

i read each word, equally important, intricately linked & inextricable, a machine moving & bending & chugging & swaying together down the page:

whare i lost my breath
underessed before myself—

it stopped me. the first time, i had read it as *underdressed*, but i realized that i had been reading too quickly, my brain seeing the letters & drawing a conclusion before it had a chance to actually notice their arrangement.

the word he'd written, *underessed*, was closer to *undressed*, a word that made more sense in structure of the sentence. but he'd accidentally added an *e*. two spelling mistakes in the same journal entry was certainly strange.

without pointing it out to mara, i continued reading:

in a midwest march
a civilization baried 100 of years ago
& i hear voices in the graund,
music scream siren explode gasp
like applause
whare

perfect black & nothing nite
& i feel these theings—

through the spelling error she'd noticed.

i feel everything & see nothing
cold evening near the
i'm crying but do not know my tears
i'm running but do not know my legs
i want so badly
to know
to bellieve—

i stopped. again, my brain had let me slide past another error. he'd accidentally slipped another *l* into *bellieved.*

coincidence will be the source of your greatest irrationality, mara had said, quoting someone. she was right, & dwelling on disconnected, totally irrelevant—

focus on the moments of difference; those are the ones that matter. that voice was louder. it was my grandfather's.

underessed.
theings.
bellieved.

undressed.
things.
believe.

believe undressed things? things undressed believe?

it was tricky, reading the words as they were & not as my brain wanted them to be. in my head, i wanted to fix the mistakes.

slowly, carefully, i wrote them again, just the errors:

under
the
bell

my heart stopped & the world of kent, ohio, & mara & my parents & kaitlin & trains & doctors stopped spinning.

under the bell.

holy shit.

the kent state victory bell had begun the protest, the bell that the students had rallied around following the shooting, the bell that had become memorialized as a testament to their will, a bell rung in remembrance of the lives lost & hope for future

generations. i craned my head around & inside of it were markings . . . letters in the bell.

here's mara, transcribing:

l

i

a

n

t

&

l

o

y

a

l

c

o

n

d

u

c

t

o

r

t

h

a

t
s
a
l
l
f
r
o
m
y
o
u
r
b
r
i
l

maybe there was more, all along, & i just had to stop looking to find it. or maybe it was exactly what it was, & the mystery was more important than the truth.

i rearranged the letters to the proper starting point, & sitting beneath the bell, his bell, i smiled at his final message to me, his final message to everyone.

that's all, from your brilliant & loyal conductor.

Acknowledgments

addison.

my family, the best & brightest on the entire planet,

steve & jill & luke & leah & caleb & seth & joe,

for racing me to the top of every mountain,

& imbuing me with a thousand beautiful, repeatable truths,

my roommates—anthony & sheppard & dylan—for making life so exciting,

my brothers—cole & lucas & jordan & marcus & michael & anthony & grant & tj & joey—for showing me the world & keeping me in the mood for a party,

my friends in los angeles—

kaitlin kay, for inspiring the character only insomuch as you're worthy of obsession,

brookie, for keeping me company on the train,

& a hundred others, for building me a home.

my friends around the country,

my paradise fears family,

anyone who ever let me sleep on their couch or bought me a pink dunkin' donut.

ben rosenthal & harpercollins, for being so good to me,

jason kupperman, for being right all the time, always,

joanna volpe & new leaf literary, for being literally just so much fun to talk to.

the people i met & the things they carried—
emily rose & christian, swifty, valerie, rebecca, heidi & kailie & emily, ben, brittany & ashley, the guy in elko who bought me the scotch, meredith & her beautiful son.

vermillion, chicago, portland, seattle, boston, minneapolis, san francisco, new york, truckee, elko, green river, denver, omaha, mccook & everywhere like it, & i guess if i've gotta, los angeles.

flor, bon iver, chance, lido, drake, this will destroy you, kanye, travis scott, porter robinson, drake, the weeknd, one republic, kishi bashi, jonsi, & drake.